FLIGHT OF THE BLACKBIRD

THE JESSICA KELLER CHRONICLES VOLUME 5

BLAZE WARD

KNOTTED ROAD PRESS

Flight of the Blackbird
The Jessica Keller Chronicles: Volume 5
Blaze Ward
Copyright © 2017 Blaze Ward
All rights reserved
Published by Knotted Road Press
www.KnottedRoadPress.com

ISBN: 978-1-943663-42-2

Cover art:

© Dezignor | Dreamstime.com - Space Battle Photo

Cover and interior design copyright © 2017 Knotted Road Press

Never miss a release!
If you'd like to be notified of new releases, sign up for my newsletter.

I will never spam you or use your email for nefarious purposes. You can also unsubscribe at any time.

http://www.blazeward.com/newsletter/

ALSO BY BLAZE WARD

The Jessica Keller Chronicles

Auberon

Queen of the Pirates

Last of the Immortals

Goddess of War

Flight of the Blackbird

The Red Admiral

St. Legier

Winterhome

Petron

CS-405

Queen Anne's Revenge

Packmule

Persephone

Additional Alexandria Station Stories

Siren

Two Bottles of Wine with a War God

The Story Road

The Science Officer Series

The Science Officer

The Mind Field

The Gilded Cage

The Pleasure Dome

The Doomsday Vault

The Last Flagship

The Hammerfield Gambit

The Hammerfield Payoff

Shadow of the Dominion

Longshot Hypothesis

Hard Bargain

Outermost

Dominion-427

Phoenix

Princess Rualoh

Earth Force Sky Patrol

Birth of the Star Dragon

Flight of the Star Dragon

Call of the Star Dragon

Shadow of the Star Dragon

Trial of the Star Dragon

AUTHOR'S NOTE

I'll blame Owen. We were at a regular Bellevue Writer's Lunch, and the topic of "literature" versus genre came up. The consensus was that so-called *literature* had to be a story about multi-generational dysfunction in an exotic (and usually ethnic) location. Whatever. But it got me to thinking about family as a topic. And that underlays this story you are about to (hopefully) enjoy.

Jessica Keller has no children. Won't have. She has Slava's family. She has her disciples. But there will be no next generation for her.

And I won't ever write a set of prequels about a young Jessica Keller (sorry, Jenny). She was never young of soul, just of body. She was already something exotic, something special. It took the influence of Miguel and Indira, as much as Nils, to turn her into the creature that will be known as Jessica Keller, but they just showed her the door. She kicked it in and stormed the place.

So here we are. Book Five. There will be Nine and no more. There will be other stories in the *Alexandria Station* universe. Some in the present. Many in the past. A few in the future.

Auberon stands on its own. Would I rewrite it, knowing what I know about craft now? Probably not. Will I make corrections and clean things up when I do the nine-volume omnibus boxed set? Absolutely.

Queen of the Pirates and *Last of the Immortals* are a duology. They need to be read back to back. In a different universe, they might be one novel, but I want all of the Jessica books to be around the same length.

Goddess of War was the departure, but even that stands on its own. It serves to open us to the other six books.

Which brings us to *Flight of the Blackbird*. This opens a new trilogy, to be followed by *The Red Admiral* and *Lord of Winter*. That gets us through Seven.

Eight and Nine will be another duology that will close out Jessica Keller's tale.

Understand that this is not all there is to write. *Siren* falls between 3 and 4. I've got another short piece planned that falls between 6 and 7. Like *Siren*, it will let me tell a compact novella that shouldn't take up a big chunk of a larger novel.

There are dozens of other people I could follow, but Jessica barks at me the loudest. I love the woman, but I want to be done with her, so I can go tell other stories. I will die of old age with so many stories untold that it saddens me. But it also excites me, because there are so many stories that I will get to tell.

More Vo. More Moirrey. Interesting other people you will meet here and fall in love with, just as I have.

I have no children, but there are five lovely step-daughters who chose to claim me when their mother died. They keep me intact. One of my grandsons already loves reading my books. That fuels me to keep writing. I have an entire army of people in my head, patiently waiting their turn for a moment in the sun.

And I have you.

Readers. Fans. People who send me encouraging notes, or just smiles. Who tell their friends that I'm pretty good at this IMHO, and they should read my books. Making it possible for me to dream of a day when all I have to do is sit around and make shit up for a living.

This is a novel about family, yes. But it is also about dreams. About making the galaxy into a better place. I'm trying. Hopefully you are, too.

blaze
January 2017
West of the Mountains, WA

OVERTURE: SIGMUND

IMPERIAL FOUNDING: 175/08/10. DITTMAR PALAC,. WERDER, ST. LEGIER

In the end, treason had required a private meeting at the palace of one of the conspirators, so Sigmund had chosen his own.

It was not a darkened back room, in a seedy bar, on the wrong side of town. The capital city of the entire *Fribourg Empire* did not have a wrong side of town, although Sigmund had discovered some of the more interesting hidden corners Dockside in his youth.

No, the room surrounding them tonight was opulence itself, representing not just wealth.

Power.

Priceless antique artworks, primarily in porcelain, combined with life-sized oil portraits of former Emperors and other famous relatives of his. A man-sized suit of armor cast in bronze to look like a Hellenic antique and hung from a mannequin. Swords of various styles, both ancient and modern, filled display boxes or hung from gold-coated racks. A reminder that he was a warrior, and not a dilettante.

This was not the Imperial Palace, nor the Grand Fleet Operations complex. It was not one of his private clubs where kin or sycophants might wish to engage him in a conversation made awkward by the compatriots with whom he was meeting.

No, this was *his* primary palace.

The Household staff were all loyal to him, or they would not be here. And they would all hang together, if he were uncovered.

Sigmund Dittmar, Prince of the Blood, Imperial Admiral of the White and a raft of other titles, scanned the men surrounding his table as the plates were removed and brandy poured. As he was one of the highest-ranking officials, a member of the Imperial Staff as well as a close cousin of the Emperor himself and a wealthy patron of the arts, it would raise no suspicion that he met with the Duke of *Osynth B'Udan*, the capital world of the *M'hanii Frontier* sector that was the center of so much combat over the last half decade.

Rodrigo Yamimura was a tall, skinny man. Rangy, with an unruly crown of dark hair that did not come by that shade naturally. Sigmund knew him as a powerful man in his home sector, with a long memory for slights and an unwillingness to ever let an insult be forgotten.

In that, they had much kinship.

The man to Yamimura's right was a small man by any standard you wished to judge. Tito Garcia-Novarella was generally considered by Sigmund's spies and sources to be Yamimura's hatchet man. He had the look of a man that might cut your throat over a silver florin found in a gutter.

It was the other two men who were the most interesting, the most obscure. Probably the most dangerous.

Certainly the most exotic.

Of the three general flavors of humans who had colonized the galaxy, the *Fribourg Empire* was dominated by the sub-type that historians generally called *Euro-American*. There were worlds representing every hue and culture that had existed in the last millennia of the Homeworld, before *Earth* itself had been rendered uninhabitable, but the seeds of mankind had scattered to the four winds with the first star-drives, like dandelions in a wind.

These other two visitors had a look unlike any Sigmund was familiar with.

If pressed, he would have called it roughly Asiatic. They had the bones and coloration one normally associated with the ancient Chinese diaspora, but of a darker color, more of a nut brown than a buttery hue. Their eyes had something of the fold of the Chinese genotype as well, but rounder, more like his own.

They had been induced to dress as Imperial merchants this evening, in slacks and blazers of a style that was utterly ancient, but Sigmund could tell by the way they pulled at their clothing that they found it uncomfortable. Possibly barbaric, from the occasional quiet word muttered.

The one with the darker skin was taller and skinnier than his compatriot, and seemed to be in charge. And his name was utterly incomprehensible, even after ten thousand years of starflight within which to explore.

Au Banop Dejha Quin. Where *Au* represented one of eight officially recognized clans of the realm known as *Buran*. *Banop* represented, in a way Sigmund had not fully grasped, his rank as a scholar and minister in his own government. *Dejha* as a crèche designation rather than family. *Quin* alone was a personal name.

The Admiral suspected that the man was more likely to answer to an alpha-numeric designation, if pressed.

He chose not to ask.

The other had barely spoken. He seemed to exist for no other reason than to provide a witness, when they returned to their homeland.

Xi Fezar Palu Dwan. Short and broad where the first was tall and skinny. Lighter where the speaker was darker-toned.

Sigmund addressed himself to the first stranger, the one who might answer to Dejha Quin. The five of them were alone, and would remain so until he summoned his staff.

"I have read your complaints, gentlemen," he said, conjuring his best Admiral's voice for the occasion. "The remedy you propose is treason of the highest order. Why? Why should we commit ourselves to this path? What will it gain each of us?"

The two Imperials blanched at the directness of his tone, but kept their mouths shut. They were delivery boys. Nothing more. And they were well aware of that.

The visitor spoke slowly, carefully. His eyes blinked too infrequently for a normal person.

"The *Eternal*, the *Lord of Winter*, wishes this war to stop, Admiral Dittmar," Au Banop Dejha Quin said in an accent that fought hard not to range all over the musical scale. "Our worlds are well beyond *Samara*, beyond even that gulf of darkness between galactic arms, but we desire to hold that system as a permanent frontier between us. The government of Karl the Seventh is aggressive and expansionary. He will not rest until he has conquered all of known space."

Sigmund nodded.

"So you propose regicide as a solution?" he inquired, his voice barely above a harsh whisper.

Even he could not bring himself to say the word too loudly.

"We propose that *Fribourg* install a new government," the stranger, this *alien* man, replied. "One that will negotiate a border, and honor it. One that will be content to conquer the rest of this quadrant of the galaxy, outward to the rims, and ignore the coreward worlds where we live. Karl does not desire peace, so we have fought his infractions. We have pushed your navies back at every encroachment, and will continue to do so. We offer to make a personal demonstration to your Emperor of the power of the *Lord of Winter* that he might learn to live in harmony with his neighbors."

"And if the Peace with *Aquitaine* is signed?" Sigmund asked, barely able to keep the snarl out of his voice.

"We do not believe *Fribourg* will honor it," Au Banop Dejha Quin said coldly. "Else we would also offer a Twenty-Five-Year Peace between us as well. *Fribourg* only recognizes strength. If this place called *Aquitaine* is so foolish as to trust your government, then one might hope that Imperial ambitions could be satisfied, sated even, there."

Sigmund nodded. He had worked to stop Karl from even considering a treaty, but the man would not budge. All because of one woman, and the emasculating fear that had arisen among grown men at the very mention of her name.

"How quickly could you act?" Sigmund asked. "If we commit to this course."

For the faintest moment, a smile might have flashed in the stranger's eyes.

"Four months round trip," the man said simply.

Sigmund felt his mouth drop open, in spite of himself.

"How is that possible?" he asked.

"The *Lord of Winter* has his ways, Admiral. Or should I say, Your Majesty?"

"My Duke, or Admiral would be appropriate," Sigmund said. "Nothing else. Until later."

The stranger bowed his head formally.

Sigmund held up his glass of brandy. The others joined him in a toast.

"Gentlemen," he said quietly. "To victory."

The dates were already set, and the invitations en route. Not only would he displace Karl and his line, Sigmund would have the Empire's greatest enemy at his mercy when it was all done.

The realm known as *Buran* might be mysterious and exotic, but they were also extremely distant and, as they had said, only defending themselves against invaders. They did not even occupy the worlds of the *M'hanii Frontier*, merely using those as an armed firebreak for their own worlds, farther yet across the deep, stygian gulf.

As Emperor of *Fribourg*, Sigmund might ignore them for perhaps another decade or more, so that he could finish the job his two cousins: the Emperor and Emmerich Wachturm; had failed to accomplish. Because his first order as the Imperial Power would be the execution of Jessica Keller.

Without her, the *Republic of Aquitaine* didn't stand a chance.

OVERTURE: MARCELLE

DATE OF THE REPUBLIC APRIL 13, 398
PENMERTH, LADAUX

Marcelle carried little five-year-old Juan-Pablo to the car, fast asleep after all the excitement of the evening. She handed Jessica's youngest nephew, maybe her own youngest nephew, depending on how one counted these things, into the arms of Jessica's sister-in-law Sasha and let the woman secure the third and last child.

There had been hugs from all the kids, but it was growing late, and they were all worn out.

Marcelle reached way down to hug the tiny, frumpy Sasha, and then Slava, Jessica's brother, and then she stepped back. She watched Jessica make her own rounds, kissing each child good night and then the two adults.

The family had never been as close as they had grown over the last few years. Marcelle took some credit for that, but she knew that Jessica had toiled to overcome the complicated family dynamics she had brought with her, first as a frequently-absent Navy officer, and then as a famous and fabulously wealthy one.

But when Marcelle and her charge came to Penmerth, it was just family. The *Republic of Aquitaine* Navy held fast at the door, unwelcome inside the cozy little home of Miguel and Indira Keller. Doubly so on a night when the extended family, including Miguel's brothers and sisters-in-law, had all gathered to celebrate the birthday of little Margaret, just turned seven and all set to grow up and be like her famous auntie, the Queen of the Pirates.

Jessica Keller.

Marcelle grinned, thinking about the last seventeen years she had spent looking after the woman. She had originally volunteered for this task as a way out of a dead-end career as a lower-decks Navy peon. Along the way, Jessica's entire family had adopted her, to go along with her own younger siblings. And nieces and nephews galore.

Marcelle watched Jessica kiss her parents good night, and then joined them, the oldest semi-adopted daughter in the household, and far and away the tallest. The party had been a rousing success, but Marcelle knew that Jessica would be ready for quiet.

The two women made their way to an armoured flitter that Jessica had finally broken down and bought with some of her accumulated wealth. It was low, and midnight blue, and vastly over-powered, but just exactly the sort of transport a young, successful Fleet Lord/Fleet Centurion was supposed to arrive in.

First Rate Spacer Willow Dolen waited patiently outside the vehicle for them.

She had been unwilling to leave the vehicle while everyone was inside at the party, taking her new job as Jessica's personal bodyguard perhaps a touch too seriously. Marcelle had gotten over such things more than a decade ago, but decided not to mention it to the young woman who was still a bit star-struck.

Indira had responded by personally delivering roasted rabbit and cake. It was that kind of family.

Dolen was standing outside the vehicle now, awaiting them, blue eyes like an owl studying the darkness, hand probably close to a beam pistol of some sort, tucked into her jacket and out of sight. She and Marcelle exchanged nods.

Marcelle opened the rear hatch and guided a bleary-eyed Jessica inside, to be cocooned by the butter-soft, gray leather and darkness, before climbing down into the driver's seat and powering the systems live. Dolen waited a long moment and then joined her up front, the other door closing like a bulkhead hatch.

The partition between the front and the back seats was down right now, a leftover from their conversations earlier as they approached the party. Marcelle raised her hand to power the switch, but Jessica stopped her.

"No," the Fleet Centurion said. "I'm good, as long as we can have no music, please."

"That I can arrange," Marcelle said.

The flitter made remarkably little sound as Marcelle brought the repulsors on-line and hovered a meter off the ground before pivoting the great beast in place and drifting down into the street.

The Kellers lived out on the quiet edge of the small city that was *Aquitaine*'s capital. Many of the roads here were still dirt, not because it was too expensive to pave them, but because the folks around here preferred it that way.

Small family homesteads, truck farms, started up not too much farther out from here. Miguel Keller's two brothers both lived within a short drive and had each been here with their wives, although with none of the next generation, most of whom had moved off-planet.

"That was lovely," Jessica announced in a tired voice from the back. "But I am so glad to be able to send them home with their parents and have quiet."

Marcelle understood, intellectually, that her boss was an introvert. She had even studied the care and feeding of such strange, alien creatures.

She still did not get them.

"Is that why you never had any?" Marcelle asked carefully.

Jessica was bone-tired, from the drawl in her voice. Being around noisy people always required time alone in the darkness, but Jessica would never let outside people see that. Some might think it a weakness, while others might be offended at the suggestion.

"Partly," Jessica replied, surprising Marcelle.

The Fleet Centurion must be really tired. Normally, she ignored those comments.

"Partly, after I worked my ass off getting a combat command, I wasn't about to turn around and get a ground assignment for several years," Jessica continued. "And any man who came along was going to be both second fiddle to the Fleet, and the house husband in the relationship."

"What about the Peace?" Dolen asked carefully, still learning what was safe ground with her boss, even after nearly a year. "If there is to be less war, would you want to start a family?"

From the silence, Marcelle was afraid Willow had crossed a line, but Jessica was just thinking.

"No," the Fleet Centurion said from the back. "I made that decision long ago. It's not worth revisiting today. Even if I thought the *Fribourg Empire* would honor such a thing."

"They won't?" Dolen asked, slightly breathless.

It was fun, listening to someone who was still that wet behind the ears.

"I would be greatly surprised, Willow," Jessica said firmly.

"Any regrets?" Marcelle ventured, trying to knock her boss off of thinking about duty tonight.

The bodyguard took her cue and lapsed into silence.

"The occasional twinge," Jessica replied. "What about you? Any regrets?"

Marcelle stopped and thought about that. It wasn't a question she had considered.

"I have my nieces and nephews, same as you," Marcelle concluded. "Plus yours by adoption. But, yeah, I wouldn't have changed anything. It's been too much fun."

"Agreed."

Marcelle left it at that. She had enjoyed occasional flings, but had never been involved with anyone, man or woman, who had impacted her own life like Daneel Ishikura had affected Jessica.

Warlock. Pirate captain. A man who had made Jessica a widow without ever making her a wife first, at least in the legal sense. Absolutely one in the emotional sense.

They drove in silence for several minutes, until a chirp from Jessica's comm interrupted.

"Wonderful," Jessica opined from the back seat a few moments later, with all the sarcasm she could apparently muster at this moment.

"Marcelle," Jessica began after a moment. "I know it's late, but we need to forgo the apartment and catch a flight up to Fleet Headquarters tonight."

"Anything I need to worry about?" Marcelle replied.

"A surprise meeting with the First Lord, first thing tomorrow morning, in full dress uniform," Jessica said. "I would rather sleep on a shuttle tonight, so I'm sharp tomorrow for whatever it is they have planned. Full dress uniform suggests politics."

"Maybe a new assignment?"

Marcelle had hope.

The *Republic of Aquitaine* had just signed a Twenty-Five-Year Peace with the *Fribourg Empire*. Nobody suggested that the war was over, but both sides needed time to recover, *Fribourg* possibly more than *Aquitaine*.

Perhaps Jessica would be out at the tip of the spear again, instead of doing paperwork and training her squadron.

Waiting. And possibly rusting.

"Hopefully," Jessica said. "What's the worst they could do?"

CHAPTER 1

In the past, trouble had always found Jessica facing the entrance to Fleet Headquarters Room 2304, the personal office of the First Lord of the Fleet, Nils Kasum. The place she always thought of as the Dragon's Den.

She took a deep breath and contemplated a completely different door in front of her now.

She wasn't sure if it was a better sign, or a worse one, that she had been asked to meet Nils in one of the major conference rooms instead. That suggested something bigger, more public.

More people than could comfortably fit into his compact office.

Jessica felt Marcelle take a moment to brush her collar and back for any wrinkles or dust bunnies adventurous enough to have joined them in the last five minutes. Not that this uniform showed them.

She wore her more-formal Fleet Lord dress uniform this morning. The usual black slacks, tight over her calves and thighs to get into an emergency suit quickly. The green and black tunic with eight visible bronze buttons, rather than the invisible joins on her regular uniform. White epaulettes on her shoulders and white cuffs on her wrists, and a white undertunic instead of the chaos green one.

It wasn't her regular Fleet Centurion uniform, the one she preferred and was always pictured in, but today was more serious business. This required her to follow the modern regulations more closely.

She looked down at her left shoulder. Mostly. *Auberon*'s red and gray thistle badge was still there.

It wasn't her unit patch any more. Denis Jež commanded *Auberon* now, in name as well as practice, but both he and the First Lord had asked her to retain that as her own, personal flag, when she was promoted to Fleet Lord.

It was her home, as much as Penmerth on the planet below.

Jessica let go of her breath and pressed the button to slide the hatch open sideways.

Her heart skipped a beat anyway as she entered the room, Marcelle one step behind her and quickly sliding to the right against the wall with several other aides and centurions.

There was a single spot open at this end of the table, so she stepped there and looked around.

Nils Kasum would normally sit at the head of any table in a Navy meeting, as was his right by being the civilian commander of the fleet. Today, he sat to one side, obviously making space for someone else to sit in the place of honor. But Nils still wore what was obviously his best uniform, including the formal, black longcoat for special circumstances.

One might expect the Premier of *Aquitaine*'s Senate, Judit Margrét Chavarría, head of the government, to take that top spot, but she sat across from Nils in a dark powersuit with a sparkling smile.

Jessica checked anyway. Judit's nails were utterly perfect.

Obviously, serious business was intended today.

Closer down the table, next to Nils, Senator Tadej Horvat. Until the affair at *Ballard*, the man had spent more than a decade as the Premier, only ceding to Judit when the good of the Republic demanded it. In the four years since, he had served as the Chairman of the Senate's *Select Committee for the Fleet of The Republic of Aquitaine*. Nils's boss, as well as one of his oldest friends, going back to boarding school in their early teens.

Across from Tadej, First Centurion Petia Veronika Naoumov. Technically, First Fleet Lord, but the woman had taken Jessica's lead after *Thuringwell*, and changed her own uniform and title. As commander of Home Fleet, her only boss was Nils, and she might take his job when he finally decided to retire to his estates in another few years.

Jessica flashed back to a meeting with Judit and Petia, and others, that had launched the assault on *Thuringwell*, two years before. This room represented an even greater collection of raw power than that dinner had.

Doubly so when she considered the man whom these four people, each powers in their own right, had granted the chair at the other end of the table.

Jessica had never met Imperial Captain Hendrik Baumgärtner in person, but she had studied the man extensively and memorized his face. Emmerich Wachturm's Flag Captain. His Chief of Staff. The man who did for the Red Admiral what Enej Zivkovic did for her, and had served Wachturm for more years than Marcelle had been with her.

He was an average-looking man. Normal in height, perhaps two centimeters shorter than the Red Admiral. Lean and clean-shaven, with short, bristly, gray hair and a deeply lined face.

Baumgärtner had an erect carriage, shoulders back, head up as he stood when Jessica entered the room.

Perhaps her greatest surprise, over and above a man like this even being here, was that he had been allowed to keep his dress saber on his left hip, hung from his right shoulder on a simple, black, patent leather baldric. That, more than all the medals and awards on his chest, spoke of great gravity in the situation, that he might be armed and left alone within striking distance of the *Republic of Aquitaine*'s beating heart, ten armed marines and centurions around the walls notwithstanding.

Baumgärtner's heels came together with a snap and he bowed at the waist, holding it for two full seconds before coming back to attention. All her Academy classes in deportment came back to Jessica in a flash.

Possibly only the Emperor rated a more pronounced show of public respect from this man that she had fought four times, coming close to killing him at least once.

"Fleet Centurion," Baumgärtner said gravely as he surfaced again. He remained standing at semi-attention.

Jessica had never actually heard the man speak.

He had a deep, baritone voice, but it had rough edges. This was not a politician, with smooth, silky tones, but an officer capable of rattling his needs off a far bulkhead, aboard a burning bridge, in the midst of chaos.

A voice not to be brooked.

The mark of a good commander.

"Flag Captain," she responded.

Jessica returned the bow. Not as deeply, nor as long, but possibly as heart-felt.

She had walked into this room expecting politics.

Nothing could have prepared her for this.

From a sabretache on that baldric, hanging at his back, Baumgärtner pulled a small bundle that appeared to be wrapped in old-fashioned, oilskin cloth. At least from the sharp, pungent smell that suddenly wafted into the room.

Jessica marked two of the marines on the far wall, exactly behind Baumgärtner, and the fact that neither of them had so much as twitched when the man had reached for his bag.

Even more interesting.

The Flag Captain unfolded his small bundle to reveal a scroll tube and three heavy, linen envelopes, all in a cream color just shy of fading to mustard.

Baumgärtner remained standing, even as the other four stayed seated, so Jessica did as well. It was obvious, and amusing, that the Imperial considered the others to be nothing more than witnesses at this point, from his body language.

Jessica stifled a laugh at the thought. This man was just as serious, just as committed to any task as his boss was. Or her.

Kindred spirits spoke across the table to one another.

Baumgärtner picked up the scroll tube first and held it like a newborn in two, careful hands. He cleared his throat before speaking.

He held out the tube in her direction.

"It is my duty, and my great honor," he said. "To present to you, Fleet Centurion Jessica Keller, Queen of *Corynthe*, these *Imperial Letters Patent*, recognizing you as *Wildgraf* Jessica of *Petron* by Imperial decree."

The table was small, but she still could not take it directly from his hands. Instead, Nils carefully received it, passing it to Tadej, who placed it into her numb hands.

Letters Patent? Her? Wildgraf Jessica? What?

Her four superiors around the table responded with polite clapping, joined a moment later by the folks along the walls, including the marines who were normally supposed to embody paranoid, armed hostility.

Stunned silence seemed to be the best option, no other course of action suggesting itself in Jessica's suddenly blank mind. All of her clever plans, subtlety, political nuance: everything just flew out the hatch like an owl spying a mouse. Or a rabbit spotting a hawk.

Baumgärtner smiled at her from his end of the table, transforming his dourness from something reminding her of Alber' d'Maine to the sort of look Tomas Kigali might have worn.

That made it easier for her heart to consider beating normally again.

Perhaps.

"In addition," the Flag Captain continued in a lighter voice. "The Duke and Duchess of Eklionstic, Emmerich and Freya Wachturm, invite you to join them for the wedding of their youngest child, the Lady Henrietta Anne Wachturm, to Lt. Commander Bernard Hourani of the Imperial Navy, as a guest of Karl VII, *Emperor of Fribourg by Grace of God*. Said ceremonies to be held at the Imperial Cathedral in Werder, on *St. Legier*, on the fourteenth day of November, in the one-hundred seventy-sixth year of the Imperial Founding."

Captain Baumgärtner clicked his heels again, and bowed, only his head this time, as he passed one of the envelopes to Nils for delivery.

Jessica placed the tube on the table top as she took the letter in her hand. The paper was almost linen. The Imperial seal was unbroken in maroon wax.

She ran her thumb carefully underneath, separating the wax without destroying it, and pulled out the invitation for a quick read. The paper stock had the dense solidity of hull metal in her hands.

Jessica smiled and looked at the First Centurion on her right.

"I believe I will need to request leave, sir," Jessica told Petia.

The First Centurion smiled up at her mischievously.

"Sit, Jessica," Petia beamed up at her. "You have no idea."

CHAPTER II

DATE OF THE REPUBLIC APRIL 14, 398
COMMAND HEADQUARTERS, LADAUX

Nils led the convoy line as they traversed the wide, well-lit hallways of Fleet Headquarters to their destination. Petia's legs were longer than his, but he was intent on setting the pace today.

Today's destination was what he liked to think of as his personal bolthole, deep in the bowels of the Officer's Club at Fleet Headquarters.

The Marquette Room.

Fleet Headquarters kept clock with Penmerth below, as much as a space station serving an active fleet could. That meant that he had managed to reserve the entire room to himself for an early lunch, following several hours of careful, verbal fencing with Imperial Captain Baumgärtner.

Brass tacks, but the kinds of things that had to be spelled out at a level of detail that would have made the fleet's lawyers preen.

Gods, he was exhausted. It had been worse than either of his daughters getting married. But neither of those had the possibility of armed conflict as a result.

Through that last hatch, and the room had not changed one bit. In at least a decade.

Folks here had been warned, so the table in back had been rearranged to seat five comfortably.

Seth stood patiently behind the bar, prepared for any eventuality, while Nils's favorite steward, Sigrún, got them all seated and took drink orders. She reminded him of his wife, Rosemonde, who had also been a similar petite redhead before her short hair turned silver. And they shared the same impish smile.

As host, he stuffed Petia and Tadej into the booth first, facing each other, and then sat next to the First Centurion and across from the Premier, putting Jessica on the end, facing everyone. She looked the most shocked, but he had been expecting that, so Nils had previously ordered two bottles of a good, red wine to get everyone relaxed. Only Captain Baumgärtner had not joined them, but he had delivered his messages and done his duty admirably.

There would be a formal, state dinner later in the week.

Nils could tell that Jessica needed the wine from the way she sat. Perfectly still, not even her hands moving. Only her eyes. He could barely see the green, as she was all pupil right now.

Fortunately, the wine appeared almost immediately, with Sigrún putting the first glass directly into Jessica's hands.

Jessica took a long sip, and that seemed to grind something off the iron walls she had erected around herself during the meeting.

Nils toasted her with a glass, waiting for the rest to raise theirs as well.

"Now imagine, Jessica," he said helpfully. "If you were the one getting married, it might have gone on like that for several weeks until everyone nailed down every last detail that some heir or ex-spouse might challenge in court at a later date."

He was rewarded by a look that told him just how hard Jessica was working not to roll her eyes at him and his opinions on the topic. Nils grinned at her.

"You did fine, Jessica," Judit chimed in. "And you will do honor to both yourself and the Republic."

Jessica's look at the Premier was less frantic, less sarcastic. Barely.

"I would ask why me," Jessica finally began slowly. "But I understand that. Why this grand of a production?"

Tadej leaned forward with a knowing smile at that point, interrupting everyone else by tapping his finger on the table top.

"Diplomacy, young lady," he said evilly. "As we once discussed in this very room. You see the Emperor's hand in this, as you should. And the Red Admiral, who, as you have previously said, once thought you reminded him of his youngest daughter, the very lady getting married. You might, again, by the way. Remind him."

He leaned back and gestured with his wine glass, smiling like a cat with the finest cream.

"What you do not see yet is how all this will play with the Imperial public."

Her response was a simple, raised eyebrow.

"If the Peace is real, if it honest," he continued, "then Jessica Keller will not be coming for them in their sleep. Karl has brought you to bay by declaring the war over, and they can rebuild their strength for a generation, until you are too old, too senior, to be a personal threat. After that, who knows?"

Nils watched Jessica lean forward to rest both elbows on the table and let some of her rigid weight settle as her spine unlocked.

"Which is why he made me a *Wildgraf*," Jessica concluded. "A noble from beyond the pale. So I can come to this event as Queen of the Pirates and represent *Corynthe*, instead of coming as a Fleet Centurion."

"Correct," Tadej smiled. "You now fit into the Imperial hierarchy of things, and they can treat you as such. Plus, you will note, he was rather inflexible that while *Auberon* was not allowed into Imperial space, *Kali-ma* would be welcome as your chariot."

Jessica turned to the military side of the table now, catching him and Petia with those sharp eyes. They had turned green again.

"I cannot remove *Kali-ma* from *Corynthe's* Fleet for the months it would take to do this," she said forcefully. "The fine merchants in *Salonnia* would try their luck, as well as some of my own worlds that just barely recognize the central government now. David's hold on power would be at serious risk."

Petia put a hand on his wrist before Nils could speak.

"I have a plan," she began with that evil grin of hers. "And I have spoken briefly with First Lord. Considering the importance of this mission, it would behoove *Aquitaine* to come to the aid of our treaty partner and insure her throne in her extended absence."

Jessica's eyes got shrewd.

"What have you done?" she asked the First Centurion sideways.

"First Expeditionary Fleet should undertake an extended cruise to *Corynthe*," Petia smirked gleefully. "If I wasn't responsible for Home Fleet, I might go myself. Navigation training. Recruitment. Showing the flag. You know, fun stuff."

"And frightening some of those worlds until they pee down their leg?" Jessica asked sarcastically.

"If they weren't up to no good, Jessica," Nils leaned forward a bit, "they wouldn't be nervous now, would they? Plus, it gives me a really good excuse to include an archaeological expedition to *Bunala* with them."

"Why *Bunala?*" Jessica asked him, shocked.

"Jessica, that is the largest wrecker yard of starships in known space," he said with rising excitement. "And resting place of the only known *Concord* super-dreadnought in the galaxy. We may have surpassed the ancients in many ways, but who knows what other things they might have to teach us, lo these millennia since. With Your Majesty's permission, of course."

"Granted," Jessica said quietly, deep in thought. "And I understand why Karl would want to reward Vo Arlo. Knighting him and making him an honorary Colonel of the Imperial 189th Division fits the rest of this. Why does he want to knight Moirrey? Everything she has done to date has come at their expense."

Nils felt his shoulders shrug unconsciously.

"Perhaps Karl wants to take her measure personally," he said. "He's never met her, only heard stories and read formal reports by people covering their asses and grinding axes."

"And maybe Dieter Haussmann of Imperial Security was hated so much that they want to reward her," Tadej chimed in sarcastically.

"So if I'm off gallivanting around the Empire, who will hold the flag for *Auberon?*" Jessica asked him carefully.

There. Nils could finally see it in the back of her eyes. The pain. The unspoken worry that someone might ruin her finely-honed crew, like an idiot hitting a rock with the edge of a sword because he didn't know any better.

"I have had a few, private talks with an old comrade of yours, Jessica," he said quietly. "I think Fleet Centurion Arott Whughy would be the perfect candidate. He and Denis get along quite well, and it's past time he got a mission like this that took him to the back of beyond."

He wanted to say something more, something about what it had done for her career, but he knew that was too sensitive a topic, especially now.

Nils could still see the ghost of Daneel Ishikura when he looked in her eyes.

That haunted loss.

Jessica Keller had gone to *Lincolnshire* to deal with a simple issue of pirates. From there to *Corynthe*.

If it hadn't been for the need to immediately plunge back into battle with Emmerich Wachturm, Nils wasn't sure Jessica's career, or her mind, would have survived that loss.

No, best to leave it at Arott. The two respected each other, and Nils knew that Petia had threatened the man to be on his best behavior with someone else's warfleet.

Jessica took another heavy drink, emptying her glass, deep in thought. Fortunately, Sigrún was arriving with an anti-pasta plate half a meter across, filled with cheeses, fruit, crackers, and cold cuts.

"So I'll be on leave for six to eight months? Off-duty?" she finally asked Petia when she set the glass down.

"You're never off-duty, Keller," the First Centurion countered knowingly. They shared a quick smile. "In this case, you are simply going to be conducting the *Eternal War* by other means."

Nils felt an ominous shiver ghost down his spine at the secret smile the two women shared. Three, with Judit.

He still hadn't gotten all of that story, from any of them.

If the war between *Aquitaine* and *Fribourg* was truly over, even for a generation, what would Jessica do? Worse, how much danger would there be on the galactic rim, if Jessica Keller truly went home to *Corynthe* permanently?

CHAPTER III

DATE OF THE REPUBLIC APRIL 18, 398 SC
AUBERON. ABOVE LADAUX

"Ma'am," Moirrey nodded as she entered Jessica's inner office. Jessica motioned the tiny woman, her own, personal, *evil engineering gnome*, to sit. Marcelle followed her into the room and put down a coffee service and began working her ritual magic.

Jessica had been plotting this since that *meeting* with Baumgärtner. Beans harvested in *Lincolnshire* and brought cold to *Ladaux*. Fresh-roasted three days ago and left to vent, using the mysterious alchemy that only Marcelle had ever mastered. Fresh cream and honey from Jessica's uncle's farm, brought up to orbit this morning.

Moirrey had grown up. There was no other way to describe the changes in the seated woman since they had first met, so many years ago, when it was Jessica's mission to rock the Empire to its core at *2218 Svati Prime.*

Moirrey no longer fidgeted when she sat. The uniform of a centurion no longer looked over-sized and wrong on her. Perhaps she had grown into herself finally. Jessica sometimes wondered if she herself would ever do the same.

They waited in warm, companionable silence as Marcelle worked before finally leaving them alone with two steaming mugs of the best coffee in the galaxy.

Jessica considered the Centurion seated across from her. So much she had asked from this woman over the years. Such great risks and rewards, as well as secrets the two of them would have to take to their graves.

Jessica could see questions flit across Moirrey's face unasked. The cute, raven-haired pixie was practically bubbling with something, and yet sat perfectly still.

Jessica smiled.

"It's because you've entered the pantheon of creatures that scare the *Emperor of Fribourg*," she said simply.

Jessica should have been surprised, but she had come to expect calm from Moirrey.

The engineer nodded at her sagely.

"So this dinna mean I have to gives up bein' an engineer ta be's an *Imperial* Lady?" she replied sideways.

Jessica laughed and smiled warmly.

"No more than I do, Pint-sized," she said, watching Moirrey's eyes flare for just a moment at the nickname.

Moirrey's best friend Dina had called her that. As had Suvi, the *Last of the Immortals*. So could the *Queen of the Pirates*.

"So what's this I hears about a crew goin' to *Bunala* and sniffin's around, Jessica? Without me, I might add."

"That's what you get for becoming important people, Moirrey," Jessica replied with a broad smile they shared. "First Lord wants to see what they can learn, what they can improve on, if we don't have to build warships as fast as we can, just to keep up with *Fribourg*."

"Gon'ta rebuilds Alber' again?" Moirrey asked with a burr.

Jessica laughed again this time. It felt good to be alone with Moirrey, a sister she had never had until recently.

After *Thuringwell*, when Alber's Heavy Cruiser Experimental, *Shivaji*, had nearly melted itself in half, they had indeed had to cut her into three pieces and scrap the middle one for metal. With the Peace, they had ended up rebuilding her with a more traditional middle section, but had done so in such a way that they could pull whole sections out as modules, with the intent of building new ones and plugging them in as engineers made dreams into steel and power systems.

Only Alber d'Maine would look forward to flying such a messy and complicated ship. Anything to be a better warrior.

"Probably," Jessica said. "It depends on what they find at *Bunala*, and what happens over the next year."

"And whats we tells the mighty Lords o'da Fleet 'bouts *Project Mischief?*" Moirrey asked with a silly grin.

Jessica set her coffee down carefully on her desk and considered the woman. Butter wouldn't melt in Moirrey's mouth right now. If she didn't trust the evil engineering gnome so much, Jessica might be worried.

"What have you come up with?" Jessica asked slowly, carefully.

The Creator only knew what might bubble up from the engineering bays, with this woman thinking evil thoughts. Her business cards read *Advanced Weapons Tech* for a reason.

Moirrey's eyes twinkled. Jessica couldn't think of another term. She was reminded of Moirrey's phrase about glitter being the most important part of any day.

And unicorns. Because, you know, unicorns.

"Lots o'craziness, ma'am," Moirrey said. "If'n's we'll be 'boards *Kalima* fer, like, months, I might ask Oz fer some leftover parts to haul out, since I know some folks who know some folks. Might be able to trade fer useful tidbits. And build me n'David some toys."

The smile on Moirrey's face looked so peaceful and innocent. And yet, this woman had been directly responsible for more deaths at *First Petron* than anybody else on the field that day, both commanders included.

One of these days, Nils Kasum was probably going to try to promote Moirrey Kermode to a ground job at a Fleet Weapons Lab.

Over my dead body. I probably will have to take her with me when I finally do retire to Corynthe. *Assuming I'm still Queen and get to retire from that as well. David needs to have the crown in fact, as well as theory.*

"We have a budget for both spare parts and for trade goods, young lady," Jessica replied. "And if Oz can't cover it, ask me. I have money I'm not spending."

On her first visit to *Lincolnshire*, five years ago, Jessica had brought with her four of the big, Mark 2 shipping containers, filled with goods normally only available in major *Aquitaine* ports, and sold them to each of four local shipping houses for the same price. Petron might absorb two easily, and there were a number of other planets that nominally offered her their allegiance. Perhaps she should plan for six, plus whatever Moirrey and Oz got up to?

"That I can do's, ma'am," Moirrey chirped as she finished her coffee. "Been playing with ideas fer beam weapons, since *Corynthe* don' use missiles and stuff lik'n's we does it here."

"Sounds good, Moirrey," Jessica replied. "I'll let you get back to your shore leave. I'm sorry we won't have time to stop off in *Lincolnshire* on the way, but have Marcelle schedule me a pair of two-hour blocks a week apart. You can show me everything, and then I can come back with questions about how we implement it."

"Aye, ma'am."

And Moirrey was gone. A little birdie had whispered in her ear that Moirrey had a hot date scheduled in twelve hours, planetside, with Digger, the Senior Centurion of the Construction Ala that HQ had decided to permanently attach to First Expeditionary Fleet, Jessica being the most likely to be dispatched on the sorts of fleet-sized *Show the Flag* missions where building roads, bridges, and hospitals was almost as important as fighting.

Peace was going to be almost as much an undiscovered country, as near as Jessica could tell.

She emptied her own mug and checked her messages. Security hadn't updated her, so she knew where her next target was to be found.

Moirrey had been easy, but the woman who had turned into her little sister was a glass-half-full kind of person. Jessica's next job wouldn't be so easy.

CHAPTER IV

DATE OF THE REPUBLIC APRIL 18, 398 SC
AUBERON. ABOVE LADAUX

Because it was a live firing line, the main hatch was locked from inside and was keyed to his voice. It would take someone with a priority override to open the door.

Vo preferred it that way right now. He still wasn't sure how he felt.

The little light continued to blink above the doorway, indicating that someone was waiting patiently outside for him to finish whatever it was he was doing and make everything safe for entry. It would also continue to beep once every two minutes as a friendly irritant.

Vo stood on the firing line and considered the target seventy-five meters away. At this range, one man with an English-style longbow was not a threat to another single man, if the target was paying attention and could move out from under the arrow. Elk and deer might spook, if they knew enough about men to be afraid, but they might not.

No, this was the time of battle where formations of archers lobbed shots at formations of infantry or cavalry, presuming their own intervening wall of steel protected them.

Vo's target was man-sized. Navin the Black had always taught him to shoot at men with a bow as if he was going to with a rifle or a beam.

You never know when you'll be shipwrecked on a hostile planet, with nothing but a knife and your wits, and have to survive.

Vo considered the bucket at his feet. A score more arrows rested there, feathers up, waiting their turn. He had hand-fletched them from stock he had bribed the engineering bays to produce. The bow in his hands was a composite, rather than traditional yew. Layers of wood glued together with care, normally a task done over a winter when planetside, shaped lovingly with heat and carved with hand-tools.

Hostile planet. You against the universe. Go.

The door beeped again.

Four times meant whoever waited was serious, and patient. That narrowed it down to a handful of people.

The Command Security Centurion would have gotten on the comm and told him to haul his ass over and unlock the door. That nobody had done so narrowed it down all the more.

Vo sighed, rested the still-strung bow on a pair of hooks, and walked over to the door. The code wasn't meant to be complicated, just to keep people from wandering in during the middle of a training exercise where they might get hurt.

Not everyone knew how to safely play with guns and knives.

He felt like an ogre when the door opened. She didn't even come up to his shoulder.

Maybe she cleared the bars on his chest.

Vo stepped back and then to one side so she could enter.

"Fleet Centurion," he rumbled noncommittally.

"Mr. Arlo."

Jessica Keller stopped in front of him anyway and looked up, studying him close enough to be uncomfortable. She did that to people.

Vo wondered what secrets she learned.

Instead of speaking, she turned and walked to the space where he would have stood to observe one of his students learning the ancient art.

Vo stood perfectly still and stared at her from across the space.

"If you think you need the practice, Vo, please continue," she said in a warm, soft voice that seemed to emanate from the heavens above.

Or the depths of hell itself.

Vo wasn't sure what he needed. He had chosen to meditate with a bow today. It would have looked awkward, at least to him, if she had walked in on him practicing kendo with his own fighting robot, a variant of the type she had made famous Republic-wide.

Oh, what the hell.

He sealed the door again with the code and returned to the firing line. Lift the bow from the hooks and find the perfect rest with the left hand.

Check the left wrist's bracer. Adjust the fingerguards on the right hand. Feet set.

Arrow picked up by the nock, then locked tight on the string. Weapon overhead, feathers brushing the cheek. Bring down to level while breathing slowly out before releasing.

Come to stillness. Find the intersection of arrowhead, target, and gravity.

Release.

The shot flew true and struck the man dead-center in the chest. There wasn't another arrow within eight centimeters of it. Vo figured he couldn't do that again on a bet.

Rather than flinch, or grow superstitious, he nocked the next and let fly.

The key to archery is muscle memory. Repeat the same shot ten thousand times. The entire act becomes automatic.

The second shot hit the man in the thigh. Good enough to wound and immobilize.

Vo stood perfectly still and took a breath.

"Navin tells me you have mixed feelings about this," she said from beside and below him, like a pixie dragon tucked away in his left back pocket.

Vo prepared the third shot. Released it.

Hip.

"Why me?" Vo finally said, realizing she would wait all day.

The Fleet Centurion was like that.

"I've watched the video from *Thuringwell*, Vo," she replied quietly. "If you slow it down and watch Horst's face, he realized that he had gone as far as he could, and that he was about to die. Anybody else in that situation, and there would have been violence. Given the hussars you were with, I would have expected them to roll over the Imperials like a plague of angry locusts."

He heard her take a breath and then move around to where she was in his peripheral vision, though still safe behind the firing line.

Vo glanced down.

"Horst and his platoon are alive because you chose to act with honor, Centurion Arlo," she bored in on him. "It's one of the many reasons you keep accumulating medals. Why I keep sending you on the hard missions."

"But this?" he finally said, head hung and shaking.

"Vo, written into the Peace Treaty itself is that the 189th Division will continue to maintain a permanent Honor Guard on Thuringwell, even as it turns into a Republic world," she explained carefully. "An Imperial Division, guarding an Imperial memorial, on a Republic world. Fourth Saxon's own Armorer is providing the swords those men will bear."

She moved the rest of the way around him, looking up from close enough he was practically breathing on her.

He didn't even flinch. Visibly.

Why was it okay that she could see him like this?

"Vo, this is the Emperor's way of personally saying *thank you*."

Her words ground through him like broken glass.

The *Fribourg Emperor* was going to knight him. And make him an honorary Colonel of the 3rd Regiment, 189th Division.

Him. City boy from *Anameleck Prime*. Street punk and former small-time cat burglar. Enlist for four years or go to jail for two. All his friends from those days were pretty much dead, imprisoned, or burned out.

Even his family barely knew him.

Centurion Vo Arlo. *Order of Baudin. Republic Cross. With Bar.*

About to become Colonel *Ritter* Vo *zu* Arlo of the *Imperial Army of Fribourg.*

How the hell did that happen?

"Because you're the one that wanted to be a hero when you grew up, Arlo," she said with a smile as she took a step back and came to parade rest.

Vo closed his mouth and turned beet red. And remembered to breathe. And to stop muttering out loud.

"When I sent Moirrey over to Alexandria Station, I told Navin what I was expected and who I wanted," she continued in a brighter but still serious tone. "I thought he would send Jackson Tawfeek. He chose you."

"JT might have managed," Vo said diplomatically.

"The only reason you aren't a Dragoon on your own ship someplace else, Vo," Fleet Centurion Jessica Keller intoned, "is that I won't let First Lord have you. Any more than I will let him take Moirrey away from me. Get that through your thick skull. Use a hammer if you have to. Remember that you're there to make the 189th proud of you, too. And not just me and the entire, damned Fleet."

Vo blinked at her. Not counting passing greetings, today might be the most words she had ever said to him conversationally.

He took a breath. There were two entire armies and at least one fleet counting on him. And he was going to go be a hero on *St. Legier*?

Vo just shook his head and hung the bow, afraid his hands would be shaking too much to even hold it right now, let alone fire a clean shot.

Colonel Centurion *Ritter* Vo *zu* Arlo.

How the hell did that happen?

CORYNTHE

CHAPTER V

DATE OF THE REPUBLIC JUNE 2, 398 SC
AUBERON. EDGE OF THE PETRON SYSTEM

Jessica told herself to breathe. And stop grinding her teeth in public, even in front of her own people. Her Flag Bridge. Her *Auberon*.

But it still felt like one of those terrible nightmares you couldn't wake up from. Not the one where you're walking naked through the hallway of your boarding school in front of everyone.

No, the one where the last twenty years of your life have all been a daydream and suddenly you're back in class, clueless, and facing a final exam you can't remember studying for.

She was back as a wet-behind-the-ears Cornet on her first cruise, on someone else's ship, watching him work.

But she wasn't. She was just out of place. Out of self.

"Battle squadron, this is Fleet Centurion Whughy aboard *Auberon*," the man's voice said deliberately. "I have the flag. All hands stand by for possible enemy action."

She must have cringed, looking around the enormous Flag Bridge of the Star Controller from her spot off to one side. Her bridge. But not hers anymore. Not today. Not for a while.

He glanced over at her with a sardonic grin. From this angle, Arott Whughy really did look like Tomas Kigali's doppelgänger. Tall, blond, and Hollywood handsome. Probably smarter. Far more serious, if quite a bit less committed to his task than Kigali.

"Seriously, Keller," he said for the tenth, or maybe twentieth time, with a wry smile. "I'm just keeping the seat warm until you get back."

That helped, barely. Technically, she didn't even belong here right now, being on detached duty and just getting in the way occasionally. At least Whughy had taken over the Ambassador's quarters while he was aboard, and let her stay in the smaller chambers she had originally customized for herself.

She wasn't in command here.

It didn't help her frame of mind that she was standing on what was now *his* deck, or that she was wearing the uniform she thought of as Admiral of the *Corynthe* Fleet. Or Queen of the Pirates.

Charcoal gray pants, so tight as to be stretched on, in case she needed to move into combat suddenly, as a Queen of the Pirates might. Knee-high, black leather, armored combat boots with metal toes, originally picked up for her first visit to *Bunala*. Over her sports bra, a light gray pullover shirt with a mock turtleneck collar. Atop that, a slate-gray, open-front jacket with a short, standing collar, in a shade midway between the shirt and the pants. It was longer than a bolero, but not much, just to the top of her hips. Much like her everyday Fleet Centurion tunic but not buttoned shut. Functional for shipboard, with pockets inside, and a useful waterproof shell she could wear on the ground on any sort of moderately unpleasant day.

On each wrist, a single band of color as wide as her hand. It was a deep maroon, almost the color of the wine she occasionally drank.

On her left breast, over her heart, a stylized logo of a beautiful woman with blue skin and four arms, holding a saber, a *main-gauche*, a severed head, and a planet, specifically Ian Zhao and *Petron* respectively, in this instance.

It was something the locals would appreciate.

At each side of her jacket collar, a single hexagon, solid and the size of a Lev coin, forged with gold from one of Arnulf Rodriguez's favorite bracers after he had died.

Had been murdered.

Had forced her to become something she had never dreamed, never wanted.

Queen of the Pirates.

And now she was home.

As much as Penmerth was the home of her youth, quaint and

comfortable, the city of Corynthe, on *Petron*, was the place that drew her now.

"Flag Centurion," Arott continued. "Please notify the Court that we are on a diplomatic mission and request orbital assignment."

Even that was wrong. It wasn't her in the command seat at the big table. And instead of Enej Zivkovic, Whughy had brought his own Flag Centurion.

Cheng Yin Dominguez was a tall, skinny woman. She had played varsity volleyball at the Academy. She still looked like she could spike anyone else in the room, most of a decade on. Her skin was dark brown, almost nut colored, and her brown hair was just barely long enough to show the rings it would grow into if allowed.

"Acknowledged, Commander," she said smoothly.

Five weeks sail getting here had given everybody time to get used to one another. The six to nine months before she got back would give this squadron time to reinforce the ties of civilization with those *Corynthian* planets inclined to act like adults. And it would let the rest have a chance to see what kind of help Jessica might be able to bring, if they did get out of line.

If she wanted to stomp them like annoying bugs for starting another war.

Corynthe was still more of a concept than a nation. If the piracy had thinned out over the last few years, that was because of the slaughter Jessica and her allies had inflicted on the kinds of men inclined to banditry, rather than letting the angels of their better selves come to the fore.

That was why First Lord had sent an entire battle squadron now.

Auberon was the biggest warship that had ever crossed the frontier, hands down. And possibly the biggest ship of any kind. And her two destroyer squadron escorts were each a match for any 4-ring Mothership by themselves. The smaller pirate carriers were even less of a threat.

Among her cruiser escorts, the Battlecruiser *Nyamboya* was the most dangerous-looking, but possibly the least effective in a space where battles would be fought between packs of beam-armed snug fighters.

On the other flank, Alber' d'Maine had apparently talked to someone with a clue about what he expected out here. *Shivaji*'s two flank modules had been filled with generators, batteries, and Type-2 beams.

Just exactly what you needed, in a world with lots of fighters flying around and hardly any hostile missiles incoming.

On one corner of the formation, *Ishfahan* was loaded with Archerfish missiles, and hallways had apparently been packed to the gills with reloads. Jessica didn't expect Doriane to need them, but she hadn't expected an Imperial coup attempt four years ago. Anyone trying their luck would run into a Manticore of Persian legend. Doubly so with Doriane Matveev in command.

And it was probably the Survey Cruiser *Ballard* that was going to have the most fun over the next year.

She was carrying a fully-funded archaeological mission from her own namesake, the *University of Ballard*, as well as a team of expert engineers from Home Fleet.

The Fast Fleet Transport *Mendocino*, who had somewhere along the way turned into Jessica's personal trucking company, had accompanied the squadron to *Corynthe*, and would be available to transport home interesting finds.

Arott eyed her speculatively.

"We're fifteen light minutes out," he began. "It's mid-morning at your palace and you've said you didn't want to combat drop on them at the edge of the gravity well. One last working lunch before a State Dinner and you turning into your other self?"

At least he was working to make it easy. And was working well with her people.

If she was going to drop into *Corynthe* and disrupt all their lives, at least they would do it in a friendly manner. After all, who liked having an entire warfleet suddenly appear on their doorstep?

CHAPTER VI

DATE OF THE REPUBLIC JUNE 3, 398 CITY OF CORYNTHE, PETRON

Five years.

Half a decade had passed since Jessica had first entered these halls, angry and ready to crack heads together, if that was what it took to bring peace and security to *Lincolnshire*'s frontier.

Four years since she had become Queen, avenging Arnulf and losing Daneel.

And starting to reshape an entire nation.

The throne room, *her* throne room, had not changed in that time. Some traditions were worth keeping. Others weren't worth the effort to overcome inertia.

At least today, things were different.

On her first trip, the room had been filled with Captains, and a few of their doxies. Jessica had been either ignored, or studied in amazement. Some sort of exotic creature from the lands where indoor plumbing wasn't considered magic.

Okay, that wasn't entirely fair. *Corynthe* was extremely technologically advanced, especially for one of the nations out at the edge of the galaxy, where stars were thin and scattered, and you often found yourself looking out at the darkness of intergalactic space.

No, it was the culture that was backwards. Had been backwards. Was coming into the future slowly, painfully, snapping and biting every step of the way as it overcame centuries of poverty.

Today was another step on that journey, she hoped.

First Lord had sent the fastest Dispatch Boat available, once her own plans were known. David Rodriguez, Crown Prince and Regent in her place, had time to prepare.

The whole Court, *her* whole Court, awaited her.

Jessica had considered arriving here today with an entire company of her marines in full battle gear. The Free Captains of *Corynthe* still reacted best to strength. But dropping into orbit with a battle fleet capable of annihilating the entire *Corynthe* Navy in an afternoon was enough of a statement, she felt.

Instead, she found herself in that last hallway with a compact group of her people. Enej as Flag Centurion to the Crown. Marcelle. Yeoman Dolen wearing her normal day uniform, with a thigh holster holding a heavy beam pistol added on the left, and a poniard on the right. Apparently the woman was adept with either, or both, and at the same time.

Marcelle had personally interviewed all the candidates for the job before Dolen made the final cut. So she was probably hell on wheels in a bar fight, too.

Marcelle thought that way.

The double-doors were five meters tall, arched at the top and plated in chrome and gold over a solid, steel core. They opened now on silent hinges and Jessica found herself facing the Court's Herald, Girisha Dhaval Misra.

He had been an older man with a noticeable limp and a shaved head five years ago. He appeared to have achieved timelessness now, with a roguishly impish smile and a decidedly excited twinkle in his brown eyes today.

Jessica had inherited him, along with the rest of the Court infrastructure. He was one of the few pieces that had remained, after she and Desianna Indah-Rodriguez finished reorganizing things to suit their desires.

He still did pomp and circumstance with a grace and style that would have impressed the First Lord and the Republic's Senate. She had considered bringing him with her to *Aquitaine*, at least once, but his place was truly here.

Misra had carried a lovely carved-wood walking staff that first time, a carryover from a limp that had healed, but tradition had turned it into his badge of office. He smiled at her, nodded formally, and turned back to the room.

The tremendous thump of his staff, capped in Sanskrit-carved bronze, echoed through the larger chamber now revealed. Jessica was taken by how quiet everything had grown.

"Her Majesty arrives," Misra commanded into the vast space. "All hands to stations."

Without looking back, Misra began to walk.

The throne room had a slight downward slope to the otherwise flat floor, a serving-dish of an amphitheater with a raised platform at the bottom. The crowd had already parted and provided her a corridor to her throne that averaged six meters wide.

The difference today was the number of women in the crowd. And their position. Perhaps a quarter of the people here, and they weren't prostitutes.

With Jessica's Peace on the frontiers, and the death of so many menfolk, women had stepped into the gap. Merchants, sailors, Captains. Even warriors.

They had always been there, but now they were allowed to be seen. To be known.

To be proud.

The two women on the platform, standing at attention on either side of the throne, would see to that. Ruthlessly, if necessary.

Misra walked slowly, partly from age, and partly from the dignity of the situation. He didn't get to show off like this very often, Jessica's duties to the *Republic of Aquitaine* keeping her away for long stretches.

Like yesterday. And tomorrow.

Jessica followed, trailed in turn by her three aides.

The throne, the physical object she had inherited from Arnulf, was a monstrous, gold and chrome thing, designed for a man who had stood more than two meters tall. The man standing next to it now had his father's size, and the man's canniness, plus his mother's wisdom.

David Rodriguez. Crown Prince. Acting Regent. The man who, if she could keep the meddlers and thieves at bay long enough, would be king in the eyes of *Corynthe*, one of these days.

He wasn't that much younger than her, but Jessica had no interest in ruling here permanently. In another decade or two, she could become Dowager. Or something.

It was enough to remind everyone that they would have to take the crown from her, and not David. The battlefleet in orbit overhead was a quiet statement of what those sorts of costs might entail. The worst of the Free Captains had all been purged or killed, and the common folk were beginning to appreciate not having to deal with pirates and brigands preying on them constantly.

Thus are civilizations changed, one mind at a time.

On David's right, his mother, Desianna Indah-Rodriguez. Dowager widow of Arnulf, but more importantly, the First Minister of the government. A woman whom time seemed to ignore, with all the beauty of her youth mostly intact. The same woman who made sure the freighters ran on time, and that any plots against the throne were discovered early and dealt with as messily as might be appropriate to make a statement.

And Desianna lost no love for men plotting against her oldest child.

It was the woman on David's left that Jessica had been looking forward to engaging, as much as Desianna on the right was probably her best friend in the galaxy.

Wiley.

As Acting Regent, David was technically still only the Captain of her flagship and temporarily only made all decisions in her name. But *Wiley* on the stage next to him told Jessica that there had been changes since her last visit home. Breakthroughs, she hoped.

Shiori Ness. Flight callsign *Wiley*. One of the handful of female, combat-certified, fighter pilots in *Corynthe*, four years ago. Since then the woman had decided that the nation could best be served by her learning to command starships. Warships.

Motherships.

She was wearing tight black pants, almost leggings, and a tunic that bore a remarkable resemblance to the *Republic of Aquitaine* Navy's standard day uniform, save that here it was gray, with the same black stripe across the chest and upper arms but square cuffs above the wrist bone. But then, she wouldn't spend as much time typing.

The uniform appeared almost stretched across *Wiley*'s frame. She was a big woman, almost as tall as Marcelle, but built more like a man in the bones. *A Polish peasant*, as Jessica's mother would have said. Broad shoulders. Big breasts. No waist at all above her hips, as her body seemed to be just a block of concrete.

Wiley's skin was almost the same liver chestnut of one of her uncle's horses Jessica remembered from childhood, with bright, russet eyes, and curly rings just long enough to move in a good breeze. She was plain in the face, almost homely, but had a smile that could light up a room, on the few occasions she used it.

She grinned down at Jessica ever so slightly when their eyes locked, and then she was serious again.

But something had happened to *Corynthe.*

On her black-clad upper right arm, three rings encircled the muscle, just as they had Jessica's, back when she had been a Command Centurion on this floor, lo those many years ago. Scarlet, but so similar. On her left shoulder, where Jessica had worn Auberon's badge, was a large gray hexagon, with a four-armed, blue goddess in the center. It was remarkably identical to the logo over Jessica's heart right now.

Jessica nodded and ascended the steps with a smile.

She had added a footstool to the throne, so she could climb into the damned thing without acrobatics, and sit without her feet dangling like a six-year-old. She did so now, and looked out over the audience, expectant and smiling faces. She hoped that it was a good sign.

"Citizens of the Court," Misra called out in a voice audible a county away. "Jessica Keller. Lord of *Petron.* Admiral of the Fleet. *Queen of the Pirates.*"

The staff sounded a single note like Doom itself on the stone floor.

The cheers and whistles seemed more energetic than dutiful. That was good.

Now she had to up-end their entire world.

Again.

***

Jessica had kept the Crown's primary conference room unchanged, save for the color of the walls.

It was a small-ish space, comfortable for perhaps a dozen people, rather than the hundreds who had danced attendance this afternoon for her first visit home in almost a year. A giant oval of a table, polished from some local, speckled orange stone, dominated the space, surrounded by a bevy of comfortable chairs and cloth-covered walls, sea-green now when they had been gray before.

It made the room warmer, friendlier.

Jessica sat at the end of the oval farthest from the door, facing Marcelle and Willow, themselves flanking the entrance and ready for anything. Although the six men of the Queen's Rifles outside should be enough.

David sat on her left, in his official place as her senior-ranking Captain. The ancient term had been Commodore. She needed to make some changes to how things were organized, now that she was sure she would hold this throne.

She needed to do many things in a short time.

Desianna, First Minister, sat to her right, dressed for business, rather than distraction. In her sixth decade, she could still entice every man in any room, if she wanted, but today she was wearing a simple green tunic over white pants, with barely a quarter kilo of gold visible in the rings, earrings, necklaces, and butterfly-shaped hair pins she wore.

Next to Desianna was one of the smallest men Jessica knew on *Corynthe*, barely a hand span taller than Jessica herself. Still, he was one of the most respected Captains, in spite of only commanding a 1-ring Mothership, and that one largely dedicated to commerce, rather than combat.

But then, this man had never wanted more, and had nothing to prove to anyone on this planet, a feeling he had made known then, and now. After all, none of the rest of them could say that their blade had killed a king.

It was apparently one of the changes that had come about without her pushing, but David had appointed Uly Larionov, formerly Captain of the 1-ring Mothership *Baba Yaga*, to be Comptroller of the Court. Her personal banker, if you will. Another sign that *Corynthe* was growing up.

Arnulf Rodriguez had always hoped to found a dynasty, but more importantly, to refound *Corynthe* into a nation, and not just a random collection of planets. It had taken his death, but Jessica and her friends were making progress.

Uly Larionov was dressed simply today: slacks, shirt, and jacket in various blues of good material, and well-made, but nothing that screamed wealth or ego.

Again, nothing to prove to anybody but himself.

Next to David, in her position as his First Officer, but really Captain in everything but name, *Wiley*, quietly measuring everyone in the room.

Finally, at the far end of the table, looking relaxed and proper, if a tad out of place, Fleet Centurion Whughy, flanked by the two Flag Centurions, Enej and Cheng Yin Dominguez.

As councils of war went, unimpressive, but she would have brought Denis, Alber', Robbie, and Tomas at a minimum, if it had been serious.

This was diplomacy.

"First off," Jessica said. "Thank you. For being prepared to move, and ready to go. It is a tremendously long sail to *St. Legier*, and you've given me enough time to make a few stops along the way."

She turned and smiled at Desianna.

"My only regret is that I can't take you away from *Petron* for most of a year to join me."

David cleared his throat diplomatically from her left.

Jessica glanced at him sidelong.

"A thought, Your Majesty," he said in a smiling, almost sarcastic tone. "In the interests of diplomacy, we will, of necessity, be working closely with Whughy's squadron for an extended period. If you would be amenable, I propose a trade, whereby Desianna accompanies you, and your Flag Centurion, Zivkovic, takes over as a senior advisor to the government here. I believe we will be able to survive in her absence."

And where Enej and *Furious* wouldn't be separated for ten months or longer. They hadn't gotten married before now only because Cho wasn't ready to settle down. They would, one of these days.

"I see," Jessica said carefully.

She fixed her Flag Centurion with a look, and he nodded with a smile.

"It was my idea," Larionov said simply, glancing right and left at any that would challenge him.

Not necessarily the most diplomatic man, but not an enemy anybody made willingly.

Jessica nodded and turned back to David.

"In that case, I need to make one important change," she said. "David Rodriguez, you are hereafter appointed Vice Admiral of the *Corynthe* Fleet, second only to myself, and senior to all Free Captains in all things. This is in addition to your other titles and duties."

Jessica turned her look to the woman next to David and locked serious eyes.

"Shiori Ness, *Wiley*, you will take command of the flagship, *Kali-ma*. Based on your uniform, I hereby appoint you to be the first Command Centurion in the history of the *Corynthe* Navy. You will exercise excellence and demand the same of your crew, that the whole reflect the greatest acclaim in serving the needs of the Nation and the will of your Queen."

It wasn't quite the orders she had received, taking over her first command, but it was close. And *Aquitaine* would provide an excellent model. *Lincolnshire* was already a close-treaty ally. In another generation, *Corynthe* might be the same.

Wiley's eyes positively glowed. Looking around, most of the table was the same way, including that old curmudgeon, Uly Larionov. His smile was perhaps the warmest.

Jessica regretted that she wouldn't have time to truly enjoy this visit, needing to change vessels and depart in less than a single, whirlwind week.

She still had to walk into that ninth circle of hell, the Imperial Palace at *St. Legier.*

And do so as a polite guest.

CHAPTER VII

IMPERIAL FOUNDING: 176/04/17. IMPERIAL PALACE, WERDER, ST. LEGIER

Emmerich couldn't remember the last time he had seen Joh, *His Sovereign Imperial Majesty, Johannes Arend Wiegand, Emperor Karl VII*, so utterly pissed. The man was usually much calmer, more diplomatic, less given to displays of emotion in public.

Or at least as public as the room where this group routinely met.

Eight men, all kin, around a conference table. The big kind, cut and polished out of a single piece of blue granite, resting atop heavy wooden legs, themselves dark with age and polish. The walls around the men were rather plain, made from a dark, expensive jade covered with a few tapestries that represented particularly important moments in the founding and history of the *Fribourg Empire*.

It was a harsh room. These were harsh men.

One measure of the emotional starkness in the room was the way many of them jumped when Joh slammed his open, right palm onto the table top to make a point.

Emmerich had seen it coming. For about the last five minutes, which was still about three longer than he had initially expected.

"I said no," Karl VII commanded in a heavy voice. "I have made my decision and you will abide by it. This is in the best interests of the Empire, your own petty piques and grumblings notwithstanding."

Uncle Kunibert, Grand Admiral Marquering, Commander of the

Imperial Fleet, scowled back. It was almost like seeing Joh's father, Karl VI, seated there.

Eerie.

"I appreciate the diplomacy of inviting this *woman* to the biggest social event of the season," Kunibert began slowly, barely taming the anger in his voice. "I do not believe that honoring her so publically is a wise choice. I care what the people will say."

"If the Peace is to last, it must be honored," the Emperor replied gruffly. Emmerich judged him as almost past diplomacy at this point. "As for the population, they will rest easier, knowing that neither of those women are coming for them. Let us not forget the impact that Kermode has had on this war, as well as Keller."

Joh took a deep breath and fixed everyone at the table with a hard look. Emmerich noted that Joh almost smiled at him, but *he* hadn't been arguing with his Emperor for the last half hour. The Emperor would make the policy. That was his job.

For the rest of them, it would their jobs to enforce it.

Being uncles and cousins just meant that this was a family intrigue, on top of everything else.

"We cannot continue to fight a war on two fronts," Joh growled. "Not with as dangerous a foe as *Buran* has turned out to be. *Aquitaine* is already nearly too big to digest."

He reached out and picked up the nearly-forgotten briefing packet that had accompanied them into the meeting this morning, quickly flipping it to a specific page with a pink tag sticking out.

"The cost of fighting Jessica Keller was spelled out for us in detailed terms by a team of economists I assigned," he said. "If you look on the bottom of page twenty-seven, you will see the absolute cost in men and materials. If you want the estimated additional costs as a factor of lost revenue, opportunity costs, and other factors, that is on page fifty-one."

His glare was back. Staring daggers at the room didn't do it justice.

Staring battleaxes, maybe.

"We cannot afford to fight Jessica Keller and Moirrey Kermode," Joh concluded. "I'm not sure we can beat her, or *Aquitaine*, on her terms, as both Em and Kozlov have attempted. That is a task I would happily leave for Ekke, when he reigns in my place. After those two women are no longer on the front line. We are bigger than *Aquitaine*, gentleman. Time is on our side, presuming we can push the *M'hanii Frontier* back and hold those people as well."

Normally, this would have been the point when Emmerich expected his cousin Sigmund to speak up, challenge Joh one last time, just to prove a point. Or perhaps Artur Marquering, Kunibert's younger brother, would step into the fray. They were like that.

Instead Emmerich noted the rigid silence of both men. Perhaps Joh had finally gotten through to them about the precarious state of the Empire. Even Sigmund might grow up, one of these days.

Pigs had been known to fly.

"If there are no other questions?" Joh announced in a heavy, challenging voice. "Hearing none, this meeting is adjourned."

The look in the Emperor's eyes was an invitation for Em to lag behind the rest.

Emmerich took his time gathering his papers and let the others of the Imperial Fleet Council depart, until he was alone with Joh and a handful of bodyguards.

"Lunch plans?" Joh asked in an entirely different tone of voice than he had used two minutes earlier.

"I was supposed to be in a meeting with you for another hour," Em replied with a grin. "My schedule seems to have an unexpected opening."

"Walk with me," Karl VII commanded lightly, rising and stepping around the table.

The years had been kinder to Joh than himself. The Emperor still had half a head of brown hair above the gray, despite being a year older. Em had given up and learned to live with everything coming in silver now. From behind, it was one of the only ways to tell the two men apart, physically.

Armed men fell in around them, maintaining a polite, paranoid distance as the two cousins exited the building and began to cross a large, overgrown courtyard to the personal part of the palace.

"Days like this, I miss Hans," Joh ventured.

Em had to agree. Hans Huff, yet another uncle, had been an exceptional Grand Admiral of the Fleet. His retirement, although long-expected, had changed the balance of things in the family. And in the Council. Kunibert and his brother were more emotional, more excitable. Hans had been the practical one, spending his focus on how to make things run smoother.

Em decided that the other two men were just too much glory hounds. It wasn't enough to be in the Inner Council that really made decisions. They wanted to be in charge.

There had been a great deal more butting of heads over the last year, as a result.

It was spring on *St. Legier*. The planet had originally been settled for the similarity to the lost Homeworld in that way. There was a calculation for adding a day to the local calendar every decade or so, just to keep sidereal time in harmony with the ancient calendar, but the rest of the time, the seasons balanced, unlike most habitable planets.

The breeze had finally lost that bitter, chilled edge, but they were down in a courtyard now, blocked on all sides by six- and seven-story buildings. Things were calmer.

"How go the Builder's Trials?" Joh asked absently as they walked.

Em felt a smile for the first time all morning.

"Officially?" he replied. "Exactly on schedule."

"Oh? And unofficially?" Joh glanced over.

"Captain Saar is confident that he'll be ready for Induction to the Fleet in time for the wedding, minus only the final loadout of missiles and consumables for a long voyage we aren't scheduled to take until spring anyway," Em replied. "His hope is that Heike will be able to Sponsor her as a honeymoon gift."

"I see," Joh said. "And the reason to keep it so quiet?"

"He's the best, but to get there, Saar has to push everyone," Em continued. "And the schedule has to be perfect. If something goes wrong, as normal, they'll miss the wedding itself, and have to do it early next year, like the formal schedule calls for. They would rather it be a surprise for my daughter."

The two men approached the door to the Family Wing of the palace. Four guards came to attention and saluted as the party came in from the sunshine, surrounded suddenly by valets and attendants. They traversed hallways in silence until Joh led him into a smaller conference room, deep inside the building.

"Coffee immediately, please," the Emperor said to one of the valets. "And then menus for lunch."

The man nodded silently and disappeared quickly from the room, leaving them alone, however briefly.

"Thank you again," Emmerich said abruptly.

"For?"

"Keller," Em replied.

It was a shorthand, but they had known each other for fifty years.

"Em," the Emperor smiled. "You ask so little of me normally. It was my pleasure to finally be able to do something for you for once. Hopefully, we can convince *Aquitaine* that we're serious about the Peace. Their spies will find out about *Buran* soon enough, if they don't already know. And I know how much you wanted to be back in the field. This is a good way to send you off to *Osynth B'Udan.*"

Emmerich nodded.

"Besides," Joh continued. "I can't think of anyone better suited to taking a new Paladin-class Battleship into the line, especially since we really don't understand how *Buran's* weapons systems or tactics are going to evolve, once we get serious. Nor why we have never been able to capture one of their warships intact enough to examine."

"I presume fanatics, Joh," Em replied. "Death before dishonor. It is something I see occasionally around us, even though we have tried to beat it out of these men. As for the other, their physics are wrong."

"Wrong, Em?"

"They don't use Primaries, Your Majesty," the Red Admiral felt himself drop into lecture mode of habit. "And, as near as we can tell, they use something akin to the ancient jump drive of our ancestors. It's like they never encountered any of our technological advancements over the last five centuries. Or they don't care."

"Interesting. I had not grasped that."

"It's not widely known, even in the fleet. At the same time, they can actually jump inside a gravity well in ways we don't understand," Em said. "Both accurately and fairly quickly. And their main weapon is some sort of magnetic shear beam, instead of an electromagnetic pulse as we originally thought. Short range, practically knife-fighting, but shields barely slow it down."

"So how do we defeat them?"

The Emperor was back now, rather than Em's best friend. A man focused on the well-being of over a thousand inhabited worlds, and several hundred billion Imperial citizens.

They faced a wolf come in from the darkness. A fox raiding the chickens, killing a few, and then vanishing back into the night.

A being known in whispers as *Buran,* the *Lord of Winter.*

"If I could," Em opined softly. "I would recruit Kermode, show her everything, and let her work her wicked magic. If the Peace holds another five years, I might submit a formal request."

"Em, if the raids continue like this, and the Peace is still there in five years, I might approve it. I already plan to Knight the woman, one of the few such women ever. If you tell me she is all that can save the Empire, we'll talk."

"She's not all, Joh," Em said in a low, tight voice.

"Oh?"

"We might need Jessica Keller."

CHAPTER VIII

Jessica expected more of a lurch on docking. A bang. Something visceral.

She looked over at Desianna and *Wiley* with a grin.

Jessica had gotten spoiled by flying with *Gaucho*. Or maybe jaded. Even Branca Rocha, the commander of her DropShip *Petron*, didn't land so softly.

Instead, a light ping, almost a docking bell, save for the slightest bump as the Royal Transport Yacht, *Baxter*, docked with Jessica's flagship. David had called the little shuttle a *lorcha*, an ancient term referring to a type of maritime sailing vessel that combined a Chinese sailing rig with a Portuguese hull, in order to get the best of both worlds. Jessica had spent much of a morning researching those terms, just to understand.

More cargo and a faster hull.

Or, in this case, a *Salonnian* administrative shuttle, manufactured by Ba Xìn Heavy Industries, with custom engines designed and built by Tomakomai Engineering Research, of *Petron*. Someone with a sardonic sense of humor had welded two halves of nameplates together and tacked it to the rear wall of the small bridge.

Ba X\T.E.R.

It had stuck. Everyone called the ship *Baxter*.

And Jessica wouldn't mind traveling a long journey aboard her.

She had been prepared for the cramped quarters she remembered from the last time she had been aboard *Kali-ma*. Instead, David had surprised her with luxury.

A so-called Royal Transport Yacht.

A fully self-contained environment, lacking only JumpSails to get anywhere, with a pair of ambassadorial cabins double the size that even *Wiley* had on the main hull as a commander, plus her own private shower, oversized kitchen with a small staff, and a hall for dining or entertaining. Stained, wood-paneled walls. Thick, handmade rugs tacked to the floors everywhere. Earth tones painted on every surface.

Jessica had been prepared to push hard on this sail, in a zig-zag, to call on friendly worlds, or at least neutral ones, so that everyone would have a chance to get away from each other for a day or so after she crammed her whole group in with the rest of the crew. Instead, she had nearly a quarter more useful living space aboard *Kali-ma*, and had a pleasant place to stay. She could work here without getting in *Wiley's* way. Plus, the interior would impress visitors when they got to *St. Legier*.

With the 1-ring Cargoship *Marco Polo* accompanying them, it verged on naval decadence.

Her thoughts must have been visible on her face. Or Desianna was thinking the same thing. Or maybe reading her mind. She did that, occasionally.

"We imported the best barbarian finery from *Fribourg* for the occasion," Desianna said with a smirk, gesturing around them as the inner airlock opened with a hiss. Unlike the pilots of the fighters and other shuttles, Jessica could walk straight across airlocks to *Kali-ma* in a dedicated hallway.

"I see that," Jessica replied as they went down a stairway into the main, spinal corridor.

Jessica followed *Wiley* as the Command Centurion turned right and passed through another bulkhead/airlock, entering into the bow portion of the flagship, Desianna and the others in tow. Unlike either of the *Auberons* Jessica had commanded, *Kali-ma* was tiny, like all 4-ring Motherships.

The bow of the vessel was an arrowhead shape with four blades, fins almost, equidistant around the centerline like points of a compass. The stern contained the engine cluster and Jumpdrive assembly.

Normally, a vessel like this was made up of parts ripped from a variety of other ships and welded together as if in someone's backyard orbital platform instead of a professional facility. The previous *Kali-ma*, Ian Zhao's chariot, the professional raider and veteran of the *Battle of Petron*, had been.

This one, *her* new *Kali-ma*, had been professionally designed and purpose-built. Jessica had dedicated a lot of thought, and a good budget, towards building a warship. She had engaged a yard in *Aquitaine* to do the work, not because *Corynthe's* shipwrights couldn't handle the task, but because they could travel to *Aquitaine* and see something built to *Republic of Aquitaine* naval specifications, and bring that knowledge home.

It has been an extremely expensive undertaking.

Looking around as she walked towards the bow, it had been worth every Lev she had spent.

The centerline of the ship, where they had docked, was a narrow cylinder, like a goose's neck connecting the two ends, but much, much longer. Around the neck, like mosquitos squatting on skin ready to bite, were rings of fighters and miniature gunships, no two designs repeated.

Like the other Motherships in the fleet, the flight wing had been thrown together in someone's backyard, if that backyard had at least three of every kind of starfighter ever flown, chopped into pieces and stacked randomly, waiting to be welded into some new configuration by a demented beaver with a laser torch. Someplace like *Bunala*.

But this was the flagship of the *Corynthe* fleet. Those craft were piloted by some of the best in the nation. Probably at least as good as the top third in *Aquitaine's* Navy.

Wiley turned and entered a noisy chamber on the port side of the main hall, rapping her knuckles hard against a steel bulkhead loudly as she did.

"Quiet," she ordered in a voice used to being obeyed. "All rise."

Jessica entered first. Desianna, Marcelle, and Willow could peek in from the hallway, and would probably enter in a bit, but Jessica wanted this moment to herself.

Wiley stood at the bottom of a small auditorium. On the blueprints, this was the pilot's briefing room. In front of her, all of *Kali-ma's* pilots came to stillness, save for the rustling as they came to their feet.

Jessica had been expecting all of the fliers to be men, as had been the case every other time she had come home.

She was almost right.

Most were, ranging in size and complexion and color across the entire spectrum of humanity.

But it was the two girls standing in the front row that caught her eye.

At least close sisters, if not identical twins. They had that same golden skin; the straight, black hair; the emerald-colored, almond-shaped eyes that were so common in this sector of space, originally colonized by descendants of the ancient colony *Nihon*. They could have been Petia Naoumov's daughters, if they had been taller.

But they were tiny. No taller than Moirrey Kermode, but built like Nina Vanek. Almost ethereal. Maybe forty-five kilos soaking wet.

And young. To Jessica's eye, they both looked fourteen at most. Not even ready to go to Fleet Academy. Maybe the Boarding School for a few years, like she had.

But they were here, in the room, obviously members of the First Fighter Squadron, *Corynthe*.

The Queen's Own.

Jessica nodded and stepped to the center of the room, resting her hands on the lectern and making eye contact with every man and woman in front of her as *Wiley* stepped to one side.

"Some of you I have not flown with before," Jessica said by way of opening. "But you wouldn't be here if David and *Wiley* didn't think you were the best."

She paused to smile at all of them.

"When we get to *St. Legier*," she continued. "I expect to show you off. The Emperor will have dress units, peacocks in pretty livery. I plan to challenge them to some real flying, like we did before at *Callumnia*, and I want you to take them for every Florin, every Lev, that you can. We'll nail the first one you win to the bulkhead on the bridge, and leave it there for as long as *Kali-ma* flies."

Jessica was rewarded by a growling whoop. These men and women were pirates in their hearts, not sailors. They wanted to be challenged, not commanded. Led, not ordered. They would have stayed on their own Motherships, to be big fish in small ponds, otherwise.

To fly with the *Queen's Own* was to skirt the edge of catastrophe with the elite. Who knew when the next batch of trouble would drop out of JumpSpace and require the awesomest?

"It will be a hard sail to get there," Jessica continued. "We'll be in Jumpspace for most of the time, except when we need to rendezvous with *Marco Polo* and take on supplies. I expect each of you to spend a great deal of time in the simulators I bought, so that we're ready to show the Imperials up. Can you do that?"

This time it sounded like an angry growl, deep and hungry.

She had them, now.

The Queen's Own.

CHAPTER IX

DATE OF THE REPUBLIC JULY 14, 398 KALI-MA. WAYPOINT 098S3Y-2D9JF4

"I've watched the two of you in the flight simulators," Jessica began carefully. "First off, I wasn't even sure they could be programmed that way. But then I remembered where I was. What I don't understand is why."

Today's meeting was aboard *Baxter*, in the front sitting room Jessica had taken to calling the *Salon*. Jessica had brought Nicolai Aoiki with her on this jaunt, rather than letting Denis and David have him to themselves. Marcelle was acting as steward, serving everyone, which today involved communal dishes of rice, vegetables, and meat, in a variety of sauces. Willow stood her shift at the front door, professionally paranoid.

They had set out a conference-style table today, dark, polished wood Jessica couldn't identify, except that it went with the wood paneling and book cases on the walls.

Jessica had been afraid the room would come across as too masculine, but then she remembered that Desianna had been in charge. The space instead looked more like a rich Fleet Lord's library. There were throw rugs tacked down. Two comfortable sofas perpendicular to each other. Several soft chairs.

Home.

Around the table, Jessica smiled at the group. Vo Arlo had kept mostly to himself, and spent as much time as he could training down and aft in *Kali-ma*'s gym, so he wasn't here. Once Chef Aoiki had retreated to his kitchen, the rest of room was entirely female. Marcelle and Willow. Desianna and *Wiley*. Moirrey. And the two newcomers Jessica has specifically invited: *Rocket Frog* and *Neon Pink*.

Identical sisters, after all. Seventeen years old, instead of fourteen, and already top-rated pilots, but Jessica could understand why now, having watched their training sims.

Their grandfather was Uly Larionov, a man who had overcome everything the galaxy could throw at him, to advance in a culture that favored giant men, when he himself had less than half a head on Jessica. One of Larionov's sons-in-law, one of the twins' uncles, commanded the Cargoship *Marco Polo* on this epic voyage.

And the girls had themselves fostered with a man who was a legend in *Corynthe*: Iorwerth Nakamura, father of Flight Centurion Cho Ayaka Nakamura, back on *Auberon*.

Furious. At one time, for however briefly, commander of *The Queen's Own*. Cho's father was the one who had helped his only daughter build her own strike fighter when she was twelve, while all her friends were busy discovering boys.

Looking across the table, and through the steam rising from fresh dishes, Jessica could see these two growing up to be just as dangerous, in and out of the cockpit.

"It's really rather simple, Your Majesty," *Rocket Frog* replied.

Jessica thought it was *Rocket Frog*. She still hadn't picked up all the subtle cues to tell the two girls apart, especially not when they had a tendency to complete each other's sentences. The color this one had painted her nails *probably* gave her away, alternating between bright yellow and lime green.

Hopefully, *Neon Pink* also lived her color scheme in her nails.

"The edges and fluctuations of a gravity well are a mass-mass interaction across the curve of dimpled space-time," *Rocket Frog* continued. "Our two fighters are stripped down of every bit of extraneous mass possible, and then maintained as close to ideal anchor mass as possible at all times. We've programmed a great deal of math ahead of time to handle the deflection."

"But a JumpSail won't even work once you cross that line," Jessica countered.

"Correct," *Neon Pink* joined the conversation without missing a beat. "We're using straight up, old-fashioned jumpdrives, scratch-built to spec under *Pops* Nakamura's micrometer. Ancient tech. The metallurgy was really the hardest part."

"Once we programmed the nav computer on *Kali-ma*, it was easy," *Rocket Frog* continued. "Input your local gravity coefficients, depth of atmosphere readings, solar wind temperature, and orbital bodies with relevant mass signatures. Then you let the jumpdrive zero your scatter down as tight as you can. We've got enough onboard battery power to jump twice, neither of them as much as a light hour, but more than enough for our needs."

"Purpose?" Jessica asked, letting her tactical brain engage and hand off ideas to the strategist in her backbrain.

"Two ways to interpret it," *Neon Pink* said with an evil grin. "We're the Law and we've come to arrest you. Or we're pirates, and your ass is ours."

"Either way, we work the same," *Rocket Frog* continued her thought. "We've got one little Type-1 beam centerline. Just enough to keep people honest. And a pair of Type-3 Archerfish rigs on the mounts outside the twin engines. We can hop right up on you and put two or four one-shot, Type-3 beams into your ass from point blank, usually with surprise, and then blink back out. This *Kali-ma* might take it. *Auberon*, sure. Anything we're likely to run into in *Corynthe* or *Salonnia* is going to be hurting."

Jessica turned to *Wiley*.

"I'll pretend we're the Law," she said, letting her smile encompass all of the women at the table. "Any other surprises in the flight wing?"

"No, Your Majesty," *Wiley* purred back with an equal smile and wicked eyebrows.

Jessica paused and turned to the rest.

"*Eel*," *Neon Pink* replied.

"*Eel?*" Jessica asked.

There had been someone named *Eel* at the battle known as *First Petron* four years ago. Apparently, he had survived, but kept a low profile in the period since. Or someone else had taken up his name. And he was apparently flying on *Kali-ma* now.

"Right," *Rocket Frog* chimed in. "Gustav had us build him a new sled."

"Did ya nows?" Moirrey suddenly put down her tea and spoke up. "'Bouts time som'tin were done about that crazy boy. What's he gots today?"

"Cold-built from the frames out from stuff in *Pops'* yard," *Neon Pink* smiled, turning to extend the conversation across the whole group.

"Engines are tuned and balanced finally, instead of doing it with those stupid, manual twin throttles. Stuffed a generator in back and took out the back seat where his girlfriend used to ride."

"Got enough power now that he can shoot and fly without the engine shutdown," *Rocket Frog* completed the thought.

"Ooh," Moirrey grinned. "Walk *AND* chew bubblegum at the same time?"

"Dunno about that," *Wiley* suddenly said. "This is *Eel* we're talking about."

Jessica joined the rest in laughing. She was looking forward to what this group of pilots, half of them new to *Kali-ma* in the last year, could do.

Hopefully, nothing more adventurous than another Promenade.

She already had enough enemies in the *Fribourg Empire*.

CHAPTER X

IMPERIAL FOUNDING: 176/08/03. IMPERIAL PALACE, WERDER, ST. LEGIER

A rustle behind her was the only indication that someone was there, so Casey knew it had to be family coming.

Anyone else would have been challenged by Sgt. Inmon, or at least acknowledged and greeted as a way of getting Casey's attention, even in the middle of the garden of the Imperial Palace.

He was utterly dedicated to those duties.

Not many people could signal the man to remain quiet as they approached. But he was excellent at maintaining perfect silence, all by himself. That was useful when Casey was doing her art.

"I'm probably supposed to be surprised to find you mostly alone," Casey's mother said quietly as she got close. "What happened to Lady Yulia this time?"

Casey, the *Princess Imperial Kasimira Helena Wiegand*, glanced back over her shoulder and went back to her painting with a shrug. She pushed a stray lock of her long, blond hair back over her ear, not willing to reclamp everything just for a few loose hairs. She'd probably end up getting paint all over everything if she tried that right now.

She was deep in the back of the Imperial Gardens this morning, near the five-meter-tall brick wall that separated it from the ancient game park outside. Another artist would probably be working in watercolors with this bright morning light, perhaps dashing off three or four canvases in a single sitting to capture the fluidity and frailty she could see around her.

Casey had chosen to work with oils instead today.

It was a richer painting. Heavier. But it also let her better communicate the fundamental emotional signature of this corner of the garden. The air was heavy and redolent with life and scent and color this morning, especially here, where a tangle of angry roses strove to conquer the brick wall and bend the obdurate stone to its will. Or climb over it and escape into the dark woods, leaving Imperial life behind forever.

"Possibly *ennui* overcame her," Casey said lightly after a bit. "Or entropy. It can be hard to tell. I would be willing to wager a quiet corner, a comfortable chair, and a binge of her favorite soap operas with headphones on."

Mother, the Empress Kati, circled close on Casey's left side, the painting side, to observe.

"You've gotten better," she said. "More subtle in your depth of shadows and expression of negative space. And yes, Yulia is not one for extended silences, is she? But nobody in the family save you has a mind to do art for art's sake."

Casey shrugged again, unwilling to pick at that emotional scab this morning. She didn't want another row with Mother. Not today. It would be nice to go an entire week without raised voices. Unlikely, but nice.

The second daughter of a Duke or important Burggraf might be allowed to become a Bohemian artist. Doubly so with an eldest son in line to inherit everything. But never a *Princess Imperial.*

Even with a father as loving as hers.

Still, he let her paint, and write, and compose popular music and symphonies, whereas Ekke, the Crown Prince, studied being a proper Emperor. And sister Steffi, the *Imperial Princess Ekaterina Stephany*a, studied more practical things. Law. Diplomacy. Politics. But Steffi was a practical girl. Boring, almost.

They would find Steffi a fiancé soon. One who was well-bred and well-connected and whom they could use to bind the man's family more firmly to the throne. That was how politics worked.

Steffi would bear the man many happy children and be content in a life of public appearances and charitable work.

Casey hadn't had *that* conversation with Father yet, but she could see it coming in another few years. Imperial Ladies were expected to wed at around twenty-four standard years of age, following an engagement of at least two years beforehand.

At seventeen, Casey had five years, at most, before they went out and found her a husband.

Imperial nobles in good repute were rarely artists. That they were Patrons of the Arts went without saying, but few had ever actually committed art themselves.

Outwardly, Casey remained still. So much to do, and so little time to cram it all into, until she was fitted with that adamantine corset called *Respectability*.

Mother here this morning was unlikely to be a positive sign.

"You have an appointment after lunch," Mother confirmed obliquely.

The Empress was one of the few people who understood how to use pauses and non-verbal communication effectively. It kept their blow-ups to a minimum. Unlike between Mother and Steffi. Or Casey and her sister.

Casey turned her head to look fully at her mother for the first time.

She saw herself in thirty years. Tall and willowy, with shoulder-length blond hair slowly turning to silver in random stripes the Empress chose not to color. Green eyes from the Alkaev side of the family, rather than the tanzanite blue Casey had inherited from father's genes.

Casey would never be as skinny, inheriting the heavier bones and broader shoulders of the Wiegand clan, but the coloration would run much the same. Hopefully, she would keep as much of the slender beauty as possible.

And the calm temperament.

"Oh?" Casey replied simply.

Sgt. Inmon hadn't reminded her of anything, and he took those duties earnestly, having forgetful daughters Casey's age back home. Therefore, something new.

"A fitting for the dress you will wear to your cousin's wedding," Mother said with a chill smile that brooked no argument from her headstrong daughter. "I've found a new designer I think you will like, and doing it this early gives the two of you time to come to a consensus. She was able to clear an entire afternoon today for the two of you to argue. Or conspire."

Truly, Mother was the only one who understood the artist in the family. And today, she was apparently willing to meet her stubborn, youngest child at least midway.

She and Casey shared a secret smile.

A thought about cousin Heike, and her upcoming wedding, struck Casey's mind.

"What's Jessica Keller really like?" she asked suddenly.

Casey's reward was a raised eyebrow, but that was better than an eye roll. Not that she had ever done something like that to her own Mother. In at least several days.

"She'll be there," Casey continued, trying to frame her words, her focus, and failing. "And she'll be fierce, and exotic, and dangerous, but I'm afraid she'll turn out to be utterly boring. Just another man in uniform, when you look close enough. I want to know if there is something more."

Mother considered possible replies for several moments.

"You should ask your uncle," she said finally. "He's probably the best judge. Everyone else will just be spiteful and jealous."

Casey nodded sagely. She didn't have any uncles.

Her father had been an only child, born and raised a crown prince. All the other nobles around were cousins of some sort, however far removed, including the currently-absent Lady Yulia, herself a distaff relative from a poor branch of the family that everyone liked. Casey and her siblings had always treated Emmerich Wachturm as an uncle.

"One o'clock, in the Peacock Room," Mother said, turning and drifting away as though pushed on some breeze nobody else felt.

Mother was trying. Casey could tell.

She could make an effort as well. Jessica Keller herself would be here. This might be Casey's only chance to meet the woman who had ever defeated the odds and overcome the men in this palace.

CHAPTER XI

DATE OF THE REPUBLIC SEPTEMBER 1, 398
KALI-MA. WAYPOINT D652G0-52S235

"All hands, stand by for emergence," Jessica heard the woman calmly announce. "Flight Wing, prepare for spiral launch."

Today, *Wiley* was seated in her command chair, Command Centurion Shiori Ness at work, surrounded by several screens, with most of the bridge crew in front of her, each facing inward towards the primary hologram projector in the center. The layout was different from what Jessica was used to, but much closer to the historical pattern in *Corynthe*.

From her observer's station, back in the aft port corner of *Kali-ma's* oval-shaped bridge, Jessica watched *Wiley* work with a critical eye. It was unnecessary to grade the woman. She wouldn't be here if she wasn't a stone-cold professional.

At the same time, every Command Centurion had her idiosyncrasies. Jessica needed to learn *Wiley's*, especially with such a radically different vessel as a 4-ring Mothership. Doubly-so, with a brand new class-vessel, hopefully the first of a new design Jessica could have built, both in *Aquitaine* yards and back home on *Corynthe*.

Kali-ma was more heavily armed than the rest of the Motherships in the fleet. Each of the four blades on the arrowhead bow had a Type-3 beam emplacement at the tip, with a tremendous arc of available fire. In addition, there was another one on the stern, below the engine cluster. Before Jessica, a 4-ring Mothership might have had at most two such beams, instead relying mostly on a random collection of randomly-placed

Type-2 and Type-1 beams for defense, and using the flight wing as her only offense.

Corynthe was going to have a proper navy, staffed by professionals. Most likely trained or mentored by *Wiley* and her crew. Jessica smiled to herself.

Wiley glanced over at that moment. Her brief smile at Jessica lit the entire bridge all by itself. The only other person Jessica could think of that smiled like that was in the aft starboard observer seat right now. But Moirrey smiled all the time.

Emergence.

Some people claimed they could not feel the difference as the JumpSails cut and dropped a ship back into real space. For Jessica, it was like falling slowly out a pool of warm water. One moment, wet, the next dry.

"Patrol Wing, fast launch now," another voice called sternly.

Yan Bedrov had been Ian Zhao's second in command, back on that fateful day. He was still tall and skinny. His short, dark hair was slowly receding from his forehead and coming in white, making him look older than forty-three standard years.

After *First Petron*, he had stayed with *Kali-ma*, and Jessica, when much of the old crew had retired, or moved on. And he had learned something useful about how to be a good Tactical Officer along the way, instead of just another of Zhao's henchmen. Both *Wiley* and David vouched for the man's competence and loyalty.

On one of the old-style Motherships, even the big 4-rings, the Captain was expected to command and fight the vessel and the fighters. That was easy when the Mothership had minimal shields, and barely enough guns to defend itself. They wouldn't go willingly into battle.

Kali-ma was a purpose-built warship.

McCandless and Daughters had built her to the same exacting standards the *Republic of Aquitaine* Navy demanded. Yan Bedrov had supervised that construction for David, and been through a six-month Reserve Commission training course while he was there on *Ladaux*.

Wiley was expected to command the battle and direct the flight wing once it launched. She was excellent at her task. The job of her Tactical Officer, Yan, was to fight the vessel itself. That was something new for *Corynthe*, but it worked.

Yan and *Wiley* were evolving into a lethal team.

Kali-ma's entire hull rang like a church bell as the twelve fighters of the Patrol Wing separated from the middle of the gooseneck almost in unison, tilted their bows outward, and lit their engines.

"Strike Wings, fast launch next," Yan commanded.

At the front of the gooseneck, *Rocket Frog* and *Neon Pink* broke free, along with *Eel* and the three heavy fighters of his element farther back. *Kali-ma* sounded like hail on a tin roof.

"Command Wing, launch and form up," Yan concluded.

There were already eighteen fighters in motion. *Baxter* went next, along with *Zorrillo*: the Royal Combat Yacht, and *Polecat*: a scratch-built, fast bomber that served the squadron in much the same manner as Jessica's own GunsShips on *Auberon*: *Necromancer* and *Sunset*.

For the old *Auberon* to launch nine fighters, one GunShip and one DropShip, roughly four minutes on a good day.

Kali-ma had just put twenty-one armed hornets into action in sixty seconds.

It was fun watching professionals work.

"Comm, I have designated Target One," *Wiley* said in a firm voice. "Flight Wing, begin your attack run. Tactical, *Kali-ma* will trail."

Yan nodded, head down over his console as he studied the paths.

"Nav, down bow plane fifteen degrees," he ordered sharply. "Come to three-five-zero, roll ten, accelerate to combat speed."

Crisp acknowledgements came from all sides. Jessica could still remember the man's bewilderment at *First Petron*, when she had taken this ship's predecessor into the combat.

Jessica watched nineteen of the craft form up into a loose spear shape and begin to track on the asteroid. *Neon Pink* and *Rocket Frog* both began accelerating madly, but in their own direction, mostly away from *Kali-ma*, but close together.

"Light Strike Team, engage now," *Wiley* said over the comm. "Squadron, come to max speed and prepare for your pass."

The two smallest fighters blinked out of space for a moment. Jessica knew where they would appear a moment later at this distance, but the scanners and computers would require several seconds to understand what had just happened and respond appropriately. Even *Kali-ma*, locked on and prepared, was slow to identify the two new arrivals.

The poor rock never saw it coming as they popped out, *Rocket Frog* and *Neon Pink* almost simultaneously. Four quick shots into the small moon blasted clouds of molten dust and lava into space as the two girls shot by at full speed.

A few second later, *Eel* opened up with his heavy lance, another Type-3, this weapon centerlined between two engines and a generator capable of recharging it. The other three of his wing let loose with a massed barrage of Type-2 beams in clusters, less effective individually at this range, but still a whole bunch of them shooting.

More rock vaporized as the rest of the squadron got close enough to pour their own fire into the stone before flaring up and starboard.

"Tactical, the Flight Wing is clear," Yan observed with a savage glee in his voice at odds with the calm smile on his face.

Wiley turned her head the other way, looking over her right shoulder this time to study Moirrey for a second.

"You're sure?" she asked the engineer in a voice that wasn't.

"You dun the maths, *Wiley*," Moirrey chirped back with a smile.

"That, I did," *Wiley* agreed with a deep, alto voice.

"Tactical," she said. "Prepare to engage."

Jessica watched the man press a button on his console that brought a smaller, personal holographic projector live in front of him. Another innovation. Or rather, a toy more expensive than *Corynthe* used to be able to afford.

Back when parties and *Events* were more important than taxes.

The projection contained a green sphere with *Kali-ma* at the center, and a score of smaller lights indicating her fighter craft. Yan pressed a button and a pink sphere appeared outside that, nearly a third of a radius larger. The outer edge of the pink was fast approaching a large asteroid quietly minding its business in a growing cloud of debris.

"Gunnery," Yan said firmly after a few minutes. "Begin salvoing your Type-3 beams now. According to Moirrey, we should be in range."

Like on *Auberon* and her squadron, every beam emplacement was tuned to a different note on a piano, letting everyone track the firing audibly. Four notes struck a single chord now.

"Three hits, Commander," Yan called from his station. "Recharging and preparing for individual engagement."

"Very good shooting," *Wiley* said, relaxing back into her chair.

Jessica was still shocked, even though she had been expecting it. After all, she had been the one to approve Moirrey's tinkering with the ship's main cannons. Those shots had been at the sort of range where ships began firing the Primaries at each other.

Back home, that was how battles were fought. You could pack more punch into a Primary than a Type-3, and they had a far greater engagement range. But they were slow to fire, and were ammunition that had to be reloaded, instead of just recharged. That made them extremely expensive, especially for the poorer nations out on the galactic perimeter. Not worth the effort or the expense.

Wiley might have been reading her mind. She turned and locked eyes with Jessica with a dead-serious look.

"This is going to up-end naval combat on the periphery," Shiori Ness said with a hard burr to her consonants. "Why has nobody done it before now?"

"Oooh, I gots an answer," Moirrey giggled. "Them folks is so rich they never'd had to does better. Rip loose with the big booms and calls it good enoughs."

"Yes, that's partly true," Jessica countered. "But you also have to consider the cost. You absolutely gain significant range effectiveness, but at what price?"

The Command Centurion nodded from her throne.

"Damage is down around thirty percent at normal engagement ranges, according to the mathematics," she said. "We'll know for sure after blasting this rock some more."

"Oy," Moirrey agreed, excitement blurring her words. "It'll no work fer fleets, unless everyone does it at once. Ya gots ta be predictables, even when yer nots. But is still daft fun, boss."

Both Jessica and Shiori smiled.

It just might up-end naval warfare again. But then, what else was a woman to do, fighting in a man's world?

CHAPTER XII

IMPERIAL FOUNDING: 176/08/09. IMPERIAL PALACE, WERDER, ST. LEGIER

On the one hand, Casey was technically too young to be drinking wine with her lunch. On the other hand, she was with family, and adults, and had cut the glass of merlot with vanilla, honey water, and cream, turning it into something approximating a purple smoothie.

And Heike and Uncle Emmerich weren't going to complain to her mother.

Imperial Valets had taken away the plates. Coffee would be delivered soon, but she could still enjoy her wine on a shadowed, second-story patio overlooking a duck pond in the early afternoon sun. It would be hot soon, but she had another hour before she needed to retreat indoors.

At least here, in the privacy of the Family wing, she could wear comfortable clothes: Capri pants and a cross-over tunic in soft, gray linen. Heike worn a sundress in cornflower blue. Uncle Em wore his usual uniform, the Red Admiral as Crimson Imperial Hawk.

Uncle Em leaned back and held his own crystal goblet of burgundy negligently.

"So what are you really up to, Casey?" he drawled. "Lunch was splendid. The view relaxing. But you've been dancing around something for the last hour."

Even his voice sounded like Father. It was fortunate this man had gone fully gray, or she might feel like confessing all her sins now and be done with it. Having shaved off the beard he had worn the last few years had made Em almost an Imperial doppelgänger again.

Heike leaned forward, resting her elbows on the table and letting her blue eyes twinkle. Had they been as close in age as Father and Uncle Em, she and Casey might be mistaken for twins. Certainly sisters, rather than close cousins. Casey's hair was a hand span longer. Heike had perhaps a handful of kilos as she started to develop a woman's curves to Casey's lean athleticism.

They even thought alike, youngest daughters of important men, smart and blond and creative. Casey was glad she had someone like Heike around her growing up, and not just her ultra-boring sister Steffi.

Casey took a sip to order her thoughts. It hadn't helped so far, but Uncle Em deserved an honest answer.

"Jessica Keller," she finally blurted out.

Uncle Em's eyes got a distant glint to them, lost inside some memory for a moment. He smiled warmly at his youngest daughter, and then her.

"Ah. She reminds me of two young ladies I know," he said obliquely. "Very smart, and with a dedicated, artistic bent. At one point, I wanted Heike to grow up to be like her, and then I hated her and tried to kill the woman. Now, she is probably the most dangerous threat to the Empire."

"Besides *Buran*?" Casey asked.

She had been in Fleet Intelligence briefings. It was a necessity for the Imperial family to know what was really going on, regardless of what the press might spin.

"No," Uncle Em replied coldly.

His Wiegand-blue eyes had grown serious and dark. His manner suggested something of a bear roused mid-winter. Casey watched the man turn from a favorite uncle into a terrible warrior in a single breath. *This* was the Red Admiral, seated before her, suddenly.

"No," he continued. "*Buran* is strange and exotic. They only fight if provoked, and then it is to the death, and they rarely want to trade. We do not understand them, but we have been able to sustain the *M'hanii Frontier* while fighting *Aquitaine*. Without Nils Kasum and Jessica Keller at our backs, we can push *Buran* back. We will start the crusade early next year."

"So the Peace really is just a means to get Jessica Keller off the game board?" Casey asked.

She could feel herself turning into her mother, that serious tone, incisive questions, nose aquiver for threats.

Not the worst role model, all things considered.

"Not just, Princess," Em countered, coming back from the dark place and fixing his softening glare on her, and then Heike. "But yes, my life, my planning becomes much easier without that woman going for my kidneys with a blade."

"So what is the person like, Father?" Heike spoke up for the first time. "We know the terrible legend, and the distorted tales spun across the galaxy."

Uncle Em smiled at that and licked his lips with a chuckle.

"Most of those lies and legends are my fault," he grinned.

"How so?" Heike asked.

"She would be a terribly dangerous role model for Imperial women," Uncle Em said. "Especially smart, impressionable ones. A blue-collar girl, identified by a series of exams that all students take when they are twelve. Sent away to a boarding school for young warriors they want to mold. Mentored by the man who would later go on to command the First Fleet, and then the entire *Aquitaine* Navy, Nils Kasum. The youngest of this and that and the other along the way."

"Our spies learned all this?" Heike asked. She had been a student before she was expected to turn into a Lady, and both Imperial Princesses had been in her charge when they were much younger.

"She told me most of it herself," Em replied serenely. "Primarily at *Bunala*, but at a few other places. None of it is secret. The secret is how smart, how capable she really is. How dangerous."

"Oh?" Casey asked, willing to let the man talk as much as he wanted, now that she had him on the topic she really desired.

"Ian Zhao was one of the most dangerous fighting men in *Corynthe*, Casey," Uncle Em's eyes bored in to hers. "One point nine meters tall, strong, fast. Physically at his peak. Smart as well. Canny. Capable. Understand that he had won several duels to the death with blades before he fought Keller. The man never stood a chance."

"None?" Casey followed up.

"None," Em exhaled definitively. "According to our spies, she is always planning, always war-gaming scenarios, political as well as military. Put that mind into a well-trained body, honed by the requirements of fighting with the blade, and you have a most dangerous opponent, child."

"Is she better than you?" Casey asked hard, almost brutally.

Heike hissed under her breath, almost silently. Her recoil was barely noticeable. Casey was keyed up and watching that closely.

Interestingly, Uncle Em didn't move, didn't flinch, didn't react at all.

Instead, his eyes got that far-away gleam to them again, trailing off over her left shoulder to find some spot on the horizon. Or memory.

"Yes, Casey, she is," he said simply after a few beats.

Heike's eyes flashed angry, just for a moment. Casey had watched the older woman long enough to spot the signs, but Heike controlled it well.

"Just like that?" Casey asked.

This was not the answer she had expected. But this was Uncle Em, and she had asked him an honest question demanding the truth. Imperial Princess Kasimira, asking the Empire's premier strategist for a specialist's technical opinion.

Casey began to understand why her Father had relied on the Red Admiral for so long. Solid thrones could be built on such men's shoulders.

"Kozlov was blinded by ego," Uncle Em explained, taking them back to the events at *Thuringwell* that had driven the *Fribourg Empire* to offer a Peace they finally meant to honor. "I let myself be taken by rage. At *Petron*, Keller was almost overwhelmed by despair, but she still overcame it and won."

Petron. Capital world of *Corynthe*. The battle to defend a newly-won crown.

Queen of the Pirates.

"Who was Daneel Ishikura, the man?" Casey probed deeper.

Warlock. Even on distant *St. Legier*, romance writers, like ancient bards, had told the tale of the pirate captain who won the heart of a beautiful queen. Casey had fantasies of a man like that sweeping her off her feet and taking her away to a beach somewhere, where she might sit and paint all day, Imperial necessity be damned.

Uncle Em's smile turned sideways and wry.

"When I first met the man, he was angry enough to commit treason," the Red Admiral said. "Would have become the next King of the Pirates, after Arnulf Rodriguez. I saw the electricity between the two long before either of them would admit it. I am still surprised she survived. I'm not sure I could have lost Freya like that and continued."

Aunt Freya. The other half of Uncle Em, largely unknown behind all the legends of the man himself.

The Fleet wife who kept the home fires burning while her sailor risked distant shores.

"So is she driven by that sadness?" Heike inquired.

Uncle Em shook himself.

"No," he said. "At the end of the day, that woman is driven by duty, Casey. By excellence. Nothing less."

Casey nodded.

That was what drove her, as well, though she would never admit it out loud, even with Em.

To do something, and be the best at it. To be judged on merit and not gender. Not social rank.

Excellence itself.

CHAPTER XIII

DATE OF THE REPUBLIC SEPTEMBER 4, 398
KALI-MA. JUMPSPACE

"So, Mister Arlo," the woman asked him carefully in her lovely voice. "What do you think?"

Vo bit his tongue. It was that or grind his teeth. At the end of the day, him being here was nothing but his own damned fault. And maybe the Fleet Centurion's, for providing him an example.

And selling him the rope.

Back home, uniforms more or less fit, and he had learned enough skill with needle and thread over the years to make necessary adjustments.

There weren't many uniforms that were sized to fit a man that was two meters tall and weighed one hundred twenty-five kilos. Less so, since all his mass was in his shoulders and thighs, rather than wrapped around his gut, like most officers.

He had never owned a *tailored* anything, much less a full dress uniform.

And never, in his wildest dreams, did Vo Arlo ever imagine wearing the full dress uniform of a Colonel in the *Fribourg Imperial Army*.

And yet, here he was.

Vo studied his image in the three-sided mirror carefully while the woman waited.

It frightened him, when he considered that the lovely woman next to him had located and brought with her a dressing mirror tall enough and wide enough for a man his size to stand in a small conference room and put everything on.

But then Vo remembered where Ms. Indah-Rodriguez came from. Men his size were far more common in the Royal Palace on *Petron*.

She might have had this *handy*.

Vo knew she and Moirrey were both experts at cloth and fashion, so he took a deep breath, amazed at how well the uniform moved with him as his ribs flexed outward, and tried to give her an honest opinion.

Impractical. That was the word that came to mind. The *Republic of Aquitaine* Navy was boringly practical in uniform choices. Everything designed to go under an emergency suit quickly. Nothing sticking out. The colors were muted and professional. The fabrics tight and light, assuming a controlled environment on a starship.

Nothing like *this*.

Vo would grant that he looked the part of a Dire Peacock. People would be in awe of his presence. Moirrey and Ms. Indah-Rodriguez would guarantee that.

But who the hell was that guy in the mirror?

Close-fitted, doublet-style jacket in cobalt blue, or maybe a shade lighter. Moirrey would know the color's hexadecimal number off the top of her head. It conformed to his waist and flared out to wrap around his broad shoulders in a way that reminded Vo of a sail. Or a big, blue tree.

Twelve brass buttons down the center of his chest. Six of them were hooked now, and the other six, from what his studies had covered, were largely decorative these days. Indeed, the top half of the front was intended to fold back into notched lapels that displayed what heraldrists and tailors called a *facing colour*, in this case, a red soft enough to be polite, when he had been expecting bold and obnoxious.

He could handle polite.

Every visible seam of the jacket was done in a yellowish color, about as wide as his smallest finger, and then embroidered over that in gold-colored thread. Down the center of his chest, around the waist, both wrists, along the edge of the jacket facing. The pattern was also worked into little, half-moon shapes that flared nearly a handspan out over each shoulder point and were apparently called wings, but looked more like something useful in armor to protect the joint.

At his wrists, a single white star was apparently his only rank insignia, the uniform stating the case for the rest.

And pearls, let us not forget the several dozen little, white pearls, apparently real, drilled off center and hand-stitched onto the fabric as part of the embroidery.

The lapels of the doublet were folded back now. He wore a linen dress shirt in cream underneath, buttoned up the center, with collars that folded down at the neck into strange, little triangles over a tiny, silk neck scarf Ms. Indah-Rodriguez had called a cravat tie. He was more than willing to let one of the tiny women stand on a footstool and tie it for him, and to put the stick pin in that held it all in place.

He would have ended up bleeding all over the nice shirt if he'd tried.

Around his waist, Vo wore a sash in a style Moirrey had called a cummerbund, two hands wide and tied into a decorative knot on his left hip with bits that dangled down to his left knee. It should have made his jacket hang funny, but the two women knew what they were doing.

It fit perfectly with front of the doublet that just covered his belt, while the back dropped down into blunt half-tails just about long enough to cover his butt if he stood still.

The pants he wore were uncomfortable and baggy, but that was by design. He was used to straight legs with lots of pockets when he was in the field. Instead, he had stirrup pants, tight around his calf to tuck into tall boots, and then poofed, almost jodhpurs, above that. With a blue stripe down the outside that matched his doublet. And the pants were made from the starkest white linen he could imagine would attract every dust bunny and speck of dirt in the room.

Plus, they had no pockets at all. None. And instead of a proper fly, they had a pair of small brass buttons, eight centimeters apart, that held up a flap embroidered in the same yellow thread as above.

Vo presumed that the overall look was designed to obscure the fact that an officer had turned into a lardass from too much sitting and too much wine, so they had just gone ahead and given everybody that disguise ahead of time.

At least there were two, small pockets inside his doublet.

It was the boots that were insane. With feet his size, Vo had a cobbler's appreciation of quality footwear. What he had on met that criteria, but the original fashion designer was nuts.

Dark brown leather with pitifully thin soles originally, Vo had required that they redo them with outdoor treads and padding inside, plus a metal cup over the toes. One put them on by stuffing stirruped feet down the tube, hooking fingers in little loops at the top, and then pulling hard. Once on, you folded the top down twice, to mid-calf, in a look Vo couldn't help but compare to a low-budget pirate movie.

And then, the accessorization began. Began, mind you.

On each deltoid muscle, there was a flap of cloth, blue with that same yellow facing line running along both outer edges. It was sewn at the shoulder and hooked with another brass button up near his neck. Vo had thought they were purely decorative, initially.

He was wrong.

Now, a white leather baldric was attached under that epaulet on his right side, crossing over to hold up a dress saber on his left hip. At least that one was from *Aquitaine*'s Fourth Saxon Legion. Another strap ran from the left shoulder to a messenger bag tucked in on his right side.

Take away all of a man's pockets, and you have to provide him a purse to carry things around.

And how had these two women done it all? Vo had seen the pallet of flat rolls of fabric that had arrived for him. Bolts. Fabric came in bolts. Lots of blue, lots of white, half as much red and yellow. Apparently, according to the women, enough material for four full uniforms, even at his size. There had been time to get one done, and get it perfect. So they did.

And it was.

Well, almost. There was currently no provision on this uniform for a pistol, and no expectation that he would need one, but Moirrey had gone ahead and made him one that would attach to his belt. Vo had left that in one of the carrying cases.

Carrying cases. He would need an entire room soon, just for the cases, and the damned hats he was accumulating, at this rate. And the small, aluminum cases to protect them during shipping.

The hats thankfully came already assembled. Custom measured for his oversized skull.

Atop his head, a tube of black leather and bangles called a *shako*. Short brimmed in black leather in front as well. Flaring out slightly as it ascended, with a brass badge on the front, about the size of his hand. Two leather and brass straps, highly decorative, but still functional, rested across the brim, but could be disconnected from each other and turn magically into a chinstrap. A short, braided rope in white hooked above Vo's left ear, dangled across the front above his eyes, to hook on the right, with a complicated, fringed knot hanging down from that.

A cropped, yellow feather, called a *hackle*, stuck up another twenty centimeters from the peak of the shako, attached to the two-centimeter red cloth band that ran around the top. It was a good thing there were three-meter ceilings in here.

Peacock.

Dire peacock. Crossed with a giant, carnivorous emu.

But, damn, he looked impressive, especially with exactly two awards pinned on his chest: the full-sized Order of Baudin, rather than the simple bar for his medal rows, and his Republic Cross. With Bar.

Vo took one more breath, deep and heavy, flexing just to see how well the doublet moved. It didn't pinch anywhere, which was a first for him.

Desianna Indah-Rodriguez, First Minister of *Corynthe*, widow of Arnulf Rodriguez, fashion expert, smiled up at him. He knew she was tall for a woman, but everyone was tiny standing next to him. She didn't feel tiny. Any more than Moirrey did.

Vo sighed.

"If I said ceremonial ox on the way to a sacrifice," he said. "That would cover it. But you two did an amazing job making me look distinguished on the way, especially with what you had to start with."

She laughed, a throaty, warm sound that filled the small room.

"Vo," she said with a broad smile. "If Jessica hadn't specifically declared you off-limits…"

She reached out a hand and brushed away something on his chest, and then looked up and grinned at him, like they were sharing a secret.

Wait. Fleet Centurion had declared him off-limits? Him? Really?

What was it about him that women found attractive?

Vo studied his look in the mirror one more time. Colonel (Honorary) of the Third Regiment, 189th Division Imperial.

Yeah, at least this ox would look good.

CHAPTER XIV

DATE OF THE REPUBLIC SEPTEMBER 14, 398
KALI-MA. JUMPSPACE

"Damn, girl," Saša, *Rocket Frog*, exclaimed at her sister, standing there on the scale. "You're nearly a kilo underweight today. You been skipping breakfast on me?"

"No," Asra, *Neon Pink*, replied with a sigh, stepping back down to the deck. "Been working too many late nights tuning the jump computer. Probably forgot a dinner somewhere."

"Well, here," Saša said, picking up her sister's bundle of clothes and then reaching for her own. "We're going down to the Wardroom and I'm stuffing a bagel or something down you right now."

Asra took the clothes and started dressing slowly.

Up close now and paying attention, Saša could see how bloodshot her twin's eyes had gotten.

"That can't be all of it," *Rocket Frog* continued. "You can't fool me, you know. I'm the only one that can tell us apart."

Neon Pink laughed at that.

"No, I don't suppose it is," she said, pulling on a fuchsia sweater to make it easier for everyone else to guess.

They would probably still guess wrong fifty percent of the time, aware of the practical jokes the twins liked to play.

"So talk, younger-by-eight-minutes," *Rocket Frog* commanded.

"It's got to be perfect, you know," *Neon Pink* replied, pulling on her slippers. "I can always board with an extra brick to bring me up to baseline. That's why we have them. But *St. Legier*'s mass base is a frigging state secret. You have any idea how hard it is to estimate all the variables when the big one is X?"

"It does NOT have to be perfect, you know," *Rocket Frog* said, always faster to dress and waiting on her. "No way Jessica wants to show us off the first week we're in system. We're her trump card, you know. All she's gonna want us do is outfly all the Imperial punks who think they know how to walk the curves of space-time."

"Then why does it matter if I'm under by a kilo?"

Rocket Frog glared at her, but Saša was there underneath the bluff façade.

"It means you're cutting corners, Asra," Saša said. "It's okay to take a little break occasionally, you know. We won't get there for another two weeks. But you've got to talk to me, you know. United front. Us against all the dipshits in the galaxy. And Gustav."

"And Gustav," *Neon Pink* echoed, her voice starting to warm finally.

It was an old joke.

Eel had made it known early on that he didn't think either of the girls was good enough to fly, certainly not with him and the *Queen's Own*.

They hadn't taken *all* of his money. Just enough to make a point.

But it had turned him into one of their biggest cheerleaders afterwards.

"Now, food," *Rocket Frog* commanded. "A week in-system and either Bedrov or Himura will have all the data we need. Plus, this is supposed to be an *Earth*-like paradise. Did you ever consider using the Homeworld's stats as a baseline?"

"Crap," *Neon Pink* giggled in sudden amazement. "That'll work, too. Now I have to deal with you being right, as well? What's the world coming to?"

CHAPTER XV

IMPERIAL FOUNDING: 176/09/22. IMPERIAL CONSERVATORY, WERDER, ST. LEGIER

Emmerich was back in his old office, while the Emperor sat in the hard, wooden, guest chair. The door was closed.

It was going to be one of those conversations.

Armed men had politely and quietly cleared the rest of the hallway. At least Joh had chosen to do this late in the afternoon, when all the other academics on this floor could leave early for the day without much guilt.

Emmerich leaned forward and put both elbows on the desk so he could lean on his thumbs as he thought.

"Am I wrong?" Joh asked sincerely.

He could do that, with the door closed. Emperors weren't generally allowed mistakes in public.

"In what you did? No," Em replied. "It is possible you could have handled it differently."

"I needed the Imperial public behind me on this one," the Emperor said.

"And you have them," Em countered. "And most of the Fleet, as well."

"But?"

"But there are some old-fashioned elements in the *Brevadel,* the old nobility, Joh," Emmerich continued. "The thought of elevating *her* to be one of *them* has roused a great many of them from their torpor, my dread Majesty. You are hearing the yapping of angry, purse dogs."

"They are still important ones," Joh replied. "Both Kunibert and

Sigmund have bent my ear on the topic in the last week. Privately, but the whisper campaigns are getting louder."

"In the interests of preventing a public break with the two men over it, what are your commands?"

Emmerich leaned back and looked at the lines just starting to trace themselves into the man's face and forehead. It was like looking back in time several years at an oddly distorted mirror.

Joh leaned back as well, relaxing some of the tension out of that face.

"We have already made Keller one of the Brevadel, technically," Joh said with a quiet smile. "I would propose that we reduce the size of the personal reception we had planned for her to something more of a family dinner. There will still be a State Dinner for Queen Jessica, but she would get that anyway, and it will be stuffy and stilted. I know Casey wants to meet her. Would Heike be insulted by doing it that way?"

"Not at all, Joh," Em said. "But I have a better idea. Let us treat it like a *fait accompli* with Keller. We can keep the plan for a big reception, but turn it slightly on its head."

"How so?"

"Make it a reception to honor Arlo, instead," Em continued. "Those hidebound, old warhorses can't really argue with that, except for the traditional rivalry for the junior service. And that would bring even more of the Army Command onto your side, mostly at the Navy's expense."

"That's evil, Em," the Emperor observed with a sly smile. "I like it. Will Keller mind?"

Emmerich put his elbows back on the desk and let his thoughts wander.

It was still odd that he was the Empire's go-to expert on that woman. But then, he had spent the most time around her, even if she had snookered him rather well on more than one occasion.

That just made him more careful about her in the future.

He smiled. It would be like all the fencing during Arnulf's Promenade, once again. But once you stripped away all the innuendo and lies, she was utterly driven by her interpretation of duty.

That she was coming here, in these circumstances, meant she should probably be safe to count as an ally, even if not a friend.

After all, the Queen of the Pirates could have easily returned to her throne and worked to raid *Fribourg's* supporters and distant outposts, had she really wanted to get around the Peace *Aquitaine* had signed.

Or she could have worked to overturn it.

It helped that they knew when she would arrive, roughly, courtesy of a fast dispatch boat making the kind of run to the capital to challenge Tomas Kigali's reputation for speed. Keller would be here in another week or so, giving them more than a month to fête and entertain her properly before the wedding.

"I believe we can rely on Keller wanting to work with us, Joh," he said finally. "And I can serve in your stead as her host, to let you maintain a polite fiction of official distance."

Emmerich smiled just as evilly at his best friend.

"That means, of course, that we will force you to come to our manor house for dinner, some night, and bring your whole family," Em continued.

"I can just imagine the trouble Freya and Kati will get themselves into, planning that," Joh said with a mock shudder.

"Oh, no, my dread Emperor," Em replied. "Imagine Casey, Heike, and Jessica Keller at one table."

They shared a laugh, but Em felt a niggle of dread in the pit of his stomach.

Was he really going to rely on Jessica Keller as an ally against his own enemies in the Empire?

CHAPTER XVI

IMPERIAL FOUNDING: 176/09/22. DITTMAR PALACE, WERDER, ST. LEGIER

It was a simple note, delivered via personal messenger. Sigmund had made sure he was alone in his office before he opened it, several long minutes after the Assistant Deputy Minister for Security for the planet of *Osynth B'Udan* had departed to wherever men like that went when you didn't want them in plain sight.

The message itself could have come via Imperial Post. There was nothing on the linen stock page that incriminated either the sender or the receiver. And the fact that elements inside Imperial Security were working to assist him in his quest to save the Empire meant that it was extra secure. Had they wanted, they already had enough evidence to have him publicly hung.

Sigmund had worked judiciously at those little details that frequently tripped up others wishing to transcend mere intrigue and commit treason.

This was a game for the Crown. Failure would end in death.

But if something wasn't done right now, the damage to the *Fribourg Empire*, to the utter foundations of Imperial culture, threatened to wipe out everything they had built.

Thuringwell was an infection, slowly poisoning the minds of an entire generation. If it wasn't excised, cut bodily and cauterized, who knew what they might demand?

Already, a new *Charter of Humanity* had begun circulating, demanding an end to the right of birth, to be replaced by some insane meritocracy, just waiting to be abused by demagogues out to amass personal power at the expense of civility and tradition.

Sigmund would not allow it.

He had seen what Johannes had done in the halls of the Imperial Palace itself. Both princesses educated far beyond need, as if they were men. And the youngest, Kasimira, wrote books and *popular music.*

Nothing good would come of it, especially not if their own father fostered such outrages against mores, to say nothing of the son who would inherit the crown in another few decades.

No, best to act now, before the Crown Prince married and had an heir that would abscond with the public's love and interest.

Sigmund could stoke the fires of discontent.

The Fleet was also deeply concerned. Worried that Peace with *Aquitaine* would mean reduced budgets, diminished prestige, lost power. And they still bore the scars that Jessica Keller had carved into their hides at *2218 Svati Prime*, at *Petron*, at *Ballard*.

Kozlov's failure at *Thuringwell* had just rammed home the risk they faced if it festered.

Something had to be done.

Every day the Peace continued, the populace became that much more comfortable with it. The *M'hanii Frontier* was an impossible distance away, and largely unknown. The war with *Buran* was barely newsworthy, especially as Johannes and his ilk celebrated a Peace.

Sigmund looked down at the paper again. Elegant calligraphy on a buff page.

His Excellency, Rodrigo Yamimura, and party will be delighted to join you in celebration of the great wedding. We will arrive at St. Legier on 8 November.

Nothing more. Nothing more was needed. It was an innocent enough message, if intercepted. The delivery by personal messenger insured that it would arrive in time, so that the final planning could be refined.

After all, the wedding was scheduled for the 14th. Security would be as tight and alert as humanly possible on that day, with various Fleet elements on high alert, and ground forces prepared for any eventuality.

Nobody would be expecting a revolution to occur a week earlier.

CHAPTER XVII

DATE OF THE REPUBLIC SEPTEMBER 24, 398
KALI-MA. JUMPSPACE

It was that late period of ship's night when Jessica found herself free to…

Worry was the wrong term. It was a wasteful act to worry, unless that was the first step to Risk Analysis. Mitigation. Reaction scenarios. Combat planning.

But those were activities either for the daytime, or, more normally, when she just woke up, having let her unconscious mind grind on a problem all night and solve it for her. The creative element, mixed with all the planning and note-taking, so that she could simply hand her team a set of code words, and let them immediately understand the overall plan, and their place in it.

Harmony. Symphony.

Art.

But tonight, sleep eluded her, lying in the dimness of her small cabin aboard *Baxter*. This wasn't planning for an engagement between ships, or even battle squadrons. Nor was it *diplomacy*, not as Tadej Horvat had taught her to understand the concept.

No, this was something else.

She was supposedly an honored guest, of a man she had publically embarrassed and nearly killed on more than one occasion.

The man who was the other half of their very personal war.

And she was also the guest of an Emperor that she could be seen as thwarting, even if she was simply the best-known of the millions of her friends and comrades working to save the Republic.

It just didn't add up.

For perhaps the millionth time, Jessica wondered if all of this was some elaborate trap on the part of Wachturm and Karl. Get her there, isolated, and have her disappear.

They didn't even have to assassinate her in public.

Ship still vanished occasionally. Pirates. Navigation errors. Something.

Random, catastrophic failures that left you stranded in the darkness between stars for years, until the life support systems gave out. After ten millennia of star flight, explorers still found ghost ships, stuffed with frozen bodies long since given over to the eternal sleep.

What the hell was wrong with her? When did she get so morbid?

Jessica sat up in bed and let her mind come to full functioning. She still slept in an old chaos green undershirt left over from her days of wearing one constantly. Her legs were bare, but the cabin was warm enough as she climbed down from her rack and paced the seven steps from wall to hatch.

Would Karl try to kill her? Would the Imperial Fleet try, regardless of whatever orders their Emperor had given?

Will nobody rid me of this troublesome priest, Henry had asked.

Back home, the Noble Lords and the Fighting Lords were in a constant rivalry for control of the Fleet that occasionally got serious enough to end careers. Her own success owed a serious debt to the fact that Nils Kasum was one of the best Fighting Lords of the previous generation, and had left his indelible stamp on the organization. If Petia Naoumov succeeded him as First Lord, like most people expected, the worst of the Noble Lords might be washed entirely out finally and the *Republic of Aquitaine* Navy turned into a fully professional force for the first time in centuries.

What were the ripples in the calm pond that was the Imperial Fleet? How many of them hid riptides, or sneaker waves?

Jessica considered getting dressed at this point. Having a go at the fighting robot installed back aboard *Kali-ma*, just to work out some of the nervous energy. But if she did that, Marcelle and Willow would feel obliged to get up with her, regardless of whatever orders Jessica might think she could give those two women.

That would quickly turn into a cascade of other folks not getting any sleep, either, at a point where they were only a few days out from *St. Legier* itself.

No, this needed to stay in the cabin with her.

Why would Emmerich Wachturm spend so much time, energy, and personal capital with Karl, just to get her, Moirrey, and Vo alone? Who would resent that presentation? And who would profit from her being there?

Jessica knew that the real control of the Imperial Fleet resided with a council made up entirely of close, male members of the Imperial Family. Karl VII. The Red Admiral. Up to a dozen cousins of one degree or another, but only by blood. There were no husbands who had married into the Imperial clan in that room when the important decisions were made.

Plus, Grand Admiral Huff had finally retired, after a career nearly as impressive as that of his much-more-famous nephew, Emmerich Wachturm. What had that done to the balance of power within that inner group? Had he been the crazed warrior, a cousin-in-spirit with Alber' d'Maine? Was that what had prolonged the war?

Or had he been the calm, rational one, the diplomat riding herd on the hotheads?

Nils Kasum's spies, little gray men and women who seemed to appear from around blind alleys, had only been able to give her so much information. Partly, to protect themselves and their methods if this was all a trap. But also, because there was so much nobody knew.

Like why the most famous, the most dangerous Admiral in the galaxy would invite his deadliest enemy to the wedding of his own daughter, under a flag of truce and reconciliation?

Jessica blinked.

Perhaps she was supposed to be some sort of stalking goat.

The only answer that made any sense was that she was intended to be someone's blade. Either the saber, or the *main-gauche*. The strike, or the block. The obvious move or the subtle surprise.

Someone was maneuvering, deep in the darkness, to set someone else up for a nasty fall. Jessica Keller being on *St. Legier* was either the catalyst, or the distraction.

She nearly growled loud enough that someone else could hear it, and not just herself. Those bastards, those *men*, were intent on using her. That made sense.

But they hadn't taken into account the second oath she had taken, the private one.

All Command Centurions swear the public oath on taking command of a new vessel. Legalisms cloaked in ritual. But that was just velvet covering the blade.

By will of the Republic of Aquitaine Navy and First Lord Nils Kasum, the undersigned, Command Centurion Jessica Keller, is hereby ordered to report aboard the RAN Auberon at the earliest opportunity and take command, subject to the normal rules and regulations. She will exercise excellence and demand the same of her crew, that the whole reflect the greatest acclaim in serving the needs of the Republic and the will of the Senate.

That had been the beginning. The Public Oath. The statement of legalities.

She will work her ass off to see that the Fribourg Empire *falls on her watch, doing every damned thing possible to advance the day when she is sitting in orbit above* St. Legier, *watching bombs level the last armed resistance that threatens the galaxy. When aristocracy gives way to meritocracy, you blue-blooded bastards.*

The unspoken words. The kind of *Vow of Excellence* that Alber' and Tomas Kigali occasionally talked about when Denis and Robbie and the other Command Centurions weren't around.

What you do when nobody is looking defines who you are.

Jessica felt the knot between her shoulder blades suddenly loosen. She hadn't even realized it was there until it vanished.

She was a Queen. She was a diplomat. She was a Fleet Centurion, which was just a different kind of Command Centurion.

But more importantly, she was a warrior.

If Karl and Emmerich wanted a war, she would happily give them one.

ST. LEGIER

CHAPTER XVIII

DATE OF THE REPUBLIC SEPTEMBER 28, 398
KALI-MA. EDGE OF THE ST. LEGIER SYSTEM

Jessica's instructions had been precisely specific, so her orders to *Wiley* were as well.

Kali-ma had emerged clear at the outer edge of the navigation field for the *St. Legier* system and waited for the local Fleet units to challenge and identify her.

After all, they were invited guests, but Jessica had arrived in a warship. One dramatically out-gunned by the tonnage of vessels plying nearby space right now, but more than an individual match for most of them, even if she doubted they realized that.

Jessica sat in her usual observer spot, port rear on *Kali-ma's* bridge, and watched the team of *Wiley* and Yan work. In many ways, it felt like a mirror of her and Denis, but that may have been Shiori studying Jessica's techniques and consciously emulating them.

It worked.

"Contact," a man's voice called from another corner.

Jessica turned to watch the Comm Officer at work. Like on an *Aquitaine* vessel, he was in charge of communications and sensors, although this ship did not carry a dedicated Science Officer, regardless of his title.

Yet.

Still, Anders Himura could have gotten that job on any *Aquitaine* vessel with a little retraining in terminology.

He was a light-skinned man, almost pale, as many in *Corynthe* were. Many shades lighter than Jessica, both in skin and in his reddish-gold hair. Right now, he was intent on three different boards at once, distilling everything quickly.

"Imperial challenge and formal welcome, Commanders," he said, turning enough to look back at both her and *Wiley* before returning to his readouts. Not quite up to *Auberon's* standards, but not that far off from her own exceptional crew. "They have also attached local navigation instructions and a flight path that will get us down to the edge of the gravity well to take up a safe orbit with all the other traffic."

Sharp. Professional.

If remaking *Corynthe* was to be her legacy, that would be an acceptable outcome. This crew didn't sound at all like the pirates she had inherited at the point of a sword, four years ago.

Wiley glanced back with a questioning look. Jessica nodded in reply.

"Comm," she said. "Acknowledge everything and send our own greetings. Nav, plot and execute, but make us and *Marco Polo* look like boring, old freighters going in, and not raiders, please."

A chorus of laughing assents answered.

Now, it was time to fly into the Gates of Hell.

CHAPTER XIX

DATE OF THE REPUBLIC SEPTEMBER 30, 398
KALI-MA. ABOVE ST. LEGIER

St. Legier.

Jewel of the entire *Fribourg Empire*. Strung out below Jessica as *Kali-ma* coasted along in the shadow of the monstrous orbital fortress that was Imperial Grand Fleet Operations.

A green and blue marble below, hanging on the firmament of night, bright and glowing with promise as they flew in geo-synchronous orbit over Werder's mid-morning sky.

Jessica couldn't remember all the times she had dreamed about floating above this planet. First, as part of a conquering fleet.

Later, leading one.

Watching fires burn as the planet fought to the last and was bombed into utter submission; the final, desperate holdouts as the Empire was ended and her people set free.

She wondered now if that made her a Visigoth, at least in comparison. *St. Legier* was an old world, re-colonized after the revival, but still occasionally throwing up lost reminders that man had first walked its surface eight thousand years ago.

But today, she was here as an honored guest.

Even now, an Ambassadorial Shuttle was approaching the forward airlock, just below the bridge on the port side of the ventral blade.

Jessica stood at parade rest in her charcoal-gray and maroon formal outfit, the one she thought of as *Admiral of the Corynthe Fleet*, or *Queen of the Pirates*, even though she had any number of costumes and uniforms she could wear back home on *Petron*.

Desianna wore her best First Minister outfit today. Formal, verging on severe. Black silk, laced and embroidered with violet. A full robe, with Jessica's personal signet, Kali-ma with her four arms, done as a panel across the chest in the ancient Chinese style. She barely looked like a woman in it, until you saw her face, still amazingly lovely, or the long hair, dyed raven black and tinted in plum highlights that accentuated the large mesh of silver rings that contained it.

On Jessica's other side, Moirrey was wearing a hand-made, wildly-decorated dress in cornflower blue linen that made her whole being light up, and not just her smile. She had embroidered it in stars, planets, and other astronomical and astrological symbols to the point she looked like a mad scientist *cum* alchemist. But at the end of the day, that was probably the most accurate description of the evil engineering gnome that Jessica had ever heard.

Behind her, as the airlock rattled, Jessica could feel Vo Arlo, like a warm mountain. She could tell he felt like a fool in his Colonel's uniform, but he looked positively distinguished today. She turned around to smile reassuringly up at him, this man whose every instinct was to act as bodyguard to the women in front of him, forcing himself instead to utter stillness at the rear.

Marcelle and Willow had that duty today. Bodyguards. And they wore identical outfits in muted brown that wouldn't draw the eye as the others moved.

Wiley reached out and triggered the inner airlock door as the pressure equalized. Yan had the bridge, but she would be returning there as soon as her charges were dispatched. There would be a round of formal events later, but today was the Arrival in State of Jessica, Queen of *Corynthe*, as the itinerary read.

Captain Baumgärtner was waiting when the hatch cleared, with two Imperial Marines in pretty, dress uniforms just visible inside the shuttle.

"Your Majesty," he said with a deep, formal bow and a warm smile. "On behalf of the Duke and Duchess of Eklionstic and his Imperial Majesty, welcome to *St. Legier*. If it would please you to join me, a reception awaits you and your party on the planet below us."

Jessica bowed in turn. This was where all her planning over the last several months had to rely on luck and timing.

It had been six months since she last saw Emmerich Wachturm's personal aide. There had been no time to stop and gather intelligence about the situation she was walking into, friendly or hostile. There was only whatever she had been able to absorb about Imperial customs and mores from her long studies on the flight out.

And a list of books on her reading slab.

For a moment, she flashed back to Daneel in his cabin aboard *Auberon*, reading a physical copy of *The Modern History of the Republic*, by Voisson, the night she had decided it was finally acceptable to kiss him. After he had carefully studied everything he could learn about an alien culture that he wanted to become part of.

And he had. And she had loved him for it.

She had a little over a month until the wedding. A month to put all that study and understanding to use. To do something Daneel had done.

Jessica could do no less now.

It were weird being a civilian, 'n'stuff. She'd no been outs of uniform this long since she joined up, fourteen years'n'change ago. Even being on a shuttle, gracefully descending into the atmosphere, didn't help.

Gaucho'd a been blasting straight down like he was racing fallin' rocks.

Moirrey wondered if this were what life would be like when First Lord finally took her away from Lady Keller and made Moirrey finally act like a grown-up.

She hoped not.

Being in a dress all the time were nice, but ever' once in a while, her hand would grip towards a non-existent welding laser in the left thigh pouch to fix som'tin she saw, or for the glitter gun on the right side.

Still, she could do this fer her sister. Look all polished and proper like a right *Ladaux* lady, since she were a guest of honor, too.

She weren't sure why, since she'd spent the last half decade blowing Impies and their friends up, but she also weren't an expert on these folks, neither. Maybe being meaner th'n them counted fer som'thin'.

Moirrey shrugged and enjoyed the feeling of silk on her skin. The dress were heavy enough that she didn't need a brassiere under it, and she barely had enough chest to matter, but this were a proper affair, with important folks, like the Red Admiral, or even an Emperer. With months ta plan, and Desianna's help, she had done herself up a chemise in white silk ta goes underneath and make her feel all girlie and stuff.

Digger'd be trying to pick his jaw up off'n the floor right now, were he here to see. Desianna'd taken a bunch of pics, just to rub it in when she got back to see him.

Her hair were still short, 'n'still black, but there were starting to infiltrate with grays here and there. Desianna'd explained hows ta fix that, too, when the time come. Fer today, she wore an enameled daisy pin in her hair, and tied a pink scarf sideways around her neck to go with all the darks and blues and purples in the dress.

Nowhere nears as bright as Vo, but she were the third on the list of peoples being honored. And they was going outs of the way with her sister and the big lug.

She'd figure out why they wanted her here soon enoughs.

Jessica and the Imperial Captain sat across the central aisle and chatted. Mostly her asking occasional questions, and him explaining in lots of details. Which were what her sister'd need.

Vo were back a row, stewing, but he'd done that a lot on the flight out. Weren't depression, or nothin' like that. Mostly shock.

Still trying to figure out how he turned into a hero.

She coulda read him the award citations 'gain. They made fer impressive feats, especially since she's helped to writes some of them. But he were just kinda on autopilot.

It were too bad Rebekah Kim weren't able to come and see all this. She'n'Vo'd been on again more than they were off again, but being light-centuries away from each other fer months on end weren't likely to be fun, and Vo dinna have anyone like Moirrey had Desianna to sit all night gossiping and giggling.

Gravity finally nibbled at her toes as the shuttle flattened out fer landing. Everyone put away drinks, and books, and stuff, and looked at the displays showing the city as they flew over.

Werder weren't like Penmerth on *Ladaux*. Penmerth were a small city, as they went. Reminded her of home. Most of the heavy industry were off-world, and the Navy were up in orbit.

Werder were much bigger. A whole, dazzling metropolis hundreds of kilometers across, buildings broken up by parks and lakes and stuff in all directions.

And fairy tale castles with towers and pennons, just like they was supposed to.

Moirrey supposed that if'n you were an Empire with lots of wealth, you might have ta have castles fit fer elven queens of *Lothlórien*.

Moirrey giggled to herself, wondering if anybody but Suvi would even remember where that were.

And then they was a-ground. Soft. Almost unnoticeable. *Gaucho*'d a probably been insulted by how easygoing a flight this had been. Especially gliding into a terminal building to keeps everyone out of any possible rain, even if it were sunny this afternoon.

Nobody moved, so she sat still, too.

After a few minutes, Captain Baumgärtner stood up, handed Lady Keller up like she were a real lady, and not a badass Fleet Centurion, and turned to the rest of them with a pleasant smile.

Moirrey fought down the giggles. Impi men were never gonna un'erstand her and her sister. She figured Jessica were planning on taking unfair advantage of that.

She certainly were.

"Ladies. Colonel," he said, making eye contact with each of them. "There will be a brief reception here, but no speeches. And then ground transportation will take us to the Palace for Colonel Arlo's investiture, followed by a State Dinner. Lady Kermode's investiture will occur the day after tomorrow, on Thursday. And Wildgraf Keller will be the guest of honor at a private banquet at the manor of the Duke and Duchess of Eklionstic on Saturday."

Moirrey's heart skipped a beat. And then started poundin' somethin' FIERCE.

Investiture.

Up until now, a game she'd played, bein' a princess in a fairy tale. She'd always wanted to be a princess when she were a kitten. Being an Imperial Knight, a *Ritter*, were just daft.

She could see it fer Vo. He done good stuff on *Thuringwell* with the Imperial Army and all. They would be happy to reward him.

But nowhere in the books on Imperial customs were there nothin' on makin' a nermal ferriner a personal representative of the Household, let alone a woman.

And in two days, she would officially be Moirrey *zu* Kermode. Lady Moirrey of *Ramsey*.

Daft.

She found Vo in the mess o' folks debarking and grabbed his hand.

He looked like he needed it.

CHAPTER XX

DATE OF THE REPUBLIC SEPTEMBER 30, 398
IMPERIAL PALACE, WERDER, ST. LEGIER

V o took a deep breath and tried to get his pulse under control. Navin the Black had taught him all sorts of meditative tricks and bio-feedback over the years, but that was for a man about to enter bloody combat, or having just come back from it.

Nowhere had the man covered anything like this.

The Imperial Palace.

St. Legier.

A long, upstairs hallway, gray tile floors covered over with long green and blue carpets. Pictures on the walls every once in a while. Art and knick-knacks on pedestals and side tables. Closed wooden doors.

Somewhere, a reception hall filled with people. Imperial people. Waiting for him.

He was about to step into that scrum, be honored by them. Smile at them.

Combat drops had been easier.

It had helped that Moirrey had sat next to him in the limousine on the ride over. Not saying anything. Just leaning against him like a fall leaf.

The piece of paper tucked into the left inner pocket of his jacket weighed a long ton right now. A special *Act of the Senate*, back on *Ladaux*, setting him on detached duty at the pleasure of the *Emperor of Fribourg*, able to accept this honor, and making him a Goodwill Ambassador between nations.

Moirrey had one, too, but he was about to be made an Officer and a Gentleman, as well as a Knight.

You need to stop being a hero, young man.

Captain Baumgärtner walked beside him now on his left as they approached the open double doors with the two men in Army uniforms flanking it.

Every other door they had passed had been guarded by Household troops. Those uniforms were showier.

These two men were line infantry.

Vo looked closely at the shoulder of the nearer man. 189th Division.

He didn't recognize either man, but he had only met a few of them on *Thuringwell* during the craziness. The rest of the division, reduced now to only a First Regiment of training specialists, had been stationed elsewhere.

Vo was about to be made the Honorary Colonel of the non-existent Third Regiment of the 189th Division. It made a useful fiction.

Both men came to rigid attention as he approached. Corporals with two service stripes on the forearm, indicating at least six years' service.

Vo nodded and smiled.

Captain Baumgärtner stopped him a half a dozen strides from the door, listening to someone talk into a tiny bud in his ear.

"I'll escort you to the door and announce you," he began, looking up with deadly serious intent. "Then walk you down the center of the room. The Emperor will be on a raised platform with the Earth Sword. You will kneel on the first step. He will touch you on both shoulders with the blade, and then order you to arise. You will take two steps back when you stand and then be formally Invested. I'll be right there to assist you. It will turn into a diplomatic reception at that point."

He paused to look Vo up and down one last time.

"Are you ready, Colonel?"

Vo turned to glance back at the half-dozen women accompanying him. All of them smiled up, reassuring and warm.

He could do this. He nodded to the man, unwilling to trust his voice right now.

Baumgärtner smiled. He reached out and caught Vo's forearm in his from underneath, lightly gripping Vo's wrist and tugging him into motion.

They paused at the door.

Vo could see inside the room now. It was a grand space, nearly the size of the Primary Engineering Bay aboard the old Strike Carrier *Auberon*.

Filled with hundreds of people, men mostly in the dark, navy blue of the Imperial Fleet, but a few in the sorts of exotic color combinations he was wearing now. The women reflected every color of the spectrum in their dresses and every hue of humanity in their bright faces.

An aisle was already opened down the center, lined on both sides by men in that line infantry uniform of the 189th. Some faces he recognized.

These men had been on *Thuringwell* when *Aquitaine* invaded. Had stood their duty right up to the moment when it should have cost them their lives, but for the actions of one *Aquitaine* Centurion.

Twenty-two men, eleven on each side, standing at parade rest, hands crossed behind their backs and feet shoulder width apart. At the far end, on the left, closest to the man standing on the dais, Master Sergeant Edgar Horst, Color Sergeant for the 189th Division.

Today, he was actually holding the colors, a red, yellow, and blue flag that matched Vo's uniform, hanging down from a polished steel crossbar atop a three-meter pole.

"Your Imperial Majesty, Ladies and Gentlemen of the Court, I present you Colonel Vo Arlo," Captain Baumgärtner called into the space.

Hush turned to utter stillness.

"Company," Master Sergeant Horst barked. "Atten-*tion*."

The twenty-two men snapped to as one, arms down, shoulders back, chins up, feet together.

Vo took a deep breath and willed his heart to start beating again.

Captain Baumgärtner's grip pulled him along. Vo didn't have the knack for falling into step that army troops got from marching together, and he was so much taller, but he was willing to be led by this man. Hopefully, he wouldn't embarrass the captain today.

The man on the dais was impressive. Vo had spent enough time around the Red Admiral, back in the day, to see the family resemblance between the two cousins. Slightly above average height. Mildly-stocky build. Hair turning gray.

The Emperor wore a cloak over what looked like Court robes, the outer cloth done in a dark maroon and highlighted in white, with the Imperial Crest: a Golden Eagle Elevated and Displayed, over his heart. He rested a sword, point down on a small pillow, by his right foot.

Vo was wearing his cavalry saber, and had been warned innumerable times never to actually even rest his hand on the hilt, let alone draw it, lest someone with a firearm get twitchy. Still, his blade probably weighed a third of the heavy longsword Karl VII held.

Vo doubted the Emperor has nearly as much training in Kendo or close combat, but he could see that the man was comfortable as he stood.

Eighteen long strides into the room. Kneel on that first step. Feel the heavy, red carpet padding protect knees from bruising.

Deep breath. Calm face.

Look up at the man you have been fighting for the last decade, smiling down at you knowingly.

Karl VII had the darkest blue eyes Vo had ever seen on a person.

"Colonel Arlo," the Emperor began. "Welcome. And thank you, on behalf of myself, my government, and especially the 189th division."

Vo watched the man easily lift the heavy blade in one hand and turn the blade flat, just touching him on the left shoulder, the right, and the left again.

There had to be a lot of muscles under those robes.

Kittens had batted him harder.

"I proclaim you Vojciech *zu* Arlo, *Ritter* of the Imperial Household," Karl said in a warm, loud voice. "Arise, Lord Vo, and be presented to the Court."

Vo let the autopilot, lizard-brain part of him rock backwards and up. Standing on a second step up, Emperor Karl VII looked him in the eyes.

The man winked at him.

"Color Sergeant," the Emperor continued proudly. "To your duty."

Vo held perfectly still as Horst passed the flag pole to the man on his right, turned, and picked up a bundle of cloth from a nearby table. It was the same maroon as the Emperor wore. A dozen or so other men in the room also wore that color.

Nobody else.

Horst approached in a slow, measured cadence reminiscent of those strides in front of the memorial on *Thuringwell.* He passed behind Vo, out of sight, and paused.

Vo heard the rustle of silk as the bundle was unrolled, flared once, and then a cloak appeared around his shoulders.

Vo reached up and caught the ties with his hands, holding them in place until Horst marched around front and tied them tightly.

The Master Sergeant turned to the Emperor, bowed low, and returned to his spot, taking back the colors.

Karl VII nodded at Vo and Captain Baumgärtner. Captain Baumgärtner turned him in place to face the rest of the room.

"Ladies and Gentlemen of the Court," he called. "Vo *zu* Arlo, Imperial *Ritter.*"

The applause was polite.

"Company," Master Sergeant Horst barked. "*Dis*-missed."

Suddenly, Vo found himself mobbed by the men of the 189th, pounding his back and shaking his hand. They hadn't become friends on *Thuringwell,* but they had become comrades.

Now, if he could just make it through the rest of the month.

CHAPTER XXI

IMPERIAL FOUNDING: 176/09/30. IMPERIAL PALACE, WERDER, ST. LEGIER

Sigmund kept his face comfortably neutral as he worked his way around the Reception Room. Bland, even. What had just happened to the soldier from *Aquitaine* was acceptable, within the confines of Imperial custom. The Army wasn't that important.

When he was Emperor, he might even do a similar thing, in light of the extraordinary situation that had dictated it.

After all, the two nations were still technically at peace. He would need some time, afterwards, to consolidate his power, his reign, after the bloody circumstances that would precede his ascension to the crown.

No, best to lull *Aquitaine* to sleep when his time came. That would make the inevitable betrayal all the more stunning, all the more successful.

Sigmund held a half-empty glass of wine in one hand and surveyed the crowd. Today, he wore his best uniform: crisp, white linen standing out amidst the dark blue or maroon around him like a supernova. As it should.

The glass served as a useful prop. Never full, never empty. It let him circulate without one of the valets coming close and risking spilling wine on him from a tray attempting to refill it.

Plus, he was not drinking anything. A clear head was needed today.

This was his first chance to observe the Keller woman up close.

Wachturm's notes from four years ago were worthless, and the man himself had long passed his time of usefulness as a spy.

No, best to send Wachturm to the *M'hanii Frontier*, as Johannes planned. It would keep his cousin well away from the centers of power and intrigue. The Red Admiral was loyal to the crown, Sigmund hoped, and not to the man currently holding it.

It would be a shame to have Emmerich Wachturm executed in the wake of the coup.

He found Keller enjoying a mild bubble of space near one corner of the room. She was not holding court, as a well-known literary star was doing elsewhere, but was just separated from everyone else, in a cluster of women that were alien to most of the men in the room. Men who lacked the context to deal with a woman like that.

It let him stand off and observe, with others doing the same, as the crowd slowly eddied, like a school of fish.

She was smaller than her legends.

Sigmund had known that, but at the same time, it was difficult to reconcile the woman he saw now with the tremendous stories that had grown up around her.

Slightly below average for a woman. As much as a head shorter than many Imperial women. Long brown hair streaking into grays. Broad in the hips and shoulders, with that build that would turn to flab at the first opportunity, if not kept ruthlessly at bay.

He preferred his women tall and willowy.

Motionless when she talked. Keller did not rock back and forth, nor gesture much with her hands. Instead, she stood square with an Imperial Captain that Sigmund didn't know on sight, and apparently chatted amiably, if serious by tone and expression.

Sigmund took a moment to study Keller's associates, the true measure of a person.

Two obvious bodyguards, both women, as one would expect from the lesser gender, both taller.

A Minister from Keller's barbaric holding on the distant fringes of the galaxy. Yet another foolish woman with aspirations to power, however beautiful she might be in the flesh.

At least Sigmund's own wife, Karya, had long since learned to be a proper Imperial hostess and mother. Seen, but rarely heard. Happiest at home, and not intriguing with other wives. Leave that to his various mistresses.

The last one in the group, if Sigmund was forced to admit it, was probably the reason behind his determination to change the course of the Empire itself, even if he had to script that future in the blood of his own kin.

Keller was at least an exotic noblewoman from beyond the pale. The entire rank and title of *Wildgraf* existed to frame such people, to place them into the Imperial hierarchy. As a barbarian queen from far away, perfect for Keller.

And it was appropriate to reward Arlo's chivalry. Sigmund wasn't sure he would have given the man both a Colonelcy and a Knighthood, but either would have easily been within the realm, given his behavior and apparent reputation.

No, those two rewards were odious, but not repellant.

It was the last person that had been a bridge too far for Sigmund.

Moirrey Kermode.

Sigmund had read the files Imperial Intelligence had assembled on the woman. She had personally killed one of their most experienced assassins at *Ballard*, and then murdered a Colonel of the Imperial Security Bureau at *Thuringwell*.

Her inventions had seriously damaged *IFV Amsel* at *Qui-Ping*, and wrought nearly incalculable economic and psychological damage across the entire *Cahllepp Frontier*. To say nothing of *Petron*, *Ballard,* or *Thuringwell*.

She had single-handedly altered the balance of power across the entire frontier zone between *Fribourg* and *Aquitaine*.

And we were going to reward her for that?

There had been six female *Ritters* in the two centuries of the *Fribourg Empire*. Sigmund had tasked Imperial Security with confirming.

Kermode would be the seventh.

And she wasn't even of noble blood. At least the Fifty Families that made up the backbone of *Aquitaine* were well-bred.

No, Kermode was a farm-girl from the barbarity of *Ramsey*, someplace out in a fringe kingdom called *Lincolnshire*, halfway to the edge of the galaxy itself.

And Johannes was going to make her an Imperial Lady.

Sigmund fought to keep his hands from clenching into fists, to keep his face from snarling. To keep breathing normally.

He and Kermode locked eyes across ten meters of space, just for a moment.

Bile and vitriol flowed both directions, behind poised, neutral smiles.

Sigmund nodded once. Short. Sharp. Promising.

Kermode reciprocated.

She actually smiled at him.

And then the bitch curtsied with a tilt to her head and a soft giggle.

Sigmund felt a knife probing his guts as he turned and made his way from the room.

CHAPTER XXII

DATE OF THE REPUBLIC SEPTEMBER 30, 398
IMPERIAL PALACE, WERDER, ST. LEGIER

Jessica had been warned by Captain Baumgärtner that circumstances had dictated a change from this evening's original planned affair. Instead of fêting her, it was a celebration for Vo. The Imperial had even delivered a personal apology from Admiral Wachturm, and a plea for understanding and promise to make it up to her later.

Privately, she marked a ledger book against a bet she had made with herself six months ago when she last saw this man.

She had doubted then that the rest of the Imperium would accept such a gesture for Jessica Keller at diplomatic value, preferring to see it on its face instead.

Still, the crowd for the occasion was large and festive. Seventeen men, including the Emperor, wore the distinct maroon cloak that marked the *Ritters*. Each had made a point to personally, individually congratulate Vo and shake his hand.

Jessica smiled like a mother hen, even as she felt like a she-bear in this midst.

As was her custom, she had abstained from all beverage of unknown provenance. If the Imperials chose to be offended, that was their prerogative, but she was not about to risk assassination here. Marcelle had a soft canteen with water in it, if Jessica needed it. Willow had several small bottles of wine in a messenger bag if the situation warranted.

Jessica found the crowd dynamics amusing as folks mingled.

Desianna and Moirrey had stayed close, of choice, as had Marcelle and Willow, of duty.

Vo was circulating and accepting words of encouragement, towering above most of the crowd by a head, even the Emperor and the Red Admiral, surrounded by one or more of the men from the 189th at all times.

In the process of the crowd moving, a space had opened around her. Folks would smile and nod in greeting and then carefully go about their way. A few had muttered hurried greetings. But none dared cross the meter-wide gulf around her that appeared bottomless.

A man caught her eye, emerging from the crowd and considering that gap, psychological rather than physical, that separated *Fribourg* from *Aquitaine*, or perhaps *Corynthe*. By dress, another Imperial Navy Captain, like Wachturm's Hendrik Baumgärtner, with the five gold rings on each cuff. She couldn't recognize the rest of the tags and badges on his chest and collar to place him past that.

That suggested the man was a staff officer of some sort, rather than a line commander.

The crowd eddied around him as he licked his lips and considered that fateful step. As though a hangman's noose awaited.

Jessica decided to disrupt the school of pretty fish around her in her own way. She stepped towards the man with a smile of reassurance. She nearly laughed out loud as the little fishies suddenly scattered away, as though a shark had appeared in their midst from the darkness.

It was a petty revenge, but it still felt good.

She addressed the man standing suddenly closer to her than he had planned.

"Captain?" she said pleasantly.

"Torsten Wald," he replied with a nod, perhaps a touch hurriedly.

Up close, he was average height, giving him half a head on Jessica, who had worn low boots tonight instead of stiletto heels. His build was verging on skinny, with curly, dark hair cut short.

"Captain Wald," Jessica smiled politely. "How may I help you?"

As she had expected, the man took a half-step backwards, separating them again by a polite meter. However, he did it with a weirdly odd hitch, shifting all his weight onto his left leg, balancing there precariously for a moment, and then stepping his right foot back and pulling himself back into balance with his hips and his shoulders.

Something must have shown on her face. Or he was expecting her reaction. His smile was somewhere between disarming and a polite grimace.

"Mid-femur amputation eleven years ago," he explained. "Accidentally traded a normal life for being a hero."

Jessica nodded. She felt the same, many days.

In an alternate universe, one where computers were allowed to push the envelope of sophistication, she could imagine an artificial limb so natural that no one could tell the difference. Certainly, Suvi had constructed herself an entire android body using the ancient technology.

But that way lay *damnation*.

Aquitaine might barely tolerate such a thing. *Fribourg* not at all. The man probably had a hinged, mechanical peg leg, like an ancient pirate.

"I see," Jessica replied neutrally.

There wasn't much to say. And he had probably heard it all by now.

Around her, she could feel the other women slowly being pulled into her new orbit, forcing the entire room's gravity well to adjust.

"How should I address you, madam?" Captain Wald asked carefully.

Jessica studied his face for a clue, but found none. The man was holding his cards close. Marcelle and Willow were probably already preparing to take him out if he presented a threat. Desianna and Moirrey perhaps as well. The latter two might also be smiling at him right now, and they might not.

She could imagine the courage it would require, for a single man to walk into that circle of strangers, of women. She would give him the benefit of the doubt.

"Militarily, Fleet Centurion," she said merrily. "Diplomatically, Queen Jessica. Socially, *Wildgraf* Keller."

Let him make of that what he would. It would slice his true intent down quickly, a Gordian knot unravelled.

The man nodded as a placeholder and considered his words.

The silence stretched.

They must be good words.

"It is a question I would address to the Fleet Centurion then," he said finally.

She could hear the stress under his voice.

"But I would not intend to give offense by suggesting you share military secrets with me, madam," he stuttered, blushing furiously.

"Ask, Captain," Jessica replied mildly. "I will judge."

"Just so," he nodded, taking a breath for courage. "If I may, I am an economist, so my studies of your campaigns are, by their nature, economic in nature, rather than military."

"Go on," Jessica prompted him.

She wondered where this would take them, especially considering the variety of naval uniforms around them tonight.

"*2218 Svati Prime*," Captain Wald explained, taking her back to the beginning of what historians on both sides of the border were now calling *Keller's Raid*, in spite of her every effort to the contrary.

"The first, or the second time?" she asked.

"Both, in fact," he stated. "You attacked other worlds on the *Cahllepp Frontier*, but this was the only place you played your so-called practical jokes. Why only there?"

Jessica smiled, a true smile. She had studied pitifully little economics in school, barely a quarter, but quite a bit of human psychology.

Admirals did not think with their pocket books. They reacted with the hearts and their guts.

"A rat will go insane far quicker on a diet of random rewards and punishments, Captain," she said. "Straight penance becomes a thing to be endured, and all creatures can endure far longer than we ever anticipate."

"So the chaos of the infliction *becomes* the value of the outcome," he said with a sigh of sudden enlightenment.

"My team destroyed less than one hundred second-line fighters with third rate crews during the entire campaign," she said. "We destroyed one orbital station, captured one hospital ship, and mildly damaged *IFV Amsel*, the *Blackbird*. What were the psychological costs?"

"Trade on that entire frontier is only now approaching seventy-eight percent of what it was before," Wald noted with growing understanding. "And that represents a five percent jump just in the year since the Peace was signed and ships, both neutral and *Aquitaine*, have begun to cross the frontier again."

The man paused and studied her far closer than he had before. He had green eyes.

"And *Thuringwell* contributed so little to the Imperial economy as to be not even a footnote on sector reports," he continued, quieter.

"And yet, the *Fribourg Empire* sued for Peace, in reaction," Jessica said in a cold, ominous voice, taking half a step forward as she spoke

The drop in noise drew him closer as well.

"What are you?" he whispered fiercely.

"Retribution," she whispered back.

Time hung cold, electric between them.

Captain Wald staggered back half a step and caught himself.

"My most profuse apologies, m'lady," he stumbled over his words. "I meant no offense."

"None taken, Captain," she smile lightly.

"Your Majesty," a rich, baritone voice rang out. "If I may intrude?"

Jessica came back into herself and glanced to her right.

Emmerich Wachturm had lost weight since she had seen him last, four years ago. The mass of bulk around the middle had melted away, showing what he must have looked like twenty years ago, at the peak of his physical prowess. His hair was completely gray now, on its way to white, but the blue eyes had lost none of their sparkling luster. He was a clean shaven as the Emperor.

And his bright crimson uniform had been tailored to his new shape with an expert eye. Jessica had two such teachers standing within easy reach. With Desianna and Moirrey around, plus growing up with Indira, she could appreciate these things.

"Absolutely, Admiral Wachturm," she said breezily. "Captain Wald and I were just having a most enlightening conversation. Weren't we, Captain?"

"Thank you, Your Majesty," Wald said diplomatically. "Thank you for enduring my pestering and curiosity."

"Not at all," Jessica replied. "I look forward to chatting again."

"Your Majesty," Wald bowed to her, and then the women around her. "Ladies. Admiral."

And then he was gone, leaving Emmerich Wachturm in his stead.

Something warm fled with him.

"And how may I be of service to the Red Admiral, this evening?" Jessica smiled enigmatically up at the man.

It was a diplomatic event. She could sense the man coming to drag her to meet various folks and blather meaninglessly. None would probably be as interesting as Captain Wald, but this was the Imperial Court, so it behooved her to deal with circumstance of birth as a governing contract, rather than excellence.

She would teach them otherwise yet.

CHAPTER XXIII

IMPERIAL FOUNDING: 176/010/01. IMPERIAL PALACE, WERDER, ST. LEGIER

Casey took advantage of this time with her mother.

The Empress had specialists who could French-braid her long, blond hair, but Mother always preferred the way her youngest daughter handled the task.

Plus, it left them alone for an hour to talk, without any of the Ladies in Waiting underfoot.

Mother Kati sat in a comfortable chair, facing a wall of glass mirrors lit to eliminate all shadows, all secrets. Casey stood behind, deftly twining handfuls of newly-brushed hair and lacing them.

"What did you think of last night?" Mother asked, her eyes closed and head leaned back as her youngest daughter worked.

Casey paused and considered her mental notes.

"Will Father want to locate a spouse for Colonel Arlo?" she asked. "An Imperial Lady?"

The Empress opened her eyes and stared back in the mirror.

"Oh?" she asked. "Something I should know?"

Casey considered mother's words and blushed furiously at the implication.

"No. Not like that," she replied. "He is certainly physically impressive, if a touch rough around the edges, but there is no art in that man's soul."

"No, I would agree with you there, Casey," Mother said. "What brings this on?"

"Power in *Fribourg* is often cemented with marriages," Casey replied, unable to help the growly edge to her voice. "We have rewarded Colonel Arlo, and made a step towards binding him to the Empire, but it is only a step, and can be easily undone later, if circumstances warrant."

"There are days," Mother said quietly, "when you sound more like your sister, or your father, than yourself. But I suppose it reflects well that you can think in those terms."

Kati paused for a moment, gathering her thoughts before she continued.

"Keller would obviously be a good candidate to seal the Peace," Mother said. "She is the most prominent *Aquitaine* commander to be single. Thankfully, she is too old to be a good match for Ekke."

Casey snorted under her breath and went back to her braiding.

"Ekke is a man," Casey griped quietly. "He wants a woman who is dumb, and beautiful, and pliant."

"And who will bear him many children," Mother agreed. "Just as your sister will do for some man we have yet to find, one of these days."

Mother paused again, her eyes focused intently on her daughter in the reflection.

"What does Casey want?" she asked finally.

Casey felt her stomach go cold. They were as alone as anyone in the palace could ever be, with bodyguards just outside the door and whole tribes of servants on call and just waiting for purpose to define their lives.

That was one of the most important reasons Casey wanted to do this, to have this very special, very private mother-daughter time.

What did Casey want?

She had almost blurted any of a half-dozen answers, before her teeth slammed shut hard enough to rattle her skull. All of them would be accurate, within some manner of context.

None of them would be true.

Mother wanted the truth.

Dare she?

Secrets whispered to herself in the dead of night, or to her grandmother's ancient stuffed bear on her shelf?

Certainly, her sister Steffi had never been one for dreams. Steffi was practical. Content.

Limited.

But Mother knew that. Knew that the rare screaming matches between sisters came from being earth and sky. Water and fire. Mostly, they stayed as far away from one another emotionally as they could, like poles on a powerful magnet.

It usually worked.

What did Casey want?

To dream.

She could not fly. Even Father would not allow that level of freedom, nor would Ekke, unless she wanted to become ostracized from the entire family.

No, never that.

Casey felt her face grow hard. Fierce. Sharp.

It reminded her of the look she would occasionally see on the face of the other woman in the mirror. Mother saw it as well, but kept her silence.

"One of these days, you are going to find a man," Casey finally growled in a low tone. "Father will. Or Uncle Em. Perhaps even you. It doesn't matter."

Casey released a breath into the fragile air, expecting rime frost to coat the glass.

"The adults will achieve consensus that he is *good enough*."

Mother flinched under the tone, just the slightest. Anyone else would have missed it, but they weren't holding the Empress by her hair to feel those nerves fire, possibly in shame.

"I will be presented with a *fait accompli*," Casey continued, implacable. An avalanche brooking no interference. "Perhaps he will even be *good enough*. We will see. But *good enough* still means a corset for me. I will still have the appearance of freedom, but will be bound invisibly. Perhaps he will understand. Perhaps not. It is the way things are. The way *Fribourg* is."

Casey took a deep breath, suddenly chilled air slashing her lungs as her nostrils flared.

"What does Casey want?" Casey continued, casting her words to the Gods themselves. "I want what *will* be."

"And what is that?" Mother asked quietly.

"*Thuringwell*," Casey pronounced grimly.

Again the shudder. Stronger this time. Noticeable by Ladies in Waiting, and other strangers, were there any to bear witness to the sight.

Of all the people in the Imperial Palace, only Mother was armed to understand those implications. Perhaps Uncle Em would, as well, but he was a man, and thus unequipped for the circumstances.

The Empress, Kasimira Ekaterina, of the House of Alkaev, understood. Or understood her youngest daughter, at least well enough.

"That will be a lonely road, Casey," she whispered.

"You didn't ask me what I would settle for, Mother," Casey whispered back, leaning forward to kiss her mother on the top of the head as the tears threatened to blind her. "You asked what I wanted. I want to be free. But that will never happen. Not for a *Princess Imperial*. I will settle for being equal. Anything less than that is not *good enough*."

Casey tied off the end of the braid before the tears in her eyes got so thick she was blind. Not that it mattered. She could have handled this task in the dark, muscle memory driving her fingers.

Mother reached back a hand to hold one of Casey's as she finished.

Thuringwell had been conquered by a woman. Jessica Keller had shown her that it was possible.

Now Casey just had to conquer the *Fribourg Empire*.

CHAPTER XXIV

DATE OF THE REPUBLIC OCTOBER 2, 398
WERDER, ST. LEGIER

Moirrey looked at herself in the mirror, mirrors even, and let all the giggles take over the whole room.

The good folks had put Lady Keller, *Wildgraf Keller* even, inta a small palace not all that fer from the bigger Imperial version. But it were decorated by men. Fer men.

Desianna had took one look at the place and had the servants that come with the place strip ever'tin' out of one second-floor sitting room and turn it into a dressing studio. Then comfie sofas had been rounded up from elsewheres and put along the walls, competin' fer space wit' trunks o'all sizes.

And the big triple mirror that were dead center, dominatin' the volume like that stupid suit of armor had dun befer.

It were Moirrey's room now. At least fer todays.

It were her day.

Staring back at her from th'mirror were a vision of utter lovely. It even had a color. 0A3200, the dark green of summer leaves in the deep woods back home on *Ramsey*. When she were just a kitten.

Ankle-length silk formed an evening gown with eggplant trim and matching leather belt. Jes'nuff onta the shoulders to draw attention to the low-cut bodice that showeded off her barely-there boobs and not-much cleavage, but did it in a way that even the Emperer might be staring down her front, stealing a peek.

'Cause she could.

And Desianna had approved. Helped, even. Nick in a bit here, loose a dash there. Add some more color in ways that maybe focused th'eye, an' maybe distracted.

Around her neck were a platinum chain Lady Keller had gotten her fer her commissioning, once they all gots back home. Digger'd added the cherry ruby in a white gold setting hanging from it.

Moirrey'd even let her normally-curly, jet black hair gets a bit too long on the flight out here, on Desianna's say-so. Now it were pulled down into a platinum binder thingee, asymmetrical and around the left side o'her neck.

And to out-ladylike the Imperial ladies, opera gloves in light dove gray with a charm bracelet she'd got in junior high around her left wrist, filled with all sorts of special things she'd *accumulated*.

Moirrey stared at this apparition in the mirror and giggled. And giggled. All that were missing were a tube of glitter, blasted into the air and left to gravity to paint with.

She had considered it.

More'n once.

"I take it you find the ensemble acceptable?" Desianna snorted from close behind, barely audible o'er the ongoing giggles.

Even in Moirrey's heels, Desianna were a head taller, but the woman were done up in her Court Robes tonight.

Staid. Respectable.

BORING.

But also completely unlikely to outshine Moirrey on her special night.

Like that were an option, lady.

"A-yup," Moirrey chirped. "Is good."

Moirrey glanced at the other faces behind her.

Her sister nodded approvingly. Marcelle jes beamed.

Willow had a cross look. Moirrey felt serious threaten to break out everywhere.

Willow could be like that, at times.

She watched her sister's bodyguard suddenly pivot and cross to one of the tables, fishing aroun' fer sometin that she finally found an' brought over to the mirror.

Moirrey felt her nose scrunch up and her eyes go kinda sideways as Willow grinned at her.

"Not quite," *Ms. Dolan* smiled as she got close.

Moirrey watched the girl hold up a hair pin, and then stick it into the knot on the left side of her head.

Willow stepped back and Moirrey *considered* the result.

It weren't her favorite hairpin, the one what looked like a Daisy flower in high summer. This one were a silver rose, a bit larger than a 2-Lev coin, with a bit of thorned stem curling down to help stabilize it.

"Yes," Willow said. "That was what you were missing."

Moirrey turned her head to see the result in all three mirrors.

Fer a bodyguard, Willow were pretty good at this. It *were* what she were missing. Even Desianna nodded.

A knock at the door interrupted further commentary.

Marcelle went and let Captain Baumgärtner in.

He were dressed to the nines tonight, both as host and escort to this shindig, all formal in navy blue and gold trim, sword and purse.

He walked close and started to say something, and broke his brain.

Er, at least his jaw. It were on the floor, along with his tongue. Moirrey'd'a said his manners, too, but he recovered them pretty quick.

There were only a few sputters. And a bit of blushing. And a few giggles from around him. Which made the blushing worse.

Not like he dinna deserve it.

He made up fer it with a bow all the way to horizontal a'fore he come to parade rest.

"Madame Kermode, Lady Moirrey," he said in a suddenly dry voice. "You are absolutely stunning. You will leave every man there tonight speechless and every woman jealous."

At least he knowed how to charm a girl right.

Moirrey grinned up at him.

"Good evening, Captain Baumgärtner," she said warmly. "Are we ready?"

He responded by pivoting around his left foot and holding out his right elbow fer her to grasp.

"Ladies," he said to the rest of the folks. "If you would accompany us. Transport to the Palace awaits downstairs."

Moirrey glanced back once and let one final fit o'giggles out.

Time to go impress an Emperer.

And maybe let him look down her front.

CHAPTER XXV

Moirrey were pretty sure Ma woulda swatted her on the bum at least once with a wooden spoon fer the thoughts chasing each other 'round 'n'her head like silly squirrels.

She'd hadta go all sneaky-like, but she had found the man who were such a shit to her at Vo's party.

Not that he'd done nothin'. Nor said nothin'.

Nope, he were just bad ju-ju, staring at her fr'm o'er there.

Admiral of the White Sigmund Dittmar. Duke of somethin'-er-tother. Imperial Cousin, his Da bein' the younger brother of the Emperer's Da.

Nasty, cruel-looking man.

It were wrong to hope he were somewhere else t'night. Ma'd'a no' approved that. But the swat would be fer the serene smile Moirrey were planning ta gives hims if'n he were.

Ya dinna argue with bullies. Ya don't fights 'em. Ya laughs at 'em. Public-like. Imperial Reception public-like.

Not necessarily proper. But Ma weren't abouts with a wooden spoon to learn her no better.

Captain Baumgärtner were much nicer ta be 'rounds, but he were the Red Admiral's man, so that were expected. An' he had at least one daughter rough' her age, from what Jessica had said, so he were extra-protective as a host.

Not that he could do much about such an important feller as Admiral

White, but she could always whisper things to the Captain, sure it'd get back to meaner folks. The Red Admiral, fer sure.

Right now, they was just coming outs the elevator at the Imperial Palace, girls in long dresses not bein' 'spected to walk up flights of stairs without face-plantin' along the ways.

Thems prolly would.

Everyone else had gone ahead, leaving her with her date fer the night, the good Captain looking all distinguished 'n'stuff.

He glanced over as they made their way down the long, empty hallway, footsteps muffled on the heavy, patterned red carpet.

"It will be similar to Colonel Arlo's *Investiture*, madam," he said quietly. "With a few changes suggested by Princess Kasimira, based apparently on her personal research. The audience will also be significantly different, this being an entirely civilian affair."

"Very good, Captain," Moirrey cooed, barely able to control the giggles that wanted to break out and paint th'very walls'o'th'place.

If he weren't standing next ta her fer scale, she'd'a been sure she were three meters tall right now. Maybe he growed with her?

And now, the door. Double-wide. Peaked arch. Open. Human scale, so she must'a nots growed, after alls.

Too bad.

Moirrey felt the Captain take a deep breath, so she did, too.

Ya never knows.

Inside, that same red carpet, to those same steps. Even the same Emperer at the top, with that big, gnarly, old sword in one hand. He even looked like the Red Admiral had, four years ago.

And the 189th were here, all fancied up.

I mean, if you gots a platoon of showmen in snazzy uniforms, best to use 'em, right?

Big difference were the two fine ladies on the platform with Karl. Tall, willowy, blond girl on his right. Redhead with a solid build on his left. Not chunky, but nowhere near as ethereal as the blond. Not smiling near as warm as the blond, neither, though not as grouchy as Admiral White.

Princess Kasimira Helena. Princess Ekaterina Stephanya.

Casey and Steffi, according to public love fer the two young ladies 'round heres.

At least Casey were competin' with her fer smile.

"Your Imperial Majesty, *Princesses Imperial*, Ladies and Gentlemen of the Court, I present you Moirrey Kermode," Captain Baumgärtner said grandly as the 189th snapped to attention at her appearance.

How did they all do that, without nobody saying nothing?

She let the Captain lead her into the room and for'd to the steps.

Moirrey had to give the man credit. He were all set to help her kneel on the riser, like she were some helpless fool that decided to wear a hobble skirt, or sometin'. Obviously, never dealt with engineers. An' never had to climb down into an engine well backwards with a welding laser and a camera to fix something.

Step, step, down. Easy as that. Even in heels.

Moirrey smiled up at the giant man above her. Maybe she flexed her shoulders forward, just a bit. Enticing-like, ya know?

He smiled back, like maybe he were in on it. Which just made it all the better.

Dude hefted that blade like it were a conductor's wand in one easy hand. Reached for'd and tapped her lights on her left, on the fabric part of the shoulder of the dress, rather than skin.

Betcha that blade would be awful cold right now.

O'er her head and tap the right. Back over and left. Then down to his side like a meter-long letter opener.

Dude had muscles.

"I proclaim you Moirrey *zu* Kermode, *Ritter* of the Imperial Household," Emperor Karl VII boomed out over the room. "Arise, Lady Moirrey, and be presented to this Court."

Only thing *maybe* topped this were getting commissioned in front of the whole squadron, just 'fore the *Ballard*-run. But that were all her friends. This were just a few of 'em: her sister, Vo, Marcelle, Willow. Desianna were a great lady'n'all, but she were Jessica's best friend. And kinda a stranger-person, although the flight in had helped.

No Digger. No Jackson Tawfeek. No Oz.

Not quite as good.

Still pretty damned awesome.

The Captain were there with an arm and all his strength, just in case she needed it. Moirrey smiled and kipped backwards onto her feet in a single motion.

Engineers and tight spaces, ya know?

She did take the Captain's arm and let him be all official and stuff.

The Emperor smiled something wicked.

Maybe he had been peekin'.

"Princess Kasimira," he said in a big voice. "Your charge awaits."

Moirrey held her breath as the blond girl turned and picked up a bolt of rich silk, almost as dark as homemade currant jam, edged in white. Same color Emperer-dude were wearing. And Vo.

The Princess stepped down and unrolled the cloak, placing it around Moirrey's shoulders. It helped that the Princess were as tall as Desianna.

Two gold-colored ropes appeared and fell down her chest, 'tween her boobs. Moirrey grabbed them and quick-tied 'em into the same knot the one guy'd done to Vo.

Princess Casey stepped 'round front and checked the tie, then kissed Moirrey on both cheeks, makin' her blush fit to her roots. But it was okay. Casey were smiling almost as big as she were. Maybe as much as Jessica were.

The Princess silently took her place again on the rise, next to her Da.

The Emperer nodded at them with a smile almost as big hisself. Captain Baumgärtner turned her softly in place by stepping around her.

Moirrey got her first look at the rest of the room.

"Ladies and Gentlemen of the Court," he called. "Moirrey *zu* Kermode, Imperial *Ritter*."

The applause were way more raucous than Vo's'd been. But the crowd were also better than half female. Way better than half. And way younger. Moirrey's age, rather than Captain Baumgärtner's. Only a handful of uniforms and them folks she mostly knowed. Cap'n B. The Red Admiral. Captain Wald from the other night. Couple of others, lookin' friendlies.

Lotsa girls in frilly and dressy, but most of them *young*.

Kinda sorta silly.

Moirrey wondered if this were the Princess's work.

If so, jes what did that imply?

CHAPTER XXVI

DAY: 277 OF THE COMMON ERA YEAR: 13,445 VESSEL - RS:32G8Y42 – "DANCER IN DARKNESS." FRIBOURG IMPERIAL SPACE. STATUS: SHADOWED

It was one star in a wall of unremarkable siblings. Nothing about it suggested why the *Lord of Winter* considered it so dangerous.

Warm and yellow. Reminiscent more of *Winterhome*'s sun than what he had known on *Korsakov* as a boy. But for the importance of his mission, nothing that would excite any attention to a passing starship.

His mission would deem that assessment otherwise shortly.

Ro Kenzo Atep Vrin meditated in his small, darkened chamber, comfortable in two decadent tatami of padded space, eyes open and studying the single screen on the wall before him. So far he had traveled from his home. So much time saved by walking the road of bonfires lit by the Survey Corps, that he could have the luxury of another forty days to lie in wait.

Another cold stone in the darkness.

Any other vessel would have taken fifteen to eighteen more days to make this historic journey, even with the path cut ahead of time. Well within time to achieve the mission, but far less than efficient.

One more reason the Ministers of the Right and the Left had chosen him.

Around him, *Dancer In Darkness* purred quietly, a stealthy shark cutting through midnight seas, her triangular portrait designed to be reminiscent of the Caribbean Roughsharks of *Winterhome*. And the Homeworld that had betrayed her children in the ancient past.

Not this, a mission for Carcharias or Megalodon. Nor for the Threshers. Not even the Hammerheads.

Only the Roughsharks, the silent stalkers, could handle this task. Best that the premier Director be sent with the foremost vessel.

A knock at the shoji interrupted what little remained of Vrin's meditations. The panel slid open a moment later to reveal his Aide, Otep.

Xi Putaz Laro Otep. A woman as petite to human scale as he was giant, each of them a head removed from average in their own direction. They shared the same straight, black hair, coarse and unruly at times, both of them beginning to fade to gray, although at fifty standard years, he had a decade and a half on the woman who was his left hand. Their eyes both came to the same folded edges.

"Director," she said patiently, as if unsure his eyes were open in the dim light. "The Advocates await your pleasure."

Vrin grunted as a placeholder.

There was little the three could say that he did not already know on a crew this small, but the ten-day meetings were both critical to the ongoing health of the crew, and for its morale.

Vrin unfolded his legs from the lotus and rose in a single motion, a monster from forgotten black lagoons appearing suddenly from the night. The lights remained their dimmest, more brightness unnecessary for now.

Something of his mood must have shown through the façade of cast bronze he maintained at all times. Or perhaps Otep knew him that well. She had been his Aide for many years now.

"It will be rapid," she said. "I will have tea steeped, Director."

Vrin grunted again and adjusted his outer robes, untying the obi at his waist long enough to draw the cloth tight again and then setting it just so.

If you act professional, it will infect your crew. Treat every day as if Armageddon awaits you. Face it with dignity and a fierce scowl.

The hallway was bright as *Korsakov's* noonday sun after his barely-lit meditation chamber. Harsh steel walls, painted in a soft, industrial green intended to sooth the mind on long voyages, jarred him, as they always did, stepping from the silk-covered walls and sumi-e paintings of his inner, personal space.

But they also reset his mind, reminded him that introspection had its place, but that it could not be indulged. Only used, like any other weapon.

The shoji to the Council of Advocates slid open easily. Inside, the two men and one woman who represented *Dancer In Darkness.*

Ro Malar Arga Rues: War Advocate. A slight man for all his savage ferocity when it came time to transform into a death dealer. Black hair grown long and coiled in delicate, gold clasps between his shoulder blades.

Wa Veren Kulo Marz: Entity Advocate. A woman who was one of the most empathic technicians Vrin had ever encountered, capable of teasing out the slightest deviations and psychological issues in the Ship's Systems, often before the Entity itself understood. She reminded Vrin of a fisherman's wife from *Korsakov*, short, stout, and occasionally braying, but harder than any shark that had ever swum. At the same time, a mother figure for the Entity, a confessor, a disciplinarian.

Ko Serek Evet Khan: Crew Advocate. Kulo's counterpart in dealing with the small cast of humans who made up the crew, rather than the intelligent systems. In many ways, Evet's job was easier, since the crew was kept on a shorter leash of behavior, and better trained from birth to serve the *Holding*. Vrin could see the tall man commanding his own Entity-vessel in another few years, even as young as he was today.

Vrin reminded himself that he had been thirty-three standard years old when he was first promoted to a Directorship, nigh two decades ago.

So, three serious faces. Calm. Competent. Focused.

Determined.

We are all so many light centuries from home.

Vrin slid the shoji shut and took his place on the fourth mat on the floor, not at the point of a diamond, but the anchor of the entire room, with three lesser satellites orbiting his greater station. His legs folded automatically to lotus, bringing his mind with it.

"War Advocate," Vrin asked bluntly. "What are the risks?"

"Remaining still," Arga replied. Never aboard ship to use a given name with his Advocates, only the clan crèche. "Something may go wrong with a system and not be picked up until we introduce stress."

"Solution?" Vrin fired back at the man.

"Retain stillness but engage early enough to work up to battle," Arga said. "The risk is exposure while closing to the target, as opposed to missing the deadline due to a surprise failure."

Vrin grunted. Nothing new from the man, but there were only so many ways to clean a mackerel.

"Crew Advocate," Vrin continued. "What are the ratings?"

Evet drew a breath before speaking, as he normally did. Cogent thought, rather than emotional reaction. A good sign in a future Director.

"Edging towards boredom, Director," he said. "This is a top crew, and they know it. They have time to relax from the peaks maintained in transit, and are doing so. I am confident they will come to the killing edge again quickly, at need."

"Proposal?" Vrin asked.

"A slow-drive cruise would work the crew up faster than a hard drop, Director."

Yes. Yes, it would. And they all knew that. No news.

"Entity Advocate," Vrin moved to the woman directly before him. "What thinks *Dancer In Darkness*?"

"Pride, Director," Kulo said quietly. "The excellence of the crew reflects and reinforces the excellence of the vessel. He was chosen first in his class for this mission and seeks to make you proud of him. At the same time, we are all veterans here, risking everything for the greatest mission in the history of the *Holding*. This tempers his exuberance, as does the extreme secrecy in which we operate."

"Resolution?" Vrin growled.

"I am at harmony with the other Advocates, Director," she said serenely. "A time to idle before the surge to toil will bring *Dancer In Darkness* to his peak when most needed."

Vrin nodded individually at the three and rose silently. As Director, it was his decision. The Advocates only proposed within their expertise: a Warrior, a Technician, and a Scholar.

Dancer In Darkness was Vrin's responsibility.

As was the greatest attack ever ordered by the *Lord of Winter*.

CHAPTER XXVII

IMPERIAL FOUNDING: 176/010/04.
WACHTURM PALACE, OUTSIDE WERDER, ST. LEGIER

When he stopped to think about it, Emmerich supposed that he had accidentally outdone himself with this plan.

If Heike's wedding were the social event of the entire season, then a small, private dinner for Jessica Keller, with the Imperial family in attendance, most certainly qualified as the most exclusive, most utterly impossible invitation to score available.

At the end of the day, there had been no safe way to expand the seating chart without starting a decade's worth of ugly recriminations and retaliation from the *Grand Dames* of Werder. Especially if he left anyone out.

The only moment of panic had been assuaged by Desianna Indah-Rodriguez, still one of the most amazingly dangerous operators he had met across his long career and all the light years they had taken him.

And the spies were still fools, unable to admit to themselves that the woman truly was Keller's right hand, her trusted confident, in ways that Hendrik Baumgärtner was his own.

Dare they invite Torsten Wald? Single him out? Risk?

No. Desianna had been right. Two families, and Keller's party. Nobody else. Nothing that might expand the circle of repercussions.

Emmerich took a moment to address himself in the mirror.

Tall. Strong.

Present.

In better shape than he had been in two decades.

Back to the being the dreaded Red Admiral, after he had lost something.

He knew that now.

It had taken Keller rubbing his face in it to drive the point home hard enough to induce the necessary introspection. And then nearly three years of consideration to find that spark that he had lost.

Emmerich smiled to himself, remembering that moment it had returned. The fire it lit in Freya's eyes, with nothing more than a kiss.

Emmerich tugged at his jacket, making sure everything was just so.

He could have worn mufti tonight. Freya had suggested it, to make the night a more relaxed affair. Certainly, everyone else would be dressed in their finest civilian attire.

But he wanted to say something to Jessica. Somehow thank her, through all the hatred that had once engulfed him, for bringing him back to himself.

Tonight, the Day Uniform of an Admiral of the Red.

But more than that.

The Red Admiral.

Conqueror. Scholar. Paladin.

And not the dress uniform, with all the silly fripperies that staff weenies had added over the ages.

No. Simple maroon. Double-breasted. Shoulder boards and two bands around the wrists done in gold. Nine brushed-chrome buttons from hip to shoulder on each side.

Brand new in the last six months as he had lost another five kilos of belly and added ten around the shoulders with a return to lifting weights in the morning after a long walk.

He wasn't even sure Keller would appreciate the depth of changes that had resulted from her pushing him off of that cliff. But he needed to honor her.

Nothing less would do, especially if the war was truly over, at least for their lifetimes.

He had been lost.

Blind.

The door connecting his dressing room to Freya's opened and the sun rose.

Like many Imperial Ladies, she was tall. Heels brought her nearly to eye-level with him.

If he was a near-mirror of Johannes, Freya was an obvious cousin of Kati, so much so that Casey and Heike looked like sisters.

Tonight, Freya wore an elegant gown in a silk so fine that it might be gold, or bronze, or cream, depending on the polarization of the light reflecting.

She walked close silently, wrapping one arm around his waist and leaning her entire self against him. A mermaid draped across the rocks.

He luxuriated in her warmth as his own arm slid around her back, lightly caressing the exposed skin he found there.

No words, just a quick kiss. Warm and promising.

He sighed and shifted backwards. Not much, but enough to break the intimacy before he lost track of the time and got lost in kissing this woman.

Most Imperial gentlemen were expected to escort a Lady on their elbow. Heike still rolled her eyes at these new-found teenagers, holding hands and giggling when they walked.

But the guests would be here soon. Joh, Kati, Ekke, Steffi, Casey.

zu Arlo. *zu* Kermode. Desianna.

Jessica Keller.

Fleet Centurion. *Wildgraf.* Queen.

The Red Admiral took a deep breath.

Dare he believe that he and Jessica Keller could be friends?

CHAPTER XXVIII

Jessica fought down the fidgets while riding in the back of the private car transporting her and her friends to the Wachturm palace, as the great, gray beast rolled to a stop in the large circular driveway. In the back of her mind, this evening's affair felt like the entire reason she had been brought to *St. Legier*, regardless of whatever cover stories were spun about a fairy tale wedding.

Wachturm wanted something from her. She would make him pay dearly to get it.

She flashed back to that night aboard *Baxter* and *Kali-ma* when sleep had eluded her. Wheels within wheels. Was she the saber or the *main-gauche*? This was too big to be merely a dinner. The guest list alone guaranteed that.

Someone would be using her to get back at someone else.

Who?

A steward in a dark suit appeared at the rear door to the vehicle and opened it with a polite, friendly smile on his face. Willow was already standing next to him, having combat-dropped out of the front door even before movement stopped. Marcelle slid out first, in dark gray pants and tunic like Willow's, designed to make both women disappear from conscious view when they stopped moving.

Desianna let the steward hand her down from the vehicle next, dressed to the nines in a lavender and black dress, with gold trim to show off her black hair and dark skin. Moirrey and Vo next in the choreography, until Jessica found herself alone in the back of the transport for the briefest second.

She took the moment to center herself, pushing everything down and inward, as she did just before bringing the fighting robot on-line. Draw on all that rage and compress it like a fire diamond. More than a year of her life functionally lost on this fool's errand into possibly the heart of darkness itself.

And yet…

What if the Eternal War was really over? Did that mean she had won, at last?

Jessica knew her own efforts over the last five years had hurt them, at least as hard as First War Fleet, and millions of others in the Republic, but why now? What had changed after *Thuringwell* that *Fribourg* was suddenly willing to draw a line on a map and honor it?

Or had Emmerich come to understand what *could* happen after *Thuringwell*, if the war continued?

The implications had all been there, what she could do, written in the language of their own, personal war. Perhaps he had been able to convince Karl, and the Imperial structure, that she was finally enough of a threat that they needed to retreat behind their walls and hope *Aquitaine* could keep her on a short enough leash, for a long enough time, to rebuild all the damage she had done?

Certainly, *Corynthe* was too far away for her to actively threaten *Fribourg* from there. And far too poor, even as the economy had grown at a rate of over ten percent per standard year since she had ascended the throne and broken the Captains to her will.

Peace and trade were suddenly becoming things in *Corynthe*, but the taxes to support a major war fleet, even a junkyard version like she was slowly mothballing as *Aquitaine* built her new hulls, that was beyond her capability.

Today.

But tomorrow…

So much unknown. Unsaid. Unpredictable.

And she was about to have a personal dinner with the Red Admiral, his Duchess Freya, Emperor Karl VII, and two extended families.

Jessica took a breath, ran her hands down her tunic to straighten it, and slid sideways to starboard. She let the young man with the nice smile give her a hand out.

At least this transport was high enough that she didn't have to climb up, or flash too much leg. She was wearing an outfit so far outside of her normal fashion sense that most of her team had blinked in surprise when she emerged from her suite. Everyone except Moirrey, her sister ever the instigator.

It was a pull-over top in white cloth, almost skin-tight in all the right places, with a navy blue cloth backing underneath that bled through when the light was bright enough. Nearly knee-length, with two centimeters of that backing blue fabric wrapped around every edge as color. It was slashed upward over the front of each thigh, with two hand-sized triangles of cloth cut out at the bottom, showing the gray leggings she wore. The only color on the dress other than the edging were a pair of blue stripes, each that same centimeter wide, that came up from the tops of the cutouts, ran along her hipbones and just outside her nipples before flaring back and coming to points underneath her arms, where the lines on each side matched lines coming up her back.

The cuffs ran high intentionally on her wrists, and open, with the same edge around the bottom as well as the opening, where she could button them if she wanted.

On her feet, knee-high boots, in a formless, blue-gray leather with zippered seams on the inside, completed the outfit.

Jessica had generally kept her hair long, but not as long as it had been. Enough to braid occasionally, but mostly she kept it tied back.

Tonight, it was loose, brushed up and over her left ear and around the right side, almost the exact opposite of what Moirrey had done two nights ago. Large silver earrings dangled and complemented a matching silver necklace with a blue-stone pendant.

Moirrey had assured her that it would qualify as high fashion meets practical, while showing off her legs and her bum. The women who knew her had been shocked. The men assigned to her palace staff had been almost lustful. Even Vo Arlo had reacted for the briefest moment, before retreating behind the iron shell he maintained around himself at all times.

That had been the biggest surprise. But Jessica knew Moirrey was an expert at these things. If Vo twitched, they had managed something special.

Certainly, the reaction from the stewards on the porch was similar. The other two women had arrived lavish and beautiful. Jessica's outfit had simply gone right past them.

As she had intended.

Jessica found Emmerich Wachturm at the top of the short stone staircase, just outside of the immense double door to his palace.

He was dressed in red.

The Crimson Hawk.

Fribourg's most dangerous commander, in a clean, formal Day uniform that made him look twenty years younger. Not as toned and powerful as Vo Arlo, but scarcely any men were. And Wachturm had lost the middle-aged middle and added a good chunk of it back to the shoulders, looking like the Captain Wachturm who had been such a scourge two decades past.

Jessica smiled as his face lit up. She climbed to his level, her party in tow, and stood before this man who was a little taller than most, perhaps 185 or 187 centimeters tall. Nearly a head taller than her, even if her boots added a finger of sole underneath.

Wachturm bowed, formally, and stood relaxed before her.

Jessica could not remember Emmerich Wachturm ever being this relaxed in her presence.

"*Wildgraf* Keller," he said formally with a twinkle in his eyes. "Premier Indah-Rodriguez. Lord Vo. Lady Moirrey. Thank you and welcome to my home."

"Duke Wachturm," Jessica replied, ignoring his uniform for the moment. "We thank you for the invitation."

He beamed down at her, some private message so at odds with how they had interacted in the past, and then turned to gesture to the door and the grand foyer visible beyond.

"Please," he continued. "Make yourselves at home."

Emmerich surprised her by offering his left elbow for her, but Jessica was intent on playing her role as *diplomat* tonight, *guest*, so she took it.

Soon enough, she would find up what devilry these men, these Imperials, had planned.

Then she could go through her mental files and pick out the next steps in her campaign.

S itting down, it wasn't as obvious, but Jessica had found the height differences amusing.

Generally, there was little physical difference between the two cultures, *Aquitaine* and *Fribourg*.

Jessica was a touch short for a female, and Moirrey tiny by any standards. Vo was half a head taller than most of the men present. It was on the Imperial side where things made her smile.

Karl VII and Emmerich Wachturm really were cast from the same mold, once you had them side by side. The Red Admiral's hair was fully gray, while his cousin was only halfway, but Wachturm was also in better physical shape.

Crown Prince Karl Ekkehard, the oldest child of Karl VII at twenty standard years, was a close knock-off of both men, obviously Wiegand in bones and coloring and height, just as seventeen-year-old Kasimira, Casey, was. At nineteen, Princess Steffi took after her mother, a slightly-stocky, green-eyed redhead, what Jessica's mother would have called the *Irish Cousins* back home. But both girls, and their mother, the Empress Ekaterina, *Kati*, were within a few centimeters in height of the men.

On the Wachturm side, it was no different. Duchess Freya had that same lean height, blond hair, and green eyes that ran through the noble class's blood. Their oldest child, Lady Jeltje, was a strawberry blond who was just barely the shortest in the family. And still much taller than Jessica. Son Tiede, *Commander* Wachturm, was another, younger version of the Imperial House male, taking after father, uncle, and Crown Prince cousin. And Heike, Lady Henrietta Anne, could have passed herself off in public as Princess Casey fairly easily.

It was only the two outsider men that differed from the Imperial family. Jeltje's husband, Commander Carsten Voight, was nearly as tall as Vo, but a pencil of a man, rather than a mountain, and both bright and charming, just from the little she had been near enough to hear him speak. Lt. Commander Bernard Hourani, Heike's fiancé, was average in height, possibly the shortest man here, and much darker than average in complexion, looking more like her or Desianna that way. He was also calmly poised and sure of himself, as well as extremely intelligent. He would be a welcome addition to the family.

The Red Admiral had made that much abundantly clear.

And now they were seated at the long table, watching the stewards clear dessert. Dinner had been a smashing success in five courses: salad, small plate, soup, another small plate, dessert.

From her spot at Wachturm's right hand, the dynamics had been interesting to watch. The Red Admiral at the head of the table as host, with Freya at the far end facing him. Jessica to the first right, with Princess Casey next to her and Moirrey beyond that. Vo across from

Jessica and then the Crown Prince across from his youngest sister. The rest of the table was a touch more random, except for the Emperor seated at Freya's left, mirroring Jessica's spot next to Emmerich Wachturm.

The conversation had been polite and rather vague up until now. Inane chatter, although Casey had asked a number of pointed questions, especially when she happened to discover that Jessica had two pilots, *Rocket Frog* and *Neon Pink*, who were her own age and flying Starfighters for a living.

Everything changed when Emmerich Wachturm picked up his wine glass and held it in the air in one mountain-steady hand, eyes ranging the whole table before coming to rest on Jessica's.

Everyone scrambled to find their glasses and raise them as well.

"I am reminded," Wachturm began with a distant, heavy tone, ominous if one was not paying close attention. "Of a dinner held at *Callumnia*, many years ago."

Jessica remembered that night. Desianna would as well. The war between the two of them had become personal, then and there. Worlds would suffer for it.

Had.

As had many men and women along the way.

Jessica kept her smile neutral and expectant. Pleasant. Polite.

None of the sea of raging emotions that she might have shown now. She had found Daneel then, and lost him, partly as a result of this man. Stopped the Red Admiral from killing the Republic's past and future in Suvi, even at the cost of *Alexandria Station*. Gotten even with him at *Thuringwell*.

Yes, their personal war went deep.

She wondered if Emmerich Wachturm had any idea.

"We spoke of differences that night," the Red Admiral continued in a lighter voice, almost lyrical. "Founding Myths. Things that separated *Aquitaine* from *Fribourg*. I have made many mistakes in my life, but thinking we were all that different was probably my greatest. In the end, we all want the same things: life, love, family, friends."

His eyes seemed to bore into hers now. Piercing.

Demanding.

Jessica breathed shallowly through her nose, keeping her own glass steady as she let the moment build.

Wachturm surprised her by breaking the rope of mad energy that flowed between them and turning to the Crown Prince, seated to his left.

That young man obviously felt the weight of that tremendous stare, but he didn't flinch under it.

"My friends," the Red Admiral concluded. "I give you the Peace between our nations. May it be long and fruitful, and both sides keep finding excuses to extend it beyond our lifetimes."

Jessica was glad she had enough breath in her to drink with the rest of the table. The shock would have prevented her, otherwise.

Emmerich Wachturm was either the greatest poker player ever born, or those were truly heartfelt words. Was it even possible that their war could fade away?

Could there be peace?

What would Jessica Keller do with the rest of her life?

CHAPTER XXIX

IMPERIAL FOUNDING: 176/010/12. IMPERIAL PALACE, WERDER, ST. LEGIER

It had been Mother's idea, originally.

Casey distinctly remembered bristling at the order, even if it was phrased as a mere *suggestion*. But even a *Princess Imperial* did not brook the Empress. At least, not without a better reason than had availed itself at the time.

So Casey found herself seated on her favorite patio, overlooking the duck pond, having a light lunch with her sister.

She would have been hard pressed to identify two people more dissimilar in the extended clan, than she and Steffi. Herself the artist, Steffi the ever-practical scholar. She might even go so far as to call her a small-dreamer. Boring. But Steffi would live a happy, simple life as a result.

More than Casey could claim.

Still, this was her sister. The least she could do was listen, and not sigh or roll her eyes. Much.

"It will never work, you know," Steffi announced as she glanced over, breaking the silence that had accumulated around their salads.

So much for that idea.

"What won't?" Casey replied, trying desperately to sound adult and not let her own tones of teenage peevishness color the conversation.

"Keller," Steffi said, munching gracefully.

Casey had never met anyone who could be as dainty and lady-like while eating, even so far as to carry on a conversation.

Casey settled for putting down her fork and swallowing.

"Could you please be a little more vague, dear sister?" Casey sarcastically half-growled. "I'm likely to start understanding you soon at this rate."

It was an old argument. Two people speaking the same language, and not even speaking remotely coherently at one another.

Steffi actually smiled at that, a rare occurrence in someone so serious so young.

And what does that make you, oh artist princess?

"I watched you at the dinner at Uncle Em's, littlest one," Steffi replied. "More importantly, I listened, which is more than anyone else did."

"Em was listening," Casey fired back defensively, still unsure where her sister was headed.

"He still thinks you're twelve and going to grow up to be a proper, little waif of a girl," Steffi said. "I know better."

"So, oh grand oracle," Casey said in a semi-mocking voice. "What am I?"

"A revolutionary," Steffi said with a serious smile, cutting Casey to the fine. "A dangerous, underhanded rebel, intent on tearing down all of Imperial society and turning us into *Aquitaine* when nobody is looking."

Casey felt her eyes threaten to swell out of her head, like the dog-wolf in her favorite cartoon. She started to say something, anything to deny her sister's words, but there were none.

How do you dispute the honest truth?

Casey barely managed a weak sputter in response, but Steffi softened her glare into a smile.

"It will never work," Steffi repeated with indomitable finality.

"I have to try," Casey finally managed to whisper, her heart and mind racing. "If nobody is willing to push against those walls, then life turns into nothing so grand as a cattle chute with the butcher quietly waiting at the end."

"I know," Steffi said. "Mother and I talked about this afterwards. About you."

Casey's blood went cold. She was sure her face went white as well. This felt remarkably dangerous, all the more so because Steffi *was* always practical. Even as a child, she had held no poetry in her soul.

"And?" Casey squeaked.

"I suggested they find you a foreign husband," Steffi's voice was like a river slowly rising over its banks, inexorably coming closer as Casey's island of stability, of sanity, shrank. "*Aquitaine*, or someplace similar. A man who would appreciate his dangerously-open-minded wife in ways no *Imperial* nobleman could possibly envision. I can just see you, in disguise, being arrested somewhere in the middle of a Chartist protest."

When had her sister gotten so smart, so cagey? Or what were her minders whispering on to others? That was eerily prescient.

Casey made a note to pay closer attention to the words coming out of her mouth in the future, lest the wrong players draw dangerous conclusions.

Even accurate ones.

"Oh?" Casey replied, unconvincingly trying to shrug Steffi's words off.

"It was that, or watch the scandal unfold when you ran away to find your own life, your own destiny," Steffi plowed on.

Casey reached for a glass of water for her suddenly-dry mouth. Words eluded her, the young woman who wrote poetry and music as naturally as she breathed.

Just hollow, fearful emptiness.

How long did she have before Father and Mother took their older daughter seriously and put the youngest in a gilded cage?

"You're safe, you know?" Steffi's voice softened abruptly. "Father also sees you as twelve, and both Ekke and I will have to be married off before anyone tries to solve the *Bohemian*."

Steffi's smile returned, warmer, like it had been when Casey was much younger and had a nightmare her sister could comfort away.

"Unless you have your heart set on becoming an Ambassador somewhere. Or a pirate captain," Steffi teased.

"It would never work, you know," Casey fired back in panicked relief.

"That's what I said," Steffi giggled lightly. "Although I know a Pirate Queen who might offer you asylum *in extremis*."

Casey's heart skipped a beat at the thought. Saša and Asra Binici. *Rocket Frog* and *Neon Pink*. Starfighter pilots, no older than she was.

Free.

Casey suddenly bitterly resented not being a sixth, or even seventh child.

Until Ekke had a family of his own, she was third in succession. The ugly shrews of the Imperial Court wouldn't stand for her stepping any further out of line than she had managed to date, even as those walls slowly began to push back harder against her.

Those high, brick walls around the Gardens would only protect her for so long.

Even the rose hadn't managed to escape.

Could she really leave everything *Fribourg* and convince Father to make her a diplomat? *Aquitaine* would certainly welcome her as such. Two birds, one stone?

Or was she better off staying right here, in Werder, spending the next several decades railing against the world? Would anyone listen?

"There are days I would like to hate you," Casey said finally.

"I know," Steffi replied breezily. "But I will be happy in a much smaller garden than you will, Casey. I'm not sure you will ever actually be allowed to be happy. That would be a shame. And a waste."

Casey refused the tears that threatened. Who was this strange creature across the table from her, and what had happened to the boringly-normal girl she had fought with for so many years?

Casey choked down another mouthful of water, rather than speaking.

What was there to say at this point? She could have her dreams, her flights of fancy, but they would never turn into the prince that would whisk her away from all this.

She was probably better off stowing away on a tramp freighter.

Or buying one and turning herself into a pirate.

Every girl needed to dream.

CHAPTER XXX

DATE OF THE REPUBLIC OCTOBER 16, 398
DOCKSIDE DISTRICT, WERDER, ST. LEGIER

By now, Vo had gotten the rhythm of his new mates.

He was a Colonel of the Regiment, however honorary and undeserved, but the men treated him as the real thing, this team of veteran enlisted troopers, friends, intent on showing their new mate, their new commander, the finest attractions that a true officer and nobleman would miss, in some of the seedier bars and establishments, in the wrong parts of town.

On the other hand, Vo had met exactly two men taller than himself in the last month. And four that might be strong enough to wrestle with, of the scores and hundreds his wanders on the docks of *St. Legier* had covered.

That size, combined with his uniform and the little, gold lapel pin proclaiming him an Imperial *Ritter of the Household*, guaranteed the best service, anywhere he went, though Vo had made it clear that he would not join the boys when they wanted another round at the bordellos.

He had made no stout promises to Rebekah Kim, Cohort Centurion of *LVIII Armored Ala Heavy (Cataphracti): The Storm Guard*. She was back with the Ninth Pohang Legion now, home and training her tankers. Hopefully, she had taken well to his letter apologizing about being unable to come visit on leave this past summer, as he had intended. The timing had been too tight, just getting to *St. Legier*, to do anything else.

And while it would have been nice to spend more time around her, she might be a tad too abrasive for Imperial High Society, as he was occasionally engaged by.

On the other hand, a dive like the current one would have been right up her alley, once the poor fools got over a woman being here who wasn't a *professional*. And who was tough enough to take any two of them by herself.

Right now, Vo *zu* Arlo found himself mostly alone, tucked into a corner booth in back of a medium-sized establishment, with only Edgar Horst seated. One group of men from the 189th were tournamenting darts along the side wall with the seriousness of brain surgery. Another squad was taking turns on a badly-tuned piano, entertaining the crowd with patriotic barbershop tunes. Again, professionally serious goofballs. Others were at the bar, sipping and lying.

It was a Thursday night, and still early. The mostly-civilian crowd hadn't really gotten warmed up yet, or even particularly here. In another three hours, a dive like this would hold twice as many men, and a goodly collection of professional girls, cheek by jowl.

The place had that feel to it.

Vo knew the newest group of men would be trouble the moment they walked in the door.

He had spent enough time as a Security marine aboard *Auberon* to see the signs in a man's stance, the set of his shoulders, the tilt of his head.

They came in like a pack of mangy coyotes, but there were still eight of them, led by a fierce bantam with a shaved pate, exotic tattoos, and scarred ears.

Vo regretted the rules that prevented him and his men from having sidearms on this planet.

The night had suddenly developed that feel.

The lead coyote locked eyes from just inside the door. Some dark fire took possession of the man's soul a moment later.

He stalked closer.

Vo rested one hand on the table, just to confirm, but he already knew there was no way to tear the tabletop loose and use it as a weapon in a fight. Probably a design feature in a joint like this.

There were stools, but none close. The mugs were a light plastic for the same reason, with none of the usefulness of shatterable glass, nor the weight of steel mugs. Something like that would be valuable about now, as the man drew closer, his pack in close tow.

Silence seemed to trail with the men.

Seated, Vo barely had to look up at the bantam. From here, the man's breath could have peeled paint.

"Yer in my seat, soldier boy," the man menaced in an ugly, rough tone.

One hand rode close to a hip in a manner that suggested a blade, either in a side pocket, or up the sleeve and into his hand with a quick snap.

Horst started to reply, until Vo fixed him with a hard, silent stare that brought the man to heel like the end of a too-short stake-chain in a squirrel chase.

Vo returned his gaze to the stranger and retained his silence.

Eight on two, them standing, but unable to deploy their numbers effectively. The leader looked tough, but the others had the swagger, the giggling, of street bullies.

Vo remembered being one of those punks, fifteen years ago. Before a friendly judge sentenced him to being a marine. Before Navin the Black. Before *Ballard*.

Before *Thuringwell*.

"I said, you're in my seat," the man rasped, louder, in case Vo were hard of hearing.

Vo blinked owlishly at the man. No other movement. No emotion on his face.

Nothing to give a punk like this a handle.

The leader snapped his hand back and forward again, a circus trick that put a stiletto shiv in his palm. It was a polished move, theatrical.

Probably impressive to most people. At least the ones who had never studied kendo.

Vo considered his options.

The piano had fallen silent. In the vids, that was always the ominous sign. The dart tournament had ceased as well, though nobody had made any outward movement.

As a *Ritter*, Vo was within his rights to have the man thrown out. And arrested just for threatening him.

This punk looked like a man who already knew what the inside of a jail cell smelled like.

Vo could order his men to fall on the strangers, twenty-four to eight with surprise and position.

But he was an officer now. Two officers, if he stopped to consider himself an Imperial Army Colonel and a Republic Centurion.

The year had been frustrating.

Not seeing Rebekah, to enjoy those sparks. Being called by the Fleet Centurion to be an example of an officer and a gentleman, when all he really wanted to do was be himself.

And now, this punk.

"You gonna move, pretty boy?" the leader growled. "Or do I have to get ugly?"

Vo nodded once to the man, slow and unthreatening.

He rested both palms flat on the table top and pushed down enough to free him from the stickiness of the pseudo-leather seat, slowly sliding sideways out of the booth and getting his feet firmly planted before he stood up.

The bantam might look the Fleet Centurion in the eyes. He didn't come up to Vo's shoulder.

The other seven began to murmur among themselves as Vo glared down at them, none any taller than average height, and either rail thin or dumpy and overweight.

Nobody here got up at dawn and ran several kilometers before chow. Not on that side of the room, anyway.

Ugliness sparked in the leader's eyes, already crazy.

"You looking at me, soldier boy?" he snarled in a coyote's low tone.

The tip of the stiletto came up to point at Vo's face.

Again, a threat, if you didn't know anything at all about knife-fighting.

Navin had taught all of them the importance of not telegraphing your movement, usually with a bamboo sword on the kendo floor. The kind that left stinging, painful welts for days afterwards.

Vo let everything bubble up. Just a little.

Enough to lash out with his left hand faster than the eye could track it.

His meaty paw engulfed the man's fist and his wrist, trapping both before the ugly man could react. And that was before Vo started to squeeze hard enough to start to grind the bones, if not shatter them. At best, right now, the punk might manage to scratch Vo enough to cut the fabric on his jacket.

Moirrey would have the man's head on a stake if he damaged that uniform. Probably Vo's as well, for letting him.

Plus, you don't negotiate with bullies. A great many people had taught him that, over the years.

Everything is a show to them. Their only power is fear.

Rather than try logic, Vo punched the man suddenly in the side of the head, as hard as he could.

Not the fragile bones at the temple. Those would have shattered to mush under the impact and simply killed him.

Vo aimed higher, the heavier part of the skull cap that could probably take the punch with nothing more than hairline fractures and a disabling concussion.

Not that he was above killing the man. Nor was he outside of his rights as an officer and a gentleman to do so, especially when threatened with a weapon.

The time spent studying Imperial law on the flight out here had covered those details.

No, let this stupid punk wake up in a hospital somewhere, chained to his bed, on the way to a prison cell.

Sometimes, bullies never learn. Those live in small boxes until they do.

Having a hold on the man, an anchor, meant the unconscious body couldn't fall away from the punch. Vo held the man's dead weight in the air with one hand overhead, dangling like a side of beef in an abattoir in front of the other seven as they fell deathly silent.

Vo made sure he had their attention before he dropped their leader like a frozen turkey and growled at the rest of the gang.

Before any of the strangers could move, twenty-four other men growled as well, suddenly arm's reach away and apparently pointedly unhappy with the turn of events.

Vo pointed to the little insignia he wore on the left side of his chest, certainly something nobody else in the bar had probably ever seen, let alone recognized.

"I am Colonel Vo *zu* Arlo, *Ritter* of the Imperial Household," he ground the words out like an angry landslide, gaining power and volume. "This is the 189th Division of the Imperial Army. If I ever see any of you again, I will have you arrested. If you threaten me or any of my men, I will have you put down in the street like mad dogs. Am I clear?"

Flies would be embarrassed to buzz in the sudden silence.

One of the men still retained the faintest hint of color to his otherwise white cheeks. He nodded. The rest stood in stony shock, mackerel suddenly discovering sharks around them.

"Your friend requires medical attention," Vo continued. "You will pick him up and take him to the hospital. Now. I have ears in this city. I will know if you disobey me."

Somewhere, in the dark, angry depths of Vo's training and lizard brain, he heard Navin the Black chuckle mightily.

"Move," Vo commanded in a sudden bellow that rang off the rafters.

The mackerel scurried to pick up their leader and flee like spooked sheep, wolves pacing them to the door.

Vo made his way to the publican, a short, fat man with terror and awe fighting for possession of his face in the silence.

"My lord," the man stammered.

Vo pulled a five-florin silver coin from a pocket and placed on the scarred wood between them.

"My apologies for the disturbance, sir," Vo said in the voice that more-closely approximated human than he had a moment ago. "If those men give you any more trouble, I will leave orders with the local gendarme to handle them as roughly as they deserve. And I will not be brooked."

The man nodded, silent, nearly as white as the few other bar's patrons, suddenly confronted with a school of sharks.

Vo smiled, and made his way back to the booth. The piano and the darts picked up again.

Hopefully, the Fleet Centurion would approve.

He had no doubts she would hear all the details from someone, no later than breakfast tomorrow.

CHAPTER XXXI

DATE OF THE REPUBLIC OCTOBER 17, 398
IMPERIAL STARPORT, WERDER, ST. LEGIER

Jessica still wasn't sure if this was a good idea, or a terrible mistake in the making, this trip. She had at least left behind a note on paper, sealed, in Desianna's hands, just in case, but there really wasn't much more past that she could do.

She found herself this morning at Werder's main starport in a small lounge, well-decorated and expensive, back around in the extremely secured, military parts of the facility, alone, but for Captain Baumgärtner, Marcelle, and Willow.

Waiting.

Time seemed to be running slow this morning, or she was just too keyed up, which was also possible, considering. She still didn't trust what was going on with these people. There were pieces of the puzzle missing.

Before she could say anything, a side door opened and Emmerich Wachturm entered the room. She supposed he had a wider wardrobe, but she only ever saw him in his Red Admiral uniform these days.

At least today was semi-official business.

"My most profound apologies for being late," he said, carrying an oversized piece of folded-up paper in one hand that he proffered to Jessica as he got close. "I needed to make a few calls and understand the situation better before we departed."

Jessica had stood as the man entered, so now everyone was on their feet. She took the paper and let it flop open to confirm what it was.

She had heard about such things, but never actually held an Imperial broadsheet before. It seemed such an amazing waste of paper, to actually print a variety of news, gossips, ads, and comics on physical paper and distribute it that way, instead of transmitting updated news regularly to electronic tablets.

But the *Fribourg Empire* was a paper culture. It made sense to them.

"Situation?" Jessica asked.

"Colonel Arlo made rather a scene last night," Wachturm replied breezily.

Jessica felt her stomach go cold. Today's trip had been planned in secrecy several days ahead, but was always subject to last-minute circumstances. Something happening with Vo might qualify.

"Bad?" Jessica inquired.

"Oh, no, *Wildgraf*," Wachturm said with a wide smile. "Quite the contrary, from what I'm given to understand. Half a dozen hoodlums decided to start a ruckus in a bar where the 189th was drinking."

"What happened?"

"Arlo knocked the leader into the hospital with one blow," the Red Admiral replied with a grin. "Chased the rest into turning themselves in to the police. Your man is something of a hero on the streets of Werder, this morning. The story is at the bottom of the righthand column, on page two."

Jessica felt her heart slow back down. But then, Vo was born to be a hero, if he could just get out of his own way.

"I see," Jessica said up to the man. "So everything is good?"

"Very much so," Emmerich said. "That was what I wanted to confirm with the local constabulary, since we'll be out of touch for two days. Now, if you will come this way, our courier is fully prepped and the pilot ready."

Jessica followed Wachturm through a door and into a medium-sized flight hangar, barely large enough for a giant Republic DropShip like *Cayenne* to fit.

There was a vessel waiting for them. While regular administrative shuttles or cargo haulers tended to be boxy affairs, this ship was sleek, a rapier poised to slice through sky and space.

Jessica followed the Red Admiral up a quick flight of steps and into the courier's guts. She was familiar with the general design architecture. The Republic used something similar, but she had rarely ever needed to be transported somewhere outside the confines of a warship.

On her left as she entered, Jessica knew she would find a cockpit with a three-man flight crew. Immediately in front of her, a cabin with comfortable seats all the way around, facing each other across a series of round tables that could be telescoped up from the deck on need. Aft of that, a set of sleeping chambers and a head, for trips that might take several days. All the way back, just in front of the engines, were crew cabins, a wardroom, and kitchen; again, fully staffed, since a courier like this was usually the personal craft of an Admiral.

Everyone quickly took their seats and buckled in as the ship came live with a hum of barely-contained power. Little vessels like this were designed to cross interstellar space as fast as one could safely navigate risks and gravity wells.

Rather than turn on the gravplates, the pilot settled for making sure everyone was strapped in as he cleared the bay doors and stood the small ship on her ass end, trying to blast a hole in the atmosphere. The g-forces weren't great, but more than enough to keep casual conversation down.

Gaucho would have approved.

Jessica took the time to read up on Arlo.

Her only surprise was that the fool who had started it was still alive.

* * *

They dropped out of JumpSpace in an unknown system four hours flight from the capital. Jessica supposed she could go calculate the coordinates later, if she really cared, but there was nothing of any military value here. If there had been, the Red Admiral wouldn't have brought her.

The only thing of any interest was a brand-new Paladin-class Battleship named *Amsel*, the *Blackbird*, replacement for the older version that had been so horribly mauled at *First Ballard* four years ago. Like the old *Auberon*, she had eventually been stricken and a new vessel built in her place.

On the screens, as the little transport approached, the new *Blackbird* was a grown-up version of the courier. She was longer and sleeker than her older namesake, a higher length-to-beam ratio that conveyed speed and danger, where the older ship had been a battleaxe.

Jessica memorized as much as she could, knowing that this ship was only the second of her class, vessels that had not yet been seen on the *Aquitaine* frontier.

Where were they being deployed to, if not the Eternal War that was now at Peace, or at least truce? Was there another foe out there?

Jessica let her strategic and tactical mind explore the possibilities that the whispered rumors were true.

Another stellar empire, on the far side of vast *Fribourg*, suddenly turning aggressive. In that light, a great deal of Karl and the Red Admiral's recent behavior made more sense. As did the requirement that she not bring along Moirrey, the evil engineering gnome capable of deducing obscene amounts of actionable information about the new ship, just from looking at her.

Moirrey would probably have been able to draw frighteningly accurate deck plans for the ship, just spending a day aboard her.

Well aft, just ahead of the engine clusters, a bay door in the gray beast's hide opened invitingly. The pilot threaded a tiny needle with his craft, passing the lock seal and landing with a jar that wouldn't have spilled tea.

Emmerich Wachturm had been uncharacteristically quiet for much of the flight. He spoke up now, in a quiet voice that conveyed grave seriousness.

"Fleet Centurion," he intoned as he unbuckled and stood. "You would have found out eventually, but I brought you here to share two state secrets. Not because I want your help, but because I want you to understand the stakes involved."

Had he offered to fight her to the death, right here on the flight deck, Jessica wouldn't have been as surprised.

From Wachturm's side, Hendrik Baumgärtner, her own minder and recent assistant, nodded intently.

"Okay," Jessica said in a slightly-disbelieving tone as she rose in turn.

She watched Emmerich Wachturm transform before her eyes, into a primeval creature, a force of raw nature.

"I know you do not believe me, Jessica Keller," he growled. "But the Peace between our nations will hold, as long as I have the power, the lifeblood, to enforce it."

Jessica felt her chin come up at the challenge in his voice.

"Why?" she fired back defiantly.

They were past *how* he could promise that. And this was no longer a conversation between *Fribourg* and *Aquitaine*.

This had come down to *The Fleet Centurion* and *The Red Admiral*.

"Because *Aquitaine* is the lesser evil, Keller," he stated flatly. "There is something, someone, far worse. *Fribourg* will not rest until that scourge is utterly destroyed. I expect that task to take my entire lifetime, and possibly my grandchildren's as well, to complete."

She could see the seriousness, the promise, in his eyes. Thoughts of second fronts danced menacingly in the back of her mind.

What could she do to convince the Senate to abrogate the treaty? They could help bring *Fribourg* down, whoever *they* were.

"Who?" she finally asked, after a moment of silent scheming.

"*Buran*," Emmerich replied. "The *Lord of Winter*. A *Sentience* in command of a star empire."

Jessica's soul went cold.

There was no greater threat to humanity than one of the deathless AIs in control of starfleets again.

The Concordancy War had ended when robot battlefleets pummeled the Homeworld, the planet *Earth* itself, with enough asteroids to annihilate all trace of civilization from her surface. All human life on the planet had vanished with it.

In response, *Earth*'s fleets had destroyed their daughters, those colonies seeking to escape the Homeworld's control. Whole worlds were crushed by orbital bombardment, *Sentiences* determining that to be the most efficient way to win the war.

Once out of the bottle, that genie could not be put back.

Worlds continued to fall on both sides. Scrubbed clean of human life.

Only after the factories had been destroyed, only after trade in specialized machine parts had been suddenly and irrevocably disrupted, did the humans and their *Sentiences* come to understand what they had done.

But by then, it was too late.

Trade failed. Colonies failed.

Galactic civilization failed.

Galactic humanity nearly went with it.

Barely one colony in fifty had even retained human survivors, with most of them fallen to Iron Age barbarism within two generations.

One thousand years of darkness had followed, broken only when *Zanzibar* rediscovered the ancient technology and began exploring, with their first stop at *Ballard*.

The Story Road.

Henri Baudin, the Founder of *Aquitaine*, had proscribed *Sentiences*, leaving only the one exception for Suvi, the *Librarian of Ballard* in her golden cage, *Alexandria Station*. *Fribourg* had gone even further, actively rooting them out and destroying them, along with anything that remotely smacked of electronic intelligence.

If one of the warriors from the Concordancy Era, the Destroyers, had survived, everything was at risk. If it controlled enough firepower to threaten *Fribourg*, it threatened the entire galaxy.

The entire species.

"You see," he said simply.

The Red Admiral took a half-step back and gestured skyward, even as they were in deep space.

Jessica grunted something under her breath, unwilling to trust words yet.

"This vessel was never meant to fight *Aquitaine*," he continued in a sepulchral tone. "If it is in my power, *Amsel* will never see that side of the Empire, except on diplomatic tours. I brought you here because I need you to understand that. Nobody else could. None that would matter."

She studied the man as closely as she could. The fire and fear in his eyes. The set of his shoulders. The shallowness of his breath.

"There's more than that, Wachturm," she finally growled, aware that the rest of the room hung poised, watching the tableau play out.

"Much more, Keller," he agreed. "But I needed you away from everyone else to hear me. What I am telling you must never leave this vessel."

Again, commitment unto death in his eyes. A man set to dedicate the remaining decades of his life to a job that would require even longer to complete.

"Then explain," she said, taking her own half-step back and falling into a parade rest stance. There was time. Outside, the crew would still need several minutes to set up the red carpet and crew.

"You and I fought once before over a *Sentience*," Wachturm said. "The reasons are unimportant now. We both did what we believed was right. She was not a threat, but a symbol. *Buran* is a threat. To everything. *Fribourg*. *Aquitaine*. *Corynthe*. If you side with him, all of the galaxy might fall."

"And you think I might?" Jessica snarled up at the man, anger warring with disbelief in her voice.

"Out of ignorance? Yes," he replied tersely. "The stakes are higher than merely possession of this section of the galaxy. About who is right or wrong. This is about the future of humanity as a star-faring species."

He fell silent at that, eyes boring into hers.

"You want me to convince the Senate to honor the Peace?" she asked, angry at where he was putting her.

"No, Jessica Keller," the Red Admiral replied sharply. "They would do that on their own. The treaty we offered was good enough. I want you to *not* convince them to break it."

"You think I have that power, Emmerich Wachturm?" she snarled.

"Yes. Yes, I do, Fleet Centurion," the man replied simply, shocking Jessica nearly out of her shoes with his blunt honesty. "You are perhaps the only person in the galaxy with that power right now. Much of my future rests on your shoulders. On your decision."

Jessica was sure the shock of his words was scribed across her face like a crimson blush. None of her strategies had covered a conversation like this, with this man.

"And I don't need your decision today," the man said. "The whole purpose of our trip here was to remind you that we are an honorable people. That we have more in common than that which divides us. That peace between us can be made to work, even as I have to face the foulest demon the ancient past ever spawned."

Jessica was speechless. A rarity, given her planning. Her preparations. Her reputation.

"I will take your silence as acquiescence for the moment, Madam Keller," he continued with a nod, turning his assistant.

"Hendrik, if you would?" the Red Admiral continued.

Captain Baumgärtner smiled carefully at the two of them, as if the last few minutes had never happened. He turned and checked the outside screen, nodding to himself before opening the hatch and descending. His voice echoed over the small flight deck.

"All hands, attention," Baumgärtner commanded. "His Excellency, Admiral of the Red Emmerich Wachturm, and *Wildgraf* Jessica Keller of *Petron*."

Wachturm nodded at Jessica with a smile and turned to the hatch, descending the steps slowly as she gathered her thoughts into something vaguely coherent.

Jessica let her training run her on autopilot, leading her to the hatch and down the steps in the Red Admiral's wake.

Outside, she found a small line of senior officers to one side, ascending in rank, with one at the end facing her. Wachturm surprised her by turning himself into line at the end, leaving her alone to face the Imperial Captain at the far end. A man she did not know.

"Fleet Centurion," the man said with a smile as she approached. "Captain Rafferty Saar, commander of *IFV Amsel.* Welcome aboard."

Saar was average height, but extremely broad across the chest. He reminded Jessica of Alber' d'Maine physically, but without the lunatic fire in the eyes. The look on his face was closer to what she would have expected from Denis Jež, with blond hair a touch too long.

Jessica was still in shock from Wachturm's words. She let her training take over to handle the diplomatic niceties as her mind raced.

After all those dreams, did she really have the power to topple the *Fribourg Empire?*

CHAPTER XXXII

IMPERIAL FOUNDING: 176/010/22. IMPERIAL PALACE, WERDER, ST. LEGIER

Emmerich looked up from his desk as a shadow darkened his door.

"Did it work?" Johannes, *His Imperial Majesty Karl VII, Emperor of Fribourg* asked as he stepped into Emmerich's office, overcrowded still with books, and silently closed the door.

Joh occasionally took great pleasure in sneaking his entire retinue into the Academy building and appearing without any warning at the door to Emmerich's old office.

Emmerich put down his pen and leaned back from his latest manuscript. This one was not another boring book on naval strategy. This would be a History, a piece only he could write.

Something for the ages.

"That woman gives nothing away, Joh," Emmerich replied wearily. "She's met Saar, toured the vessel as much as she could in a day, and heard my spiel."

"But?"

Joh settled into the emptier chair by piling everything on the floor instead.

"What if her hatred is too great?" the Red Admiral asked. "What if she would rather take a few years rebuilding their strength, and then swoop in on us from the flank, trusting that they can crush us between them, and then deal with *Buran* on her own, afterwards?"

"It was always a calculated risk, Em," the Emperor replied. "It will always be one. As you said, we can bring her here. We can show her what our side is like. If that fails, the only person we could bring that might overrule her in the long run is Nils Kasum."

"No, it won't be Kasum," Em said forcefully. "Petia Naoumov will most likely be First Lord by then, after Kasum retires."

"Will *she* deal?"

"I don't know, Joh," Emmerich said. "She's good. Not in Kasum's league, or Keller's, but close. Canny, capable. Dangerous. And she's got Arott Whughy on her staff now, except when he's got *Auberon* out defending *Corynthe* from all comers while Keller's here. The man was at *Ballard*, with the Battlecruiser *Stralsund*. He knows his stuff as well."

Silence passed as the two men ruminated.

"Em," the Emperor finally broke the impasse. "You are still the best strategist I have. Your judgement said to do this with Keller. I'll trust that. I would rather die with honor, doing as much damage to *Buran* as we can, for Keller to clean up afterwards, than to do it any other way."

"I know," Emmerich said with an exasperated sigh. "I just wish there was some way we could show her everything, get her fully on our side. To trust us."

"Everything?" the Emperor blinked hard. "Em, you're insane. Trust Keller?"

"Joh, she's the best opponent I've ever fought," Emmerich replied harshly. "Period. Probably better than me, although she caught me at a bad stretch. I'm back now, healthier than I've been in a decade or more. You know that. Imagine what we could do if she was with us."

"Em, we're her worst nightmare," Joh said.

"No, that was a week ago, Joh," the Red Admiral fired back. "*Buran* is her worst nightmare come to life. What I don't know is if she hates me, us, enough to watch us go down in flames first."

The Emperor sat back, silent, his face a harsh mask.

Emmerich knew his own face looked nearly identical. Two men, almost mirrors.

Emmerich knew that history would record them as such, for what was the one man, without the other?

"There's one avenue left that we haven't explored, Em," the Emperor said quietly. "One ambassador left that might get through to Keller, might convince her."

"Who?"

"Casey," Joh replied simply.

"That's not a topic I can broach with either of them, Joh," Emmerich drew a figurative line in the sand.

"I know," Joh replied. "I have talked to Kati, and even Steffi. Keller inspires Casey in dangerous ways, and I have come close to putting my foot down. But what if Casey is the key we need to break through to Keller?"

"Then we might be doomed, Joh," Emmerich replied seriously. "And we might be saved. How much latitude do we allow her?"

"As much as you and Kati think she needs, Em," Joh replied. "But it must be done in the strictest secrecy. This is not something that the Imperial public would understand, let alone appreciate."

Em nodded. If Keller represented all that the people of the *Fribourg Empire* feared, Casey growing up and emulating her would be even worse.

CHAPTER XXXIII

IMPERIAL FOUNDING: 176/10/25. DITTMAR PALACE, WERDER, ST. LEGIER

I t was a Saturday, and the Empire still kept the old calendar: five days of hard laboring for one's self, a half-day of labor for the Imperium, and a holy day for rest and reflection. Banks were open for a time, and the Imperial Post, but most offices were closed as the population scattered to their volunteer pursuits: cleaning parks, fresh paint, assisting neighbors.

It was too cold to hold barbeques outdoors at this northern latitude, but too early for the innumerable rounds of winter holidays that came with the change of seasons. A time for family, for small gatherings, with the windows closed and curtains drawn against the chill.

A time to conspire.

Sigmund studied the man seated across the desk from him in his inner office, a visitor making a simple social call. Dinner would follow, when other guests, less interesting and less dangerous, arrived as a cover.

Geoffrey Grundman was a tall man, but corpulent in ways that almost made him round. A naval officer would never be that far out of shape if he wished to retain his office, but the rules were different for a General of the Imperial Security Bureau. Especially Section Eleven, the so-called *Midnight Knock* department.

Sigmund did not trust the fat man as far as he could have thrown him, but the conspiracy had originated in the one place where it was supposed to be thwarted.

Quis custodiet ipsos custodes?

Who will watch the watchers? Especially when *they* have determined that the Empire itself is risk, and that only a change at the top will put it on a path to survival.

Sigmund Dittmar considered for a moment that desperate men can talk themselves into almost anything.

"General," Sigmund finally inquired in his most majestic tone. "Are there any issues with the plan?"

The big man squinted his pig eyes, as if smelling for back-sliding on Sigmund's part. It was far past that point. If anything, Sigmund wasn't even sure they could call it off at this point, with so many moving parts relying on radio silence and precise timing.

Revolution was coming. And it would be neck or crown. Almost momentarily.

"No, Admiral," the man replied a moment later, apparently certain that everything proceeded as expected, even here. "My teams have already prepared to arrest key dissidents at the precise moment necessary to hobble the Fleet response. Section Seventeen will disable critical elements of Grand Fleet Headquarters and the station's defense array."

"And Karl?" Sigmund asked, barely able to keep the angry snarl out of his voice.

"The Imperial family will hold with tradition," General Grundman oozed oily confidence. "Even though the woman is but a cousin, they will be gathered at the Imperial palace with only family invited, in preparation for Church services the next morning at the Imperial Cathedral. The Wachturm Palace will be the same. Everyone can be rounded up and disappear from history as necessary after the coup."

Sigmund nodded. As planned. Simple, direct, efficient. A minimum of moving parts meant a minimum of places where friction could alter details.

"And *Buran*?" Sigmund asked heavily. "Do we trust them? After all, you will have disabled most of the planet's defenses."

"Only temporarily, my lord," the General said. "Plus, there will still be loyal Fleet elements that you can call on, rally in our time of need, to drive them off. And all the important facilities and palaces will retain their orbital shields, so even if the strangers decide to bomb the planet, the damage will be cosmetic, and only serve to heighten anger and drive people to your side."

Sigmund leaned back and let the chair's back take his weight. He was a figurehead at this point. Armies of invisible worker ants toiled out of sight, moving things to fruition. He could neither control nor deny them.

But at the end of the day, this was the only way to save the Empire from falling into the decadence and decline that was destroying *Aquitaine*.

"See to it, then, that we can move quickly, if *Buran* decides to double-cross us in the end," Sigmund Dittmar commanded. "Once I have the crown, we will move quickly to arrest Keller and the rest. Arlo we will send home, but the two women will be tried as common criminals."

"Will they be executed, my liege?" the Security officer asked.

"That remains to be seen," Sigmund said. "Perhaps, after enough time has passed. After all, without Keller, they will not be able to stop us from striking at will. Nothing will be able to stop us. If *Buran* can be ignored for a decade, we will own all of *Aquitaine*. Then, we will be in a position to turn on the *Lord of Winter* as well."

Sigmund ground his teeth. Politics might stay his hand from executing Keller outright, but that smiling bitch Kermode would not be missed.

CHAPTER XXXIV

DAY: 306 OF THE COMMON ERA YEAR: 13,445 VESSEL - RS:32G8Y42 – "DANCER IN DARKNESS." FRIBOURG IMPERIAL SPACE. STATUS: SHADOWED

The Temple of Command hummed with an excitement Vrin could not attribute merely to the crew. He sat on his command throne and faced the three Advocates as the timer clock wound itself down to nothingness.

"Crew Advocate, bring your team to maximum readiness," Vrin commanded the tall man on his right. Ko Serek Evet Khan was a scholar. He would be a good Director of an Entity-vessel after this voyage. Vrin knew a moment of sadness that the elite team he had built would soon be broken, but this would go down in the history of the Holding as one of the greatest days.

The man nodded back to Vrin and pressed a button on his own console. Lights took on a reddish hue and a ringing bell sounded four times.

"Entity Advocate, bring *Dancer In Darkness* to his full potential," Vrin continued, turning his attention to the harsh woman on his left. She would stay with the Entity as long as the scholars of *Winterhome* would allow her, probably longer than Ro Kenzo Atep Vrin commanded.

The fisherman's wife nodded sharply and scaled a series of controls from partial to full. An Entity left at its peak for too long would begin to develop mental issues, frequently either *God Complexes* or *Philosophical Distraction*. Best to leave them at a much lower level of cognition most of the time, bringing the mind to his fullest potential only at the moment of need.

"War Advocate, prepare yourself for conflict," Vrin concluded, facing the man in the middle.

Around *Dancer In Darkness*, special crew would come into their own now, soldiers trained to do one task, and do it better than any Technician or Scholar. *Dancer In Darkness* was no longer just a starship, not even just an Entity-vessel.

He was about to become a warship.

They would take a long, looping pass through an empty stretch of nearby space, dropping back into physical space only in the darkest interstellar reaches, and then only to test the weapons and navigation equipment for final tuning.

In one hundred and twenty hours, *Dancer In Darkness* would drop into space close to that one, nearly-insignificant yellow star, and remind both foolish Emperors that the *Lord of Winter* was a far more dangerous foe than they realized.

CHAPTER XXXV

DATE OF THE REPUBLIC NOVEMBER 3, 398
KELLER MANSION, WERDER, ST. LEGIER

Jessica found Moirrey committing art on the long dining room table, far earlier in the morning than the evil engineering gnome was normally awake. At least there was no glitter.

Currently.

Jessica had even managed to sneak by both Marcelle and Willow this morning, or maybe they were finally beginning to trust the building's security enough that they didn't need to be in her hip pocket every waking moment.

Or the sun not being up had confused them.

Jessica had even managed to make her own coffee this morning.

"What are you up to, half-pint?" Jessica asked as she snuck up on Moirrey.

The tiny woman stopped her drawing long enough to pop her head up and gaze seriously in Jessica's direction.

It was like looking at an owl.

"Seventeen to one, beam-line ratio?" Moirrey asked.

When she got this serious, this intent, her accent nearly disappeared. Today, she almost sounded like Oz, Command Engineering Centurion Vilis Ozolinsh, Moirrey's boss, back on *Auberon*. Scion of one of the poshest families in the Republic.

Jessica moved around the table to look over the woman's shoulder.

Moirrey was working with a graphite pencil on a roll of white paper a meter wide and several meters long. There was a remarkably accurate drawing of the *Blackbird*, taking shape under the woman's hands. Jessica could see a variety of deck plans scattered around the table.

She wondered if Moirrey had slept since Saturday.

"I didn't have access to the courier's scanner logs, Moirrey," Jessica replied. "But that feels about right. The lines look close, other than I would move the primary emitter arrays forward a frame or so, just from memory."

"Wondered about that," Moirrey replied. "This dinna feels right, but I knew I had achieved a rough semblance."

"You planning to take all this home and design a new Battleship, half-pint?" Jessica teased.

"No, Fleet Centurion."

Jessica was amazed at how serious the woman's voice had suddenly turned.

"It will all be burned shortly," Moirrey continued. "Anything else would leave us open to charges of espionage. However, the Bureau of Ships will need this for the next generation design I will be submitting on our return."

Jessica pulled out a chair and settled, amazed at the transformation she was watching. This was not the goofy engineer with a glitter fetish that frequently infected *Auberon*'s engineering bays with her silliness.

Centurion Kermode, *Moirrey* zu *Kermode*, sounded more like an Advanced Research Weapons Technician, the job she was born for.

"Purpose?" Jessica probed, aware that the conversation had just gotten far more serious than a Monday morning coffee originally warranted.

"*Fribourg* is now engaged in a new Arms Race, Jessica," Moirrey replied.

Jessica knew it was serious when Moirrey used her given name. She only did that when they were alone, and it was *Very Serious Business*.

"Previously, their only arms race was with *Aquitaine*, and we generally held an edge there, being more willing to explore new technologies while they were happy to rely on the brute-force capabilities of their ship-building infrastructure."

"Who are you, and what have you done with Moirrey, you amazingly-nerdy imposter? I don't see any unicorns on this page."

Jessica grinned. Moirrey broke her own seriousness long enough to grin back and giggle, and then waved at the meters of designs on the paper in front of them.

"The Paladin-class is a bloody revolution, boss," Moirrey chirped, dropping back into serious too soon. "Fast, mean, tough. We're gonna need something even better in response. Gonna talk to a few folks on *Kali-ma* 'bouts some crazy ideas I gots. And yes, I will keep it all very, very secret, at least until we get back to friendly space."

"Why a revolution?" Jessica asked.

She had told Moirrey everything she could remember, and answered every question. Sure, the *Blackbird* was a new design, but what made her so dangerous?

Moirrey leaned in to point at key installations on the drawing.

"Fewer missile racks and more beams," Moirrey replied. "And the beams are all wrong. Type-3 and Type-2. Almost no Primaries nor Type-1."

"So what are the implications, young lady?" Jessica could hear Nils Kasum's voice come out of her mouth. Not the worst comparison, considering.

"I am an engineer, and not a line officer, Fleet Centurion," Moirrey grinned back. "That strikes me, however, as a weapons load-out for engaging battleships and corvettes, rather than cruisers and carriers. Hopefully, that tells you something about who they're engaging. Are you sure they weren't hiding nothin'?"

Jessica let her back-brain process, memories floating up from the thirty hours they had been aboard Wachturm's new chariot.

"I'm sure," Jessica said after a stretch of silence. "Captain Saar happily showed off everything I wanted to see, and a few places I never would have asked for. And I agree. The engines are also oversized for the design, but that's to better power all those beams while maneuvering at high speed. Nothing about the shield arrays struck me as odd."

"But they're ready for the wedding?" Moirrey probed. "All the Acceptance Trials complete that far ahead of schedule?"

"Yes, Moirrey, they are," Jessica agreed. "Excepting only that they had just enough Primary rounds aboard to fire everything four times in testing, and the same to test the few missile systems, they'll be here and ready for the wedding, and then start loading up for their next destination a few weeks later."

"Good," Moirrey said. "I'll have th'folks on *Kali-ma* run all the passive scans they can on her, 'n take that home, too."

Jessica nodded and rose.

"I'll let you get back to your unicorns, then," she said, walking more somberly back to her quarters as she let the implications sink in. Behind her, Moirrey went back to furiously sketching.

Fribourg really was up to something. Wachturm was up to something. The *Paladin*-class was a whole new way to build warships, unlike anything *Aquitaine* was currently building.

What did that say about the Peace?

CHAPTER XXXVI

DATE OF THE REPUBLIC NOVEMBER 5, 398
KELLER MANSION, WERDER, ST. LEGIER

A knock at the door to her sitting room caused Jessica to look up from her book with a scowl.

She had taken enough day trips, toured enough factories and schools, eaten meals representing every planet in the Empire by now.

She just wanted a day to herself. Had even scheduled such a thing.

Desianna entered a moment later and closed the door behind her silently.

Jessica didn't feel the look on her face softening.

"You have an unannounced visitor," the woman said with a careful smile, barely above a whisper.

Between Desianna and Marcelle, there was no such thing.

Those two women worked intimately close to handle everything in the background, usually coordinating with Hendrik Baumgärtner to make Jessica's schedule magically full in such a way that she had just enough time to make it to every appointment and appearance and no time to actually think.

This was *her* Wednesday. Nobody was allowed to bother her. Jessica felt like pointing that out.

But Desianna knew that. Knew that most people should be turned away, slotted into a meeting sometime after the wedding. Jessica could always delay her departure a few days, if needed.

Unless something came up that needed to be dealt with right now.

Jessica bit back the first words that came to mind. And the second.

"Will I regret asking who?" she finally settled on.

Desianna's smile got predatory.

"I would have lost money, betting on this one, Jess," she replied.

Considering that it was Desianna's job to stay on top of all the threads, and the threats, that was an impressive admission. Jessica felt an eyebrow creep up her forehead.

"Fine," she said, releasing her breath. "Out with it."

"*Her Imperial Majesty Kasimira Ekaterina, Empress of Fribourg,*" Desianna said grandly, with only a hint of sarcasm. "In disguise."

"Disguise?"

"Mufti," Desianna clarified. "Unmarked ground vehicle. No bodyguards. Civilian attire. She literally walked up to the front door and knocked."

Jessica looked down at the dark slacks and blue tunic she was wearing today. Not a Centurion's Day Uniform, but damned close. Old, broken in, and comfortable.

It was her day off.

Jessica put down her book on the early history of the *Fribourg Empire* after marking the page.

Reading paper was strange. Paper bookmarks were archaic.

Fribourg was a paper culture.

She supposed that she should make an effort to get cleaned up and fully presentable in a diplomatic sense.

But if the Empress wanted to just show up, on a day Jessica had no meetings planned, she should have been prepared for what she found.

Or perhaps she was, and showing up in disguise was her chance to escape the bubble of publicity as well.

Only one way to find out.

"Show her in, please," Jessica sighed, ever so slightly.

Desianna grinned.

"Marcelle is already boiling water for you," she smirked as she opened the door and slipped out.

Jessica stretched as she rose, popping her back and rotating her shoulders ninety degrees each direction. There hadn't been enough sessions with the fighting robot lately, but Jessica didn't want to risk pulling anything and walking gimpy at the wedding. Not something that would probably be seen by several billion people. The only wedding that would be bigger was when the Crown Prince got married, one of these days.

Would they invite her back for that one, as well?

Desianna opened the door with a dangerous gleam in her eyes and a wicked smile.

"Jessica, your guest is arrived," she said with only a hint of formality as she stepped to one side and gestured to the woman trailing her. "Kati, please, be welcome."

Kati?

Jessica could think of a number of things that Desianna might call the Empress. *Kati* was not anywhere on that list. They had obviously planned this to be a rather informal discussion.

So be it.

The Empress was tall, even in flats. Taller than Desianna. Not as tall as Marcelle. Still a head above Jessica.

Kati exuded grace and warmth as she came into the room and shook Jessica's hand.

"Jessica," she said politely.

"Kati."

Jessica hadn't had that much time to speak to the woman at the dinner Wachturm had thrown. Nor had Desianna.

Where had this sudden comradery come from?

Marcelle followed them into the room last, carrying a portable table with all the accoutrements of coffee, laid out as if on an ancient altar.

Jessica saw Kati to the other chair and sat as they watched Marcelle work in silence, Desianna standing watch by the open door.

A two-century-old burr grinder for the beans to be reduced to potent flakes. Poured into a clear cylinder atop a ceramic mug. Steaming water poured over that and stirred to produce a skim of bubbles. Pressed through and then cut with more water. Fresh cream and locally-sourced honey to take the edge off the bitterness.

Imperial culture was odd, in that Jessica was expected to take the first mug as host, with guests being served in order of importance next.

Kati sat on the edge of her chair, poised for something, or perhaps waiting for a photographer to capture her relaxed perfection and ready smile.

She looked like a fashion model.

Kati accepted her mug and sipped appreciably as Marcelle packed up and the other two women departed, leaving Jessica alone with this sudden visitor as the door closed.

Jessica thought again about Tadej Horvat, and his lessons on the tools and techniques, and limitations, of *diplomacy*. She smiled at the woman.

"I find it hard to shave that fine of an edge," Jessica said carefully. "Important enough to bring you to my door, and quietly, but not so critical that official notice must be taken. How can I help you, Kati?"

The woman grinned over the edge of her mug and then swallowed.

"It is not actually official business that brings me, Jessica," she replied. "But rather, a request. And not, as you observe, an official one. A personal favor."

Yes, she and Desianna would have both lost money, making those bets.

"I am your guest here, at least through Emmerich and Freya Wachturm," Jessica said carefully, wondering what kind of personal favor this woman, this *Empress*, might need. "What do you need?"

"This might rise a bit above and beyond," the Empress grinned lightly. "To use one of Joh's favorite sayings."

"Joh?" Jessica let confusion creep into her voice.

"I'm sorry," Kati said, waving her hand by way of apology. "My husband. *His Sovereign Imperial Majesty Karl VII, Karl Johannes Arend Wiegand.* Joh."

Right. Joh. Just another guy.

Uh huh.

"Ah," Jessica nodded.

"I have a rather headstrong daughter," Kati continued. "Who would love nothing more in the galaxy so much as a tour of your flagship, and a chance to meet your pilots, including the two girls who are apparently her own age and flying combat Starfighters for a living. She is not in a position to ask, culturally or politically. She asked me."

"*Rocket Frog* and *Neon Pink*," Jessica said around a sip of coffee. "Saša and Asra Binici. Identical twins and granddaughters of my Comptroller of the Court, Uly Larionov. Their uncle Galen is the commander of the cargo vessel that accompanied me, *Marco Polo*."

"Interesting," Kati leaned back slightly, settling into the chair.

"An exceptional family," Jessica agreed. "*Corynthe* is best classified as a meritocracy of ability."

"Well, don't let her run off and become a pirate, please?"

Kati was only half kidding, from the look in her eyes.

"Do you approve of this trip, Kati?" Jessica asked carefully. "I would be happy to act as her host and chaperone. Emmerich Wachturm recently did something similar for me aboard *Amsel*, so it would be the least I could do to return the favor. What would make Casey happy?"

"What would make Casey happy would be to wake up suddenly and find that she was a princess in *Aquitaine*, rather than *Fribourg*," Kati teased lightly. "She is a Renaissance Thinker in a deeply conservative society, and will soon begin to find doors closing on her as her adult responsibilities crowd her. I want her to be as happy as she can, while we figure out how to keep her scandals to a minimum."

"Scandals?" Jessica inquired. Nothing she had heard had suggested anything but the broadest love for the child among the Imperial population.

"Moirrey *zu* Kermode's Investiture was highly irregular," Kati replied with a wicked smile. "It should have been an exceedingly stuffy, formal affair. A crowd of perhaps a dozen old men and a few matrons of society. Nothing like the party it turned into."

"I see," Jessica kept her tone neutral.

"You mentioned *Amsel*?" Kati pivoted suddenly. "Here? How is that even possible? I didn't think the new one would be ready until the spring."

"Apparently, Captain Saar and the Red Admiral have been burning the candle at both ends to have her ready for Heike's wedding," Jessica said. "The *Blackbird* will actually be in system, secretly, in a day or three, according to their schedule, giving them time to get everything spiffied up for a commissioning ceremony for the blushing bride."

"Secretly?" Kati asked archly. "And yet, Em took you."

"Diplomacy, Kati," Jessica replied. "I'm not entirely sure what he's up to, but I can certainly behave and show proper appreciation while I'm here."

"Heike will be thrilled. But I suppose some of that blame should also be laid at your feet, Jessica," Kati's voice turned teasing. "If not for *Thuringwell*, these young ladies would have settled for finding a good man and having a happy family. You've corrupted an entire generation of Imperial women."

"I have?" Jessica asked, surprised.

And thrilled.

This was what victory tasted like.

Kati looked friendly, but this woman was still something of an enigma. It might yet all be a trap of some sort.

"You've shown them that it's possible to want more, to have more," Kati agreed. "That they don't have to settle for what little bits the male chauvinists of the Empire are willing to allow them. You've started a discreet, slow-burning Revolution, Jessica Keller."

Which was exactly what she had intended, dropping out of the darkness to pounce on *Thuringwell* like a sparrowhawk. Men backed by the divine right of kings were dangerous. Forcing them to rule by consent of the governed was a dominantly powerful way to cage them.

"And Casey?" Jessica asked, wondering where this woman, this *Imperial Highness*, fit into the mixture.

"I have a daughter who won't be happy waiting her whole life for what is your native birthright," Kati said, turning the charm up. "But she's also seventeen, and convinced that thirty is ancient. You remember what it was like."

Jessica laughed. She had turned forty in the flight out. Kati had another decade on her. But teenagers are always convinced that nobody understands them or how they could make the world better.

"Yes. Yes, I do," Jessica agreed. "How can we assuage her?"

"I realize that it's short notice," Kati said. "But the two families are scheduled to stay home for the entire day Saturday. If we could, would it be possible to sneak Casey out before sunrise and have you take her up to *Kali-ma* for the day, and then bring her back late Saturday night?"

Marcelle and Willow would be quite busy, keeping a beautiful, headstrong, *Imperial* princess safe around the coarse and salty pilots and crew, but *Wiley* ran a strict ship and would crack the whip hard if she had to.

Jessica's only fear was that the young woman would decide she had to run off and have a pirate princess adventure.

Jessica couldn't think of a worse social or diplomatic outcome.

Still, *diplomacy*. And Casey herself represented another front in Jessica's lifetime war to bring down *Fribourg*.

Not the Empire itself, but the mindset of the men who ran it, who owned it. The *Divine Right of Kings*. Rule by birth.

That she would happily obliterate.

Casey could probably help. If nothing else, she would make a potent symbol to the Chartists, those men and women demanding that society change, that *Fribourg* accept the so-called Charter of Humanity that Jessica had heard whispers about.

"It would be my pleasure, Kati," Jessica agreed.

Jessica was happy to plant another worm in the Imperial apple.

KASIMIRA

CHAPTER XXXVII

IMPERIAL FOUNDING: 176/11/08. IMPERIAL STARPORT, WERDER, ST. LEGIER

Casey wasn't sure if vibrating with excitement would help, or ruin Keller's opinion of her.

She settled for a case of fidgets. At least Lady Yulia would stay home for the day, happily ensconced in her latest shows rather than off seeing the galaxy and complaining non-stop. Not even Sgt. Inmon was allowed to accompany them today.

Instead, Casey found herself seated in a private lounge with Keller and her two assistants. Or rather, a (female!) bodyguard named Willow and another woman who looked like a bodyguard, but didn't quite fit the mold. She wasn't exactly sure what a *dog-robber* actually did, and Marcelle Travere looked too fierce for Casey to come right out and ask.

Still, she was going to have an adventure. She was only sad that the other two women, Keller's Prime Minister and the wonderfully silly engineer, Moirrey, wouldn't be able to join them. That more than made up for the fact that the sun wouldn't even come up for two hours.

"Is anything wrong, Princess?" Keller asked, looking up from her book.

"Please, call me Casey, *Wildgraf* Keller," Casey replied. "And no, nothing's wrong. Just nervous and excited."

That got a wry smile.

"Casey," the woman said. "Please, call me Jessica."

A man entered the room and interrupted the conversation before it could go much further. He was young, not more than a few years older than Casey, and walking on eggshells as he approached.

"*Wildgraf. Princess.* Your shuttle is ready," he said, eyeing a spot on a distant horizon rather than make eye contact.

Keller was already on her feet, along with the others, before Casey could move.

"Thank you," she said to the man, who immediately turned and retreated from the room.

Willow moved first, stalking quickly like a big, fierce cat for such a small woman. Jessica was right behind the bodyguard, and Casey found herself next, with the willowy tall woman Marcelle bringing up the rear.

The flight bay held a type of shuttle Casey had never seen before.

Imperial models tended to be big, ugly boxes. Even Republic designs tended to be cubes.

This craft reminded her of a swan in flight for winter, long and lean with a cockpit up front, and a long, thin neck that flared out into a rounded body at the rear. Stubby wings out each side ended in small gun turrets, to go with a monstrous searchlight of a turret atop the beast's skull.

The paint job took her a moment to recognize, and then she couldn't contain her giggles.

Jessica glanced back with an eyebrow raised in Casey's direction.

"It's a skunk," Casey managed between giggles.

Jessica smiled back at her.

"A Western Spotted Skunk, specifically," Jessica said. "*Zorrillo.* The Royal Combat Yacht. Welcome aboard."

A hatch let them into a small space. Casey found herself hunched over to avoid bashing her head on things overhead as she followed Jessica to a set of four jumpseats in the swan's neck.

A few moments later, Marcelle had her buckled in and had thrown herself into the last chair.

Casey watched Jessica press an intercom button.

"Flight deck," Jessica said forcefully. "Ready for launch."

"Roger that, Admiral," a man's voice replied crisply.

Around her, Casey felt the craft suddenly power up with high-pitched whining as various systems came live.

"Normally, we would ride up in the small cabin aft," Jessica explained. "But time is short today, so I've told them to push. We're better off strapped in for an hour. *Gaucho* has infected them all with his insanity."

Casey nodded, unsure exactly what the other woman was saying, or who *Gaucho* might be, until *Zorrillo* began moving.

Every shuttle Casey had ever ridden in was a staid affair. Calm. Smooth. Comforting.

This was a racecar. On a curvy track. In the rain.

Casey felt the surge of the engines as they cleared the bay doors. A moment later, the pilot turned slightly onto one wing, such that Casey was suddenly almost lying on her back, and then the afterburners kicked in and the rear of the vessel was suddenly almost straight down.

If she hadn't been strapped in tight, she might have plummeted into the door to the rear section. Her stomach wanted to, and would have happily taken her breakfast with it.

Casey sucked a breath deep to keep her oatmeal down.

Well, she had wanted an adventure.

K *ali-ma* looked unlike any ship Casey had ever seen. Again, the swan motif, with the front end dominated by four arrowhead blades like a compass, and then the long neck, filled with a mish-mash of smaller craft, before flaring out to the big, lumpy rear of the craft.

Rather than docking at an airlock, as Casey had expected, they were actually landing in the middle of the swan's neck, riding small thrusters carefully into place until they touched with a thump.

"All hands, prepare for gravity transition," the pilot's stern voice intoned from the speakers.

Casey was about to ask what that meant when her bottom suddenly found down.

Ah, turning on gravplates. Why weren't they on earlier?

Marcelle Travere was unbuckled and across the aisle, helping Casey get free and stand.

Again, she had to stay ducked, as the ceiling was made for someone Jessica's size, rather than her own.

Casey watched Willow kneel and press a control in the floor, just rear of the cockpit. A hatch opened and Willow's upper half disappeared for several seconds before she popped back out and stood up.

"We're in A-slot," Willow said cryptically. "Climbing into gravity."

"Sounds good," Jessica replied. "You first, then me, then Casey."

Rather than reply, Willow dropped back down and climbed into the hole, disappearing down into *Kali-ma*.

Jessica turned to her now, a serious look on her face.

"We'll be going nearly face-first down the ladder, Casey," she said seriously. "Just inside, you'll encounter a reversal, and about fifty centimeters later you'll be climbing up. For a few seconds, both your head and your feet will be in gravity, pointed opposite directions. Just keep going and we'll be there if you run into problems. Marcelle will be following. Everything will be fine."

Casey nodded silently as Jessica disappeared next.

Adventures.

Then it was her turn.

The tunnel wasn't claustrophobic, but seemed to go on forever, climbing face-first down into the bowels of the earth. Casey could just make out Jessica's feet as she reached the other end and climbed out of the tunnel, leaving her alone for a moment as she went up.

The discontinuity was sooner than she expected. Casey was in it and slightly disoriented before her brain caught up.

Down stopped being down, right around her belly button, and her inner ear insisted that she was suddenly climbing up.

Casey clenched the sides of the ladder firmly for a second before moving.

"Everything okay?" Marcelle asked from below her. Above her. Behind her.

"Fine," Casey gritted her teeth and willed her feet and hands into motion.

Adventures.

Once through, Casey's head popped up out of *Kali-ma*'s deck. Willow was there, along with Jessica and a dark-skinned woman Casey knew only by reputation. *Kali-ma*'s Captain. Command Centurion.

Shiori Ness.

Wiley.

Standing, Casey was surprised at *Wiley*'s size. The woman was taller and broader than she was, almost Uncle Em's size, or father's. She was built rather like a man, blocky and solid, but with a huge bosom.

Casey found her plain, but the woman was smiling ten million watts right now.

"*Wiley*," Jessica introduced them. "May I introduce our guest, who wishes to be known, at least for today, as Casey?"

"Casey," the woman said in a warm alto voice. "Welcome aboard."

Not Princess. Just Casey.

At least for today, she could have an adventure. All too soon, life as she knew it was going to be over.

CHAPTER XXXVIII

DATE OF THE REPUBLIC NOVEMBER 8, 398
WERDER, ST. LEGIER

A pounding on the door brought Vo up from the darkness of his dreams. Nothing good, but no nightmares either.

It took a moment to place where he was.

Rather than return to the mansion where they were staying every night, Vo had taken to crashing frequently with Edgar and the men at the motel closer to the docks where the Army was putting them up for the month they were here. All too soon, they would all be returning to *Thuringwell,* or to *Carufel,* where the rest of the division, now just the 1st Regiment, acted as training cadre for cold weather and mountainous conditions as other divisions cycle through for the experience.

The owner had been quite happy to give Vo a private room. That's where he was.

Wooden door, locked and chained, but nothing that would keep out a determined person.

Vo had been careful last night. It was too easy to drink too heavily with these men, but the wedding was getting close and he wanted to stay out of trouble.

Trouble seemed to be pounding on his door this morning.

"Coming," Vo called, loud enough to be heard from the hallway.

The knocking stopped.

Vo climbed silently from the bed and slid into his pants and tunic.

Socks and boots were quick as well. Navin the Black loved surprise inspections and training missions. Everything was close at hand.

He stepped close to the door and braced one big foot about a boot-length back, and set his shoulders. If someone was going to kick in the door, they'd be in for a bouncing surprise.

He reached out and slipped the chain, and then unlocked the door and pulled it open a crack.

"Colonel Arlo, there's trouble," a young girl's voice called quietly.

Vo leaned around the door to confirm that the owner's twelve-year-old daughter was alone, and then opened the door wider.

"Annette?" he said. "What kind?"

She was pale this morning. Wan and drawn in ways no child should ever be.

"Tanks in the street, sir," she replied. "Poppa told me to wake you and your men, in case you needed to hide."

"Hide?"

Vo wasn't sure he was awake.

"She's right, Colonel," a man's voice intruded. "Serious shit going down outside."

Corporal Danville appeared a second later, already dressed for combat in his field utilities, rather than the colorful parade rig.

Danville had always struck Vo as one of the most dangerously-slick killers he had ever met. A born assassin. Fortunately, completely loyal.

"Annette," Vo said to the girl. "Go tell your father we'll be safe."

"Yes, sir," the girl chirped and disappeared.

"Colonel, in here," Edgar Horst called gruffly. "Morning news. Quickly."

Vo got there a step behind Danville.

Horst was pulling on his boots as a man on the vidscreen spoke in serious tones.

"And now, we return to the top of the news," the announcer said sternly.

Vo realized that the man was wearing a military uniform, rather than the usual dress jacket he had grown used to from newspeople on this planet.

And then he recognized the color.

Imperial Security.

"The government of the traitor, Karl VII, has been overthrown and the Emperor and his suite arrested. Admiral of the White Sigmund

Dittmar, His Imperial Highness and a loyal prince of the blood, has been chosen to assume the throne in his place. The Imperial Navy has acted to overthrow the treasonous government before their evil conspiracy could unfold. They have taken control of all of *Werder*, while saboteurs and dissidents are rounded up for the good of the state. Imperial Security has declared a curfew on all civilian traffic and all citizens are required to remain at home for the next twenty-four hours under penalty of law. Stay tuned to this channel. More information will be made available at a later time."

The words faded into martial, patriotic music at this point. Obviously, the news stations had been taken over and were just going to continue playing the same music and warnings against going outside.

Vo felt like the world had just turned inside out. This was supposed to be a wedding and a party. How the hell had it turned into a revolution?

And whose side was he on? Well, the Fleet Centurion's, but first he had to find her. Then he could ask.

"Colonel?" Horst asked as he turned off the repeating announcement. "Orders?"

Vo started to say something about him only being an Honorary Colonel, and not the real thing. And how this wasn't even his war.

His pocket comm chirped before he could do more than open his mouth.

And it was the signal that whoever was at the other end was using the scrambled frequency. That meant trouble.

"Arlo," he said, pulling it out of his pocket.

Around him, the room was filling up with his men, like someone had pulled a bathtub plug in the hallway and drained them all into Horst's room.

"Vo, I gots issues," Moirrey said in a harsh whisper.

"Go ahead," he said, sensing the men around him getting ready to growl.

Moirrey was probably more popular with the 189th than he was.

"Vo, they comes to th'door five minutes ago and arrested everyone," Moirrey said in an angry tone. "Well, Desianna. Jessica's no' here, an' Marcelle and Willow went with her first thing."

"What about you?" Vo asked, unsure how Moirrey could have been missed if someone was already arresting the *Aquitaine* mission.

"Nobody here as sneaky as a watch goose, city boy," she growled.

That made no sense, but Moirrey did that to him too frequently anyway.

"Okay," Vo said, shifting suddenly into the sort of combat mode Navin had pounded into him over the years. "Can you get to that one park with the ducks we found the second week we were here?"

"Can do," she chirped back. "What 'bouts you?"

"We'll be along as soon as we can," Vo replied, looking at the tense, angry men around him.

Vo cut the line and took a breath.

"Colonel," Horst said before Vo even could get a word out. "We're with you."

"We might be on the losing side," Vo countered.

"And we're dead on *Thuringwell* without you, sir." Horst replied. "Plus, if they're overthrowing *my* Emperor, they're doing it over my oath and my dead body."

That did get a growl from the men, all long-serving veterans chosen for that loyalty. The 189th might be reduced to a parade unit and training cadre these days, but the men were all hardened veterans.

Vo went into mental overdrive.

"All right, break it down into fire teams and move," he ordered. "Comms, cash, weapons if you have them. As much out of uniforms as we can so we look like civilians. Check the weather forecasts. Be ready to sleep rough if we have to go into the brush. Our target is the park about three blocks north of Keller's palace. We need to be out of here before some bureaucrat remembers us and decides we might be dangerous. Move out."

The room emptied around he and Horst.

Vo jogged back to his room and quickly dug out his weekend gear: blue dungarees in a heavy denim, a seaman-style wool sweater Rebekah had gotten him, rain shell, and a floppy hat. The weather had been tolerable, but that was going between taxis and bars, not sleeping under trees.

A weapon would be nice, but there was nothing at hand.

"Colonel Arlo," a new voice called from Vo's half-closed doorway.

Annette's father, the hotelier himself, was standing there, holding something covered in his hands.

Vo was set to move already, so he smiled at Walter as he approached.

"Thank you, Walter," Vo said. "For taking care of me and my men."

"Sir, have they really overthrown the Emperor?" Walter asked.

"It looks like they intend to," Vo replied, sizing up the small, pudgy, middle-aged man standing before him.

"And you're going to go stop them?" Walter asked with a plaintive smile.

Him?

He was going to stop an Imperial coup? Take on the entire Imperial Security Bureau and the Navy and demand that they behave themselves?

Vo laughed silently.

Yes. Yes he was.

Vo Arlo, Hero at Large.

"We're going to try, Walter," Vo said quietly, hearing his words echo down the hall and out into the crisp morning, a challenge to the entirety of *Fribourg*.

"Then you'll need this, sir," Walter said, holding out the cloth-covered lump in his hands.

Vo took it and unwrapped an antique, slug-throwing pistol in a leather holster. It was a glossy, black, semi-automatic, of a medium caliber, with rounds stacked in the handle. Probably older than either of them were.

"Are you sure, Walter?" Vo asked.

"Yes, sir. And you'd best hurry."

The little man turned and scurried away quickly.

Vo found himself in the hallway with Horst, Danville, and one other man, Sgt. Street, one of the quietest men in the platoon, and a pretty good darts player.

"Orders, sir?" Horst asked.

"Out and gone first," Vo replied. "Then I need to contact the Fleet Centurion. After that, we're going to go have a chat with Imperial Security."

That got a chuckle from the three men. It sounded more like a pack of wolves than anything else.

It felt like it, too.

CHAPTER XXXIX

IMPERIAL FOUNDING: 176/11/08. DITTMAR PALACE, WERDER, ST. LEGIER

Sigmund hadn't slept.

He had tried. Laid down with the lights out and the house quiet. Karya had taken something and slept next to him like a corpse, purring occasionally to show she wasn't actually dead. Sigmund couldn't risk doing the same, not when so much was at stake.

All he could do was lay there.

He might have even dozed, however briefly.

Nothing had helped.

Several hours before dawn, he had given up trying and gotten dressed.

Today, he wore his formal robes. Not quite Imperial, but as close as a cousin of the blood was formally allowed.

At least until he rectified that situation.

Emperor Sigmund I.

The birth of a new dynasty, a new direction.

Never peace with *Aquitaine*. Only enough peace with *Buran* to swallow the rabbit that the Republic represented, before turning on the so-called *Lord of Winter*.

Sigmund sat in his office now, lights still dim, but bright enough to work as he watched various news feeds and received regular, cryptic updates from General Grundman.

Friday night was a bad time to initiate a revolution. At least, this one.

The common populace was in the midst of a week-long pre-wedding celebration for the youngest daughter of *The Red Admiral*, the largest civic, social event any of them could imagine, until Prince Ekkehard was married off.

Not that they realized how little chance that had of ever happening.

No, best wait until after the bars have closed. And the all-nighters finally caved to the need to sleep and go home.

Strike early on Saturday morning, just as the sun was coming up. Catch the population of Werder hung over and confused. Both Karl and Emmerich would be at home with their entire families.

Pigeons facing the hawks of Imperial Security, of Section Eleven.

The midnight knock coming at dawn instead.

Sigmund sipped his coffee and fought the urge to preen.

Only villains in bad videos cackled aloud, but Sigmund finally understood the desire, the urge. That rising force of excitement demanding that he bubble over with evil glee.

Mad scientists always failed.

He was an Admiral, and a Prince of the Blood. Calm, rational, prepared.

A chime sounded on his computer, the first alert coming in on the secured channel he shared with the creatures of Section Eleven, Imperial Security.

Wachturm Mansion secured. All accounted for.

Lovely.

Emmerich Wachturm had been Sigmund's greatest fear. The man was utterly loyal, but was that loyalty to the throne or the inhabitant? Best to remove him from the game board first, so that the Red Admiral didn't have the opportunity to escape and rally other forces to Karl's side later.

Revolutions got messy when emotions got involved with what should be rational discussions.

News One secured. Prepared broadcasts on loop on all channels. All citizen ordered to curfew.

Marvelous. The beginning of his reign as Emperor was clear now.

People would awaken in a new world from the one where they had gone to bed. They would slowly ignore the curfew and begin to gather in public places, or rally in small, familial clusters. Churches would overflow with confused cattle. But nothing would come of it.

Imperial Security had predicted as much.

And it wasn't like he was planning on actually shooting anyone. The troops on the corners in their armoured vehicles were there to reinforce the change, and remind people that he retained the monopoly on force.

Karl and his family would be put on trial, facing trumped up charges of treason and secretly conspiring with *Buran*, everything Sigmund was doing, in fact. This afternoon's *demonstration* would just hammer the point home, and make Sigmund a hero as defender of the realm when Karl's *supposed allies* turned on him with the whole Empire watching.

And then the Imperial family would be found guilty and sentenced to death. *Emperor Sigmund* would commute that to exile, a safe, quiet place, far from the halls of power, where their sudden and accidental demise later could be kept quiet. There would be no blood on his hands.

Directly.

Thus are revolutions successful.

The most important message was late. The critical one. That thing that would cost Sigmund his life, if it went wrong.

A chirp finally signaled success.

Imperial Family secure. Princess Kasimira unaccounted for.

The artist? How could they miss one seventeen-year-old girl? This was the Imperial palace. It was not possible that Kasimira could simply vanish.

Still, how much damage could a child like that do, in the face of everything he had assembled?

CHAPTER XL

DATE OF THE REPUBLIC NOVEMBER 8, 398
ABOARD KALI-MA, ABOVE ST. LEGIER

Corynthe had always been a poor nation. Jessica knew that. Children frequently grew up with bad nutrition that resulted in them being stunted compared to places like *Aquitaine*, or even *Lincolnshire*.

This morning, standing on the deck, Casey rammed that point home without even trying.

Jessica was slightly shorter than average for a woman of the Republic. *Rocket Frog* and *Neon Pink* were absolutely tiny by any standard. Many of the men were barely taller than Jessica. *Eel* was probably the tallest man in the flight squadron, and Casey had at least a centimeter on Gustav. Only *Wiley* and Yan were taller in the room, excepting Marcelle.

Still, the young woman was all smiles, slathering the charm on everyone and asking pointed, intelligent questions as she shared coffee with the flight squadron and several members of *Wiley's* command staff. She seemed especially smitten by the twins, but that was to be expected.

They represented everything Casey could never have.

A sound brought everyone to utter silence. Probably the last sound that Jessica had expected to hear in orbit of *St. Legier*.

The ascending triple-note reserved for emergency communications. Loud enough to be heard over any sound, even in Engineering.

"Command Centurion to the bridge," the Watch Officer's voice calmly filled the ready room, the entire vessel. "All hands, stand by for battle stations."

Jessica took two steps at a dead sprint before her brain stopped her. The pilots and bridge crew were all in motion. Casey would have no idea what she was supposed to do.

Jessica turned to find Marcelle close to the princess, pointing her in the right direction.

"This way, Casey," Jessica said, waiting for the young woman to nod.

Casey blinked in shock, and then processed everything and began to move.

The corridor was largely empty, *Wiley* and her people already well ahead, with the pilots racing aft to their locker room to dive into their flight suits and climb aboard their combat chariots.

It made for quick going for Jessica to get to the bridge and badge herself and Casey through the secured hatch.

Inside, everything had faded from that immediate surge of chaos to the hum of a well-trained team. *Wiley* and Yan had dropped into their stations, evicting the younger officers who had been earning their ratings two minutes ago.

A projection dominated the middle of the room, the man speaking in stern tones.

"The government of the traitor, Karl VII, has been overthrown and the Emperor and his suite arrested. Admiral of the White Sigmund Dittmar, His Imperial Highness and a loyal prince of the blood, has been chosen to assume the throne in his place. The Imperial Navy has acted to overthrow the treasonous government before their evil conspiracy could unfold. They have taken control of all of *Werder,* while saboteurs and dissidents are rounded up for the good of the state. The Navy has declared a curfew on all civilian traffic and all citizens are required to remain at home for the next twenty-four hours under penalty of law. Stay tuned to this channel. More information will be made available at a later time."

Casey had gone white. Jessica was seeing red. *Wiley* looked angry enough to actually chew nails.

"Orders, Admiral?" Yan asked, breaking the tableau.

Jessica took a moment to draw a heavy breath. There was nothing in her planning catalog for something, anything, like this. Nowhere.

Not in her wildest dreams.

Damn them.

Dittmar in charge would probably mean an abrogation of the treaty as fast as he thought he could send the official word to *Ladaux*. And the fool probably had no idea how fragile that frontier was.

For a moment, Jessica considered blasting for deep space immediately, confident that diplomatic protocol would keep Desianna, Moirrey, and Vo safe from harm until they could be rescued or traded back.

Jessica could be back on station with *Auberon* and her squadron almost as fast as *Fribourg* could do anything. Poised for the next pearl on the string, the next rabbit to be swallowed.

The next Imperial target.

There was only one fly in that ointment.

What to do with an Imperial Princess who might be one step from being declared a homeless refugee?

"What's the chatter on Imperial frequencies?" Jessica asked.

They hadn't broken any Imperial codes, but not everything sent would be encrypted. Some signals would be in the clear, bouncing off stations, ships, or even the atmosphere. Questions. Comments. Dirty jokes. If you listened close enough, there was always a soft undertone of emotion floating on radio waves, just in the voices alone.

You could learn a great deal, without even understanding the words themselves.

Himura, the comm officer, had been listening intently with one ear.

"Fleet's freaking out, but nobody has given them any orders, other than to maintain their current patrol patterns and be on the lookout for spies and saboteurs," Himura called, looking up for his console to fix Jessica with his stare.

"In other words," Jessica replied sharply. "This originated with the Security Bureau and their people, and the Navy was caught with their pants down?"

"That'd be my guess, boss," Himura said.

"If anyone hails us, there is no mention of the Princess," *Wiley* interjected. "Nothing. Nobody. Nowhere. Am I clear?"

The whole bridge rang out on that one.

"Any noise from the Army?" Jessica continued.

The 189th Division was represented by a score of men, but there were thirty or forty full divisions of troopers available on the ground, both as garrison, and in barracks.

"They've gone stone cold, Admiral," Himura said. "Nothing on any frequency and nobody even answering the Fleet boys."

So. A *coup d'état*. Bloodless surprise, so far, but things like this were never completely innocent.

"All hands to battle stations," Jessica said finally. "Flight wing, get loaded and ready to launch on command, but remain locked on for sudden maneuvering."

Lights on *Wiley's* console began to go green almost immediately. Everyone had just been waiting for that command. A good crew.

But what could they do, sitting in the middle of an entire Imperial Fleet, flying in the shadow of their main orbital base?

"Admiral, I have a ground signal," Himura called suddenly. "Stand by. Go ahead Arlo, you're on bridge comm."

"Roger that," Vo's voice cracked slightly with distortion. "Fleet Centurion, this is Arlo. No doubt you've heard the news by now. We have a situation on the ground. Desianna was arrested this morning. Moirrey has gone into hiding. I'm moving to get her with my team now."

Arrested?

Jessica felt her teeth grind until she stopped.

"Understood. Stand by, Vo," Jessica replied. "In fact, we'll call you back in ten minutes. Move in case they are tracking your signals."

"Acknowledged."

One did not arrest foreign diplomats under immunity and invitation. Not unless you wanted a war with Jessica Keller. Dittmar was seriously pushing his luck.

Jessica considered some of Moirrey's *opinions* of the man who would be Emperor.

She had stopped being just a witness to history.

"Yan," Jessica ordered. "Drop us back out of range of the station's big guns, but do it slowly and make it look like poor ship handling on our part."

"Roger that, Admiral," Yan replied, furiously typing into his console. "Pilot, execute this flight deviation."

"Yes, sir," the pilot replied.

Jessica ignored the men. Yan was a consummate professional and could handle his tasks without supervision. She gathered Casey and *Wiley* and moved to the rear of the bridge, where they could talk quietly.

"Casey, I can't return you to the surface in the current situation," Jessica said. "I have no idea what your reception would be."

"I would most likely be executed, along with my family, Jessica," Casey said flatly, her face a hard rictus. "If Dittmar fails in this, that will be his punishment. I can't imagine anything less for me."

"Someone will figure out where you are, soon enough," *Wiley* said. "There will be signals, notes, logs."

"I'm aware of that as well, Command Centurion," Casey replied.

Jessica could see the anger and pain in the young woman's eyes.

"I have two options at this point," the Princess continued, her voice threatening to break. "I can flee and ask for refuge with *Aquitaine*. Or I can fight."

Something changed in the girl's voice as she spoke.

Jessica remembered the moment she first ordered Moirrey to break every law imaginable, and possibly commit treason against the entire human species, orbiting above *Ballard*. Something had bled out of Moirrey's soul at that moment, replaced by a hard, quiet energy that had never dimmed since.

In Moirrey's case, it had been growing up as trial by fire. Perhaps Jessica was watching the same thing happen before her eyes.

"Fight?" Jessica challenged. "With what?"

"If my father has been deposed," Casey's voice ground harshly across the words. "Then my brother would replace him as Emperor. Failing that, my older sister. They might all be dead right now. Had I been there this morning, I would probably be dead as well, or on my way there now. If they have all been taken, then I am the next in line to ascend the throne."

"You?" Jessica asked sharply.

There had never been a ruling Empress. Older daughters had been stepped over for sons, from even before King Gunter became the first Emperor.

Casey stopped and drew a harsh breath. Her shoulders flexed down in way that reminded Jessica of drawing all the anger into her belly, compressing it, before facing the fighting robot.

Fire diamonds.

"Madam Keller," Casey, the *Imperial Princess-nee-Emperor of Fribourg* began in a dark tone. "I must ask one favor of you before I can release you to seek your own safety."

"Madam?" Jessica asked. "Don't you mean *Wildgraf?*"

"No," Casey replied firmly, drawing herself back up to that amazing height of her family. "Madam Keller. A *Wildgraf* would be required to become personally involved in this situation. That would be unacceptable for you, and either of your governments. This is a *Fribourg* task, and must be handled as such."

Moirrey had turned into a grown-up in those few, precious seconds. Jessica wouldn't have recognized it now, had she not watched then.

A young girl had joined her on this bridge, all of five minutes ago.

An Emperor had just replaced her.

"How can I help?" Jessica asked with a nod, recognizing the fury and terror at war with each other in Casey's eyes.

"Not all of the Fleet will have gone over. At least not quickly. They will, eventually, given time," Casey said. "I need to make it to friendly forces before I declare myself. Otherwise, I can simply be arrested and disappeared."

"But will they take orders from a woman? Even a woman Emperor?" *Wiley* asked bluntly, but warmly.

Alone, of perhaps everyone in the entire planetary system, only *Wiley* could ask that question, understanding what it meant to be *first*.

Casey's chin came up sharply. Her shoulders came back. A fire took root in those bright, blue eyes.

She turned to Jessica with a snarl.

"What was it you said before the *Battle of Petron*? To the assembled Captains?" Casey asked. "I will have their oaths, or I will have their souls."

Not quite the words Jessica remembered speaking, but close enough. And it would convey to those men out there the seriousness of the situation.

They could honor their oaths to the crown, or their allegiance to power. But not both.

Not with Casey. Never with Casey.

Jessica smiled secretly, in the deepest parts of her soul, where the goddess Kali-ma still danced.

Something like this might tear the Empire apart.

Either a usurper would hold the throne, driving fragments of chaos into the population, or a woman would ascend, unraveling all the power of male chauvinists to their prerogatives.

Some of Jessica's wildest dreams were suddenly much closer to fruition. And there was nobody she could tell, even whisper it to, until she saw Nils Kasum again.

"So, who can we trust?" *Wiley* asked in a voice gone hard and tactical.

Jessica fought her attention back to the present.

She could dream evil dreams later.

"If you went to the effort to launch a palace coup this detailed, this extensive, would you let Emmerich Wachturm run around loose?" Jessica asked back.

"The Red Admiral?" *Wiley* smiled conspiratorially. "Hell, no. I'd nail him down first. He's more dangerous than any Emperor."

"Agreed," Jessica said. "The man's loyal. Everyone knows that. Everyone. That means his people are as well."

"So where does that leave us? Right here, right now?" Casey asked sharply.

"Well, Princess," Jessica stammered. "Uhm, Emperor…"

"Please, call me Casey," the young woman said. "There will be enough time for Emperor later."

"Casey," Jessica nodded. "I know a place that should be safe for you while we sort things out."

"Where?"

"*IFV Amsel*," Jessica replied. "The *Blackbird*."

"But she's not here," Casey countered, confused.

"She is," Jessica said. "Captain Saar was planning to arrive in-system Friday morning, without any fanfare, and prepare for a formal commissioning ceremony next Thursday for your cousin's wedding."

"Can we trust him?" Casey asked tightly.

Jessica could still see the young girl, the artist, carefully hidden underneath, peeking out as if from under the blankets during a frightening storm.

"If you cannot trust Rafferty Saar, the Red Admiral's hand-picked man," Jessica said with funereal tones, "then there is absolutely nothing you can do here but flee into the wilderness like a princess in a fairy tale."

"I'll die fighting first," Casey growled defiantly.

Jessica nodded. Not necessarily the most intelligent move, considering the odds, but the correct emotional response. As with the crown of *Corynthe* that day, this would be for everything.

"Comm Officer," Jessica called out over the entire bridge. "Ping *IFV Amsel* quietly and ask Captain Saar for a secured channel."

"Aye-aye, Admiral," the man replied.

"Will it work?" Casey asked.

"Is there a choice?" Jessica replied.

"No," Casey's tone was subdued. "Thank you."

Jessica nodded in understanding. What was it about *Jessica Keller* that caused the men of the *Fribourg Empire* to act insane when she was around?

And what would a female Emperor do to them?

Jessica could only hope.

"Imperial Captain Saar on channel six, standing by, Admiral," Himura called out. "Three second lag on signal."

Jessica took Casey by the hand and guided her to a spot near *Wiley's* console. Close enough to listen, but out of sight of the video pickup.

A red band appeared around the border of the screen as Captain Saar's face appeared. Encrypted. At least enough for now.

"Captain Saar, thank you for taking my call," Jessica said, patiently waiting for the signal to route and arrive at his end.

"*Wildgraf* Keller," he replied after the long pause. "Considering the circumstances, I will presume you have a compelling reason for signaling me?"

"That is correct, Captain Saar," Jessica said patiently, breathing as the lag ran. "I need to come aboard your vessel as soon as possible. I have information vital to the future of the Empire, but it must be delivered in person."

There. Nothing more. Nothing useful. Nothing incriminating. No reason to suspect that she had the future Emperor herself aboard *Kali-ma*, in the middle of a revolutionary crisis.

The man had to read between the lines if he wanted to know.

"And you cannot share more than that?" he asked after a pause. "Even over an encrypted line?"

"Captain Saar," Jessica replied. "I give you my word as an officer, a *Wildgraf*, and a Queen, that you will find it interesting. If not, I will immediately return to *Kali-ma* and bother you no more."

Unsaid, that she would be in his power. That Battleship might be without Primaries and missiles, but it was still capable of simply annihilating a shuttle at short range like an annoying fly, assuming he didn't just arrest her when she arrived, seeking to curry favor with the new regime.

Those were the risks at this level of play.

There was a long pause as the man considered.

"Very well, Keller," he said. "I look forward to your message."

The line went dark.

"Can we trust him?" Casey asked again.

Jessica looked up into the woman's glacial-blue eyes.

"This is where the die fighting part comes into play," Jessica said.

CHAPTER XLI

DATE OF THE REPUBLIC NOVEMBER 8, 398
WERDER, ST. LEGIER

The early-morning fog helped.

Vo and his three men could move quickly in the fading swirls of billowing clouds. Later, it would grow warm enough to evaporate like dew, but for the next hour or so, unseen tides would push it between buildings and vehicles, limiting sight to dozens of meters, instead of hundreds.

Danville had point.

Vo would have said it was like watching a dachshund hound go into a burrow after a rabbit, but no dog had ever moved like that. Weasel, perhaps.

No stores were open this morning. A few normally would have been, but nobody was apparently willing to challenge the curfew yet.

That would probably happen tomorrow, but by then it would be too late to stop this avalanche.

If the Fleet Centurion wanted it stopped.

In his pocket, the comm vibrated silently.

Vo looked around at the alley he and his men were traversing.

"Hold here," he whispered. "Incoming call."

Danville nodded without looking. Horst and Street took opposite sides facing each other to watch flanks. Vo moved to one wall for something at his back.

"Arlo," he said quietly into the comm.

"Vo, are the men with you?" the Fleet Centurion asked simply.

No, she wouldn't ask that simple of a question. Not her.

The Chess Grandmaster was already nine steps ahead.

Her tone indicated questions about loyalty, not mere presence.

"They are," Vo answered firmly.

"Armaments?" she continued in her cryptic voice.

"More than expected," Vo replied.

Indeed. The men were supposed to be completely unarmed when traveling to the Imperial capital. But they had also been on-planet for nearly two months, and had connected with the local black market. Every team had at least one firearm this morning, and every man had a close weapon, be it a knife, a stunner, or a club. Vo had Walter's pistol, and also ended up with a matte black, telescoping baton that was light as air, fifteen centimeters long, and would pop out to a meter-long club at need.

Just the way to celebrate a wedding.

"You have a mission," she said.

The words sounded like they weighed a ton each.

"Acknowledged," Vo replied.

"I will work skyside with the Navy," the Fleet Centurion said. "Your team will rescue the Flag. Questions?"

There was only one flag in this town. An Emperor in need.

So. That simple.

Cross the Imperial Capital during a daylight curfew in the middle of a revolution. Break into the palace against unknown, renegade forces. Rescue the Emperor and his family from whoever was holding them.

Save the *Fribourg Empire*.

All by himself.

Navin the Black believed in you. He still does. Fleet Centurion thinks you can do this. She's always right. Edgar Horst and the men are with you.

Get out of your own damned head and do this.

"No questions, Fleet Centurion," Vo finally answered in a tone that brooked no questions.

"Go dark then, Vo," Jessica Keller ordered him. "We'll talk later."

And that was it.

Vo closed the comm and glanced at the three men with him.

"After Moirrey," he said quietly. "Our job is to rescue the Emperor."

They nodded back, silent.

There wasn't anything else to say at this point.

Except perhaps *see you all in hell.*

CHAPTER XLII

IMPERIAL FOUNDING: 176/11/08. IMPERIAL PALACE, WERDER, ST. LEGIER

It was a small and expensively-decorated salon, almost overflowing with people packed uncomfortably together.

The *Imperial Princess Ekaterina Stephanya*, Steffi, found herself seated on a long couch between her father and her brother. Mother sat in an overstuffed chair, holding hands with Father across the armrests.

Poor, little Lady Yulia sat in another chair, shocked out of rational thought entirely, from the slack appearance of her face. Part of that might be her isolation from her slab and the chance to disappear into her shows. Yulia was not a particularly social creature, being far too much the introvert.

It was what generally made her such a good companion for Casey.

Steffi had no idea where her sister was, why she wasn't here with the rest of them, dressed in whatever clothing had been at hand when armed men rudely invaded their personal chambers, pointing guns at her and ordering her about, before taking the servants and Ladies-in-Waiting somewhere else.

She didn't think Casey would have provoked the men, but Steffi couldn't think of any other reason for her sister to be absent.

And she had started to ask Mother, only to be shut down before the words even emerged from her mouth.

So they waited in silence.

None of the men of Imperial Security were in the room with them, but Steffi knew that a handful guarded the locked door from the hallway. Several others paced on the patio outside the locked windows, guns at the ready and watching everything that might move.

At least nobody had been hurt. So far.

The door opened suddenly into the room.

A hideously-fat ogre waddled in, preceded by the stale flowers of a commercial aftershave that had met its match in the man's body odor.

Father made to rise, but Mother squeezed his hand. Steffi leaned into Ekke before he did anything irrational.

"General Grundman?" Father asked in a harsh, quiet voice instead.

"Where is Princess Kasimira?" the voice emerged from the many chins like a ghost in the wainscoting.

Silence greeted him.

"Have you checked the starport for stolen vessels?" Steffi asked impulsively. "My sister always had a notion to run away and become a pirate. Perhaps now was simply the right time."

She heard the man growl in frustration under his breath. Or maybe it was a wheeze, trying to escape the layers of blubber encasing the ugly walrus.

Mother obviously seemed to want to say something, but restrained herself to a simple grin, as if holding in a bout of giggles.

Casey hadn't really run off like that, had she? Was that why Mother and Father were so relaxed, facing the situation? Had they helped Casey escape?

Nothing else made sense.

None of this made sense.

Of course, what was daughter Steffi, the so-called practical one, doing, goading Imperial Security and mocking them?

Too much time around Casey, obviously.

"Fah," the walrus growled. "We will find her. She will simply be first on the list, instead of last."

He turned and stomped out. As much as his waddles would allow. Ripples in gelatin, perhaps.

Steffi snarled at his back, once it was turned.

The door closed like a vault, or a coffin.

Father surprised her by putting an arm around her shoulders and tugging her close for a kiss on the forehead.

Steffi had never been one for emotional displays, but this was Father. She relaxed and leaned into his strength and his touch.

Maybe Casey would escape all this.

Would she be happy as a pirate?

CHAPTER XLIII

They were in the same seats on the skunk-colored yacht as before. Jessica turned her head far enough to smile at the Princess, *Emperor*, seated next to her.

"Will it be safe, flying there?" Casey asked in a tight voice.

"It should be," Jessica replied soothingly. "Nobody knows you're here. We're generally outside of the range of everyone, scooting up and out of the gravity well. This ship has a minimal sensor signature already, and we can always short-hop up to maybe half a light-year if things get really bad."

"You've planned for this," Casey said in a tone verging on accusation.

"I've planned for almost everything, Casey," she replied. "Almost. And where planning fails, right now for instance, we'll improvise as best we can."

Like how to surf the chaos of a palace coup and possible impending Imperial civil war from the inside. Nothing in the manuals or her notes covered this.

Jessica would rectify that when she got home.

Not if. When.

The pilot up front had the comm relay audible in the neck of the yacht, so his Queen could keep track of things.

"*Amsel* Flight Control," the man drawled in a reasonable facsimile of

Gaucho's laconic voice. "This is KM-two-zero on final approach. Please confirm your lock seal status."

"KM-20," the man at the other end replied in a professional tone. "Seals are green. I show you centered on the beam. Land as you bear."

"Roger that, Flight Control. See you shortly."

This pilot wasn't as silky-smooth as the man who had brought her up with Wachturm, but it was close. He was also flying a combat yacht, and not a purpose-built flag officer's courier designed to be pleasant.

Still, they landed quickly and the *Blackbird's* deck engineers swarmed out to lock everything down and plug them into ship's power.

Jessica was up quickly, but Willow and Marcelle were still standing before she was. And Casey was getting good at shedding the harness. At least she didn't stand too quickly this time and bang her head on the ceiling again.

"Boss?" Willow asked apprehensively.

This wasn't a friendly visit, or an inspection. Everything might be about to go completely sideways, and there was nothing she or Marcelle could do about it except watch.

"I'll go down alone," Jessica replied. "You three wait here until we know what's going to happen.

"Roger that," Marcelle growled back before Willow or Casey could object. The two women fell silent.

A fist outside banged on the tiny airlock, letting them know that they were in a pressured environment and safe to open the door.

Jessica pressed the inner hatch override and watched both heavy panels open inwards. She took a deep breath and pulled herself up to her full height, however short that might be.

Everything rode on first impressions and political calculations right now.

Weakness would be death. Therefore, be strong. Be dominant.

Be *Queen of the Pirates*.

Jessica set her jaw and went down the three steps to the deck at a measured pace.

She hadn't been sure who she would meet, given the crypticness of her original message. She wouldn't have been surprised to be met by a lowly flight engineer.

Instead, Captain Saar awaited her, with a couple of men who were obviously marines. Bodyguards.

They looked almost as professional, as competent, as Marcelle and Willow.

Jessica would still bet on the two women in a bar fight.

"What would be the correct term of address today?" Saar asked abruptly as she got close. "Fleet Centurion? *Wildgraf?* Your Majesty?"

It bordered on rude, given the rules of Imperial culture, but it also cut to the heart of why she was here. The man had made a good impression on her before with his professionalism and his instincts. She could cut him some slack in a testy environment.

Still, time to *push back.*

Jessica forced herself to smile, in spite of the bitter anger underneath. That man's uniform also provoked her at an unconscious level, even if they were now at peace, just as hers probably did with men like this.

This was not her fight. It was not her war.

"I have been informed that Madame Keller would be most appropriate today, Captain Saar," Jessica replied tartly.

"Madame Keller?" he said tightly with a slight nod and a tight voice. "I see. Given the excitement of the day that has preceded, what brings you aboard my fine vessel, *Madame* Keller?"

"First, I must ask your personal opinion of that excitement, Captain Saar," Jessica said. "I understand that this verges on unacceptably rude in polite company, but the future of the Empire might rest on your answer."

His face went from serious to closed. It was like watching Vo Arlo when that man folded in on himself and refused further comment. Brothers, however far removed.

It was a promising sign, she hoped. She understood Vo.

Several moments passed. The two gunmen behind Saar were wary, but unmoving, except their eyes.

"Admiral Wachturm has an exceptional opinion of you, *Madame* Keller," Saar finally said to her. "Of your trustworthiness. And your tact."

He waited a moment, but Jessica refused to rise to the bait.

"I find the situation personally distasteful," Captain Saar continued with the faintest sneer. "However, I am bound by my professional duties to think otherwise. Does that satisfy your morbid curiosity?"

She could almost feel the angry heat boiling off the man, for all the calmness in his face. No doubt, he was clenching his teeth so as not to grind them in front of her. Again, so much like Vo that they could be brothers under the skin.

Walking up and slapping him probably wouldn't have been as rude as asking that particular question in public, especially today.

"It does," Jessica replied, calm finally entering her voice. "Sigmund Dittmar stakes his claim on being the closest relative in the line of succession, were the Emperor and his family to fall. Am I correct?"

"That is so, madam."

The tones were sharper and more clipped. He must really dislike that man. And yet, would no doubt serve him just as loyally, if required.

Jessica kept her face serious.

"And if there was a legitimate challenger to that claim?" Jessica continued. "A better one?"

Saar's expression closed that last, little bit, like the light going out in the wardroom refrigerator when the door shut in the middle of the night.

"It is my understanding that the entire Imperial suite, Karl and his family, is under house arrest, pending trial for treason," he said quietly, verbally probing her suddenly like a bladesman. There was anger under his tones. "Would you suggest otherwise?"

"I would," Jessica said, parrying deftly. "Would that alter your opinions?"

"It would provide greater options for maneuver, madam," Saar politely snarled back, a swipe to engender a block. "If it were actually possible."

"Captain Saar," Jessica said in her best royal voice, verbally thrusting at him with her *main-gauche*. "The Red Admiral also has a pronounced opinion of you, as a man to be trusted. I am willing to put myself in your power right now, as an outsider doing what I think is right, instead of what would be politically expedient. *Do you understand?*"

Saar's shoulders twitched back at her tone. His eyes slitted. The two gunmen got twitchier, but held their peace.

"Yes, Your Majesty," Captain Saar finally said in a quiet, sharp voice, coming to utter stillness.

But still deadly.

Again, so like Vo.

Not Madame Keller. *Your Majesty.*

Whether this was a hunter baiting a trap, or a warrior accepting orders remained to be seen.

Jessica nodded. She even smiled at him.

"Princess, if you would," she called back over her shoulder.

All three men audibly gasped as their eyes found a spot over Jessica's left shoulder.

Casey's boots rang on the metal deck as she stepped closer, coming to rest exactly beside Jessica.

"Captain Saar," Jessica announced quietly. "I present you Princess Kasimira."

"No," Casey said firmly, raising her voice enough that even the shocked flight engineers watching silently in the background could hear her. "If the Imperial House is fallen, then I have become your Emperor by right of law and precedent. You will address me as *Her Imperial Majesty, Karl VIII.*"

Again, the men gasped.

Saar's eyes flickered to Jessica's with a moment of unreadable, almost vulnerable, emotion.

Jessica smiled up at the man.

"Options, Captain Saar," she said finally with a firm nod.

He nodded back.

"Thank you, Madame Keller," he replied. "I cannot ever repay you the debt of honor you have done me today."

It was a cultural response that had no equivalent in *Aquitaine*, except perhaps to establish the kind of relationship Jessica had as a disciple of Nils Kasum.

But more. So much more. Perhaps more than the man owed the Red Admiral for the right to stand on his deck.

She had chosen correctly, coming here. That much was obvious in his eyes.

"Come," Captain Saar said, gesturing to the women. "Let us retire to a conference room and determine our next step."

"Marcelle, Willow, would you join us, please?" Casey called back over her shoulder before Jessica could.

Jessica had turned to speak, and saw Casey's harsh face show a flicker of a grin. Just a ghost.

Enough.

A siren suddenly filled the landing bay. Lights went red at the same time.

"Red Alert," a man's voice intoned severely. "All hands to your stations. I repeat, all hands to your stations."

Captain Saar gestured for them to join him, and then took off at a fast jog for the nearest hatch.

Outside the *Blackbird*, something had gone desperately wrong.

CHAPTER XLIV

DAY: 313 OF THE COMMON ERA YEAR: 13,445 VESSEL - RS:32G8Y42 – "DANCER IN DARKNESS." FRIBOURG SYSTEM: "ST. LEGIER". STATUS: DEPLOYMENT MODE

Ro Kenzo Atep Vrin checked his harness carefully, and then confirmed that two sealed bottles of chilled black tea were close at hand, also locked in place.

He glanced once around the command deck, from farthest right to farthest left, pausing on each crew member visible. Each nodded their own readiness.

Communications had been monitoring traffic in the system for long enough to determine that the mission was still moving forward as designed. There were foxes in the hen house, on the world deeper into the planetary system.

Shortly, a hungry shark would join them.

Satisfied, Vrin turned to the three Advocates facing him across the small command altar.

"Crew Advocate," Vrin questioned. "Are you prepared?"

"We are, Director," Ko Serek Evet Khan replied calmly.

"Entity Advocate," Vrin continued. "Has he meditated on his cause?"

"He is at peace, Director," Wa Veren Kulo Marz nodded back at him.

"War Advocate," Vrin ordered. "Prepare for battle."

"*Dancer In Darkness*," Ro Malar Arga Rues commanded aloud. "Detach the *Energiya Module*."

Around him, Vrin felt the gravity system power to nothing suddenly.

Down disappeared, leaving only the horizon of the command deck itself to provide direction.

Vibrations in the hull felt like a minor earthquake for several seconds, as the three-thumbed grip of the transport system let go and retracted, separating *Dancer In Darkness* into his two constituent parts: *Buran* and *Energiya*.

Like a blade, the forward section, the fighting module portion of the ship, slid out of his scabbard, long and deadly, leaving behind the bulky base section with the Jump Drives and their terrible engines.

Energiya would wait here for the combat module to return from its mission, quietly hiding in the darkness at the edge of the Imperial system.

Stripped down like this, *Dancer In Darkness* became the avatar of war. Without the bulk and mass of the Jump Drives and long-range engines, he was compact and deadly, particularly compared to Imperial warships equivalent in size. Not a Carcharias or Megalodon, the great monsters of deep space, but more than enough for the mission at hand, the greatest raid ever undertaken by the *Lord of Winter*.

Vrin allowed himself the luxury of a quick grin.

Tomorrow, *Fribourg* would truly desire peace. But first, they must be made to appreciate the value of such a thing.

"Entity Advocate," Vrin commanded. "Have we detached?"

Rather than answer immediately, the woman looked down at her screen for a moment.

"We have, Director," she finally replied, taking the moment to be certain.

"War Advocate, prepare the Capriole Drive," Vrin continued. "Coordinates have been identified and calculated. The Mauler is charged. The First Stage Exciters are ready. State your readiness."

Like his Entity Advocate, the War Advocate took a moment to check his panels and confirm that everything was in readiness before speaking.

"Combat preparedness is confirmed," the man replied with a steely gaze.

"Make your jump," Vrin commanded.

Dancer In Darkness flickered out of the physical universe on a ballistic path.

The *Fribourg Empire* used a different technology to sail between the stars. It was more accurate over vast distances, but they did not believe in using intelligent systems to control those calculations, relying on *human feel* for such things. Thus, they could only land a significant distance from any planet, or risk random scattering.

The Entity could do the same calculations as a human, but fifty thousand times faster. Thus, he could land well inside the zone a human-piloted vessel would risk, and do it accurately. And he could use the short-range blink drive, the *Capriole*, to leap across the planetary orbit. It was far easier to maintain a specific altitude when doing so, like electrons falling into a series of valance shells.

Below, the Imperials would have their eyes cast down, watching the planet below them and hoping for a sign from their new masters.

None would be watching the heavens for an avenging archangel to descend.

A tone sounded. Three seconds warning.

Emergence.

It was a fine construct, this Grand Fleet Orbital Headquarters that the Imperials had lofted into the skies above their capital. But it was a child's balloon, mostly empty space contained within a metal ovoid.

Large energy cannon mounts, too big for the First Stage Exciters to absorb easily, protected points of an imaginary cube around the base.

Or would have, if they had been unlocked and charged. After all, this deep in the gravity well of the planet, what vessel would be able to get close enough to threaten them without plenty of warning?

What vessel, indeed?

Dancer In Darkness had plotted his first leap with surgical accuracy, passing above and along the longer axis of the station at a high-enough speed to be a difficult target, but perfectly aligned for the Mauler.

Sensors showed the presence of energy shields around the station. Not at a combat setting, but enough to protect it from the vagaries of everyday orbital rubble.

Not that even the combat shields would make much of a difference to the Mag-Shear, the *Mauler*.

"Engage," Vrin commanded his crew.

From this point, his task was to provide oversight, rather than command. To plot strategic maneuvers. In a fleet action, to control the gears like fingers in a raking and grasping claw.

The War Advocate and the Entity would fight the battle at a tactical level. They did that well.

"Activate the Mauler," the War Advocate said calmly.

Without gravity plates active, every erg of generated power could be routed through the Mag-Shear. Even the lights flickered heavily for several seconds as a beam of ravening fire emerged from the three points on the Roughshark's snout, came to a focus, and engulfed the top of the station like molten frosting poured on a cupcake.

Shields stopped perhaps thirteen percent of the incoming energy. Combat shielding might have deflected as much as ten percent more.

The rest poured into a tremendous magnetic field that induced a transverse shear powerful enough to shatter entire sections of the station. Even humans caught in the beam could be devastated, the iron in their blood suddenly a weapon against them.

The lights came back to full power.

Vrin only imagined he could smell ozone, considering the beam that had just hammered the station. Everything was still clean and spring-fresh on his command deck.

Nobody would be prepared to shoot back for longer than it would take for them to escape.

"Begin Firing Sequence One," the War Advocate continued in his smooth growl.

The cost for all the stealth and long-range sailing properties of the Roughshark was mostly in offensive weaponry. The Makos also relied on the Mauler, but carried more Pulse Beams: medium-range energy weapons designed to kill small escorts at the sorts of engagement ranges made possible by the Capriole Drive.

Dancer In Darkness had the normal complement of Flicker Beams, rapid-firing and point-blank range, but he lacked the longer-range weaponry of his cousins.

At this range, Vrin could hit the badly-staggered orbital fortress with a thrown rock if he wanted.

Still, three Pulse Beams and six Flicker beams lashed out, a staccato symphony. Normally, the station would shed them like water on a duck's back, but the Mag-Shear had also shattered a number of shield emplacements, or power conduits, so there were holes in the fortress's defenses.

Beams pierced them like ice picks.

Vrin watched the charge levels on the various battery arrays race towards zero. The Mauler took some time to recharge, as did the Capriole. Normally, that could be greatly assisted by letting the First Stage Exciters act as power accumulators, absorbing incoming fire and routing it into the batteries, rather than shrugging it off like Imperial warships did.

Today, at least right at this moment, nobody was firing back. The shock was too new on their part.

That would not last.

"War Advocate, make the first bombing run," Vrin commanded.

He smiled to himself a cold, thin smile. The Makos and the Threshers had more offensive firepower, but they did not carry missile racks. The *Lord of Winter* had chosen to adopt that singular Imperial technology. *Dancer In Darkness* was the first to use them in battle.

Vrin watched the projection of the planetary system turn gray as *Dancer In Darkness* leapt across JumpSpace again, dropping down low, almost to the edge of the atmosphere. Four seconds, and they emerged again, this time with a jar as the upper reaches of the stratosphere caused a thickening of space around them.

It was almost like hydroplaning in a land vehicle that had hit a patch of sudden, black ice.

The hull rang around him suddenly. Three missiles ejected manually from mechanical catapults, beginning their long, lazy fall.

And then their gyroscopes engaged, pointing them down like needles into flesh, and engines ignited.

The scramjet bombs did not have much warhead. Only a small core of radioactive metals that would generate a quick triple-thermonuclear explosion at a relatively high altitude. The first electromagnetic pulse would generate soft damage over a widely dispersed area, while the actual destruction would be fairly limited in scope.

The *Lord of Winter* had made careful calculations about doing a demonstration with small casualties, versus attempting to wipe out one of the major cities on this planet. Plus, even the medium-sized cities would be protected by automated systems that would bring defensive shields online fast enough to protect them from the death about to rain from the skies.

One of the first targets today was simply an Imperial hunting lodge on the far side of the planet from the capital, the sort of place that should be largely empty on this date, with the impending celebrations half a world away. Only caretakers would be killed in the making of this omelet, rather than personages whose death would demand retribution.

Bounce again.

Dancer In Darkness was suddenly over the north pole axis of the planet. Three more scramjet bombs launched, this time intended to trigger a series of tsunami on every shore by detonating simultaneously at sea level. Again, far enough from any inhabited shore that the humans on the planet should have time to get to high ground. Only a single weather station on an isolated island, too close to explosion number two, would have no time to evacuate before destruction.

Controlled devastation.

A lesson from the *Lord of Winter* as to *What Could Have Been.*

Tomorrow, negotiations with the new lord of *Fribourg* to ensure it never had to happen again.

Dancer In Darkness leapt.

CHAPTER XLV

The fog was mostly gone, out on the streets, but it clung tenaciously in the burrs and hollows of the park, cool ground heating slower than the asphalt of the surrounding roadways.

Vo felt more at home amidst the greenery, which surprised him, considering he had never even gone outside a city, out into the raw wilderness, until ground infantry training when he had joined the Navy at eighteen.

The time on *Thuringwell*, riding a horse and hiding in the bush, had obviously rubbed off. Even if Moirrey still called him City-boy from time to time.

Corporal Danville up front found a large bush and squatted down behind it silently. They were in a small glade, invisible from outside the park, the last wispy fog still poking fingers of chill into collars.

The four of them took a moment and relaxed, to recover a bit after nearly walking right into an armoured troop transport and a platoon of troops, two blocks away.

All that time with Fourth Saxon and *LVIII Heavy* had truly taught Vo the bushcraft he needed to keep them alive. Danville was good, but another city boy. Still, nobody had seen them.

Vo pulled his comm from a pocket and selected Moirrey's channel.

"We're here," he said simply, waiting.

"Yup," she chirped back instantly. "Watched you. Yers about thirty meters away, fifteen degrees right o'the line you'd been on."

She had been watching them arrive? Knew where they were right now?

Suddenly, the stories that the men and women of the Construction Ala had shared about the dangerous, little girl from engineering made more sense.

"Okay," Vo said. "What now?"

"Stand up and turn a bits to yer right," Moirrey said.

With nothing better to do, Vo did.

Sure enough, Moirrey leaned out from behind a tree and silently waved at him to come to her.

Vo tapped Danville on the shoulder, nodded to Street and Horst, and set out.

For a city boy, he made far less noise than the soldiers behind him, even a silent killer like Corporal Danville. Good to know.

Moirrey was inside a stand of trees that was almost a room in the middle of this forest when he got close enough. Certainly, if they were quiet, someone could walk within meters and not see them.

Vo decided that it probably wasn't an accident on Moirrey's part.

Maybe Moirrey really could give someone like Danville a run for his money.

"What's the mission, Vo?" she asked as they got in and settled.

"Imperial Security arrested the Emperor and the family," he replied, watching her bristle. "Apparently, they got the Red Admiral, too, but the Fleet Centurion wants us to rescue Karl first."

"Fitting," Moirrey announced. "Seein's we's important Imperial folks now, an'all."

Vo grinned at her.

Moirrey *zu* Kermode. *Lady Moirrey.*

Vo *zu* Arlo. *Lord Vo.*

Cost of doing business, he supposed. If someone had done this to the President, or the First Lord of the Fleet, he'd be doing the same thing right now.

Funny how doing the right thing always seemed to put him in the position to do more of it.

One of these days, he was going to have to go home, his old block on *Anameleck Prime,* and pay a visit on that old judge, the man who had offered to make him a marine instead of a felon, once upon a time. Let him know how it had all turned out, fifteen years later.

He just had to survive this.

"Danville, Horst, Street," Vo ticked off their names. "I am aware that you arrived on this planet unarmed, a situation you rectified in good order. Might you have also given thought as to a means of accessing the Imperial Palace grounds undetected? Perhaps have even implemented such plans?"

Vo was rewarded by three sheepish faces suddenly blushing, eyes down.

Yup, thought so.

"What've you got?" Vo turned to Horst, the most likely man of the three to give him a complete answer.

"Security's good around the place, sir," Edgar replied after a moment. "But there's a game park around behind that, surrounded by a fairly significant green belt."

"Okay," Vo acknowledged.

He really hadn't paid close attention to the terrain when they'd arrived, focusing mostly on the city grid itself and memorizing streets.

The Fleet Centurion probably would have known all this. Lesson learned.

"So the greenbelt is marked," Edgar continued. "And it's something of a large park that snakes around. Much of it follows a small river, really not much more than a creek in many places, but a psychological barrier to the locals. We cross that, and we're inside. From there, a wall runs around most of the palace grounds proper. Don't figure the park rangers came to work today, so we should be able to get to the wall. Once inside, dunno how good security will be. Doubt Imperial Security knows the grounds as well as the house unit, but probably doesn't trust those folks, so they're doing it themselves, at least for now."

"Risk?" Vo asked.

"I'd bet they're counting on surprise to hold the field for them today, Colonel," Sgt. Street spoke up suddenly. "Hit hard and fast, and chance nobody being able to do what we're up to."

"Why not?" Vo fired back.

"They'd be focused on the palace troops, sir," the man grinned. "Plus city gendarmes, Shore Patrol, and nearby military units. Even if they're looking for us, they ought to expect we'd be defensive, not offensive. Hiding to escape notice, rather than attacking the Imperial palace ourselves."

"He's right, sir," Danville murmured. "Imperial Security is a passive force. Sit back and watch. They would never immediately attack like this out of the blue. Nor expect it. The faster we move, the better. Less time for them to lock everything down on us."

Vo let his tactical and strategic training take over. He knew every alley and sidewalk in the area, but not the best way to the park. But he didn't need to. He had the 189th Division with him. Mountain infantry specialists.

"Horst," Vo commanded quietly. "Contact the other teams and route them to a destination you know. We'll coalesce there and move in."

"What 'bouts me?" Moirrey snapped.

"I need your help with the electronics," Vo replied. "And once we can get you a gun, I'll turn you loose. It'll be just like *Ballard* or *Thuringwell*, all over again."

"You knows 'bout thats?" she asked evasively.

"Fleet Centurion told me parts," Vo said. "Enough."

Moirrey actually blushed up at him.

"Rights," she muttered. "Ne'er ya minds, then."

Vo nodded.

Moirrey *zu* Kermode might really be one to give Corporal Danville a run for dangerous creatures. He wasn't about to suggest it out loud, though.

Not yet.

CHAPTER XLVI

DATE OF THE REPUBLIC NOVEMBER 8, 398
ABOARD AMSEL, ABOVE ST. LEGIER

It wasn't that many steps to get to *Amsel's* bridge, up only two decks and forward some. Jessica followed Captain Saar at a hard jog, with the other three women keeping pace behind her. The two male bodyguards were trading off racing ahead and opening hatches so that their group didn't need to slow down as they crossed frames.

The bridge hadn't changed from the last time Jessica visited, except to possibly be cleaner. As if expecting a wedding party to come aboard in a few days and commission her into formal service.

Today, everyone was dressed in regular uniforms, dark blue pants and heavy jackets over white shirts. They kept the temperature in here several degrees cooler than any vessel Jessica had ever served on. That was probably the result of having an all-male crew in heavy clothing.

The cultural differences you noticed when the stress went high.

"Status," Captain Saar called as Marcelle brought up the rear and closed the hatch.

"Surprise attack on Grand HQ, Captain," a man said as he stood up from the Captain's chair.

Unlike an *Aquitaine* vessel, where everyone faced inward on the bridge, every man here was facing forward in descending ranks of importance and looking at a single large screen on the far bulkhead, in addition to his own screens. It felt inefficient, but Jessica supposed it probably worked.

"How is that possible?" Saar snarled only vaguely at his crew as he sat.

Jessica moved around to his right, bringing Casey with her and letting Willow and Marcelle move to either side defensively.

"Roughshark-class cruiser short-jumped right on top of them and let loose, sir," the other man continued, turning to face them. "Then they short-jumped out and started hitting the planet with missiles. Nothing important was targeted, but we've got four salvoes downward so far and it's going to be messy."

Jessica recognized Commander Corbeil, *Amsel's* executive officer. Another one of Wachturm's protégés.

"Damn it, how could they do that?" Saar cursed again.

Jessica stepped forward just enough to get Saar's attention.

"Probably not an accident of timing, Captain?" she said firmly.

That seemed to break through the man's hot rage. She needed him calm right now.

He nodded and drew a breath.

"All hands to battle stations," he said. "Engineering, bring everything on-line. Weapons systems, do the best with what you have. Navigation, prepare for maneuvering."

"What do you intend, Captain Saar?" Casey said in a heavy voice.

That brought the man's head around.

"That's a warship of *Buran*, Your Majesty," he said after another calming breath. "We've got to do something."

"What were your orders before, Saar?" Jessica stepped up another bit.

"To remain in our patrol patterns until further orders were issued," he said slowly.

"And what better way to weld the Fleet to you than to ride to the rescue from an attack?" Jessica replied.

Jessica watched the lightbulb go on in his eyes.

"They knew that it was coming," he continued in a deadly voice.

"Something like this would take months to engineer and execute," Jessica agreed. "What are the odds that they happened to be in the neighborhood to attack *St. Legier* today?"

Silence greeted her.

"Captain," a man's voice called out. "Fleet orders from the planet to form up in battle squadrons and pursue the enemy vessel."

"You said short-jumped, Commander," Jessica turned to the man on the other side of the command seat. "What does that mean? I've never fought *Buran*."

"They can do the impossible, sir," he replied. "Hit jumpspace from deep inside a gravity well and bounce around all they want. It's almost impossible to chase them. And if they're below you, you can't use Primaries or you might hit the planet instead. You have to wait for them to get close and then hope you can hurt them before they kill you. The only thing that saves us most of the time is that their beams are extremely short range compared to ours."

"So forming up and giving chase will do no good?" Jessica asked. "Other than to pull you out of your current defensive positions?"

"Quite possibly, Fleet Centurion," Saar bit the words off. "However, there is nobody that can belay that order."

"Yes, there is," Casey, *Her Imperial Majesty Karl VIII*, said with utter conviction.

"Casey, we don't dare say anything at this point," Jessica spoke politely but there was steel in her words.

She felt Casey's hard stare boring in and accepted it.

"Why not?" Casey finally demanded.

"We cannot know who would be friendly, and who would sell us over to Dittmar," Jessica replied. "I took a chance on Captain Saar, largely based on the Red Admiral. I don't know who else would could trust. Do you, Captain?"

"I do not, Fleet Centurion," the man replied in a quiet voice. "Yesterday, I would have spoken up for any of my brother Captains. Today?"

"Today indeed, Captain Saar," Casey said in a regal tone. "However, they are attacking my home, my *Empire*, and we must do something about it. And I do know one Captain I can absolutely trust to assist you."

"Who?" the man asked.

"Command Centurion Shiori Ness," Casey grinned suddenly, breaking through the seriousness of her mien. "*Wiley*."

Jessica nodded. She would be happy to throw *Kali-ma* into this mess, with her flight wing, but she wasn't sure it would work. At best, Casey could take command and issue orders to every other vessel to stay put and guard the planet.

But how would they entice the invader to come close enough that they could shoot back?

Jessica felt her own lightbulb go on, staring at the tall, blond Emperor standing before her.

She turned back to the two men.

"All short range weapons you said, correct?" Jessica queried them.

"That's right," Saar said. "The big one they use, the Mauler, scarcely slows down when it hits the shield wall, but has barely the range of a Type-2 beam. They appear on a flank, shred you, and then blink out. And they don't have shields, near as we can tell, but some sort of absorption system that captures incoming energy and routes into their batteries. You have to overload it all at once to get through."

"And missiles are useless, since he can leap away from you," Jessica said. "Primaries are extremely slow to reload, so he might get away before you get a second shot off."

"Which is why the *Paladin*-class Battleships were designed this way," Corbeil agreed. "Fewer of both and more beams that can fire fast enough to hammer him."

"He's attacking the planet, but nothing important?" Casey asked. "Is that what you said?"

"Yes, Your Majesty," the Commander said. "One salvo set off a trio of nuclear weapons low over the Western Ocean, well out to sea. That will generate significant tidal waves, but not for hours in most places. Other targets are similarly illogical."

"It's a demonstration raid," Jessica stated flatly.

She felt it in her bones.

"A what?" Saar asked.

"*2218 Svati Prime*," Jessica replied in a cold, quiet voice.

This was all about the psychological damage one vessel could do.

The warship out there had to be working with Dittmar. And there was just the one vessel, when they might have sent an entire battle fleet instead. Enough damage to rouse everyone, but not outright devastation. Just enough to get the population behind a new Emperor with a shaky claim to power when he drove the invader off.

Just exactly the sort of thing you might want if you overthrew the previous government under highly questionable circumstances.

The two men wanted to argue with her, but she could see the fire drain out of their conviction.

Casey seemed to make the same leap. She nodded fiercely.

"And if that is the case," Casey said. "Then we must entice him to get close enough to fight us."

"How do we do that?" Captain Saar asked warily.

"The same reason I came aboard your Battleship, Captain Saar," Casey replied. "To raise the Imperial Banner and rally the Fleet to my cause. Father and Uncle Emmerich have always said that the true power in the Empire is the Navy. Now we will prove it."

Jessica wanted to say something, but she held her peace.

This was no longer her fight. She had done her duty by getting Casey this far. The new Emperor and Rafferty Saar would have to see it through.

She could go back to *Kali-ma* and watch. Help, even if the *Fribourg Empire* tore itself apart.

Casey turned to her anyway, her smile peeking out through the harsh mask that had fallen back over her features.

"There is one other task," the new Emperor said. "Jessica, I need you in charge. It's the only way it will work."

"Your Majesty, I must politely decline," Jessica said carefully, fully aware of how close she was to violating any number of ethical and legal standards. Court martial wasn't even a worry at this point. When she got home, it would a given. "As you said earlier, this must be an Imperial task."

"I agree, Jessica Keller," the Emperor said in a new voice. Heavy. Hard. Implacable. "However, I did not ask Queen Jessica to assist me. I am ordering *Admiral Keller* to take command of the Imperial Fleet. Those bastards are attacking *my* home. You will SEE THEM OFF. Are there any questions?"

Jessica felt her shoulders snap back and her head come up, as though Nils Kasum had just snapped the whip of his voice on a new cadet, twenty-five years ago. Or Alber' d'Maine taking charge of the room to commission a new Star Controller just two years ago.

Some things went bone deep.

A day ago, this woman was an artist pretending to be a princess to make her parents happy. An hour ago, a refugee on the verge of fleeing and becoming a pirate.

And now, an Emperor made flesh, right in front of Jessica's eyes.

Jessica took a deep breath.

She turned to Rafferty Saar, still seated at the third point of a triangle.

"Captain Saar, will you serve?" she asked in a pointed voice.

This was no longer friendly officers, planning a battle over a beer. It had come down to this, his honor, overcoming his culture.

He smiled warmly.

"Admiral Keller, it would be my honor," he said.

Jessica nodded. She nodded to Casey as well.

No. Not Casey any more.

Her Imperial Majesty, Karl VIII. Emperor of Fribourg.

Death, or glory.

"Captain Saar," Jessica commanded. "I am aware that the Red Admiral was going to bring his new Flag Staff with him when he took command. Lacking that, I need to command from your deck, and I need you to assign me a Flag Lieutenant who can work with me."

Saar nodded. He paused and looked over his deck thoughtfully.

"Emshwiller," he said loudly. "Turn over your duties to your assistant and take over Flag Communications."

Jessica watched a Lieutenant Commander rise from his station off to one side and approach quickly. He had a broad face, with Asian eyes and thin lips. Unlike many of the men on this deck, his brown hair was cut severely short, almost shaved on the sides.

He came to a stop and snapped off a salute, edge of his hand tapping his forehead and then slicing straight down across his chest. It looked silly, but made the man's point.

"At your command, Admiral," he said in a heavy, baritone voice.

"Get the Emperor secured, with my two assistants on either side," Jessica said first. "Then you and I need stations where we're out of the way, but still in the battle. Finally, open a secured channel to *Kali-ma* and get our comms synched with Yan Bedrov, the tactical officer over there."

"On it."

The man was a whirlwind as Jessica watched, never a step wrong, as though he was doing a high-speed, Argentinian Tango with professional judges grading.

Less than two minutes passed, but it felt like a hurricane had passed over the ship, centering the eye of calm above them, with devastating winds all around, just waiting their chance.

Jessica watched a calmness take possession of the men around her, poised, even as the Goddess of War awakened in the depths of her soul and drew blades.

Everyone here knew that history was about to happen.

"Captain Saar," Jessica called in a voice loud enough to be clear in every corner. "You will raise the Imperial Standard and order all vessels to remain on their stations. We will do this ourselves. All ahead full and get me to a higher elevation, with *Kali-ma* and her wing on one soft flank. Get us away from everybody else and find me the Plain of Megiddo."

"Megiddo, Admiral?" he asked in an unsure tone, turning to look at her across the four meters of space, and the lifetime of study, that separated them.

"An ancient, Biblical reference, Captain," she replied. "Armageddon."

CHAPTER XLVII

IMPERIAL FOUNDING: 176/11/08. DITTMAR PALACE, WERDER, ST. LEGIER

Sigmund had moved from his first-floor salon to a personal office in the basement of his palace. Deep below ground and safe, even if *Buran* managed to pierce the shield protecting the city.

They were not allies, even today. Merely fellow travelers, both intent on removing a dangerously-reckless man from power, before he undid two centuries of stability with his stupidly-foreign ideas.

Dittmar was surrounded by a cadre of men he trusted with his life at this point. Every one of them would hang with him if this failed. It made him feel even safer.

Sensors from a loyal Heavy Cruiser in orbit showed the effect of that first savaging of Grand Fleet Headquarters. Pieces were still floating away in a cloud of destruction that had no scale, until one realized how big the station itself was. And then the pieces were the size of Starfighters.

"What's the status of Fleet Command?" he asked the room gruffly.

Someone would answer. That was the mark of a good staff.

"We're not sure, Admiral," a man called back. "Attempts to reach them have been unsuccessful. We're also seeing significant communications degradation as a result of multiple electromagnetic pulses in the atmosphere."

The nuclear warheads had been a small and unwelcome surprise, but they weren't attacking the big cities. Sigmund wasn't sure the station would be able to respond, effectively, if that shark jumped back for a second round, but hopefully the big Type-4 beams and Primary installations protecting an imaginary dodecahedron would be live if *Buran* tried.

Even Imperial Security wouldn't be that stupid.

Would they?

Still, the station had been hurt. Best to protect it. He would need it tomorrow, after he had removed the troublesome elements from thwarting his reign.

"Communications," Sigmund said tersely. "Order all units to coalesce into battle squadrons and pursue the enemy vessel, under my authority as Acting Emperor. Hold First Squadron close to Headquarters in a defensive array and launch all fighter craft."

"Acknowledged."

Sigmund accepted a mug of freshly-brewed coffee from someone. He didn't bother looking up. As long as his needs were met, he was satisfied. It was going to be a long day, he would need the caffeine to maintain his edge as issues popped up.

Something like this had never happened before, either the coup or the raid. There were certain to be wrinkles in the plan that would need ironing. Plus, he would need to guard against it ever happening to him in the future.

A second screen showed real-time imagery from satellites looking down at the surface of *St. Legier*. The Western Ocean had three, rippling pulses, charging outwards from holes that had been blasted in the surface by high-powered nuclear detonations.

"Someone get me an oceanographer," Sigmund growled. "How big will those waves get?"

That had been another surprise.

He had been thinking in terms of the first trio of missiles, dropping on unimportant portions of the planet, too irrelevant for planetary shielding, and causing flashy damage that would be easily repaired later.

Tidal waves were a whole new level of threat. Who knew what they might do when they reached land?

"And sound the global alert for tidal waves," Sigmund continued. "Get people to high ground immediately and keep them there. We can repair wharves and cities later."

Someone acknowledged. Again, it didn't matter who.

The men around him were largely faceless. Interchangeable cogs in a vast machine, who showed their value by not rising to the level of recognition.

"Sir," a voice impinged on his planning. "You need to see this. Immediately."

Did he now?

Sigmund made a note of the man's face for later. One did not give the Emperor orders, even in the thick of battle.

A projector came live in the middle of the room. Sigmund recognized the opening notes of the Imperial Anthem, with the Imperial Flag blowing in a soft breeze, something normally only played for official pronouncements.

This was the planetary emergency communications network, overriding News One.

Since he had no news to send out presently, someone out there was playing with fire. Sigmund would have to roast them over it slowly later. Especially since this signal was on the emergency band, over-riding all of his broadcasts on every frequency.

Someone was absolutely going to die for this.

And then *she* appeared. The missing Princess, *Kasimira*, looking stern and self-important for all of seventeen years of uselessness in a palace.

At least her sister, Stephanya, would have known how to act Imperial right now. This child was obviously on the verge of tears.

So, little girl. You wish to challenge me?

"Imperial citizens," Kasimira began slowly, attempting to sound so much more grown-up than she knew how. "It has dawned a terrible day in the history of the *Fribourg Empire*. A usurper has attacked the throne and imprisoned the Emperor, my father. As the traitor has also captured my brother and my sister, the Imperial duties must, of needs, fall on my shoulders, by law and custom, making me your Emperor in duty, at least until my father can be freed from his captivity."

The girl paused to take a breath.

It was obvious she was reading from a script, but who had written this speech for her? All the major players were either in custody, or on Sigmund's side, at least passively.

None would dare challenge him. The Fleet would not follow a child into battle. Only a proven warrior could command their allegiance, especially today.

"Where is that signal originating?" Sigmund demanded.

"Furthermore, our enemies have chosen to strike on this very day, killing both sailors defending us and innocent civilians on the ground," the Princess continued after a beat, pausing again to fix the camera with a hard stare. "This will not stand. I have taken the Imperial Robes and I will protect you, as is my duty. My first act as your Emperor is to appoint Admiral Jessica Keller as supreme commander of the Imperial Fleet for the duration of the emergency. You will follow orders from her as if from me. Treason will not be tolerated. Admiral Keller?"

Keller!

Sigmund's teeth ground. How had she done this to him? Were there no limits to the evil that woman would do to *Fribourg* before he had her killed?

"Sir," a man's voice rattled around the silent room. "The broadcast is originating from *IFV Amsel*."

"The *Blackbird*?" Dittmar rounded savagely on the man. "How is this possible?"

"Investigating, sire."

"Captains of the Imperial Fleet," Keller began after the camera panned over to her. "You know me. I have given my oath to the new Emperor, and I give you my oath now that we will protect *St. Legier* together. Further orders are forthcoming, but all vessels are expected to follow my commands without hesitation or question. You will stay on your current stations and defend the planet. If you cannot accept those terms, you have no place in this institution and I expect you to turn over command to a subordinate who is willing to take my orders. This is not negotiable. Now, all hands to battle stations."

The signal cut out.

Sigmund had no doubt it would be looped frequently, at least until he captured those two women and had them shot, possibly on camera so everyone could see the risk they took, thwarting him.

And worse, he was trapped on the ground. Yesterday, it had made perfect sense to be nowhere near the orbital fortress on the day that it faced devastation. They would be hours just getting enough repairs done to talk to the outside world meaningfully.

And he could not get aboard a friendly Battleship now without attracting notice, either from the Raider, or Keller and her possible allies, any of whom might take the opportunity to do greater mischief while he was at risk.

Sigmund unclenched his jaw and sipped coffee to center himself. It would not do to show weakness in front of these men.

"Get me General Grundman," he seethed, moving to a small conference room to one side where he could close the sound-proofed door and rant.

A light was blinking on the secured landline when he was alone.

"Geoffrey?" Sigmund snarled into the comm.

"Here, Sire," the security leader replied soothingly.

"How could your men miss Keller?" he demanded. "What fools need to be shot for this mistake?"

There was a small pause at the other end of the line.

"We believe that Keller took the Princess aboard her flagship secretly this morning," Grundman replied. "A goodwill tour that just managed to be horribly timed from our standpoint."

"Why was I not notified immediately?"

"Sire, we captured the rest of the Imperial Suite, plus Admiral Wachturm and his family. Other undesirables are being rounded up as the day progresses. There is nobody on the ground that represents a threat right now."

"And the Fleet?" Sigmund snarled.

"The raid will be over soon, Your Majesty," the Security officer replied. "He cannot carry that many bombs, and will be facing the entire Fleet in the system now. Our deal was always that he would depart after making his point, chased off by loyal forces to help solidify your power base."

"And if Keller splits the fleet?"

"Sire, do you really think these men would follow a woman?" Grundman purred. "Moreover, if the Peace truly holds, how many of these fleets and squadrons will be demobilized by those women, putting these self-same commanders and their clients out of work ashore? No, Keller might lead them for a bit, but they will not hold."

"See to it, General," Sigmund snarled. "I expect no more surprises."

He slammed the handset down in his frustration. All of this planning and it might be for nothing. Naught but his own death.

Still, that one Roughshark had managed to savage the station.

What could it do to a single Battleship? Quite possibly enough that his loyal elements could finish those two women off for good.

Sigmund allowed himself a small, petty smile.

CHAPTER XLVIII

DATE OF THE REPUBLIC NOVEMBER 8, 398
ABOARD KALI-MA, ABOVE ST. LEGIER

iley opened the electronic file from Jessica and smiled to herself.

So many firsts in the lifetime of a little girl named Shiori.

First woman to qualify in combat Starfighters in the history of *Corynthe*. First one invited to join a crew. First woman ever acclaimed to Captain.

First Command Centurion, ever.

And now, the first woman to join the *Fribourg Imperial Navy*, as a Captain no less, albeit of an Auxiliary warship sworn into service. Still, another notch. A dangerously-large one, considering.

She was looking forward to helping Jessica bring *Fribourg* into the modern age, she, a little girl raised in a ramshackle flat on the edge of Petron City, where the water occasionally ran brown from the faucet.

But they were still more open-minded than this place, these people.

She would so enjoy this.

The words across the top of the file left no doubt as to the seriousness of the situation.

Warning: Imperial Security Rating O-4.

Command-level. Line officers only.

Ha.

Men.

Wiley quick-scanned the document and routed it to her full staff, as well as all the pilots.

Rough technical specifications on the stranger, a so-called *Buran Roughshark*, at least as much as Imperial Engineers could reverse engineer from destroyed ships and scanner logs. Apparently the firepower equivalent of at least a pocket dreadnaught. Weapons systems. Whatever the hell it was that they used instead of shields. The ability to leap inside the envelope of a planet's gravity well.

The latter was impressive, but not impossible. *Rocket Frog* and *Neon Pink* could do the same thing, but they had refined the calculations over months of work and then both dieted with iron discipline to maintain their exact baseline mass. A vessel that size would need a super-computer to handle the math.

There. Yes. A super-computer. An actual, *Creator-be-damned-for-all-eternity Sentience* flying the vessel. One of the darkest demons ever to cross space. In command of a warship.

Wiley had already seen the monster bomb the planet below them. Every child of *Corynthe* grew up with the stories of *Lost Earth*, bombarded by robot spacefleets until no humans survived. Or the other colonies that suffered the same fate, until there were no factories left to build the parts, or make the drugs, or process the food.

Wiley felt a growl build deep in her stomach.

Trillions had died as a result. Humanity had almost died. And here was an entire stellar nation founded and run by a *Sentience*.

No wonder *Fribourg* went a little crazy. The Dark Angel himself wouldn't push more buttons in their culture, if he came down from Heaven and offered them the apple personally.

"Yan, check your plans against what this thing can do," she said aloud. "I'll call Jessica in a few minutes and see what she has planned."

"Roger that," he called, never looking up as he read.

"Engineering," *Wiley* continued, opening a line aft as well as yelling at the folks here on the bridge with her. "I know we don't have Moirrey today, but there are implications here. Find them. Get me an ace in the hole. And see what we can do if that Mauler hits us."

Probably, that Mauler beam would simply snap *Kali-ma* in half along the gooseneck like a chicken's wishbone. That would be a more tempting target than the engine and jump clusters aft. And more easily repairable tomorrow, if they survived. Blowing the engines apart might take them all down in one, ugly fireball.

Assents echoed back. No *Corynthe* warship had ever fought a pitched naval battle before. They were all carriers that dueled with their squadrons. Or chased pirates off.

But *Corynthe* had also never had a warship built this tough, this dangerous. *Kali-ma* was built to the old *Auberon*'s standards: launch the wing, and then follow them into battle.

And there, *Wiley* knew she had an edge.

Those fine folks from wealthy places fought battles with expensive Primaries and scads of disposable missiles, like they just grew on trees in pallet loads.

Kali-ma was all beams. Her squadron were all beams, even *Rocket Frog* and *Neon Pink*, who would have to reload after they shot their Archerfish. *Wiley* was used to having to get close in to make her point, at least in training.

Plus, Moirrey had given them an edge by tuning the Type-3's to what Shiori had taken to calling Three-Ex. Extended range focus. Not quite Primaries for range and nowhere near that for damage, but way faster rate of fire.

Against a teleporting imp, that would be important. Especially when he was going after the *Blackbird*.

Her comm chirped. Erik Doležal, Primary Engineer. A big, burly, rough-looking customer whose grandchildren turned him into a giant teddy bear when he wasn't looking.

"Boss, got an idea," he said.

"Go," *Wiley* replied.

"So, those things absorb incoming fire and explosions, and transform it all to power and feed that into batteries, from what this thing implies, right?"

"That's my read, Erik," *Wiley* said, paging down to that section and reading along with him.

"Right," Erik continued. "When our shields fail, they just collapse and you have to regenerate them. Takes time, and you have to maneuver 'cause you got a hole taking on water. This thing, when they get full, there's nowhere for all the extra energy to go. Doesn't look like they can bleed it off. Has to route to engines, jump, or weapon systems."

"Okay," *Wiley* said, not quite following his line of logic, but she was a pilot, not a physicist.

"So, timing, boss," Erik said. "Everybody beams him at the same time. Battleship lights up St. Elmo's fire if you do that, because y'all hit various shield facings. There's really only one here. It will all get absorbed at once."

"What happens if the bucket gets full?" *Wiley* asked.

"Page 938," he replied. "Looks like that's how they usually kill them. Overload just keeps filling. Something breaks, and the whole array cascades into a compact, short-lived supernova."

"Thank you, Erik."

"My job, boss."

And he was gone.

"Comm," *Wiley* said. "Get me Jessica."

CHAPTER XLIX

Vrin studied the tactical as his brain weighed the strategic.

Dancer In Darkness had sent off all eighteen of his scramjet bombs in six, tight salvos. Mushrooms of fire in the atmosphere below, visible even from space, hashing the same communication channels the *Fribourg Empire* required, even as they sundered the ties of Empire itself.

Those fools could give chase, but without reliable comm links, the Imperial Fleet could never coordinate the complex movements necessary to net him.

His task appeared to be nearly complete, after a navigation feat for the ages, crossing nearly a fifth of the galaxy itself to be here, now, in order to teach these barbarians what it meant to respect a border and their civilized neighbors.

The *Lord of Winter* cared little for what you did in your own little mountain valley. When it spilt out and threatened to upset *The Holding*, you must needs be chastised.

Hopefully, like a young dog, these Imperials could be trained.

And there was the crux of it.

The *Lord of Winter's* deal was to support the Usurper, Dittmar, in the hopes that his spleen would be satisfied venting on another of the rabble on the fringe, something called *Aquitaine*.

Nobody expected the traitorous fool to actually honor his word for any period of time. Another could be found to replace him, if the time came.

Either *Fribourg* would learn, or it would be erased from history. Thus had the *Lord of Winter* commanded.

And now, the Usurper was already challenged for his supremacy.

Vrin was not a student of the fringe cultures, but he did understand that this particular one believed in gender-based aristocracies. A distinctly visible mark of their backwardness that they felt females incompetent by their biological nature.

Vrin watched the video transmission again, with a running translation across the bottom. He did not need the words. What he wanted was the emotional lading. The surety underneath. The rage. The fears.

Those tones were there, if you closed your eyes and listened to the odd, flat way both women spoke, barely shifting their voice up or down the scale. Such a strange, a-tonal language.

"Imperial citizens," the first woman spoke with a heavy tone that threatened to crack with emotion. "It has dawned a terrible day in the history of the *Fribourg Empire*. A usurper has attacked the throne and imprisoned the Emperor, my father. As the traitor has also captured my brother and my sister, the Imperial duties must, of needs, fall on my shoulders, by law and custom, making me your Emperor in duty, at least until my father can be freed from captivity."

Yes, a young woman, as she appeared. Apparently the youngest child of the ruling family, not yet even considered an adult, at an age when Vrin had already been a promising deck hand.

She was overwhelmed by the day.

"Furthermore, our enemies have chosen to strike on this very day, killing both sailors defending us and innocent civilians on the ground." More emotions, harder, but brittle. Wrought iron, rather than damascene steel. "This will not stand. I have taken the Imperial Robes. My first act as your Emperor is to appoint Admiral Jessica Keller as supreme commander of the Imperial Fleet for the duration of the emergency. You will follow orders from her as if from me. Treason will not be tolerated. Admiral Keller?"

A pause as the camera panned across the deck.

The other woman was a generation older. More composed. More sure.

A Director used to executive power, but riding today atop the restless tiger's gender-based aristocracy. She could not simply command these men. She must seduce them with guile into following her into battle.

"Captains of the Imperial Fleet," the one called Keller spoke. "You know me. I have given my oath to the new Emperor, and I give you my oath now that we will protect *St. Legier* together. Further orders are forthcoming, but all vessels are expected to follow my commands without hesitation or question. You will stay on your current stations and defend the planet. If you cannot accept those terms, you have no place in this institution and I expect you to turn over command to a subordinate who is willing to take my orders. This is not negotiable. Now, all hands to battle stations."

Vrin opened his eyes as the recording ended. He had heard what he needed to know.

Both women were putting on a brave front, what historians used to call *playing to the galleries*, but neither had the surety to move the men commanding other vessels, these male Captains, into a place their culture had left them ill-equipped to grasp.

"Crew Advocate," Vrin began ritually. "Define your place."

"We are prepared, Director."

"Entity Advocate," Vrin continued. "Speak for your charge."

"He is at the top of the scale in all dimensions, Director."

"War Advocate," Vrin concluded. "One final charge, and then home. Prepare your lance and your shield."

"We are victory, Director."

Vrin's chair did not lean back more than a few degrees. Nonetheless, he slouched a touch, letting his muscles relax from the rigid solidity that had held him for the last two hours.

Games of cat and mouse were never fun for the rodent. One false step, one bad calculation, would see *Dancer In Darkness* accidentally land amidst a squadron of vessels powerful enough to annihilate him before he could recharge the Capriole Drive and flee. Fifteen such leaps had just been that many more chances that something would go wrong.

Now, one lone vessel had challenged him across the field of battle.

A Battleship, no doubt, but one badly out of position, without support, and bereft, its only consort some manner of alien carrier platform. And even that was badly ordered, a score of mismatched gnats remaining around the consort in a loose, globular formation, vessel and craft all well removed and somewhat distant from the warship that had raised the Imperial standard and threatened to undo all Vrin's labors today.

The War Advocate plotted several options for him on a screen. Most

Directors would instinctively jump into a rear, flanking corner when making an attack run like this. They would pass over or under their suddenly-damaged foe and then prepare to escape.

Few considered that such a path inevitably brought them into the range and arc of the big, slow cannons that *Fribourg* seemed to prefer on their capital vessels.

Others would cross directly on the beam, crossing its T.

That risked spending the most time within reach of the most weapon installations.

Vrin's War Advocate was among the best, the shrewdest. Vrin had brought the man's career along as quickly as his student could absorb the lessons of the great masters of maneuver: Sun Tzu, Musashi, Kublai, Burke.

His projected course brought them out of their jump right above the bow of the Battleship, traveling down the ship's centerline at high speed, passing up and over, where the usual design for such a vessel left the cannons with a slight downward tilt. Not much, but eight to ten seconds difference at that speed before passing out of their firing arcs. No time for the Imperial to get off a second shot, even if he was prepared enough to fire his first.

Plus, if they were lucky on the first shot of the Mauler, they might rupture enough of the weapon turrets fore to allow them to come back for a second pass, once the great beast was rendered toothless and blind.

He felt like a single panther hunting a mammoth. It was truly a shame he had been unable to bring an entire pack of wolves with him.

Vrin nodded to his disciple with a warm smile. Truly, a genius move. Abrupt. Decisive. Potentially game-changing.

"Engage."

CHAPTER L

DATE OF THE REPUBLIC NOVEMBER 8, 398
ABOARD AMSEL, ABOVE ST. LEGIER

Jessica studied a map projection of the surface of *St. Legier* with a guilty twinge in her soul.

How many times had she dreamed of doing this? Of flying her flag in the skies above this planet, watching bombs shatter its defenses, as a final step towards bringing down an Empire?

And here she was now, trying to stop it. Trying to uphold both an Emperor and an Empire.

Obviously, the Creator has a supremely black sense of humor.

Eighteen scramjet bombs had fallen on the fringes rather than the cities, just reinforcing her opinion of the nature of the attack.

To cross that much empty space and launch a surprise bombing raid, and then do so little actual damage.

She had a powerful realization as she watched. Apparently, it showed on her face, as well.

"What is it?" Casey demanded in a fierce whisper.

"That commander over there understands *2218 Svati Prime*," she said back, loud enough that Emshwiller, Saar, and a number of other men close by could hear her.

Casey gave her a confused look, but Saar nodded with an angry grimace similar to hers.

"Where it all started for me, Your Majesty," Jessica continued. "We got your fleet's attention by raiding a frontier world and dropping a gigantic bomb on the place. Ours did barely any damage."

"Physical damage, Admiral," Saar corrected her.

"Correct," Jessica agreed. "The psychological effect staggered the entire Empire. Captain Wald asked me why we would do something like that, but he had been thinking of it in military terms. It is the same here."

"So *Buran* is doing this to move an Empire?" Casey asked.

"Not *Buran*, Your Majesty," Jessica replied. "Dittmar."

"But why?" the Emperor's face grew clouded and confused. "We're already at war with *Buran*, even if it is far away."

"What better way to rouse a population?" Saar interjected. "It is rumored that Admiral Dittmar did not want the Peace with *Aquitaine*. If he has accused the Emperor, excuse me, your Father, Your Majesty, of treason, it would not be hard to convince the population that *Aquitaine* was at the root of it, given that several officers of the Republic are here being celebrated at the highest levels."

"And tomorrow, we are at war again," Casey said. "Jessica, if we fail, we'll have undone everything my father and Uncle Em worked so hard to accomplish. I'm sorry."

Jessica fixed the young Emperor with a steely eye.

"I don't plan to lose, Emperor," she growled. "If I have to shatter the entire Imperial Fleet to make my point today, to have peace in the wake of this coup, that is the price that I must take to my grave."

At what price peace?

Today, perhaps, everything.

"Captain Saar," Jessica began. "This vessel is brand new and had just passed her Builder's Trials with flying colors. I will need you to use her up entirely in the next hour."

"Admiral?" he looked askance at her.

Jessica turned to glance at Emshwiller as well, including him in the orders she was about to give.

At what price, peace?

"*Amsel*, and *Kali-ma*, are to uncouple and override all of the interlocks and safety features on every beam installation," Jessica ordered in a heavy, almost primal voice. "When that vessel arrives, everyone who can bear is to immediately open fire, without orders. Further, they are to continue to fire everything they have, up to and including the overload and destruction of the weapon itself or the generators behind it, on my authority. Both warships are new, but I expect to age them a decade today. Both can go back to drydock tomorrow, if we are successful."

Saar and Emshwiller both nodded soberly and relayed her orders.

Casey grew a little white around the edges, jaw clenched and lips pursed, eyes straight ahead.

Silence descended on the bridge as they waited for *Buran* to make his next move.

"Alert," a man's voice called in a warm tenor tone. "The Raider has jumped. Repeat, the Raider has jumped."

Jessica could feel it in her bones.

"All hands, stand by to receive a charge," she ordered in a voice that didn't waver.

CHAPTER LI

It was a weird way to fight a battle, by any standards *Wiley* had ever studied or experienced.

In a classical engagement, like *Fribourg* and *Aquitaine* had routinely fought, one squadron dropped into space and marched down into the gravity well to fight, with the loser fleeing back up and out.

This felt more like how *Corynthe* did it. Pirates waiting outside in the darkness, with every bit of stealth they could arrange.

Someone would drop out of JumpSpace and slowly bring everything on-line.

If you were a pirate, you snuck up on him and caught him from behind, like chasing a cute boy and grabbing his ponytail when you got close enough.

If you were the Law, you did the same thing, for the same reason, but got to be the good guys in the eyes of the population, stopping those pirates and hauling them off to jail.

Here, Jessica had apparently chosen the worst of both worlds.

The *Blackbird* was sitting a little inside that zone that would generally kick a ship out of JumpSpace. She couldn't jump herself without ruining the tune on her sails, but someone coming at her at full speed would be able to leap away fairly quickly, even without the weird jump drives *Buran* was using.

Kali-ma, for instance.

And *Wiley* was protecting a high flank.

Amsel was traveling in a counter-clockwise orbit, looking down on the planet's northern pole. *Kali-ma* was above, behind, and off to starboard, on Jessica's orders, right at the edge of the JumpSpace line.

But just outside it.

Around her, the whole Flight Wing held station with both vessels, a cloud of angry mosquitos, but they were orbiting around *Kali-ma*, rather than *Amsel*.

They should have been orbiting both. Plus, they were laid out all wrong for a standard engagement.

Wiley smiled, imaging the thought processes of the other guy.

It almost looked like she and Jessica were amateurs, here.

They would never be so sneaky as to be luring the guy in, or anything.

Normally, the Combat Team was on point, twelve mixed *Uglies* with beam weapons and minimal shields, at best. Today, they were back aft, a girdle of mice circling an elephant like tiny moons.

In their place, *Eel* and the other three boys of the Heavy Team were surfing *Kali-ma*'s bow wave. These were the bigger craft, frequently two-man jobs designed to crack shields and heads interchangeably, led by the craziest pilot in the Navy.

At least until the Twins had joined.

Rocket Frog and *Neon Pink* had redefined crazy in their own ways. With any luck, their brand of crazy would be just what was needed today.

Actually, with any luck, the alien would decide discretion was the better part after all the damage he had done, facing all this firepower, and disappear forever, letting the Imperials sort their own shit out.

Wiley didn't believe that for a moment.

Still, how many people got to serve under both a Queen and an Empress?

"Commander," Himura's voice broke into her reverie. "Orders from the Flag."

A chime indicated the message on her board. She opened it and read the implications, keying a comm back to Engineering.

Erik Doležal appeared on her small screen.

"Boss?" he asked, looking up from whatever he was doing.

"Orders from Jessica," she replied, sending the message along.

A moment passed.

"That's gonna be expensive," he muttered, mostly to himself.

"Empire's paying," *Wiley* replied. "Or we're running like hell for home and trying to convince the Republic to pay when we pull in there with news. Make it happen quick."

A thought struck her, lost in all the excitement up until now.

"Speaking of which," she pressed a series of buttons to close this comm and open an intership relay.

Galen Estevan appeared on a screen.

"*Wiley*, what's the news?" he asked in a breezy voice that masked the man's hard-driving demeanor. Nobody had shared anything useful with him, even over secured channels.

Galen was tall in that family, a man of average height when Uly and the twins were so much shorter than average. Galen's wife, Kara, was another short one, making Galen look like a giant, half a head taller than the rest and still two or three centimeters short of *Wiley*'s height.

"Jessica thinks it's going to happen shortly," she replied. "I might suggest you get your ass and *Marco Polo* out of the gravity well. If it goes bad, we're going to have to bug out, and I don't look forward to having to get to Republic space without fresh coffee."

"Glad to know my place in your universe, *Kali-ma*," he laughed at her. "Remind me to buy a battlecruiser to fly when we get home, so you can haul cargo for me, next time."

Wiley laughed back. Galen flew *Marco Polo* because the tiny, cargo-carrying Mothership could go anywhere, cheap, and serve even the smallest colonies amazingly profitably.

He probably could afford to build a battlecruiser, if he wanted. The man had learned money from Uly Larionov, after all.

"Deal," she said, closing the channel.

It might be interesting, seeing what a *Corynthian* ship yard could do along those lines, if they went away from the basic Mothership design that had been their bread and butter for so many generations.

"*Wiley*," Himura called. "Bad guy just jumped."

"Flight Wing," *Wiley* called into the open push. "Everyone shut it down and roll on your gyros right now. If this is it, you have about five seconds to be in position. Light Wing, prepare for phase two."

She didn't bother to wait for their answers.

Yan had *Kali-ma* lined up on a parallel track with the *Blackbird*, rolled over on her side. From here, he could bring every single of the five Type-3's to bear: all four blades and the stinger on the tail. It was a great deal of firepower for *Corynthe*.

Nothing compared to what the Imperials could bring to the table, but it might be enough.

She would settle for letting loose with all the hounds of hell right now. Combined with *Amsel* and the flight wing, it might be enough.

She would know, shortly.

CHAPTER LII

Vrin felt *Dancer In Darkness* almost shiver in excitement as he rose from the dark depths of otherspace to rend this new foe. The Entity recognized the value of this last run, at least as much as his crew did.

Already today, they had shaken an Empire, even one as barbaric as *Fribourg*.

Now, they might manage to slay an Emperor.

The jump seemed to stretch into an eternity, when a run on the Capriole Drive over this short of a distance usually flashed by too quickly to notice.

Shudder.

Realspace.

Vrin felt like Jonah, confronting the whale.

A Roughshark was built on a much smaller hull than his foe, the base design itself a modification of the Mako. *Fribourg* might call it a light cruiser, if it was possible to make such an equivalence.

Facing him, passing beneath as Vrin saw the stars again, an Imperial Battleship. Twice as wide, almost three times as long.

Well-matched opponents, when Vrin could do this.

"Fire the Mauler," Vrin commanded calmly.

A firehose of energy erupted from *Dancer In Darkness*'s mouth, that hollow spot at the center of the three tines that housed the beam weapons forward.

Against the gray hull of the beast, the blanket of energy looked almost pink in hue, a salmon fleeing madly from the shark's closing jaws.

His own hull hummed with the furious release of batteries and generators emptying as rapidly as they could without melting.

Vrin could only imagine the sound aboard the Battleship.

He had never been the victim of a Mauler, to hear the sound of metal tearing, the whistle of air suddenly free to escape into the vacuum of deep space.

To listen to a warship dying, even one that had never been truly alive in the first place.

He imagined it as the dying bellow of a gutted whale.

The massive beast beneath him had been apparently surprised, even as she made herself a tempting target. Not one of the big cannons fired as he traversed the top of her hull. Only the lesser beams appeared to have any preparations to fight.

Still, at this point, it was the rest of the suite that would hurt, because something was wrong.

Imperial warships fought predictably.

Slow, staccato bursts of energy designed to wear him down, like a river content to cut a new bank.

As Vrin watched the incoming pulses of light sparkle and vanish into the First Stage Exciters, he finally understood the importance, the value of placing the older woman in charge.

She had done something new, in a star nation that valued conservatism of thought and action over all else.

She had understood the stakes, and the timing.

The ship below him fired far more rapidly than any Imperial he had ever seen.

There would be time for only one tilting pass, armored knights charging one another with energy lances poised and shields held close.

No tournament this, passing with a single blow and then lining up for the next shot.

No, she was intent on hitting him with as much energy as she could, hoping to overload him before he could escape.

But even an Imperial Battleship lacked that capacity. Not in the few seconds *Dancer In Darkness* would be close enough to rend.

"Director, we are taking fire from the escort and his attendants," the War Advocate called with a taut voice.

Yes, he could see that.

They had not bothered with missiles. There would be no time. Nor the slow, over-powered cannons.

And the escort should not be able to hit his shielding this accurately. Not from that distance.

They had done something to change the focus on their main beams.

Worse, both vessels were firing everything at a rate that would risk burning out the weapons themselves out in the few seconds while this combat yet raged.

Never had an Imperial vessel been so profligate, so reckless.

It was an unwelcome revolution in naval warfare, if *Fribourg* and his allies were beginning to fight like the *Lord of Winter*.

Short. Fast. Hot.

Worse, while *Dancer In Darkness* was equipped with such rapid-firing weapons, but they could barely range on the Battleship. He might as well throw rocks at the distant escort.

The effect would be similar.

And then the little craft, the things called Starfighters, fired again.

Not as a wave of random pulses, as he had expected.

No, they had held to some private command, pivoted until every tiny fish was suddenly facing him, and fired in unison.

"War Advocate," Vrin called sharply. Sharper than he intended. "Can we hold?"

That much energy, that rapidly, might actually overload the First Stage Exciters. At this engagement range, *Dancer In Darkness* would be annihilated, unable to charge the batteries fast enough to prevent catastrophic overload.

"I think so," the man said tersely.

Vrin had never seen Ro Malar Arga Rues unsure.

But they had never been here, either.

On one screen, the countdown until the Capriole Drive was recharged and they could leap to safety.

On another, the rising, red tide as the First Stage Exciters filled, like a bucket left out in the rain.

Only they would face death, and not simply a spill on the floor, when the crimson reached the top.

Vrin felt his breath grow shallow as adrenaline pulsed.

Never had he come so close to death.

Others had failed, their Entities and crew unable to react rapidly enough to achieve success.

Dancer In Darkness had never failed him.

And he had never failed the Entity.

He would not fail today, either.

The Capriole Drive signal turned green on the screen.

Dancer In Darkness shuddered once as he twisted space and slipped away into the night.

On the other screen, high tide struck and began to recede.

Less than two percent of the bucket remained empty, death averted by the thinnest edge of the blade.

But averted nonetheless.

In six seconds, they would drop into a hollow spot. Safety, clear down at the edge of the planet's atmosphere, the last place anyone would expect them. And then, a brief respite to recuperate and flee into the deep darkness.

Something had changed. *Fribourg* had up-ended warfare itself.

The *Lord of Winter* needed to be warned.

CHAPTER LIII

DATE OF THE REPUBLIC NOVEMBER 8, 398
ABOARD AMSEL, ABOVE ST. LEGIER

Jessica thought she had prepared for an aggressive foe. As her triangular-hulled adversary dropped back into space, she understood that she had planned too small.

The image that crossed her imagination in that moment truly was a shark emerging from the depths to strike a swimmer in coastal waters.

Except this swimmer was a whale, and woefully unprepared.

"All guns fire," someone yelled.

It might have been her. Or Emshwiller. Perhaps Saar.

Maybe *Amsel* herself.

The Battleship rumbled like a small avalanche picking up speed at the top of the hill as her gunners let loose a torrent of hellish energy.

And then dust and bangs as every screen went blank.

Jessica would not have believed survivors later, had she not been here at this moment.

Had not seen electricity physically arc between metal bulkheads and humans close by, even this deep inside the great beast.

Had not watched a man be knocked across the room, still strapped into his chair, as it torqued under some unimaginable load that ripped it loose from the deck and cast it and him sideways into a bulkhead.

The Mauler.

"Medical teams to the bridge," Jessica yelled as she took it all in.

Captain Saar's command station had landed closest to her, so she disconnected her safety harness and raced to his side as the noise began to settle. At least the gravplates had held.

"Corbeil," she continued, waiting for the Executive Officer to turn her direction. "Saar's injured. Take command."

He blinked, absorbed the situation, and turned back to the rest of the room.

"All guns, continue firing as long as you have a weapon and a target," he commanded. "Damage control teams have priority on every deck."

Jessica understood that her value right now was in not being seen. Not by these men.

She had prepared them for this attack, as much as anyone could. Gotten them mentally into a place where they could return fire, surprised as they were by the ferocity of the foe they faced.

Now she needed to let them do their jobs. If she understood *Buran's* tactics from the file she had absorbed, he wouldn't be here long anyway. A quick flit in, and then another hop away.

The same as he had been doing for however long it had been today.

Saar's heart was beating as she put a hand on his neck, even if his eyes didn't focus on her. His hair was even beginning to settle back down, static discharging itself into the deck.

He started to lurch upright, and Jessica's weight was barely enough to hold him in place.

A moment later, an Emperor appeared at her side and added her own mass.

Jessica heard the man growl, low and deep, a naval officer to his deep core, unwilling to miss a battle, even one he couldn't follow any longer.

"Rafferty," Jessica commanded. "Stay put. You're injured. Corbeil has command."

That seemed to get through to the man.

Jessica felt his tense muscles begin to relax under her fingers.

A moment later, a man appeared on her other side, sliding into place on his knees.

"Admiral," the medic said calmly. "Your Majesty. We've got him."

Jessica lurched upright and looked around, giving Casey a hand up as well, as two other men began to treat their injured commander.

There was smoke in the air.

Not much.

The smell of a cooking circuit someplace close, rather than an insulating wrap igniting.

Dust jarred from cracks and seams hung heavily as the air systems strove mightily to suck it away from human lungs.

The voices and hums and pings had fallen largely silent as Jessica took notice.

"Commander Corbeil," Jessica called out, still the Admiral on her deck. "What is our status?"

"Intact, I think, Admiral," the man replied, looking at his screens. "Could have been much worse. Navigation, flank speed. Get us somewhere else before he can come back for more. Any heading, ahead full."

Up front, the pilot acknowledged the command and began rapidly pushing buttons on his various consoles to turn the big beast and dive to deeper waters.

Somewhere out there, the shark had disappeared back into the depths, lurking.

Jessica had goaded him, that *Buran* commander. Waved the shamrock-colored Imperial flag in his face like a red cape before a bull.

Amsel had nearly paid the price. She could see that on her screen. The newly minted Battleship had suffered greatly, from the sounds of various damage control parties furiously cutting, pasting, and welding to get the ship back to readiness.

"Admiral," Corbeil called, snapping her eyes from the screen to meet his. "Engines are nearly undamaged. Maneuverability is generally stable."

"Guns?" she asked, knowing that nothing else would matter if the Raider came back for a second pass.

"Better than I expected, sir," the new commander replied.

"Roll to two-four-zero and begin a yaw," Jessica ordered.

She could see the man wanted to ask a question. Demand an explanation. A moment later, he nodded to himself and relayed the command.

They had been thinking two dimensionally, against an enemy moving in three.

It was necessary to throw the invader off his line of attack.

Now, would he come back to finish the job?

CHAPTER LIV

Yan Bedrov had served aboard a warship named *Kali-ma* for most of his twenty-five years in space.

First, under Georges Basserman, and then rising to Second in Command under Ian Zhao.

Before.

He had no other way to describe his life.

Before. After.

Before, when he was a thirty-eight-year-old, dumbass teenager pirate.

A dead-ender happily dead-ending.

Ian Zhao had been a charismatic man, a leader men wanted to emulate and follow. Popular, successful.

For a brief time King of the Pirates.

He would have been a good one, too, as those things went.

But that was before the hurricane known as Jessica.

She wasn't a woman. No, not even a queen.

No, Jessica Keller was a force of nature.

Even *Wiley* was just a determined bad-ass, by comparison.

Before. After.

After Jessica happened, Yan had been forced to grow up, if he wanted a place in this new world. A lot of them had.

Many others had just walked away, or retired, or crawled into a bottle or a gun barrel, unable to cope.

Unwilling to change.

There was no middle ground anymore. Not with Jessica Keller.

There were nights where Yan still woke in a cold sweat, staring up into those eyes from his knees as she approached him, anger radiating off her body like speed lines, still dripping Ian Zhao's blood on the deck.

A monster coming for his soul.

But she hadn't killed him that day. Had taken a chance on him. Several.

She could have just as easily had his head on a pike as Zhao's at any point along the way.

Instead, she had kept him. Promoted him, even, when you considered what she had done to upgrade the battle fleet Yan had served his entire life.

Sent him to *Ladaux* to supervise the construction of her new flagship, a task that left him suited to become *Corynthe*'s Master Builder when he wanted to return to the ground. That was a respected job, especially in the Keller household. Maybe he could give *Pops* Nakamura a run for design aesthetic.

Yan had even been invited to dinner with Jessica's father, himself a Master Builder, and her mother as well, an event arranged under the auspices of the First Lord of the *Aquitaine* Fleet himself.

But even that was something of a before.

Before *Kali-ma*, the new goddess of war.

Before this trip, deep into Imperial space and an unknown future, had changed him.

Before *After*.

After, when he had turned into a grown-up, a knight on a silver steed, rescuing a princess.

And Jessica was here. Now.

Flying under the flag of the *Fribourg Emperor*. Commanding that other woman's fleet. Trying to make the galaxy a better place.

Counting on him to be there when she needed him to be. Saving her ass, after all the times she had saved his. Given him purpose. Given him hope.

Given him place.

Yan popped his shoulders up and back, and then rotated them individually forward.

Stress distracted. And there was just no time for proper yoga to get the body loose.

It would be enough for the mind to come to stillness.

"Pilot," Yan called suddenly, struck by a thought bubbling up from the evil, black depths of his tactical mind. "Roll us up three. Bad guy's coming in high, but tight. He'll buzz the *'bird* and then jump. Centerline me here."

Yan spun the projected image of near space with both hands, like holding a bubble blown by one of his grandsons, and then stuck a hand in and triggered a glowing pulse of red where he wanted things.

"Gun Captains," he continued, triggering the push out to the whole ship anyway, so everyone would know what was coming.

There was nothing worse than sitting in Engineering, or a Wardroom, listening to the ship hum and crackle, with no idea what was happening outside.

Plus, he had personally trained those five men. And only had to break and demote three others out of the way to get the kind of crew he wanted.

Demanded.

The Command Centurion might be in charge.

Tactical Officer fought the ship.

Yan Bedrov drew the lines everyone else toed if they wanted their place here.

Kali-ma was the flagship. If you were going to serve on her, you were going to be the best, but this was a team effort, just like him and *Wiley*. There was no space for ego on a gun deck.

"Center your guns here and prepare to traverse them to port," Yan commanded quietly. "Vector will be unknown on emergence. Use your best judgement. Lowest accuracy rate team buys beer for the top team."

A good dose of competitiveness, on the other hand, was healthy. And it gave the boys an outlet, since dueling and blades were no longer acceptable ways to handle disagreements.

Not after Jessica.

"*Wiley*," the sensors dude called. "Bad guy just jumped."

"Flight Wing," the Command Centurion replied. "Everyone shut it down and roll on your gyros right now. If this is it, you have about five seconds to be in position. Light Wing, prepare for phase two."

Good.

Yan wasn't responsible for the pilots out there. He only had to fight a single ship. And that would take every gram of his attention right now.

He took a deep breath.

The man over there had jumped at least a dozen times so far today.

Those drives were cute, but not all that dangerous. Strategically amazing, but still tactically predictable.

If you were paying attention. Or angry.

Or protecting the life of the woman who had turned you into someone your grandkids could be proud of.

"All guns, commence firing now," Yan ordered.

There was nothing in that spot but hollow space, suddenly filled with pulses of energy as the modified, long-range Type-3's Moirrey had gifted them with fluoresced against tiny wisps of atmosphere, even at this altitude.

In any other circumstances, folks over on the *Blackbird* would throw a hissy-fit right now about how close his shots were trailing above them.

Tough luck, buddy.

Pause. Breathe.

Shark.

Got you, bastard.

Almost on cue, bad guy popped into existence, barely more than a ship length away from the center of Yan's targeting circle, flying right into the hornet's nest of heavy beams.

You're good, buddy, but you were never a pirate.

"Pilot," Yan ordered. "Roll me down left and yaw hard upwards."

Kali-ma was still a cruiser-class warship. She couldn't dance on her axis like the killer bees around her, but she had been designed by someone who expected crazy maneuvering in tight quarters. Her gyros could do some amazingly stupid things, in the hands of a man crazy enough to try.

Downrange, the Raider lit up like a winter tree briefly.

It was weird, watching all that energy disappear. Normally, you hammered on a guy's shields and it was like watching sparks flair off or water splash. Here, everything just faded, sucked into whatever the hell those guys used, like water poured over sand.

Still, there was only so much sand to suck up that much water. He and Jessica could still drown that asshole, if he stayed around long enough. Science Officer was tracking with every ear and eyeball he could bring to bear.

Hopefully, it would be enough.

Around him, the bridge lights went dim as every single beam, even the little, defensive Type-1's on both flanks, let loose with everything they had. Generators on every deck were already overheating. Cooling systems would be laboring for hours to bring it all back to green. There was no spare juice for anything.

Not for the next however many seconds he had until the other guy could move clear and escape Yan's wrath.

Just as quickly, empty space.

And not the kind of emptiness you got when some stupid mook exploded, either.

Nope, gone.

"All guns cease fire," Yan yelled, reaching out and tripping an override that would cut them out of the firing loop anyway.

It was an eerie calm.

The lights came back up to normal. The air system had apparently shut down briefly, because fans kicked on again and there was a breeze with a hint of staleness underneath that he could taste.

But the bastard got away.

Blackbird looked like street pizza right now. Hopefully, everyone was okay, but that wasn't his responsibility right now. Tactical Officer stayed inside the hull.

Wiley was a big girl. She knew her shit.

"Got him," the Science Officer practically sang as his sensors located the Raider. "Transmitting now."

"Strike team," *Wiley* channeled calmness. "Phase Two."

Yan leaned back and let go a heavy sigh.

Yeah, you got away from me, buddy. And Jessica.

You still haven't gotten away.

CHAPTER LV

DATE OF THE REPUBLIC NOVEMBER 8, 398
ABOVE ST. LEGIER

Rocket Frog* had actually stopped firing a few seconds early. At this range, her Type-1's were a joke. Instead, she had sent a text-only comm to her sister on their private channel.

Neon Pink had stopped firing almost at the same instant anyway.

Outsiders were always surprised when the two of them thought so much alike. Insiders knew better.

Gustav just always assumed that whatever he told one of them would instantly be transmitted via telepathy to the other one.

It wasn't really instant.

Silent now, Saša took a moment to spin her little knife back to center on the gyros before red-lining her engines. Somewhere close, Asra was doing the same thing. There wasn't much time to do this, not if they wanted to do it right.

"Strike team," *Wiley* channeled calmness over the airwaves. "Phase Two."

A file popped open on a side screen, showing her a destination and making the first, rough cut at a flight vector calculation.

Saša was the artist with the welding laser and grinding wheel who tended to lead. Asra had always been the nerdy one who did math. But the compact Starfighter known as *The Rocket Frog* was centered and accelerating, with her sister in *The Neon Pink* hanging tight on her right back corner. Just like the training runs on asteroids and dipshits.

And Gustav.

Two identical arrows in flight, a tiny flight cockpit with a weak gun on the front, generator and jump drive behind her, and two huge engine pods on the sides. Underneath, the payload.

The *Buran* Raider had been in place for thirty-three seconds engaging on this pass. Considering the amount of fire he had been taking, Saša baselined that as the fastest he could jump again. That gave her and Asra nineteen seconds and counting.

Piece of cake. Every variable they could plan ahead was already in the difference engine, just waiting for the last numbers and the lever to be locked down before some crazy chick lit a jump drive inside a gravity well and expected the machine to take her where she demanded.

Raider had obviously thought he was being cute, going down so deep. None of the warships would usually risk coming so low after him, where atmosphere might grab them as they went by and make their flight an adventure.

And you sure as hell didn't light a Primary pointed at an inhabited planet you liked. Even this one.

So. Mouth pointed forward. Three tentacle-looking towers on the triangular corners up front, with probably more on the flanks and something aft, like her Mothership.

Saša plotted a high-speed pass at an even-crazier angle, locked the gears on the drive into place, and waited.

"*Neon Pink*, transmitting," she called, letting Asra and the rest of everybody know they were in motion and riding to the rescue.

Asra already had the same primary settings. It took her all of two more seconds to set the rest and blink a green light back at her.

Computers did stupid things when you bounced in and out of JumpSpace so quickly. Lost their bearings, sometimes their marbles.

Too much risk of something drifting out of alignment when a servo went wonky.

Pops had solved that by going old school. An honest-to-Creator Difference Engine, a box of gears assembled out of super-lightweight alloyed components, bulky, but actually lighter than a small jumpsail would've been.

Ya scrolled yer wheels on the doohickey by your right hand, and steam-age-looking teeth underneath came into alignment with the stellar age.

"Three, two, one," *Rocket Frog* called the cadence. "Gone."

Push the big red button and do the impossible.

Blink.

Back.

Gotcha.

The Rocket Frog was in lawn-dart mode right now. Straight down. Engines wide open.

And right there was the ugliest shark she had ever seen, trying to hide down in the rocks and reefs, all casual and sneaky and stuff.

Saša glanced over her right shoulder just enough to confirm that her awesome doppelgänger sister was along for the fun, and then pushed the engines to the last stop, afterburners leaving it all on the table this time.

"Weapons lock," *Neon Pink* called, setting the table.

"Confirmed," *Rocket Frog* answered. "Three, two, one, shoot."

You could only pull a stunt like this with someone after you had developed a semi-telepathic link. Shared wombs were strange places.

Four thumbs detached from flight yokes in perfect harmony. They each traveled inward two centimeters to find four red buttons, rested briefly on them, and pushed extra-hard to overcome built-in friction.

Contact opened four circuits, connecting four solenoids underneath a matched pair of identical lawn-darts diving towards an ugly, triangular shark, at ludicrous and accelerating speeds.

Four Type-3 Archerfish warheads on rails fired as one. Two more Type-1's on the centerlines between them joined the chorus, mostly because they didn't want to be left out.

But every little bit helped.

CHAPTER LVI

Vrin drew a heavy breath.

Dancer In Darkness had emerged from his jump as deep as the Entity had considered safe, and even that was lower than Vrin would have commanded, in any other circumstances.

At this altitude, the upper edges of the planet's atmosphere brushed up against the naked metal of the hull, a rasp like occasional grains of sand on wheels.

The First Stage Exciters were critical. Even background radiation, the warm solar wind itself, might tip them over into a cascading failure right now.

Dancer In Darkness had never been so close to the edge.

"Entity Advocate," Vrin commanded calmly. "Begin charging all banks."

"It will be so, Director," she replied in a tight voice that betrayed her own stress levels.

"War Advocate," he continued. "Normally, I would authorize weapon's fire to draw off the extra energy we will not need, but right now, that might engender return fire from someone. Even outside of range, they might be too dangerous. Lock down all weapons systems and prepare to run silent."

"Acknowledged," the man who had just fought the greatest battle in their lifetime responded. He toggled a number of switches as Vrin watched.

Vrin took the moment to pull the second bottle of cold tea from its holder and deployed the nipple. Otep always made sure he had two, knowing that he would hoard the first, drawing it across an entire battle slowly, before emptying the second when the excitement finally died down.

Truly, that woman understood him as no other person he had ever known. It was a pity that the *Lord of Winter* had forbidden them any romance.

Vrin made a note to tell her how much he appreciated her constant efforts, once they were safely away in deep space and could dock with the *Energiya Module* to go home.

"Warning," a young man's tenor voice spoke suddenly. "Enemy vessels incoming."

It took Vrin a moment to place the sound. The Entity spoke to the general crew so infrequently.

Only when it was critical did he talk to everyone.

Vrin spun the screen until he saw the attack.

Two of the Starfighters had just emerged from a Capriole Drive-style jump, deeper inside a gravity well than any Imperial ship had ever attempted, let alone managed.

"War Advocate," Vrin yelled madly. "Engage."

There was time for Vrin to see Ro Malar Arga Rues press the first button on his console, and then the two tiny craft fired.

Vrin tasted time slow to almost nothing.

No. Not nothing. He had just run out.

Four beams struck like lightning bolts from the heavens above.

The First Stage Exciters caught the first beam and absorbed it, pushing the red bucket to ninety-nine point seven percent full.

The second beam arrived a step later and struck. Amazingly, the red bucket managed to go to one hundred and one point three percent.

A third beam, a beat later, and the upper grid of the First Stage Exciters collapsed. There was time to watch it rupture like a soap bubble on a calm day.

All of the energy contained in the grid flooded backwards through the housing, a white hot plasma eating the hull like a riptide chasing sand as the fourth beam struck raw metal.

Dancer In Darkness screamed in sudden pain. Mercifully, the Entity died a moment later.

Around him, Ro Kenzo Atep Vrin felt the ship explode.

And then darkness.

CHAPTER LVII

Vo felt safer surrounded by a score of hard men in drab street clothes. One of the teams had even produced a pocket beam pistol suited to a woman's hand for Moirrey.

She had insisted on taking point with Corporal Danville as they moved. He hadn't grumbled aloud, but Vo had watched the man's body language turn into a sulk.

For about five minutes.

Danville had brightened up considerably when he realized that she was apparently at least as good at forest craft as he was.

Vo still wasn't sure, however, what she meant when she referred to the rest of them as watch geese.

Not that it mattered.

The deer and other creatures had vanished into the depths of the woods. Only the occasional rabbit was about, immediately bounding into cover when Vo's team approached.

"Sir, they've arrived," somebody close whispered.

Vo and most of the group had been strung out in little groups, oozing slowly along various trails in the trees, resting and waiting while Danville and Moirrey broke trail. Nobody knew what kind of security they might run into. Imperial Security troops would be better armed, but not better trained.

But a firefight in the game park would ruin everything, so they had to move like thieves in the night.

Vo nodded to the man who had spoken.

"Everyone hold here," he said. "I'm going to check it out."

Being in charge meant that some decisions were on his shoulders, even as skilled and independent as these men, and woman, were.

Cost of wearing that uniform, he supposed, even if he was only supposed to be an Honorary Colonel. He was still the officer these men had chosen to follow.

Up front, Moirrey, Danville, and Street were clustered at the base of a red brick wall, ancient and heavy, covered in places with ivy that looked tough, but wasn't strong enough for a man to actually climb. Roughly five meters tall, it stretched out of sight in either direction.

They were squatted down, so Vo did the same.

"Situation?" he asked.

How many other officers would demand to have an opinion here, because they were supposed to be in charge? Not the good ones. Not the Fleet Centurion. But he had served under a few.

And nobody here was a rookie.

Street pointed to his right.

"Nearest gate should be roughly two hundred meters that way, sir," he said. "Access for gardeners and rangers. One hundred percent chance it's wired. Fifty percent chance there's a live guard close with a radio."

"I see," Vo replied as a placeholder.

This was probably one of those places where everyone was better off with him not asking the obvious follow-up question.

"How do we get over the wall?" he asked instead.

Danville grinned, as if Vo had passed some test in the man's head.

Maybe he had.

"Brick's rough enough, Colonel," the tiny assassin said. "I can get up and over easy enough. There's rope somewhere on the team. That gets us all inside."

"Is gonna be wired fer stupid, Hans," Moirrey chirped quietly. "Is what I woulda done."

Danville grinned huge back at her, like two teenage siblings committing rivalry.

"Gosh," he said. "Do we know any engineers who could possibly bypass and disable dangerous security systems?"

"Very funny, watch goose," she replied. "I'm not a rock-climber, thank-ye-very-much. How's y'suppose I'm'a do that?"

"I'll lift you," Vo said quietly.

Moirrey turned on him with a look of utter surprise.

She studied him for a second, but didn't say anything. Then she nodded with a half-shrug.

"Rights," she muttered. "Let's does it, then."

She stood and the men joined her.

From a thigh pocket Vo hadn't noticed before, she pulled a small multi-tool of some sort and a palm-sized computer.

Vo studied the woman. She was dressed today in heavy, cotton pants with thigh pouches and a sweatshirt of some sort under a light rain shell. Everything was dark, from the coal-black pants to the dark green shell to the navy blue sweatshirt.

"How?" she asked simply.

Vo responded by shifting over onto a small rise close to the brick and catching her by the belt with his left hand. He put a giant paw flat on the grass.

"Stand on my hand," he said.

She did, somewhat awkwardly, and then held rigidly still as Vo stood up and leaned back into the wall.

"Brace yourself," he said, letting go and feeling her lean forward to place a hand on the brick.

Vo lifted his arm slowly. Not because she weighed anything at all. She didn't. Maybe forty-five kilograms. Not fifty.

He pushed his arm straight up over his head, rising up onto his toes to put her as high as he could.

Danville blinked in surprise at what was probably a display of raw strength he hadn't imagined possible, and then attacked the wall himself, going up it like a spider.

Vo shared a grin with Sgt. Street. He was two meters tall in his boots. With another meter of arm in his ape-hangers. Moirrey was only a meter and a half tall, but with the high spot he had picked, that would put her right at the top to peek around.

Vo willed his muscles to iron as Moirrey worked. He could hear Moirrey and Danville whispering back and forth.

"Street," Vo ordered. "Go get the rope Danville was talking about and round everybody up."

The man nodded and jogged out of sight, leaving Vo standing there like a weird piece of Imperial statuary. Fortunately, Moirrey really weighed about as much as a feather.

Sgt. Street returned quickly with half a dozen others silently trailing in his wake.

At a soft whistle from above, Street tossed the coil into the air.

A few moments later, one end dropped to the ground and Moirrey's weight suddenly vanished from Vo's hand. He glanced up to see her scramble up and out of sight, over the wall. Danville waved down and gestured for the men to follow.

Vo went first because he could. No other reason.

Until they needed a decision made that went beyond their own comfort zone, the men of the 189th, and especially Moirrey, could operate independently quite well. He might as well join them.

Vo was pretty sure he was at least as dangerous as most of them. Maybe not Danville and Moirrey.

Then he thought about some of his adventures in the brush on *Thuringwell*.

Yeah, maybe as dangerous as all of them, after all.

Beyond the wall, something changed.

Maybe it was the difference between the rough chaotic nature of the Game Park, and the more-orderly confines of the Palace grounds. Hard to explain, but the air felt different.

Heavier, perhaps.

It wasn't just the vastly overgrown rose bush close at hand on his left, although it helped.

They were committed now.

That was it.

Up until this moment, he and the men could have stayed back. Walked away. Found a bolt hole until everything else was sorted out.

Now, they were on the grounds.

He couldn't see a single building, but they were out there, beyond arbors and paths and orchards. The deciduous trees had gone to winter, but someone had carefully planted a whole bunch of evergreens, both stands of trees and hedges, to break things up.

It was still wild. Contained and pressured to conform, but not a simple park.

And he had invaded it with a score of men and one tiny, dangerous woman.

If something went wrong now, lives would be lost.

"Danville," he murmured. "Find me a sheltered spot to plan out the next steps."

The man nodded rather than answering, fading quickly up a narrow trail made of grayish-green pavers.

"What 'bouts me?" Moirrey sneered. "I coulda dun that."

"We still have to penetrate the palace itself, Moirrey," Vo fired back, keeping his voice above a growl by force of will. "Danville's expendable right now. You aren't."

"Oh…"

Again, that blink of surprise.

He and Moirrey had never really been that close. Jackson Tawfeek was still the guy she went to get coffee with, and gossip, at least when Digger wasn't around.

She still seemed to think of him in terms of the big, dumb killer she had first really met at *Ballard*.

For Vo, two lifetimes ago.

So far.

At least she was willing to open her mind, rather than her mouth.

And she had never commanded troops in the field. Never sent someone to die in enemy fire, distracting enemy gunners so a force of cavalry could slip around and take them from the side.

Never had to write letters home to families.

Vo felt ancient compared to the woman, even when she was a handful of years older.

Her miles hadn't been nearly as hard.

Danville reappeared silently with a nod. He turned, and Vo followed, Moirrey in his wake and the rest of the men behind that.

They came out of the trees into a small space that someone had cleared, and then covered over with a solid roof and concrete floor. Just the sort of place to sit in the winter, when the rains came and you wanted to be outside, but not that much outside.

Vo watched as four of the men detached themselves automatically and took up positions watching outward from the four faces of the space.

He gestured everyone close and kneeled on one knee. Everyone joined him low.

"You men organize into teams based on skillset," Vo began. "I want one back there at the wall, covering our retreat. One needs to scout the gate Sgt. Street pointed out in case we have to transport wounded through it in a hurry. One with a medic stays just outside the Palace when we penetrate. Horst, Danville, Street, Moirrey, and I will break into the place, locate the Emperor, and get him out. Questions?"

There were a few. Mostly technical. Many of these men had at least a decade in service, much of that as experts training younger troopers to do their job. Vo had no reservations about taking any of them into a firefight with Imperial Security, even under-gunned as they were. But that sneakiness wouldn't last any time at all, if they weren't sneaky enough.

Plus, they were already in five rough squads of men, although it was interesting watching them trade members with nothing more than a quick whisper and a nod.

Again, experts.

Competent, hard men.

Vo stood.

He could have done it from his knees, but the energy had taken hold of him like an electric current.

For a moment, he was back on *Thuringwell*, about to charge down into the valley of death to rescue *Gaucho* from the bad guys.

Half a league, half a league, half a league onward…

"We are about to launch an assault on the Imperial Palace," Vo stated his case plainly. "I will expect you to kill your fellow countrymen with no compunction whatsoever, under the orders of a foreigner pretending to be your commanding officer. Even if those men are Imperial Security."

That got a chuckle out of them. As was intended.

"They have taken the Emperor prisoner," Vo continued. "Your Emperor, and not mine, but I swore the same oaths as you did before this started."

He paused to fix them with a hard glare. This was where all that bottled-up anger was going to come out. He couldn't help it.

And didn't care to.

"We are going to teach those bastards the difference between right and wrong," Vo snarled in a quiet voice. "We all signed up to the colors to make the galaxy a better place, a safer place. Some people don't understand that, don't appreciate it. They want a place where the strong rule and the weak cower. I will not allow that. That is not how we work. Gentlemen, mount up."

There was a moment of emptiness to the men around him. Sheer nothingness that separated them from the wider universe around the clearing.

A growl somewhere broke it. Vo wasn't sure who it was, because the others joined it a moment later as the men of the 189ᵗʰ surged to their feet.

Moirrey surprised him the most, by throwing her arms as far around his waist as she could and hugging him fiercely.

By the time he got himself disentangled from the pixie, half the men had vanished, already moving to their positions for the coming assault.

"Danville, take point," Vo ordered as the rest sorted themselves into small groups. "Shoot first."

"Negative, sir," the small man answered, handing his beam pistol to one of the others and drawing a long, skinny shiv from his boot.

It reminded Vo of a skinning knife someone in *Fourth Saxon* had used on a deer they had spooked from cover during a patrol.

Danville met his eyes and they both nodded.

Shoot first was the wrong order to give, if they wanted to do this in relative secrecy. And Danville understood that.

He should have said *kill first…*

CHAPTER LVIII

Somewhere, a deck above and a little forward, Jessica knew that there was a Flag Bridge she could use, so new that most of the screens were still covered with that thin, factory-installed plastic film dockyard crews left in place.

She supposed she should be there, taking the Emperor with her and getting out of everyone's hair here, but she chose to stay put.

Corbeil had things well in hand. Saar had only been mildly injured by the explosion, but was down in Medical right now getting everything checked out. She would probably have to talk to the Chief Surgeon at some point, and see if she would have to order Saar to bed. Nobody else on this ship could.

Besides, these men deserved the honor of this day, regardless of how it turned out. King Gunter Wiegand, *Gunter I*, the first *Fribourg Emperor*, had been the last monarch to lead a warfleet into battle.

Until fate had made it necessary for *Karl VIII*, Kasimira Wiegand, to do the same.

Jessica glanced over at Casey, seated between Marcelle and Willow as if she held Court with two Ladies-in-Waiting at hand.

Casey smiled back, but Jessica could see the rigidity underneath her mask, a seventeen-year-old pretending she knew exactly what she was doing.

In a way, she did.

Casey's job was to be seen. To put a spine in the backs of men who might otherwise be willing to let the situation go.

To let the *coup d'état* happen on their watch without stopping it.

It took a lot of guts to simply stand up and say "No," when everyone else said "Sure, why not?"

Jessica looked forward to her own grand and magnificent Senatorial Court Martial when she got home, regardless of the fact that she was acting here as a private citizen with the explicit approval of that same Senate written down in documents secured on the planet below as well as back home on *Petron*.

She still had enough enemies in *Aquitaine's* Senate. Someone would be baying for her blood.

Jessica simply hoped that Nils, Tadej, and Judit would see her actions in the broader context. If she won today, she might have truly won the war.

That thought suddenly rocked Jessica to her core.

She could win the war. Today. Now.

She looked around the deck with new eyes.

Up until this moment, she had been on the defensive, reacting to circumstances she could not dominate, running across a series of rolling logs and hoping not to be crushed between them on her inevitable misstep.

"Confirmed kill, Admiral," her Science Officer called, or whatever *Fribourg* called the position. "The Raider has exploded. I'm not sure how far out his transport is, but we'll watch for that explosion as well."

Energiya.

A separable transportation module that contained Jump Drives and generators and engines. Designed to be detached before battle, allowing the warships to be amazingly small and compact for their firepower. Especially considering how big the ancient jump drives were.

According to the Imperial file, every single one self-destructed as soon as it got the signal that the *Buran* half of the equation was destroyed. Without fail, as if they were two halves of one being.

Who knew what the Old Gods were capable of?

"Sir?" Corbeil asked suddenly. "How did those two fighter craft manage that attack? I've never even heard of *Aquitaine* being able to do something like that."

Jessica smiled enigmatically back at the man. Neither had she, until she had watched it the first time on her flight out here, but she wasn't about to tell these men.

She still might have to fight them tomorrow.

"That's the *Corynthe* Navy, Commander," she temporized with an enigmatic smile. "Once upon a time, pirates. They see *impossible* as a challenge, Corbeil, not a limit."

"I see," the man replied with a wry smile. "And the *impossible* range on those Type-3's, as well?"

"Your engineers will be able to tell you how, once they study the logs, Commander," she said. "You just have to listen to them, first."

He grinned, rather than replying.

"Comm Officer," Jessica raised her voice to fill the entire bridge. "Order all vessels to stand down and maintain their current station under Imperial authority and my position as Karl VIII's Admiral of the Fleet. Notify me if anyone deviates. Then broadcast our scans of the Raider exploding to the surface. Override every transmitter and every ground station you can. If you had a proper art department on this vessel, I would have them spin us up a quick documentary to ram it all home."

Half the bridge actually turned to look over their shoulders at her, utter befuddlement writ on their faces.

"The War is over, gentlemen," she said with a harsh smile. "Now, it is necessary for us, for you, for them, to win the Peace. And then the Emperor can take back her throne."

That got through to them.

History wasn't over yet.

CHAPTER LIX

IMPERIAL FOUNDING: 176/11/08. DITTMAR PALACE, WERDER, ST. LEGIER

The image was shaky as Sigmund watched.

A scan log, zoomed up until the image itself turned grainy with pixelated distance. *IFV Amsel,* Wachturm's new *Blackbird,* sitting in a trans-gravity orbit as the Roughshark emerged from jump into a fury of defensive fire from Keller's flagship.

Savaging the Battleship with the same Mauler that had heavily damaged the orbital fortress, before then leaping to safety.

Cut.

The *Buran* Raider, now sitting low in orbit after his jump, quietly holding space, with the green and blue marble of *St. Legier* below and the curve of space in the distance.

The shot pulling back until the ship was a triangular, gray knife.

Two unknown, tiny Starfighters *appearing out of thin air* as he watched, racing downhill at full speed and firing simultaneously.

The Raider imploding in a plasma burst rather than exploding, like a soap bubble popping, leaving barely any debris to fall to earth.

Sigmund had turned off the words so he didn't have to hear the woman's voice again. It didn't matter which of them spoke. The rage they engendered would be the same.

He hadn't come this far to fail to a woman. Either woman.

Any woman.

"Security," he yelled as he stood. "I'm going to the Imperial Palace now. Arrange it."

One man, a Lieutenant in Imperial Security livery, looked as though he might argue the point until Sigmund focused his anger on the man like a spotlight.

The fool finally nodded instead, but Sigmund memorized his face and added it to the list in his head entitled *Monday*.

Everything had hinged on holding that fool Karl out of contact while bluffing the Fleet into accepting Sigmund in his place. There were enough Admirals and Captains that would be put out of work by a true Peace with *Aquitaine* that they would have been willing to go along, given a *fait accompli*.

All that had been required of him was to be someplace safe when the day dawned. Someplace remote, but not too remote. Out of the direct action, so nobody could blame him.

Plausible deniability.

It was not my choice, but I have been forced by circumstances to ascend to the throne in this time of need. Anything to save the Empire from chaos.

Around him, all his careful plans were on the verge of falling apart if he didn't act quickly.

He grabbed his mug of coffee and drank the last, cold, bitter dregs from the bottom. Transport would take time.

"Communications," he rasped heavily. "Get me a secured channel to Admiral Bakemann aboard *Adler*."

There were still enough squadrons in orbit to destroy the interlopers, if he could just get them to move.

It would take only one squadron to crystalize the decisions of the rest. They could join him in saving the Empire, or throw their lot in with a pair of women intent on overthrowing the natural order of things.

With nearly forty major warships of various sizes, he had been counting on twenty percent supporting him outright, ten percent opposing him briefly, and seventy percent sitting tight to see which way the solar wind would blow.

A steward came by with fresh coffee.

Sigmund waited briefly while the man refilled his mug, drank half, and then had the man top it up again. At this rate, he would need to urinate profusely in another hour, but that could wait.

Everything could wait until he wore the crown.

"Communications?" Sigmund yelled. "Where is he?"

It had been several minutes. That fool should have been on the line within thirty seconds, especially if he wanted to keep his uniform.

Another one for the Monday list.

"Atmospheric disturbances and electromagnetic echoes are causing communications problems with our satellites, Your Majesty," the man replied in a careful voice, aware that he was the messenger that might be shot. "*Adler* is currently on station on the far side of the planet from us, moving slowly relative to the ground."

"Keep trying," Sigmund snarled.

That doomed Lieutenant from Imperial Security appeared in his line of sight and snapped his heels together smartly, as if professionalism at this point would somehow protect the man.

"The motor pool is prepared, Your Majesty," he said simply, careful to stare at a horizon somewhere over Sigmund's left shoulder.

At least the man realized how thin the ice he was on had gotten.

Sigmund threw himself to his feet. The monitors around him had nothing new. Nothing he wanted to see.

"Send a signal to Grundman," Sigmund commanded. "Tell him to meet me at the palace so we can talk."

At this point, he needed to meet with Grundman personally, and take possession of Karl and the rest of the former Imperial family before anything else slipped through his fingers.

For a moment, Sigmund seriously considered divorcing Karya so he could marry the older daughter. Not the most promising start to his reign, but at a swoop, it invalidated any claim by the younger.

Plus, Stephanya was only nineteen, so she had few legal rights to resist him. She might even be useful to produce a new generation of heirs, to go with the children Karya had borne him. She wasn't an unattractive woman, just far too headstrong and opinionated.

He would enjoy correcting those aspects of her personality, if he chose to keep her alive.

Perhaps that was the easiest path to unifying the Empire.

Kill two Emperors and a Crown Prince, and marry the surviving girl. The current Empress would be easily controlled at that point, perhaps he could even keep her around as some sort of Dowager, along with Karya.

Sigmund smiled at the men around him.

Yes, this would all work out fine.

Now he just had to go shoot his cousins.

CHAPTER LX

DATE OF THE REPUBLIC NOVEMBER 8, 398 IMPERIAL PALACE GROUNDS, WERDER, ST. LEGIER

Vo had never known anything like it to compare. *Anameleck Prime* had a few public parks and former estates preserved like this, but he had grown up in the poor parts of the capital city. Folks like him never got to visit the countryside.

Worse, all this greenery around him literally amounted to someone's backyard, when all was said and done. Kilometers and kilometers of trees and bushes, large and nearly overgrown, but for paths carved here and there.

At least Moirrey and Danville were at home, slowly working their way along, disabling sensors occasionally, marking others for the rest of the group to walk around. It had gotten the team here.

A mild rain had engulfed them at some point. Nothing ugly, just a miserable, thick curtain that hung over everything, filling leaves that would drip onto the top of your head when you brushed them. Still, it would keep everyone else indoors, and hopefully distract those that weren't.

It had helped so far.

Now, they were penultimate, Vo and his team, squatted down on the edge of a grassy clearing.

Before him, the Imperial Palace itself. Or part of it. The residential parts. A horseshoe-shaped courtyard nearly two hundred meters across and five hundred long, formed by parts of four red brick buildings.

There were at least another dozen other buildings beyond these, maybe two dozen. Maps were kinda iffy on the topic and Vo hadn't paid that much attention.

Navin the Black would never let him hear the end of it, not memorizing all the possible terrain. Fleet Centurion would just smirk at him.

But how frequently had he been in a major revolution in a foreign country?

Doesn't matter, punk. Always out-prepare your enemy. Think like the Fleet Centurion.

Vo chuckled to himself, hearing the Dragoon's bass rumbles in his head.

"Sir?" Horst whispered from close by.

Vo smiled at the man.

"Too much time having fun, Edgar," Vo said. "Not enough studying maps in case I needed to assault the Palace. The Fleet Centurion would have been better prepared."

Horst smiled back.

"Aye, sir," he said with a firm nod. "That she would have."

Vo was slightly taken aback by how deeply Keller had become part of *Fribourg*'s culture. That an infantryman from a training division on a remote planet could have that level of surety about the habits of one of their deadliest enemies was an interesting development.

Was that why they got so crazy when she was the topic of conversation? Was she the Devil, as far as these men were concerned?

Vo had seen some measure of that in his time on *St. Legier*, but only from the military. The public considered her some sort of avenging angel.

Weird.

Danville and Moirrey interrupted his ruminations by appearing like ghosts out of the brush on one side.

Cats with canaries in their mouths wouldn't have smiled so broadly.

"And?" Vo inquired.

It must be good.

"Gots 'em," Moirrey chirped happily.

"Oh?"

"Sir," Danville picked up the thread. "Building on the right appears interesting. Most buildings have single guards on portals, but this one also has four men posted together on a patio. My guess would be high-value prisoners secured inside that room."

"Show me," Vo said. "Do we know what it is?"

Moirrey handed him a pair of optics: cute, little, opera glasses barely the size of two of his fingers together. She moved him around and then forward to a new spot in some bushes, before she pointed over his shoulder like a sniper.

"There."

Vo found the spot and flipped a switch to go to three hundred zoom.

At the college he had attended, after *Ballard,* a quad like this one would be all open grass, for students walking every which way between buildings.

This was an overgrown garden. Almost a forest.

The buildings here were all four stories or more tall, but the trees were that and higher in places, with hedges two and three stories tall, carving everything into little, green valleys and mazes.

Someone dumb enough to try could probably sneak into the Palace grounds and get himself within three to five meters of the buildings with a little work.

Of course, most days, there would be guards around who knew the grounds well enough to intercept you. Tomorrow, there might be.

There.

Four men in Imperial Security Gray holding rifles, standing guard in the miserable mist, on an open patio itself surrounded on all sides by low bushes.

Vo counted windows from the nearest corner and memorized the location.

While it might be nice to come at them from the outside, anyone even halfway competent would have locked that outside door, giving whoever was inside enough time to raise alarms or do other evil things.

They would need to do this from the inside.

Vo smiled to himself.

Good thing he happened to have a reformed cat burglar handy. Although, cats were small. Would that have made him a tiger burglar, back in the day? He'd had the height and the reach, but not the layers of muscle.

Free climbing building facades had left him long and lean when he was seventeen. Navin the Black had turned him into an ogre.

But he still had the silent step.

Vo handed Moirrey back her lenses and turned to Horst.

"Do we have any stunners in this team?" he asked with deadly intent.

Horst shrugged silently and moved out of sight.

"Why stunners, sir?" Street whispered curiously.

Vo fixed the man with a serious stare. The 189th was a mountain division. Alpine in elevation and climate. Outdoor specialists.

They'd never been through Navin's version of a Hogan's Alley. Star Controller *Auberon* had one they could set up that covered three decks and four hectares, divided into five different environments.

Assaulting a secured building was one of them.

"It would be helpful if we had stunners, Street," he replied after a beat. "So that we could kick in the door firing indiscriminately at everything that moved, and then sort out the friendlies later."

Horst was back already.

"None, sir," he said. "Thought not, but wanted to make sure nobody had one stuck in a boot that they forgot to mention earlier. You know how the boys can be."

"Aye," Vo agreed, looking over his First Team. "Horst, you and Street do not fire your weapons inside the building until the alarm has been raised, or you get an order from me or Moirrey. Clear?"

Both men nodded.

"Danville, you have your knife," he continued. "The only people authorized to fire are myself and Moirrey."

"Me?" the woman chirped in surprise.

"I've read the Fleet Centurion's reports of your actions on *Ballard* and *Thuringwell*, Centurion," Vo replied. "I don't have time to run the rest of the men through their paces for three days to see if any of them are as good as you are. I know I am. Understood?"

He watched her face fall, just a little bit, meeting a blush slowly coming up.

Moirrey nodded.

Vo missed the goofball girl who used to come kidnap Jackson Tawfeek and drag him off to get coffee and gossip. The Centurion who had replaced her was a much more poised woman, but some of the fun had slowly bled out of her over the last three or four years.

And Moirrey certainly didn't look dangerous enough to be a Marine on the front line.

Vo wasn't fooled. Not after reading her own words about tracking down and killing an Imperial Security Colonel in some sort of personal duel on *Thuringwell*, in the middle of a major, pitched battle for the future of the planet.

"Street," Vo continued. "Find me someone on Team Two who is the same size as the man guarding the door on the far right. We'll take him out and put our man in the jacket, pretend a radio broke, and hope we can do this faster than they can react. Team Two will hold this door and cover him. Questions?"

"No, sir," the three men rumbled back, splitting and heading in different directions. Vo found himself momentarily alone with Moirrey *zu* Kermode, Imperial *Ritter* of the Household.

"C'n we do this, Vo?" she whispered with a touch of nerves.

"When we took Imperial colors, this came with it," he replied.

"Aye," she replied mournfully.

Those costs hadn't been weighing on her shoulders for nine months. Not like his.

This was why the Fleet Centurion had come down to the archery range to kick his butt into motion. This went beyond being an officer. Now he had two masters to serve. At least today.

Actually, no. Just one master. It just wasn't *Karl VII, Emperor of Fribourg*, just like it wasn't the Fleet Centurion.

No, today, his only mistress was Justice.

CHAPTER LXI

DATE OF THE REPUBLIC NOVEMBER 8, 398
ABOARD KALI-MA, ABOVE ST. LEGIER

From here, she could see the damage. Brutal, angry.

It really did look like a shark had mauled the big Battleship.

Wiley could only imagine what it must smell like on the inside.

"Tactical," she called, loud enough to be heard across the entire bridge, even though a speaking voice would have worked for the three meters that separated her from Yan. She wanted everybody listening.

Yan glanced up from his screens with an eyebrow raised.

"The emergency situation appears resolved," she said in the formal words that indicated to everyone that she was taking command again. "Prepare for squadron maneuvers."

He fought the ship. And did it well. Almost art, watching Yan outthink the other guy fast enough to shoot first.

But it was time to come back from that place where he had been.

Wiley outlined her maneuvers and transmitted them to all stations on the bridge with a click.

"We will assume *Blackbird* is seriously messed up until the Admiral tells us otherwise," she continued. "We're moving into a close escort position, with the Flight Wing taking up defensive layers outside that. Get the twins aboard and reloaded soonest."

Heads bobbed. Voices growled.

They were professionals. Nothing more was needed at this point.

Amateurs hadn't lasted long on her deck when she took command. Just like Yan's teams had gone through the wringer to get to stay.

"Science Officer," *Wiley* called across to the far left corner. "Get me the Admiral on a secured channel. I'll take it in the day office."

"Roger that," Himura called as *Wiley* unstrapped herself and moved to the closet where she did paperwork when she was in charge, rather than her own office down by the Flight Deck.

The screen was already lit and blinking when *Wiley* closed the door and sat.

She touched the screen and watched Jessica's face appear.

"Admiral," *Wiley* said.

"Command Centurion," Jessica replied in a serious, formal voice. So, not alone. They had spent enough time in each other's pockets by now to communicate at that level. "What can I do for you?"

"We're moving into an escort formation, Admiral," *Wiley* replied, slightly stiff. "What are your combat capabilities at this point?"

In other words, how bad did he fuck up your ship on that pass, Jessica?

"*Amsel* has no Primary shells or missiles loaded, *Wiley*," Jessica said carefully, with a glance to her left at someone that was out of the camera. Probably the new Emperor. "All but one of the Type-3 beam installations are intact. We've lost two Type-2's on the starboard flank, but all of the Type-1's are working. We've lost an interesting pattern of the dorsal shield generators and are working to replace those as soon as possible, but the bridge crew understands the need to fight in three dimensions if we have to. You come in high and distribute the Wing normally and we should be good."

Wiley digested everything. Jessica had included stats on the new *Paladin*-class Battleship in her original packet, so *Wiley* could fill in the gaps in the conversation.

That thing had hammered the shit out of *Blackbird*, and another Battleship coming along to fight might be enough to finish the job, even with *Kali-ma* and the Queen's Own helping out.

So it was going to be a game of bluff with all the other Captains and Admirals in orbit right now, at least until something broke.

Wiley smiled.

She had started her career as a pirate, taking on all comers. She could easily fall back into that pattern of thought.

"Understood, Admiral," *Wiley* said. "Anybody in this mess we trust?"

Jessica shook her head.

"If the Red Admiral was here, he could probably list them off for me in mind-numbing detail," she replied. "Saar was injured on the pass, but his team has everything covered. Once he gets out of medical, I'll interview him. Your job is to talk tough, because nobody is allowed inside gun range until we know who they are. Neither of us have Primaries or missiles right now, but they don't know that."

Wiley nodded.

Kali-ma could annihilate a squadron of Imperial fighters by herself, if somebody sent one over. Two, once she threw in the Queen's Own.

Pops Nakamura had designed a junkyard dog of a 4-ring Mothership for Jessica to build.

Still, not a lot either of them could do about cruisers or capital warships coming in, except back away, especially if it was one of the three battle squadrons that was protecting the planet, and not just a single ship.

But with two Emperors, three if the father wasn't already dead, the chessboard was a complicated mess. Hopefully, that would keep most of the other players honest.

After all, nobody had ever promised *Wiley* she would die in bed.

CHAPTER LXII

The mist had deepened ta rain. *Monsooninating* would be the next step, but fer naow it were still that nasty wet that annoyed cows and kepts ya inside with grilled cheese dipped in Ma's tomato soup.

Moirrey had planned better'n th'boys fer today. As thin's got wetter, she'd dug out a cute, little hooligan cap she'd rolled up inta a pocket this morn, slickered her hair back, and stuck it on.

Let the rests of 'em look like a street gang. She were stylin'.

And it were about to get kinda messy 'rounds here.

Moirrey and the nine ogres. It were a fairy tale in reverse. One o'th'ancient ones, backs ta th'beginnin' of recorded civilization. Maybe if she were four meters tall, they could all be dwarves. But then she'd hafta be a princess er som'tin.

No fun in that, t'all.

Hans were poised with a shiv that couldna make up its mind if it were a skinnin' knife er a short sword. But he were thumb'n'forefinger gripped at his thigh, so she hads no worries that he were good enough ta use it.

And Vo dinna t'ink any o'th'rest were good enough to shoot, 'ceptin' him'n'her, so it were gonn'be serious work.

Jes one watch goose today.

She'd'a felt sorry fer 'im, but the lad had joined Imperial Security instead o'th'Army er th'Fleet. That made him a bully, fer as she were concerned.

An' she liked bullies even less'n Vo, which were sayin' some'tin' fierce. Vo were big enough to handle them hisself.

She put away the rest of her gear, tucked it all in special pockets and rolled up in cloth t'protect it. She'd no' need the goggles here. Nor the engineering sensor pad, though that might change when they gots inside.

Only thin' at this point were to wrap a cloth around her pistol hand.

Ya weren'ts supposed'ta do that, on count of heat bleed havin' nowheres to go, but it also made the little thin' mouse-like fer noise. At least fer a few shots until ya started cookin' yer hand.

That mights be imp'rt'nt inside.

Vo looked like someone had carved a god of doom outs of an angry mountain and set it in the trees to scare peeples.

The rest of the boyz were nice'n'all, and probably pretty good at whats they did, but she and Vo and Hans were likely to do all the killin' needed doin' today.

Moirrey weren't sure how she'd got here, any of the heres, but that were a problem fer a glass of hot chocolate, maybe with a shot of peppermint schnapps, sometime tamorrows.

The rain had at least made the watch goose miserabler than afore.

He were tucked inta the lee o'th'buildin' on the handle-side. Kept him mostly dry and largely out of the yuck, but it also meant that nobody were sneakin' up on hims with a knife.

Hans were prolly beside hisself, beside her.

Moirrey kept the grin off'n her face and turned to Vo.

She held up the pistol wrapped with a headscarf to gets his attention as a question.

He took a moment, then nodded.

They were all three as close as you could get in the brush, which were prolly closer'n most folks would'a thought without gettin' antsy 'bouts it.

Still, it were four meters at a slant from here.

Watch goose lifted his radio'n'answered someones with a callsign'n'a checkin. They'd been watching him close. Fifteen minutes on the dot.

Imperial Security sure did love patterns of organization.

Moirrey would'a liked to extend her hand to make the shot, but a bright purple scarf comin' outta th'leeves woulda got even the watch goose to looking.

She took the shot from her hip, like she were some kinda cowboy.

Beam still caught a leaf anyway, though.

She got watch goose in the right shoulder with a wallop, instead of the heart. And not nearly hard enough. At least the microphone he were holding had fell outta his hand at the same time he dropped his rifle.

And she did bounce him off the bricks o'th'building pretty fierce.

But it weren't gonna be enough to drop him. That were sure.

Moirrey extended her arm fer the second shot, sure she'd one chance to finish the dude off. Any more'n he'd get the radio.

She had never seen Vo Arlo move like that.

She weren't sure she had ever seen a human move that fast. Someone else, but she weren't human. Technically.

Three steps in a flash, an' Vo had the guy by the neck in one o'those doom hands, while th'other grabbed the radio hand and squeezed.

Even a slick, little, killer bunny like Hans Danville were a step and a half behind Vo gettin' there.

Wow.

Cartilage er som'tin crunched like a plastic sandwich tub being stomped, and then watch goose stopped fightin' back. Collapsed like a puppet with cut strings.

Had Vo just broke the guy's neck one-handed?

Could you do that?

Vo and Hans were heads-on-sticks, but nobody seemed to be around.

Moirrey glanced back over her shoulder.

"Team Two," she called quietly. "Next watch goose, move."

They understood her words, which were good, 'cause she weren't really all here right now.

Maybe up in that high place where Vo had gone.

One man slipped past her pretty quiet'n'all and jack-rabbited to where Vo were just now setting the dead goose back against the wall.

Moirrey kept watch while they stripped the dude's jacket. Weren't worth the pants er those tacky, black leather, shiny boots. If someone were that close already, thin's had already gone sideways an' there were no recoverin'.

Radio and rifle stayed with the new watch goose from Team Two. With any luck, he could buy them time in fifteen minutes'r more, assuming they dinna roll passwords er any'tin.

Hans had the keycard to open the door in his off-hand and stood poised, all set to stick a point in anyone openin' th'door right now.

Vo caught her eye across the space with a look of pain so dark and intense that Moirrey nearly cried.

She hadna realized how much it might take outta a big, tough goon like Vo Arlo to kill a total stranger fer no better reason than the guy were in the way on a bad day.

Huh.

Still, he were countin' on her.

She moved, bringin' Horst and Street in her wake like vengeful ghosts.

Vo nodded. Hans keyed the panel next to the door. Moirrey pulled it open and stepped boldly into the hallway.

They'd planned it out like this. If'n ya looks like you belong, people tended ta agree and ignores you. Plus, Imperials might hesitate to shoot a woman without a damned good reason. That would give her a chance to shoot first.

It were likes ta get messy afore it got better.

CHAPTER LXIII

IMPERIAL FOUNDING: 176/11/08. WERDER, ST. LEGIER

Sigmund let the rain drumming on the roof of the vehicle sum up his afternoon, but he refused to let the gray, wet misery define it.

Into every life…

He snarled to himself, alone in the back seat, and watched the cityscape rumble by.

It would have been faster to fly there, but Imperial Security had ordered all vehicles grounded as a control measure, and there was always some fool who would be willing to shoot first and investigate later. On the ground, there was more time to approach each checkpoint in a less threatening way.

Slower, yes, but enough things had gone wrong today.

Still, only one had to go right at this point.

Sigmund found his left fingers drumming the arm rest in rhythm with the rain and the pavement. A tone rang out in the otherwise empty space.

"Sire," one of the men in the front part of the vehicle began. "We've gotten through to Admiral Bakemann finally."

Finally? Long past finally.

Still, if the man would get off his ass, he could make the girl give way. She had one untried Battleship and a pirate escort.

Bakemann commanded a full battle squadron that could easily overwhelm the interlopers.

"Put him through," Dittmar replied after a breath to crush the anger in his voice.

"Your Majesty."

Bakemann's voice was that of a man giving an interview on the radio. Soothing, warm, calm. Like he was playing both sides of the equation equally.

Sigmund Dittmar realized that the man would have to go, just as soon as he could be set up by Imperial Security and arrested.

Every man had a skeleton in his closet that wouldn't bear public scrutiny. Otherwise, they would have never gotten where they were.

"Have you broken orbit and moved to engage Keller?" Dittmar snarled.

That was really the only question worth discussing at this point.

There were two flags on the battlefield. Bakemann was going to commit to one of them, right now.

Or Sigmund would have him shot tomorrow. Simple as that.

"Not all of my Captains are prepared to break with tradition," Bakemann replied. "Even to save the Empire. Additionally, Keller complicates their loyalties. And I couldn't sound them out ahead of time, Your Majesty. It will take some time yet to bring them around, but we're making good progress."

Sigmund ground his teeth rather than answer.

It had sounded so plausible when Grundman first suggested it. Let Imperial Security organize things, only bringing people into the conspiracy who were well-placed enough to nudge it along at critical junctures.

You just sit back and be prepared to step in when the situation demands a strong hand of the Imperial blood.

Above, Bakemann in command of one of the fleets in orbit should have brought over the rest at the right moment, chasing *Buran* off and providing a sound example of the need to maintain a war footing at all costs.

Instead, Keller and the girl had managed to kill the intruder and survive. And now apparently, the Captains were wavering.

It was beginning to look like there would need to be a pitched battle in orbit. The fate of the *Fribourg Empire* might depend on it.

Perhaps Bakemann would successfully martyr himself along the way, so he could be a hero, after all.

Sigmund could see a future where the entirety of his throne rested on the shoulders of Imperial Security, especially if the Fleet was turning into a morass of uncertainty. Had this been their plan all along, or were they merely the only ones reliable enough to sustain his rule?

Sigmund Dittmar cast the dice in his head.

In fifteen minutes, he would be in a place to eliminate Karl and the Crown Prince, and then announce plans to divorce Karya and marry the elder daughter to nail everything down.

Karya would, well, if not understand and support his needs, at least be too weak to thwart his plans. She was a passive woman, one he barely noticed anyway. Sigmund would have it no other way.

Breaking his young cousin to the bit, on the other hand, would be necessary. It might even be pleasurable.

"You have your orders, Bakemann," Sigmund finally said definitively. "I expect you to carry them out."

He closed the channel before the fool could equivocate anymore.

There was little time to bring the Fleet fully into his orbit. At least this way, he offered them a future of glory and tradition.

Gods above knew what those two women would do to the Empire.

CHAPTER LXIV

I t were an eerie field trip inta an empty museum on a Tuesday morning. That early stretch o'day when even mosta the docents weren't up yet, let alone followin' along as she traipsed quietly through empty halls committin' culture.

Moirrey kept her internal commentary to herself. T'weren't the time n'r th'place to offer up silly historical facts about the art work'n'how it comed to be here. Regardless of how silly some of th'stuff here looked.

She were up front, lookin's all innocent'n'stuff. Inside th'building, she'd stuffed the hooligan back in a pocket and left her jacket with Street. She were dry underneath, so her shirt weren't stickin' to her boobs er'nuthin', but it were obvious she were a girl, with curves and hair and maybe a little makeup.

Girl's got to be lookin' good when we go rescuin' Emperers, ya know.

Her wrists were kinda crossed in front of her, right hand holding left wrist, left hand still all wrapped up in the purple scarf.

With a pistol.

From far enough away, it outta look like she had frilly sleeves and someone had hand-cuffed her.

As if.

All the frilly stuff were for parties. Real engineers added buttons to sleeves so's you could roll 'em up when it were time ta gets ta work.

Mountain o'Doom walked right behind her. Vo were doing the same thin' with his hands as her, but countin' on them payin'ttention to Moirrey'n'her hips and only kinda lookin's at the dude twice her size, or the ruffians th't apparently had 'em both supposedly under arrest.

It were a long hallway. They'd entered th'palace in on a weird, lil side corridor 'tween rows o'offices thet was all empty t'day. National holiday from work, kinda thin'.

She'd stuck the end of her slab 'round the near corner and took a pic, so's they could plan it all out an' ever'one knows their job.

Now, it were showtime. Lights down. Curtain up. Makeup perfect. Glitter ready.

'Cause, you know, glitter.

Long hallway, completely empty, 'ceptin' four fellows facing each other in pairs across fr'm th'door Vo wanted.

They weren't even that bad, as far as professionals went. Moirrey could see that as she got close.

The nearest two detached themselves from their walls'n'turned her way. Th'other two paid attention to their left, away from Moirrey, like this were all some elaborate trap. Which it were, but not that kind.

"What's going on?" the older man on the left demanded.

Moirrey kinda drifted to a halt, almost in synch with Vo.

"High value prisoners," Street replied in a drawl gone laconic. "Gamma Command said to bring them here for storage."

"Gamma Command?"

The man were confused now. Which were the whole point'o'th'thin'.

"I've never heard of them," he continued.

"If you've never heard of them, buddy," Street fired back. "Then your security clearance probably isn't high enough to even be talking to us in the first place. Is the Emperor in there? This is where we were told to bring these two."

"Who are they?" the man stammered slightly.

"*Aquitaine* spies," Street declared harshly. "Unlock the door and let us get back to doing our job."

"The Emperor and his family are our responsibility," the man puffed up officiously.

"You're babysitters, punk," Street growled. "Open the damned door so the real teams can get back to wiping your asses for you."

Not exactly th'way she'd a 'splained it to Street, but close enough. More or less on script.

Dude in charge wanted to growl'er'somtin, but apparently figured this weren't the time to muss. He turned to the other guy on his side and nodded.

That guy pulled a badge out of a pocket and turned to the magical door that were the center of Vo's existence right now, far as Moirrey could tell.

That were her cue.

Moirrey took three quick steps that put her right up in th'other guy's face. Or, chest. He were tall. Not Vo-tall, but tall like somma her cousins. Not near as big. Just tall.

He reacted placidly, like a cow, kinda bugging out his eyes a little and staring at her boobs rather than payin'ttention to what she were doing.

There were little time fer subtle, so Moirrey reached out with her free hand and jes punched him in the balls as hard as she could.

Some things from junior high stayed wit' ya ferever.

He even tipped like a cow, too, going down in a great big heap of painful groan as she slipped the keycard outta his hand. Behind her, more thumps as angry men used unnecessary force on unsuspecting villains.

Moirrey turned around, all set ta shoots someone, but all the bad guys were seeing stars. 'Cept hers.

She kicked him in the head once, just so he dinna miss out on the fun of his own, personal kunkussion, and then looked 'round to scope thin's out.

Museum were still way too early on a Tuesday morning kinda quiet, which was good.

Vo nodded, still in that God of Ugly Doom place, from th'look on his face. Street, Horst, and Danville were pulling bodies towards her and stripping tunics theys could wear.

Nobody were actually dead yet, mostly because Vo'd told them not to get blood'n'brains all over uniform jackets they might need, the rest o'th'189th all being in mufti 'til now. Still, apparently she weren't the only one knew where to take a bully down, fast'n'silent.

Good to know.

Nobody here were near big enough fer a jacket to match Vo. Nor her. But they'd figured that, going in.

Instead, Edgar pr'ceeded to pull eleven pairs o'handcuffs from belts and pockets of their new playmates and truss 'em ups like turkeys, then Street, Edgar, and Hans swapped themselves inta Imperial Security ruffians.

Why did four men need eleven sets of handcuffs?

Still, nobody comin'er going. Maybe they'd pull this thing off, after all. Door across the way were a small utility closet, filled w'mops and buckets and shelves.

And four fast-bound and gagged doofuses. Apparently, none of them managed to get themselves deaded, so they could hang out there until someone noticed the problem.

Moirrey took her spot at the door with Doom standing ahind her and Street playing watch goose.

Hans badged the door. It clicked with a nice, solid thunk, and Street pulled it into the hallway.

Okay.

Empress-Lady-Mom on the left, in the big chair. Holdin' hands with the Emperer, then Steffi and Cute Prince on th'sofa. 'Nuther girl in a chair in th'corner, trying to be invisible.

Must be Lady Yulia.

Watch goose just inside the door. Four more goobers outside, beyond the door, butts more or less against the glass facing outwards, in outta th'rain that had gotten right nasty in the last few minutes.

Amazingly-fat dude in a frilly uniform standing on th'far side'o'th'room, apparently ranting at th'Emperer 'bout somet'in' important-like.

The goober on her right woke up outta his doze as she stepped past him into the room.

Moirrey ignored him and took another step, smiling huge and flirty with the guy. Doom and Street could handle the one guard. This one were an officer of some sort.

"Hi, cutie," she said, taking another step. "Who'r'yu?"

"I am General Grundman of Imperial Security," he wheezed at her, totally knocked off track and distracted. "What's the meaning of this?"

Yup, story as old as boys noticin' girls. His face went kinda blank as he stared at her boobs.

Eyes are up here, watch goose.

Still, there was no way she were gonna get close enough to kick him. Moirrey took one more step and let go of her wrist, bringing the pistol up in a smooth motion and shooting the fat man square in the chest with a thump.

Hopefully, the glass were heavy enough thet nobody outside would hear it or feel it, butts up against the glass, and all.

This shot were cleaner. Navin th'Black'd be proud o'her shootin'iron skills, nowadays.

Fat man went down like a bag of ugly potatoes.

Behind her, dead silence.

Hopefully, a good sound.

Moirrey kinda turned with a sidestep, in case somebody were about to whomp her upside the head. Not that this were a bar or a lockerroom, or nothin'.

Goon by the door were looking at Doom and his big, gnarly pistol from just far enough away that the eyelashes on the right eye would brush metal if'n he were to actually blink.

Smart boy done froze, kinda like a department store mannequin back home.

Street pulled the door in from the hall with him and closed it while she watched, leaving Horst and Danville to guard the hallway.

Mountain o'Doom took possession of the guard's pistol and then they both watched as Street cuffed and stuffed the guy, with one of Moirrey's eyes still kinda on the glass wall and the butts outside.

They weren't all dumpy and outta shape, but none of them was lookin' in. That were good.

Moirrey nodded, mostly to the room, and kinda to the good luck fairies, and turned to his Empererness, who had remained utterly still and quiet fer the three seconds the whole op had taken.

Moirrey blanched as her junior high geometry teacher come back from those regular nightmares to point out the path o'th'shot she'd took to get the fat guy.

If Steffi'd been taller through the torso, maybe the size of the boyz on either side o'her, Moirrey'd'a just about perfect split the gap between Steffi's right ear and Karl's left one with that shot.

From the look on the Emperer's face, he were kinda aware o'that, too, and politely not bringin' it up just yet.

Whoops.

"Your Majesty," Vo rumbled like an avalanche wakin' up. "Time is short. We need to get you to safety."

Karl fixed her with a knowin' eye and bounced upright in one fast kip, like he were an acrobat er sometin'.

Who knowed with Emperers?

"Lord Vo," the man said graciously. "Lady Moirrey. Thank you. What about the men outside?"

"This is a small op, sir," Vo replied. "Surgical, until we can get you to a secure facility and call in the fleet."

Vo gestured and the others were in motion, too.

Moirrey found herself at the short end of a really tall hug. Two of them. From Steffi and then Empress-Mom.

She felt eight again, around people this tall.

"The Fleet?" his Empererness asked.

"Yes, sir," Vo said, moving towards the door and rapping lightly three times in slow cadence. "Princess Casey has declared herself Emperor in your stead and appointed the Fleet Centurion as her Admiral. Whoever was bombing the planet has apparently been neutralized, but we've been off the newswaves, so I couldn't tell you who or how."

"Casey got away?" Steffi asked, hugging Moirrey again with a gleeful giggle. "Good for her."

Moirrey'd seen the looks the older princess had given everyone durin' Moirrey's special show. There were a little sibling rivalry goin' on, but more of it were a family tryin' to deal with an oddball kid were too smart fer the farm.

Not that she had ANY experience with THAT sorta thing.

Vo knocked four quick raps on the inside of the panel to signal.

Danville opened the door and peeked in. He mostly had the blade outta immediate sight. Ya had to ken how he were standin' to know how quick he could stab, block, or maybe throw it in pinch.

"Danville on point," Vo ordered in that doom voice. "Street and Horst on the flanks, running uniform interference. Empress first. Crown Prince next. Then the Emperor, and the Princess and Lady Yulia last. Moirrey and I will be on the rear."

"Colonel?" the Cute Prince asked.

"Everyone else here is expendable in layers, sir," Vo rumbled. "Including you."

That were apparently good enough. Kid nodded and fell into his place in line, behind his mom and with Edgar and Street covering his wings.

Hallway were still museum on a quiet mornin' as they got out into it.

But there was a weird echo before they got more'n a few meters.

"What's going on here?"

CHAPTER LXV

IMPERIAL FOUNDING: 176/11/08. IMPERIAL PALACE, WERDER, ST. LEGIER

To top it all off, the fools guarding the palace had dropped an armoured fighting vehicle in the middle of the main driveway and dug it in to the point that it would take half an hour to rearrange things so that his driver could deliver him to the covered part of the driveway. Wheels instead of lift, again.

Any other day, Sigmund would have considered making them move the damned thing, just to put a razor-fine point on the kind of power he normally commanded, even before his Ascension to the throne.

Peons needed to be reminded of their place occasionally, even if it required a rolled up newsprint to do so.

Today, time was too tight for the grand gesture. Sigmund settled for walking the last three hundred meters in a bitter, stiff rain. Of course he didn't have a jacket, but his white Admiral's uniform would stay dry enough.

Around him, men of the Imperial Security Bureau let him know they felt his indignity by taking out their own anger on everyone they met.

As praetorians, not the worst fit today.

Sigmund paused just inside the door to run his hand backwards through his brown hair. One of the troopers handed him a small towel pulled from a dry pocket. Sigmund memorized the man's face and nodded. At least someone had managed to think ahead of the situation.

Around him, a dozen heavily-armed men and two officers could wait while he dried himself off. What was about to happen would be in the history books. It would not do to come in dripping and disheveled, except possibly for the propaganda posters he would need to put up soon.

Sigmund Dittmar as some sort of action hero from the videos, with wet hair and a lantern jaw. That would probably sell well in many parts of the Empire, not that he required more groupies. But it might be a useful recruiting tool for the Navy, one of these days.

Sigmund handed the damp towel back to the soldier. He tugged his jacket down and smoothed out any wrinkles.

Catching a glimpse of himself in a side mirror as they passed. Nodding in approval. He looked Imperial.

Now he just needed to convince his people of that.

One other thing that caught Sigmund's attention as they walked was the amount of noise generated.

Sigmund had spent his entire career, and most of his life, surrounded by naval officers. Those men tended to be noisy when they walked, a giant drunken centipede on metal floors.

The Imperial Security troops accompanying him today were remarkably quiet, by comparison. Had he closed his eyes, Sigmund would have guessed less than a handful walked with him, rather than the dozen men he actually had.

He supposed that made a perverse sort of sense.

These were the sorts of men you sent for the midnight knock. You didn't want your prey alerted to their presence until it was too late to do anything but disappear.

Thus were empires upheld.

Sigmund hadn't spent that much time in the personal quarters sections of the Imperial Palace. He had his own palace that was just as sumptuous not far away, and had spent large portions of the last two decades elsewhere, either serving aboard a ship, or at Fleet Headquarters.

He had forgotten how large the palace was.

Still, he was making good time. If Bakemann would get off his fat ass, and Grundman, as well, they could bring this to a head shortly and then begin the laborious task of remaking the *Fribourg Empire* into someplace he could finally be proud of.

The group came through a set of secured doors that split the office parts of the building from the private spaces. The building had been under lock-down for several hours, with most of the inhabitants rounded up and secured in a separate building.

So it was a surprise to see a large group of people moving away from him at the far end of the hall.

Worse, when he recognized his cousin among the group, as well as the foreigners, including that bitch Kermode.

"What's going on here?" came out of his mouth in a harsh snarl, even before his brain processed the scene.

But he already knew.

Imperial Security had failed him, just as the Fleet had. The former Emperor, Karl VII, was in the process of escaping.

"Stop them," he commanded in a voice best suited for a burning bridge.

Around him, his troops opened fire at long range. Sigmund's dress uniform lacked a sidearm, or he would have joined in.

None of them would be allowed to live.

CHAPTER LXVI

DATE OF THE REPUBLIC NOVEMBER 8, 398
IMPERIAL PALACE, WERDER, ST. LEGIER

This hadn't been his war.

That hadn't stopped Vo from becoming personally involved. Emotionally involved.

From breaking into the Imperial Palace and killing people whose only crime had been being in the wrong place.

From trying to be a hero.

No, he wasn't trying to be a hero.

He was trying to do what he thought was right. What Navin the Black had been pounding into him for better than a decade.

Dignity. Duty.

Honor.

Ahead of him, Danville had that blade low against his thigh, all set to slide between ribs and seek hearts. Edgar and Street held his rear corners. The Empress, the Crown Prince, Karl himself, and then the two girls, hurrying along down a back hallway, fleeing to that corner where they could escape, shepherded by he and Moirrey.

They just might pull this off.

"What's going on here?"

Vo hadn't realized until that very moment that he had been subconsciously expecting those words for better than an hour.

Time seemed to slow to a crawl as he glanced back over a shoulder.

Imperial Security troops. Bunch of them.

The gig was up.

Open field. Minimal cover. Hostile force closing from the rear. Outmanned. Outgunned.

But not surprised. Oh, no.

Navin had pounded those lessons home.

"Stop them," a man in the center commanded as Vo's team kept moving.

Even from here, Vo could see the white uniform standing out against the gray of the other boys.

And he recognized Admiral Dittmar, an Imperial cousin, Pretender to the Throne, as the one giving orders.

The man was unarmed, so Vo ignored him and opened fire on the troops around him as they moved to open up.

Walter's old slugthrower made an impossibly loud noise in the confined space.

Moirrey's beam shot was barely a beat behind his.

"Get them to safety," Vo ordered over the din.

Someone would handle it. Probably Danville, since Horst and Street had pistols that could range and cover.

Vo slid sideways into a doorway and fired again. He had been on the right going forward, so his left shoulder was tucked in as he fired again.

Downrange, a third man fell and the rest woke up.

Vo glanced back as Street moved up and grabbed Karl by the hand, dragging him forward.

The girl, the young Princess, Steffi, did the thing Vo should have done, before his training had taken over and moved him out of the way.

She stepped close to her father like a proper bodyguard, nearly hugging him from behind as she pushed him forward.

The shot took her high between the shoulder blades with a sick, meaty thump.

Even from here, Vo could smell the Princess die. The heavy body armor he normally wore in the field would have barely made that shot survivable.

Silk burned.

Everything turned red.

Somewhere, deep in the ugly parts of his brain, Vo heard the Fleet Centurion speaking again.

Remember that you're there to make the 189th proud of you, too. And not just me and the entire, damned fleet.

He had screwed up, and it had killed the girl. She was the one doing the right thing.

And it just cost her her life.

Someone howled in primal rage. It might have been him.

Time had slowed before. Now it stopped.

One man was responsible for this. For all the men and women that had died today. For all the damage done to the planet and the citizens.

For that girl never growing up.

Vo raised his pistol as an extension of Justice itself. No, not Justice.

Vengeance.

He drew a line that connected his rage, his soul, and eternity.

The shot rang off the marble hallways like Rebekah's tank slamming into a brick wall and crushing it.

Downrange, the Imperial troops were just starting to scatter, intending to pin Vo down while they called for help. Nothing more was needed at this point, surrounded by an army of men in gray that could be vectored in on the radio.

Sigmund Dittmar, Admiral of the White, Imperial Pretender, would not be able to appreciate the tactical situation.

What was left of his face was a bloody ruin. Vo could see that, even from this distance.

Vo fired several more shots as fast as the pistol would cycle, noise be damned.

He glanced over, to be sure, but the rest of his men had done their jobs, better than he had. The Emperor and his family were moving smartly away, protected by Street and Edgar, both backing and firing, while Danville took point.

Moirrey had done the same as Vo and taken a doorway. She was firing almost as rapidly as Vo, although she was taking time to aim, instead of just forcing those men to evade.

The only other person close was the Princess. And she would not be moving again.

"Cease fire!" a man called from the other end of the hallway. "Stand down!"

Incoming fire tapered off and stopped as the man repeated himself at the top of his lungs, so Vo and Moirrey did as well.

Silence fell as the Emperor and his family got around the corner to safety. Hopefully, Team Two could get them to the wall and freedom.

"Sir," a young man's voice sounded. "I'm moving out into the open so my team can surrender to you."

Surrender?

Even from here, Vo could hear the murmurs of surprise and shock from the Imperial Security troops over there. The survivors, anyway. More than half of those men weren't available to surrender at this point.

Moirrey really was at least as good as he was.

"Go ahead," Vo called back.

At least those men hadn't been issued grenades as part of their duties today. Just one, and it would have all been over already.

The officer over there was serious about this, stepping into the open with his hands out. Not up over his head in the universal signal, but obviously trying to be not-dangerous.

He was young. That much was clear.

Ramrod straight, clean-cut blond hair, perfect uniform slightly marred by sudden activity.

Vo watched the young man carefully draw a pistol from a holster and then bend down to place it delicately on the marble tile, like it might bite. He stood, and walked into the middle of the hall, turning to face the men on his left.

"Weapons down," he ordered in a sharp, parade-ground voice. "Form up."

Around him, the men looked confused.

"I said down, damn you!" the kid snarled savagely.

That got through to them.

Bewildered men lowered pistols and short guns to the floor before falling into a rough line in front of their officer.

Vo detached himself from the doorway with a nod to Moirrey. She could cover him just fine.

Vo moved forward, back itching like he was about to get shot. He got all the way up to the young officer commanding the team.

From here, Vo could see Dittmar's corpse, face up in the middle of the hall, draining blood in a pool.

Dead.

Based on the similarity of the uniforms, the man dead next to Dittmar on the floor was an Imperial Security officer, like the kid who had come to attention at one end of the line of much older men. Higher ranking, given the two stripes on the corpse's arm to the kid's one.

Dead Centurion, roughly. Live Cornet.

"Sir," the kid began. "My men and I are surrendering to your authority."

"Why?" Vo snarled, unable to keep the white-hot rage out of his voice.

Unwilling. There was a dead girl behind him. He should have protected her.

It was all he could do to not kill every single one of these men.

The kid gestured to the dead Admiral that made a weird, artistic symmetry to the scene.

Noble blood spilled at both ends of the hallway.

"Admiral Dittmar, the man who would be Emperor, is dead," the young man said with utter gravity. "Emperors Karl VII and Karl VIII are both still alive. Our actions no longer have purpose, sir."

"Your men have committed treason, Lieutenant," Vo growled angrily, the legalisms of his centurion training finally coming to the fore, in spite of the rage underpinning.

"No, sir," the kid snapped back harshly, his own officer training backing him up. "These men were acting under Commander Hauss's authority, and then mine. I am the only surviving officer present, so the act of treason was mine alone. These men are at most guilty of knowingly following illegal orders. That is a Court Martial offense. I'm the only one who should hang."

Vo had to give the kid credit.

He hadn't met that many officers willing to die on the same sword that they lived by. This was up there with a Command Centurion going down with his ship.

"You probably will hang, Lieutenant," Vo replied, rage bleeding slowly out of him.

Some of it.

"Should I have lived as an outlaw, sir?" the kid fired back with a chip on his shoulder almost as big as the one Vo frequently saw in the mirror. "I took an oath."

"No, you should not have," Vo granted him. "Do you have a radio on the command frequency, Lieutenant...? What is your name?"

"Lieutenant Grantholm Safavid, sir," the kid replied, reaching slowly for a radio unit on his belt and handing it to Vo. "Channel six is the command frequency. Channel three is general push."

Vo nodded.

He had to give the kid points for dying with honor. But he was pretty sure what the outcome of that trial would be.

Vo turned and signaled Moirrey to come closer as he stared down at the faceless corpse at his feet.

Channel three.

"Members of the Imperial Security forces, this is Army Colonel Vo Arlo," he let all of his rage focus down into his voice and broadcast it across the entire planetary system, a bass so deep that whales might answer him. "Admiral Sigmund Dittmar is dead. I repeat, Admiral Dittmar, the pretender to the Imperial throne, is dead. All Security units will stand down immediately and return to barracks. Officers will identify the nearest Naval or Army unit and turn themselves in. Failure to do so is no longer an option. In six hours, you will be considered outlaws and dealt with accordingly."

Seven men stared back at Vo in various states of shock and horror. He really didn't give a damn.

What he did do was hand the comm back to Safavid and pull out his own unit.

"Horst, this is Arlo," he said. Much of the emotion was gone from his voice now, crammed back down into his soul where it belonged.

"Sir, we heard your broadcast on the other line," Horst replied instantly. "What is your status?"

Vo could tell that Horst thought someone had a gun to Vo's head, issuing orders.

"Find a safe spot and stay quiet for now, Sergeant Major," Vo replied. "I'll send Moirrey when we have friendly reinforcements. Let me know if anyone in gray presents a problem."

"Will do, Colonel," Horst replied.

Vo flicked to another channel and took a deep breath. Moirrey reached over and laid a friendly hand on his arm, even as she watched the unarmed troops like a hungry raptor spying mice.

"*Amsel*, this is Arlo," he finally said.

Best to get this over with quickly. There was no good way to do this.

The Fleet Centurion was there instantly.

"Go ahead, Vo," she said.

Her own tone let him know that she had been listening in on the other channels.

Now he just had to explain his failure to two Emperors.

"Dittmar is dead, Admiral," Vo said. "The survivors of his personal guard have surrendered and I have ordered the rest to follow suit. Request Shore Patrol and Army troops to reinforce my position at the palace soonest."

Vo fell silent for a moment. There was no easy way to say these words.

"The Emperor is safe," he continued in a voice that threatened to break on him. "The Empress as well, and the Crown Prince. Princess Stephanie was killed in the fighting."

Another voice came on at that moment.

Vo probably could have handled it if the Fleet Centurion had said the words, but this was the Emperor.

The other Emperor.

The younger sister of the woman he had just failed to protect.

"Thank you, Colonel Arlo," Princess Casey, *The Emperor Karl VIII*, said quietly.

Vo felt hot tears run down his face.

Rage. Hatred. Failure. Self-loathing.

It didn't matter.

What he really wanted to do right now was break something.

Anything.

Everything.

From the look on Safavid's face, the kid was expecting Vo to start with him.

It was tempting.

"You confirm that Dittmar is dead, Arlo?" Keller was back on the line, official, authoritative.

Speaking to future historians.

Again.

"Affirmative, Admiral," Vo replied quietly. "I killed him myself."

EPILOGUES

EPILOGUE: VO

DATE OF THE REPUBLIC NOVEMBER 19, 398
DOCKSIDE DISTRICT, WERDER, ST. LEGIER

It had become his bar. Vo had no other way to describe it.

The Maltese Cross had been just another pub down by the docks two months ago. A dive with a rough clientele, spacers and professional girls mostly. One place in a dozen just like it on this stretch of road. Nothing whatsoever to rate it above any of the rest.

Until Colonel Vo *zu* Arlo, Hero of *St. Legier*, happened to be drinking here one night when a criminal gang came in to make trouble. And ran into the 189th Division.

The legend had already outgrown him. At his size, that was an impressive feat.

The Maltese Cross wasn't normally closed on a Wednesday night, but the men of the 189th had arranged a private party. By invitation only. And those invites were not available on any black market. Family only.

The piano had been tuned. By someone from the palace, no less. Someone else had provided six new sets of darts and a custom board. Imperial Caterers had parked their vehicles out front, nearly blocking the street, but the local gendarme were out there with batons and attitudes, making sure nobody bothered the guest of honor on his night.

Twenty-four men in their best field uniforms filled the tables as food and drink was consumed in prodigious amounts. This was not a party for formal attire, although Vo wore the maroon cloak that was his badge.

He sat at the center of the bar, being served by one Foster Calderin, owner and publican of *The Maltese Cross*, a footnote all his own.

On Vo's right, Moirrey, in her own cloak. She wasn't as serious as she might be, but there was no glitter in the air tonight, either.

On his left, twelve-year-old Annette Fuchs, the innkeeper's daughter who had sounded the alarm and saved the day, as the legend went. Beyond her, her father Walter, the man who had supplied *Excalibur*, and mother Frida, looking a touch nervous at all the energy and attention.

One ugly fist held a shot glass of something on the bar. Vo could probably shatter it if he wanted to. Just squeeze until it came apart and drove shards into his palm.

It was tempting.

"Colonel Arlo, are you okay?" Annette asked in a shy, tiny voice.

On his other side, he felt Moirrey's hand on his arm. Warmth. Solace.

Vo came back to himself from that cold, dark place.

He drew a breath and wondered.

He was alive because he had screwed up. Steffi was dead for the same reason.

Would there ever be okay, again?

There were no words.

Annette hesitated for only a moment, then scooted her stool over and leaned against him, like he was a great, big, puppy dog.

She had no words, either. Or so he thought.

"You saved the Emperor and killed the bad man," she announced with all the seriousness only a twelve-year-old can manage.

Vo felt tears well up. Again.

Moirrey leaning on him from the other side didn't help.

Annette leaned away enough to turn and look up at him.

"And you saved all of us," she continued.

Whatever reserves he had shattered. Tears poured down his face.

Vo sniffed and drew a deep breath into his lungs. Maybe it would warm his soul.

Vo reached out his left hand and hugged Annette close, smiling over her head at her parents and whispering *thank you.*

One more deep breath.

Vo raised his glass high in the air.

"My friends, I give you a toast," he called.

The room had already fallen silent as people watched. He saw other tears as well, as glasses came up.

"The Empire."

EPILOGUE: JESSICA

The changes were subtle, but Jessica had come into this meeting keyed up to spot them.

In the past, Vo had always been rigidly in control of himself, sitting perfectly still in her office, even just drinking coffee and talking.

She had been accused of never being off duty, but that was untrue. She just never stopped thinking, planning.

Vo was never off duty around her. Never relaxed.

Or hadn't been.

Something had changed.

He was leaned back in the chair across from her desk, one leg crossed and the hand not holding a coffee mug draped out across the back of the other chair.

His breathing was regular, when he was normally tight.

She hadn't pried in the last few weeks, realizing from her first look at him after the revolution that he needed time to find himself.

Apparently, he had.

"I have a document here," Jessica said, picking up the offending parchment and glancing at it. "It is a note from the Emperor himself asking for some clarifications about a clemency petition filed by one Vo *zu* Arlo."

Vo nodded in his serious way.

Did he just grin at me?

It was gone in a flash.

Perhaps she imagined it.

"Anything you want to talk about?" Jessica continued.

"He is a kid, doing what he thought was right," Vo replied gravely. "He was willing to take the responsibility, to hang alone, so as to protect his men from doing the same."

"And?"

"At that critical moment," Vo continued, his eyes suddenly light years away, "he could have killed us all. Wouldn't have taken much. He had us pinned down and could have easily called in others to bottle us up. And he chose to surrender instead. Everything was over at that moment. We won."

"And you think the Emperor should pardon him?" Jessica probed.

"I think that he shouldn't be put to death for following what he thought were legal orders, Fleet Centurion," Vo fired back. "He acted with honor. Very few others did. Very few were in a position to influence the final outcome that much. Even Grundman, the man behind the whole coup, got off easy. Moirrey had no idea who he was when she shot him, except that he was one of the bad guys. Safavid was the junior-most officer present, just a kid, and suddenly in charge when it all fell apart. I don't know if they will rehabilitate him, but he shouldn't be put to death."

Jessica let the silence hang. That might be the most words Vo *zu* Arlo had ever spoken to her in one breath. Normally, he was much more reticent, at least around her.

He must really be involved.

"Would you have him serve under you, Centurion Arlo?" she asked. "Could you trust him?"

She watched Vo turn back into the ominous, terrible creature Moirrey had described, the *Mountain of Doom*, for just a moment.

His eyes were still on that horizon.

"Yes," Vo finally said with a tiny sigh. "Yes, I think I would, Fleet Centurion. It would be a stupid shame to throw that kid away. Even as much as I understand why they are going to do it. I just had to speak up. Do the right thing. Does that make sense?"

Jessica smiled up at the man.

"It does, Vo," she replied. "And Karl understands that, as much as he owes me and Casey, he owes you everything. And is willing to listen."

She held out the paper for Vo to take, catching him off guard, however briefly.

"Karl is willing to commute a sentence of death to one of permanent exile," Jessica said. "There will be enough others to make negative examples of, going forward, but Karl asked me if I can find a place for one Grantholm Safavid, either in *Aquitaine*, or *Corynthe*, as a personal favor to you."

She watched Vo consume the paper quickly, blowing air out of his lungs in one long, shocked sigh.

When he looked up, there might have been tears in his eyes, however brief.

Jessica contented herself by taking a long drink of her coffee, eyes elsewhere, while this normally-taciturn man got his emotions back in order.

"I'll take him," Vo finally said, voice still not quite back down to where it normally rumbled. "Give me until we get back to *Petron*, and I'll know if the Fleet can use him, or if we need to turn him into a pirate."

Jessica smiled. That was the least she could do for this man.

EPILOGUE: EMMERICH

IMPERIAL FOUNDING: 176/11/23. IMPERIAL CONSERVATORY, ST. LEGIER

A knock at his door caused Emmerich to look up from his desk.

The latest manuscript was finally done. Edited. Complete.

It would be headed off to the publisher soon, where it would no doubt be extremely successful, and probably have a print run hundreds of times larger than the normal thirty to fifty thousand copies for naval students and historians that his professional books usually justified.

After all, who else could write a biography simply entitled *Jessica Keller: Volume 1?*

He supposed Nils Kasum might, but that man would never be willing to declassify enough secrets to improve on what would probably be the definitive document for this generation of Imperial scholars, at least until she wrote her own stories down.

If she ever did.

A silent stranger shadowed his doorway.

Em suspected the man enjoyed that part the most.

"It's not often I find myself *summoned* somewhere," Joh, *His Sovereign Imperial Majesty Karl Johannes Arend Wiegand, Emperor Karl VII by Grace of God*, announced to the otherwise empty room.

"Pity," Em replied in a droll voice. "I must have a chat with Kati about that sometime."

His reward was an Imperial eye roll as Joh entered and closed the office door behind him.

Em had already cleared a chair for the man, knowing he was coming.

Joh fixed him with a sardonic glare as he sat.

"Have you changed your mind?" the Emperor asked simply.

"No," Em replied with a smile. "I will do this thing for you, but those are my terms. Take it or leave it."

"And you drag me here to tell me that again, Em?"

"Yes, Joh," Emmerich said. "You don't seem to be listening."

"That's because you're insane, Em," Joh fired back. "And your demands are completely irrational."

"Maybe," Em's smile grew wider. "And you're still going to give them to me. I have something better than blackmail, this time."

"What could you possibly have that you think will move me?" his Imperial Majesty growled sulkily. "What might convince me to surrender to your outrageous demands, you blackguard?"

"Casey."

Em rather enjoyed the shudder that passed through Joh's whole being.

"It's not about Casey, Em," Joh said in a tight voice.

"No," Em agreed merrily. "But you'll have to face her on this one if I don't get my way."

Joh growled at him. No words, just a low growl. The kind that indicated surrender to a greater power.

"Okay, master strategist," Joh finally fired back in turn. "And what do I do about Casey?"

Em nodded as a placeholder.

Heike's wedding had gone off without a hitch, right on schedule. She had even insisted on going up afterwards and commissioning the new *Blackbird* from the ship's orbital drydock, a slightly banged-up Rafferty Saar standing proudly at her side as she did so.

Steffi's state funeral three days later had served to bring the entire planet together as one family in mourning. As news spread, it was doing the same to the Empire.

But now Casey. *Her Imperial Majesty Karl VIII.*

"First, Joh," Em finally said. "Come to grips with the fact that she's a grown up. The bright, little thirteen-year-old you have in your head is a woman now. She has done us all proud, and will continue to do so, but she's never going to fit into the sort of life that Steffi would have enjoyed. You will only drive her away by trying to force it upon her."

"And *Fribourg?*" Joh asked, stepping outward to his broader duties to the Empire, and not just his family.

"Joh, the woman just saved the Empire," Em snapped. "The people here understand that. The rest will as soon as the newsreels make the planetary rounds. There will be people out there demanding that she become the Crown Princess and that Ekke step aside."

"No," Joh bristled sharply.

"I agree," Em said soothingly. "But that will be what some want. Mostly Chartists, who will find in her a champion of their cause. You, your government, and your Empire will have to come to grips with that, embrace it, and politely blunt the calls for the *Charter of Humanity* at some point."

"So what do we do with her?" Joh reiterated.

"Have you asked Casey what she wants?" Em asked.

"No," Joh said, exasperated. "I was too busy being blackmailed by you to get to that topic."

Em smiled evilly.

"So sign the paperwork to give me what I want, solve the rest yourself, and go have a chat with your daughter. I suspect she'll surprise you in happy ways, Joh. She's already done that with me."

Em got a second Imperial eye roll, which he was pretty sure was a record for a single conversation, at least in the last thirty years.

Joh stood and stretched.

"There are times I would like to hate you, Em," he said sternly.

"That's because I'm right and you know it, Joh," Em replied with a shooing motion. "Now. Go away, I have work to do."

Joh, *His Sovereign Imperial Majesty Karl Johannes Arend Wiegand, Emperor Karl VII*, scowled briefly, huffed once in Imperial exasperation, and departed without another word.

Em knew that he had struck true at that point.

He did have work to do. A great deal.

Fribourg would never be the same.

Keller hadn't caused those fractures. She had merely identified the gaps, even as he and everyone else had missed them, and then happily hammered home shims to spall off jagged fragments.

2218 Svati Prime.

Ramsey.

Petron.

Ballard.

Thuringwell.

And now, *St. Legier.*

At least the rest of the Empire had awoken to the threat of *Buran*, and the need to hold the Peace with *Aquitaine*.

The task would take quite possibly the rest of his life.

He looked down at the cover of his manuscript one last time.

Jessica Keller: Volume 1.

Would she write his story, one of these days?

EPILOGUE: CASEY

IMPERIAL FOUNDING: 176/12/05. KARL V
IMPERIAL STADIUM, WERDER, ST. LEGIER

The event had been moved, of necessity. There was simply no place in the safe confines of the Imperial Palace to hold it.

Even the arena was packed, sixty thousand tickets awarded initially by lottery and going for a duke's ransom today on the secondary market.

Casey watched the soldier in front of her step onto the grass from the tunnel under the arena, holding the bright green Imperial Standard on a tall, wooden pole as he slowly made his way to the center of the pitch.

There was an announcer handy, but he had been instructed to remain silent unless needed.

He was not.

The entire crowd fell utterly silent. Casey hadn't known a group that large could all hold their breath so carefully at the same time.

Two lines of armed men marched crisply forward next. The 189th Division's Color Guard was on her left. Marines from *IFV Amsel*, her flagship, for however brief that moment had been, on her right.

They formed a corridor.

Not facing out, protecting the inner area from the crowd, but facing in, representing the masses in the stadium, as well as the entire Empire.

Again, utter silence.

There was no precedent for this ceremony, so Casey had written one.

The first notes of the Imperial anthem could be heard, and then disappeared as sixty thousand men, women, and children came suddenly, noisily, to their feet, singing quietly along, Casey included.

Quiet as the anthem ended, men and women poised.

Anxious.

Father went next, moving just fast enough to billow out his maroon cloak as he strode to the center of the field.

Again, the crowd fell utterly silent.

Casey glanced out of the tunnel, but she could only barely make out the Imperial box where Mother and Ekke sat, along with Aunt Freya and her family. Even Saša and Asra had joined them, along with Yan Bedrov and especially *Wiley*.

She could feel everyone's love from here.

Out on the pitch, she watched Father reach under his cloak and draw the Earth Sword, reforged of steel that had originally come to *St. Legier* from the Homeworld itself.

There had been sound before. Casey could only tell because the crowd gasped once collectively, and then fell to a silence that was almost painful to endure.

Casey turned to glance back at each of her escorts. Like Father, they wore the long, maroon cloak with the Imperial crest on it.

Lady Moirrey beamed up at her.

Lord Vo smiled down like Odin atop his throne, listening to his crows.

She wanted to say something, reassure him again, but it was unnecessary now.

He had been broken after the battle, but had found peace. Perhaps he had reforged himself, just as the Earth Sword had been.

His look said that he understood, and he nodded down at her.

Casey took a deep breath and faced forward again.

"Kasimira Helena Wiegand," Father said in a conversational tone that the microphones picked up and echoed. "You will present yourself before this Court."

She started off in a slow, measured stride. Vo could have kept up with her, but Moirrey's short legs would be churning like a children's cartoon, so Casey moved at a relaxed pace.

The crowd let out a sigh when she appeared, which almost undid her and all the careful planning and effort she had done to hold everything together this long.

Focus. You faced down the entire Imperial Fleet and the Usurper. You can do this.

Still, it was hard.

Steffi should have been here. Her sister who had been her rock for so long. Heike had helped, but she was a married woman now and didn't need Casey's tears staining her blouse anymore.

And Saša and Asra had shown her that it was possible to do anything she demanded hard enough, but they would go home soon.

Casey was on her own.

So be it.

Father looked like the Sun God Apollo, standing perfectly still in the middle of the green sward, the Earth Sword point down in the soil before him. Between them.

Casey had worn white robes today.

Purity. Innocence.

Mourning.

She stopped three steps before Father and kneeled in the grass, uncaring if she stained the robes. They would never be worn again.

Either she would offer them to the Imperial Museum, or burn them. It was a hard choice.

Silence.

Dead eerie calm.

The day had dawned clear and crisp. Casey was out in the wan sun now rather than the chill confines of the tunnel, but she would need more than that to leach the chill from her bones.

The blade of that sword would be so much colder.

Father lifted it easily and stepped forward. He tapped her lightly on the shoulders: left, right, left.

His face was serious, but she could still see the proud gleam in his eyes.

Again, an effort to hold the tears at bay.

For both of them.

"I proclaim you Kasimira *zu* Wiegand, *Ritter* of the Imperial Household," Emperor Karl VII boomed out over the stadium's public address system. "You will speak in my name as my personal representative in all things, and you will do me proud. Arise, Lady Casey, and be presented to this Court."

Father stepped back and Casey rose carefully to her feet.

She lost it at that point.

The dam broke and tears just poured down her face, visible on the video monitors placed around the stadium as she stood.

But she could finally breathe.

She was not free. She would never be free.

But she had the chance to forge her own destiny now, a Princess who had been raised to be a *Ritter*, something the galaxy had never seen.

She was not the Emperor anymore. Would never be, unless something catastrophic happened.

More catastrophic.

Good Lord willing, never.

But she was an Imperial Knight now. One of the movers and shakers of Empire.

She would never again be just a girl.

"Lady Moirrey. Lord Vo," Father continued. "Your charge awaits."

Moirrey appeared in front of her with a smile that warmed the entire city, and much of the Empire with it.

She pulled a maroon bundle from under her own cloak and caught it like a bull fighter in the ring. She flipped one of the cords up and around Casey's neck, where Vo grasped it and lifted the cloak into place.

Moirrey quick-tied the two cords and briefly placed a hand on hers, before stepping back and out of sight.

Casey swallowed hard in a mouth suddenly gone dry as Father stepped close again.

He stuck the Earth Sword into the grass and held the pommel with a single finger as she stepped close and placed her hand carefully around the warm grip.

As she took control, Father let go with a smile and stepped back, leaving her standing before the entire arena alone.

Casey turned.

Moirrey and Vo had taken spots in line on either side with the troops.

Glancing back, Father stood next to Master Sergeant Edgar Horst and the Imperial Standard.

She took a deep breath, conscious of the entire population hanging on pins and needles with her.

"Emmerich Wachturm," she said in a conversational voice that emerged from every speaker in the city. "You will present yourself before this Court."

Uncle Em emerged from the darkness of the tunnel next.

Casey had briefly considered using the Earth Sword as part of this ceremony, but trying to look impressive while hefting a two and a half kilo, meter-long blade had shown her just how strong Father must be to make it look so effortless.

Uncle Em appeared to be in even better shape. She hadn't truly realized until now what a powerful figure he cut, v-shaped and moving like a panther as he approached.

The crowd gasped.

The man had worn that uniform for so long that he had come to be identified by it.

Imperial Admiral of the Red Emmerich Wachturm.

The Red Admiral.

Today, he wore black.

It had taken the crowd a few, collective seconds to grasp that.

It was a sable uniform with a single, silver band around each wrist. Still the uniform of a naval admiral, perfectly styled to make the man look like a giant.

But the color of the darkness between galaxies.

The Imperial Fleet only recognized one black uniform.

Grand Admiral of the Fleet.

Commander In Chief.

A few cheers broke out, and then turned into a roar so loud it was painful.

It went on for nearly a minute before Casey raised her right hand, the one not holding the blade.

Silence fell as though she had chopped it with the Earth Sword.

Uncle Em didn't kneel before her. That was reserved for the special occasions, like making someone a *Ritter.*

Something else he had refused time and again.

Instead, Uncle Em stood at perfect attention, waiting. Smiling at her.

Even Father had come around, and agreed to her and Uncle Em's plan, eventually. The whole galaxy was going to change, starting today.

"Emmerich Wachturm," she said, again carried to every corner of the city, and quite a few radios in system. "You are hereby promoted to the rank of Grand Admiral, and charged with commanding the Fleet. The future of the Empire we place in your hands and direct you to keep us all safe. Will you accept this charge?"

"Lady Casey," Uncle Em nodded. "Your Majesties, I will."

The crowd erupted again, thunderous applause and cheers filling every nook and cranny of the ancient stone edifice.

Casey let it go longer this time, let the people have this moment, when they could look forward to the man who had been the Red Admiral being in command of everything.

Protecting them from things in the night.

Again, she raised her hand.

It took longer for the noise to subside, but eventually, it did.

"Jessica Keller," Casey said in a voice that boomed over the entire city. The entire Empire.

The entire galaxy.

"You will present yourself before this Court."

Again the gasp. Sixty thousand mouths falling open at once in shock.

One man would be nearly silent. Sixty thousand was a pop of sound audible even down here on the pitch.

Uncle Em moved to Casey's side and together they watched Jessica emerge from the tunnel, covered in a dark gray cloak that hung to her knees.

After the gasp, stunned silence.

Jessica's face was unreadable as she walked, but Casey had come to understand that the woman held her emotions close.

Command face.

Casey had seen it on Father and Uncle Em occasionally, but precious few others.

Until Jessica.

Jessica came to rest and stared up at her.

Casey blinked in a moment of surprise, until she remembered that she had half a head of height on the woman.

Jessica Keller was so much larger in her memory.

"*Wildgraf* Keller," Casey began, sounding as calm as she could, even as tears continued to pour down her face. "The Empire makes no special demands on you, beyond that which you have already given us, as an outsider willing to see that Justice be done. Will you stand ready to aid us again, in our time of need?"

"Lady Casey, Your Majesties, I will."

"Then join us, Admiral Keller, and be welcome."

Casey watched as Jessica let go of her cloak and shrugged her shoulders.

The cloth fell to the grass in a gray puddle.

The crowd blinked in a silent shock so profound that Casey thought she could hear hearts beating.

And then they erupted in joy.

Under the cloak, Jessica was wearing the uniform of an Imperial Admiral.

Crimson.

Emmerich Wachturm had become *The Grand Admiral*.

Jessica Keller would replace him.

As *The Red Admiral*.

FLIGHT OF THE BLACKBIRD:
CAST LIST

Corynthe

Name/Rank/Position

- Jessica Marie Keller (F)/Fleet Centurion/Queen of Corynthe
- Marcelle Augustine Travere/Chief/Jessica's Personal Aide
- Willow Dolen/First Rate Spacer/Jessica's Bodyguard
- David Rodriguez/Vice Admiral/Regent to Queen Jessica
- Desianna Indah-Rodriguez/Counsel to the Crown/First Minister of *Corynthe*
- Uly Larionov (M)/Counsel to the Crown/Comptroller
- Galen Estevan (M)/Captain/Commander, *Marco Polo*
- Vo *zu* Arlo/Centurion / Ritter/Honorary Colonel, 3rd Regiment, 189th Div. Imperial Army
- Moirrey *zu* Kermode/Centurion / Ritter/Engineer, detached duty
- Nicolai Aoiki (M)/Master Chef/Master of the Wardroom

Kali-ma

Name/Rank/Position

- *Wiley* / Shiori Ness (F)/Command Centurion/Captain, *Kali-ma*
- Yan Bedrov/Exec/Tactical Officer
- Anders Himura/Science Officer/Command Sensors
- Erik Doležal//Head Engineer
- *Rocket Frog* / Saša Binici/Pilot/Light Strike Wing
- *Neon Pink* / Asra Binici/Pilot/Light Strike Wing
- *Eel* / Gustav Marquez/Flight Lead/Heavy Wing

Auberon

Name/Rank/Position

- Denis Jež (M)/Command Centurion/Commander, *Auberon*
- Enej Zivkovic (M)/Centurion/Counsel to the Crown of *Corynthe*
- Tamara Strnad (F)/Senior Centurion/First Officer
- Tobias Brewster (M)/Senior Centurion/Tactical Centurion
- Aleksander Afolayan(M)/Centurion/Gunner
- Nina Vanek (F)/Senior Centurion/Defense
- Nada Zupan (F)/Senior Centurion/Pilot
- Daniel Giroux (M)/Senior Centurion/Science Officer
- Vilis Ozolinsh (M)/Command Engineering Centurion/Chief Engineer
- Phillip Navin Crncevic (M)/Command Marine Centurion/Dragoon
- Nadine Orly/Yeoman /Flag Marine
- Jackson Tawfeek/Chief/Marine

Pilots, Auberon

Name/Rank/Position

- Iskra Vlahovic/Command Flight Centurion/Flight Deck Commander
- *Jouster* / Milos Pavlovich/Command Flight Centurion/Flight Commander

- *Uller* / Friedhelm Hannes Förstner/Flight Centurion/*Jouster's* Wing
- *Vienna* / Avril Bouchard/Flight Centurion/*Jouster's* Wingmate
- *Bitter Kitten* / Darya Lagunov/Senior Flight Centurion/Wing Commander
- *Hànchén* / Murali Ma/Flight Centurion/*Bitter Kitten's* Wingmate
- *Furious* / Cho Ayaka Nakamura/Flight Centurion/*Bitter Kitten's* Wingmate
- *da Vinci* / Ainsley Barret/Senior Flight Centurion/Scout Pilot
- *Gaucho* / Hollis Dyson/Senior Flight Centurion/Commander, *Cayenne*
- Takouhi Taline Nazarian (F)/Chief/Loadmaster, *Cayenne*
- Murphy Alexandru (M)/First-Rate Spacer/Tower Gunner, *Cayenne*
- Branca Antía Rocha (F)/Flight Centurion/Commander, *Petron*
- Anastazja Slusarczyk (F)/Senior Flight Centurion/Commander, *Necromancer*
- Leila Ketevan (F)/Flight Centurion/Commander, *Damocles*

RAN Squadron

Name/Rank/Position

- Tomas Kigali (M)/Command Centurion/Commander, *CR-264*
- Alber d'Maine (M)/Command Centurion/Commander, *Shivaji*
- Robertson Aelieas (M)/Command Centurion/Commander, *Nyamboya*
- Doriane Matveev (F)/Command Centurion/Commander, *Ishfahan*
- Kanda Lungu (F)/Command Centurion/Commander, *Ballard*
- Elzbet Aukley (F)/Senior Centurion/First Officer/Science Officer, *Ballard*
- Teuta Uzodimma (F)/Command Centurion/Commander, *BrightOak*

- Yezekael Jarogniew (M)/Command Centurion/Commander, *Rubicon*
- "Siran" Akpabio (F)/Command Centurion/Commander, *Vigilant*
- Tonći Östberg (M)/Command Centurion/Commander, *Andover*
- Calista Katsaros (F)/Command Centurion/Commander, *Albena*
- Ionuţ Yannic (M)/Command Centurion/Commander, *Advocate*
- Waldemar Ihejirika (M)/Command Centurion/Commander, *Mendocino*

The Republic

Name/Position

- Indira (Chastain) Keller/Jessica's mother
- Miguel Keller/Jessica's father
- Petia Naoumov/First Centurion. Commander, Home Fleet
- Nils Kasum/First Lord of the Fleet
- Kamil Miloslav/Personal Aide to First Lord Kasum
- Judit Margrét Chavarría/Premier, Republic Senate
- Tadej Marko Horvat/Senator, Republic Senate, *Chairman*
- Calina Szabolcsi/President of the Republic of Aquitaine
- Seth/Bartender, the Marquette Room
- Sigrún/Steward, the Marquette Room

The Fribourg Empire

Name/Rank/Position

- Johannes Arend Wiegand/Emperor/Karl VII
- Kasimira Ekaterina/Empress/Imperial Household
- Karl Ekkehard Szczęsny/Crown Prince Ekke/Imperial Household
- Ekaterina Stephanya/Princess Steffi/Imperial Household
- Kasimira Helena/Princess Casey/Imperial Household

- Emmerich Wachturm/Admiral/The Red Admiral
- Freya Wachturm/Duchess/Wife of Emmerich Wachturm
- Tiede Wachturm/Cmdr/Son of Emmerich Wachturm
- Jeltje Voight/Burggraf/Daughter of Emmerich Wachturm
- Carsten Voigt/Cmdr/Husband of Jeltje Voight
- Henriette Annne Wachturm/"Lady Heike"/Daughter of Emmerich Wachturm
- Bernard Hourani/Lt. Cmdr/Fiancé of Heike Wachturm
- Hendrik Baumgärtner/Flag Captain/Aide to Admiral Wachturm
- Sigmund Dittmar/Admiral/Eldest son of Prince Reinhart
- Karya Dittmar//Wife of Sigmund Dittmar
- Geoffrey Grundman/General/Imperial Security, Section Eleven
- Karl Bakemann/Admiral/Flag, IFV Adler
- Antoine Hauss/Cmdr/Imperial Security
- Grantholm Safavid/Lt./Imperial Security
- Walter Fuchs//Hotelier
- Frida Fuchs//Wife of Walter
- Annette Fuchs//Daughter of Walter
- Foster Calderin/Owner/Publican/The Maltese Cross

The Blackbird

Name/Rank/Position

- Rafferty Saar/Captain/Commander, *Amsel*
- Dieter Corbeil/Commander/Executive Officer
- Guy Emshwiller/Lt. Cmdr/Flag Officer

M'hanii Frontier

Name/Rank/Position

- Rodrigo Yamimura/Duke/Ruler of *Osynth B'Udan*, Sector Capital
- Tito Garcia-Novarella//Merchant

Buran

Name/Rank/Position

- Buran/ The Lord of Winter/God/Emperor/Ruler of Buran
- Au Banop Dejha Quin (M)/Scholar/Ambassador
- Xi Fezar Palu Dwan (M)/Scholar/Ambassador
- Ro Kenzo Atep Vrain (M)/Scholar/Director – *Dancer in Darkness*
- Xi Putaz Laro Otep/Technician/Aide to the Director – Dancer in Darkness
- Ro Malar Arga Rues (M)/Soldier/War Advocate – *Dancer in Darkness*
- Wa Veren Kulo Marz (F)/Technician/Entity Advocate – *Dancer in Darkness*
- Ko Serek Evet Khan (M)/Scholar/Crew Advocate – *Dancer In Darkness*

ABOUT THE AUTHOR

Blaze Ward writes science fiction in the Alexandria Station universe (Jessica Keller, The Science Officer, The Story Road, etc.) as well as several other science fiction universes, such as Star Dragon, the Dominion, and more. He also writes odd bits of high fantasy with swords and orcs. In addition, he is the Editor and Publisher of *Boundary Shock Quarterly Magazine*. You can find out more at his website www.blazeward.com, as well as Facebook, Goodreads, and other places.

Blaze's works are available as ebooks, paper, and audio, and can be found at a variety of online vendors. His newsletter comes out regularly, and you can also follow his blog on his website. He really enjoys interacting with fans, and looks forward to any and all questions—even ones about his books!

Never miss a release!
If you'd like to be notified of new releases, sign up for my newsletter.

http://www.blazeward.com/newsletter/

Buy More!
Did you know that you can buy directly from the KRP website?

https://www.knottedroadpress.com/shop/

Connect with Blaze!

Web: www.blazeward.com
Boundary Shock Quarterly (BSQ):
https://www.boundaryshockquarterly.com/

ABOUT KNOTTED ROAD PRESS

Knotted Road Press fiction specializes in dynamic writing set in mysterious, exotic locations.

Knotted Road Press non-fiction publishes autobiographies, business books, cookbooks, and how-to books with unique voices.

Knotted Road Press creates DRM-free ebooks as well as high-quality print books for readers around the world.

With authors in a variety of genres including literary, poetry, mystery, fantasy, and science fiction, Knotted Road Press has something for everyone.

Knotted Road Press
www.KnottedRoadPress.com

9 781943 663422